MALICE

Ewell E. Greeson

PublishAmerica
Baltimore

© 2002 by Ewell E. Greeson.

All rights reserved. No part of this book may be reproduced in any form without written permission from the publishers, except by a reviewer who may quote brief passages in a review to be printed in a newspaper or magazine.

First printing

ISBN: 1-59129-482-7
PUBLISHED BY PUBLISHAMERICA BOOK PUBLISHERS
www.publishamerica.com
Baltimore

Printed in the United States of America

To my loving wife Rose Marie, who has always been by my side with her help and support.

PROLOGUE

Alex's stomach began to tighten as he lay there waiting. He had never killed a man before. He had been trained to kill in the army, but he had never killed. Alex wiped his sweaty hands on his shirt and took a deep breath, trying to still his mind for what was to come. There was no way out. He knew that they would never give up trying, and he knew that he couldn't. The tracker was closer. He had stopped three hundred yards down the mountain and was studying the trail again. Alex held his breath. That was the area he had backtracked to. He had left the softer ground and keeping to the hard rock, circled to where he was now. He had tried so hard not to leave any marks on the rock, but then he wasn't the expert that the Indian was. The tracker stood and slowly followed Alex's first trail.

Alex eased the bow forward and notched the arrow. He thought about laying another arrow out but dismissed the idea. He would only have time for one shot. His hand shook. The tracker was one hundred yards away and then seventy-five. Alex was above and to one side of the trail. He had to wait until the tracker was directly across for the best shot. The Indian would stop when the trail ended and realize that Alex had backtracked. He would turn back, and Alex knew that he would have to shoot in that split second. The man with the rifle would be in range within minutes. Alex put tension on the bow string and waited.

Chapter 1

Alex Bradley leaned back against the small pile of luggage. He stretched his long legs out and pulled the shades down over his blue eyes. A familiar shape moved at his side, and he turned to look at his sleeping wife. To him she was the most beautiful woman alive, but then he was prejudiced. Her sandy hair flowed out over the duffle bag she lay on. Her face had the classic look of a model, spoiled only by lips that were slightly too big but made her even more sexy. Her loose clothing did little to hide the shapely contours of her body, and all of it was on a five foot four frame. Her lips pouted at him in her sleep.

Alex turned toward the road as a truck came toward them, but it turned away at the last moment. They should have been picked up over an hour ago. Alex took his sunglasses off and studied the empty road behind the truck. Giving up on seeing anything else, he brushed his black hair back and slid the shades back down. He settled back on the luggage and with his eyes half closed, let his thoughts drift back to last week.

Alex had just started his latest book and was busy pounding away on his computer keys when Jan had burst into their modest home in Atlanta, Georgia and pulled him away to celebrate her latest assignment. She had been picked to do a photo layout of the Rockies in western Canada. It would be great for both of them. The quietness of the wilderness would be the perfect place for him to work on his book. Alex smiled as he remembered how she had rattled on, not giving him a chance to get a word in edgewise.

Jan had already rented a cabin fifty miles away from everything. The rental information showed a small cabin overlooking a beautiful mountain lake. She couldn't wait to get started.

They had arrived at the Prince George airport more than two hours ago and after grabbing a sandwich for lunch, piled their luggage against the south wall of the hangar, near the parking lot, and sat down to wait for their ride.

Alex looked at his wife again. He needed to wake her, but she looked so peaceful. He leaned over and blew gently in her ear. A long eyelid opened slowly and a striking green eye peeped out at him. The eyelid blinked at the sunlight.

"Has he come yet?" she asked lazily.

"I haven't seen him," Alex answered.

Jan stretched slowly and sat up, looking at her watch. "It's two o'clock," she said. "We'll be lucky to get unpacked before dark. I was hoping to get some pictures of the sunset."

"I know, honey," Alex said. He started to explain that country people kept their own time, when a van turned into the parking lot and came barreling toward them. The vehicle slid to a halt, and a thin, bearded man jumped out.

"I'm sorry I'm late folks," he said. "I had to deal with an asshole this morning." The man grabbed a duffle bag and started loading the van. Suddenly he stopped and turned back to them. "Where are my manners? My name is Robert Owens and that's right," noticing Jan's look, "I'm an American from the great state of Texas. I still wear my cowboy boots." He stuck out one foot. Alex and Jan laughed. Robert had the weathered look of someone who had been outdoors a lot. He looked to be two or three inches under six feet and his face had a hard, chiseled look to it, but his easy grin changed that. He looked more like a cowboy than a helicopter pilot. Alex wondered if he was just a driver, sent to collect them.

Robert closed the back doors and motioned for them to get into the van. Alex slid his six foot, slightly plump frame into the back seat. Jan had talked him into working out again but so far all it had gotten him was another ten pounds. Maybe the mountain air would take some of it off.

"How far do we have to drive?" Jan asked, as she bounced into the front seat.

"Oh about fifteen miles or so," Robert answered, stopping at a stop sign and checking the road. "By the way, I'm your pilot. My plane is waiting for us at the lake."

Alex couldn't believe that Robert was a pilot. He just didn't seem the type. "What asshole did you have to deal with?" he asked.

Alex could see Robert's gray eyes in the mirror, giving him a good going over. Robert didn't answer right away but swung into the light traffic. They soon left the airport behind.

"Someone wanted to rent my cabin," Robert finally said, swinging wide to miss a parked truck. "I told him that I had already rented to you folks, but he wouldn't take no for an answer. My brother and I own the cabin. We rent mostly to hunters in the fall. Hell, we haven't rented the cabin in six months and were glad to get your business, being in the off season and all. Anyway, this butt hole just kept on until we had to tell him where to stick his money."

A sign for highway sixteen flashed by. Robert kept talking, pointing out different landmarks as they flashed by. His voice became a drone, and finally Alex blocked him out, as he began to take notice of the wild, beautiful country they were passing through. Jan had her camera out and was snapping shots off every chance she got. Robert finally stopped talking, and Alex leaned back and closed his eyes. He was still tired from the long trip.

Alex jerked his head up as the van bounced over a pothole. He had dropped off to sleep. They had left the pavement and were on a gravel road. The gravel made a drumming sound under the van. Alex looked down at his watch. They should be there shortly. Alex sat up and began to watch the scenery flash by. Five minutes later, they topped a mountain and dropped toward a green valley far below.

In the center of the valley, a small lake sparkled in the bright sun. As they drew closer, Alex could see several buildings clustered around the lake. A yellow plane floated at the end of a small dock.

"Is that your plane?"

"That's my baby," Robert answered.

"It looks kind of small," Alex said nervously.

"It's bigger than it looks," Jan assured him. "I flew in one just like this when I did that layout in South Carolina."

Alex remembered, she had been gone for two months. The photos she had brought back were breathtaking. He felt a flash of pride. Jan was really good at her job.

Jan reached back and squeezed his arm. "You'll love it," she said. "The larger planes don't give you half the thrill."

"She's right," Robert agreed, as he turned toward the nearest building. "Hey," he said, turning to Alex, "Would you folks like a bite to eat before we take off? My wife can cook up something before we leave."

Jan looked at her watch. "It's after three," she said, looking back at Alex. "It's getting kind of late."

"We really need to get started," Alex said, taking Jan's clue. He knew that she couldn't wait to get to the cabin and start taking pictures.

"No problem," Robert said. "Let me unload your luggage at the dock, give me two minutes at the house, and I'll be ready to go."

Robert brought the van to a stop next to the dock. Alex and Jan jumped out to help unload. Minutes later, they stood by their bags and watched the van disappear behind a building at the far end of the settlement. Without a word, Jan joined Alex as he grabbed a couple of bags and headed for the plane. About halfway there, a man jumped onto the dock from behind the plane. Alex grinned and nodded at the man as he passed. The man gave Alex a hard look and kept going.

"Boy, talk about a sour puss," Jan said, turning to look at the man's back.

They reached the plane and dumped the luggage, turning back in time to see the man get into a utility vehicle and drive off.

"Did he come from the plane?" Jan asked as they headed back for another load.

Alex spotted a boat tied up next to the plane. "He could have come from the boat," he answered, pointing. "He was probably fishing. Maybe he was in a bad mood because he didn't catch anything."

"Dammit," Jan said, looking back over her shoulder at the sun. "It's going to be too late for any shots."

"Don't worry," Alex said. "You'll have plenty of time tomorrow."

They had just picked up the last of the bags when Robert drove up. He parked the van and jumped out to take the two bags from Jan.

"I didn't mean for you two to haul all of the luggage out," he said, as they walked to the plane. Robert vaulted from the dock onto one of the pontoons and started taking the bags from Jan and Alex. He began to cram them into the baggage area.

"Hey! Be careful with that one," Jan cried, as Robert started to throw her camera bag in with the rest of the luggage. Robert hesitated and then carefully slid it on top of the luggage. Shutting the baggage compartment, he turned and held the passenger door open for Jan.

Jan insisted that Alex take the copilot seat so that he could get the feel of a small plane. Alex found the seat slightly cramped. He drew his legs up and pulled the door closed. Robert gave him a grin as he slid into the pilot's seat and started the engine. The sound of the engine blasted at Alex's ears as Robert increased power and, seconds later, they were skipping across the smooth lake.

Alex didn't know much about planes, but to him it seemed kind of sluggish in the water as they headed for the lake's end. Robert turned the plane around and with the whole lake in front, pushed the throttle forward. The engine sound went from a hum to a roar. The plane hesitated at first and then began to pick up speed, until they were skimming across the lake's surface. Alex grabbed the seat with both hands as the plane lifted into the air and cleared the pines at the end of the lake. He felt his stomach lift and then settle back down as the plane climbed steadily toward the blue sky.

Alex could see for miles in the clear air. The mountains of north British Columbia lay before them, their white tops glistening in the sun.

The feel of the small plane was nothing like the bigger planes Alex was used to. He could feel every change in the air current as the plane climbed toward the snow-topped mountains.

Robert flew the plane with a relaxed hold on the controls and didn't seem to notice the up and down motion. Alex tried to relax but found his hands gripping the seat at every sudden drop and rise of the plane. He saw a blue lake below and forward of the plane.

"What's the name of that lake?" he asked, trying to get his mind off flying.

Robert dropped one wing. "That's Naltesly lake," he answered. "I carried some folks there yesterday." He suddenly dove to avoid a flight of birds and grinned as Alex grabbed the seat again. "You have to keep your eyes open up here," he said. "All kinds of wildlife around."

Jan leaned over the front seat. "Look at the river."

Leaning over, Alex could see a blue river winding its way through the mountains. He could pick out the rapids by the white caps. Further up, the river dropped over a steep mountain side, forming a huge waterfall that ended in a foaming pool far below.

"Do you want me to go down for a closer look?" Robert asked and, without waiting for an answer, dropped one wing and fell toward the river. Alex's stomach climbed to his throat. Seconds later they were skimming along, fifty feet over the raging waters.

"Boy, I wouldn't want to go swimming in that," Alex said, swallowing hard to force the contents of his stomach back down.

"Me either," Robert agreed. "That water is straight off the mountain snow. It's icy cold."

The river became another waterfall and then disappeared suddenly into the ground, only to emerge again two hundred feet down the mountain. It continued its winding way to a valley hundreds of feet below. The rock formation it left behind made a natural bridge across the river.

Robert circled the plane to let Jan take pictures of the waterfall and the pool below. Then he turned back and followed the river upstream until it ended in a large, blue lake. Dipping low over the still waters, he skimmed over its surface until he reached the other end. Just before the trees, he pulled the plane's nose toward the blue sky and turned north. The sun was sinking low in the western sky. Alex could hear Jan's camera clicking away. She was getting her pictures after all.

"How long?" Alex asked.

"About ten minutes. It's just over that mountain range," Robert answered and then added, "Oh shit!"

"What's the matter?" Alex asked. Jan stopped taking pictures.

"This can't be," Robert continued without answering.

"What can't be?" Alex asked, beginning to get worried.

"We're low on fuel," Robert answered.

"How low?" Jan asked.

"Damn low," Robert answered, as he eased the throttle back. "And it's getting worse. We must have a leak."

"Can we make it to the cabin?" Alex asked.

"I don't know," Robert answered. "We're almost bone dry now. One thing's for sure, we don't have enough to get back home."

Alex looked ahead. The mountain range loomed closer with each second. What a wild place to go down. He drew in a deep breath. His heart pounded in his chest. *My God!* They could die in these God forsaken mountains. He grabbed the side of the seat as Robert dropped the wing and began to circle.

"Shouldn't we try to make it over the mountain?" Jan asked.

"No," Robert answered. "I would have to increase power, and our fuel wouldn't last five seconds. Our only hope is to find a lake on this side of the mountain and quick."

The engine sputtered and caught again. "Do you see anything?" Robert shouted, trying to keep the plane's nose up. Alex could hear the panic in his voice. The engine missed again.

"There! At the base of the mountain!" Jan yelled.

Alex caught a flash of white water. It was a stream and, judging from the foam, a rapid moving stream. Alex couldn't tell how big it was because of the trees, but streams make lakes.

Robert saw it too and headed for the spot, trying at the same time to gain altitude. Suddenly, the engine died and everything went quiet. The only sound was the air rushing by. Robert began pumping the choke and tried to restart the engine. Nothing! "It's no use folks!" he yelled. "Tighten your seat belts! We're going down!"

Alex reached up to wipe the sudden sweat from his eyes. His hand shook as he tightened his seat belt. They had lost sight of the stream. All three searched as the plane dropped toward the trees below. The trees were getting bigger fast, too fast. "There!" Alex shouted, pointing ahead. He could see blue waters. It wasn't the stream. It had to be a lake. "There!" he shouted again. "To your left!" They could all see it now. The lake was more like a big pond. Alex could see the stream, no it was a small river, flowing into one end of the lake and out the other.

Robert dropped one wing, trying to align the sluggish plane with the river. "The lake is too small!" he shouted. "We'll have to use part of the river."

Alex could see white foam around half-submerged rocks. It didn't seem like much of a river to him. The rocks could tear the small plane apart, but he knew they didn't have a choice. The plane was going down one way or the other. The forest rushed up at them. The plane shook as one wing hit a tree limb. Everything was happening too fast. Alex could hear Robert shouting at them.

"Hang on!" he shouted again.

Alex looked back for Jan. She had her head between her legs.

The plane touched the water. Alex heard the harsh grinding as the pontoons slid over the rocks and then they were into the deeper water of the lake. They didn't seem to be going any slower. The engine was dead. The plane rushed toward the opposite shore. They couldn't stop. They were going to hit the trees.

Alex was thrown forward as they hit one tree and then another, throwing the plane sideways. The trees disappeared as they fell into something – a hole, a gully. Alex could see sky as the nose climbed, and then he felt the plane crash to a stop. His head slammed forward, hitting the windshield, and the plane was falling again. Alex could hear the tail collapsing behind him as it hit bottom, and then suddenly he was thrown backward. The seat was moving. He tried to hold on, but something hit him in the face. He felt no pain as everything faded away into blackness.

A squirrel fell from a tree at the sudden impact and landed on the plane. Its feet worked feverishly against the smooth skin until it caught the branch of a tree and scampered up to a higher limb. The squirrel sat there chattering at the strange monster that had invaded its territory.

It finally vented its anger and darted away into the trees. The forest was still and quiet.

Chapter 2

Alex opened his eyes. Something was pressing down on top of him. He tried to get up but couldn't move. It was the front seat. Somehow, he had been thrown behind the seat, and it had landed on top of him. Fear creep through Alex as he thought about Jan. Where was she? Was she hurt? He yelled out her name and the fear was replaced by relief when he heard her voice. He slowly drew his leg up and pushed with all of his might. The seat slid away to one side, and he could crawl out. He looked up, toward the front, for Robert, but couldn't see in the dim light. The plane was at a crazy angle, with its nose straight up. He knew that Jan's voice came from somewhere below, but all he could see was luggage, and where was Robert? Alex eased over the seat and slid down toward the back of the plane. His feet came to rest against a piece of luggage. He yelled for Jan again.

"Alex!" Jan shouted back. Her voice seemed closer.

"Are you hurt?" he yelled back.

"I don't think so, but I can't get through this luggage."

Another voice joined in from outside. "I'm trying to get the luggage door open!" Robert yelled. "Can you get out?"

"Yes," Alex yelled back. He made his way up to the door and pulled himself out feet first but couldn't feel anything below but air. Holding onto the door frame, he let himself down until he dangled over the blackness below.

"Let go!" Robert shouted at him. "You're about three feet from the ground."

Alex dropped to the slope and slid down toward Robert who grabbed him as he slid past. Alex's whole body was sore, and he felt pain in his chest every time he breathed. He wondered if he had broken any ribs.

Together they climbed back up to the luggage door and started pulling luggage out. A hand emerged, waving at them, and then an arm. Jan's face suddenly poked out of the small door. "Are you going to take all day?" she kidded.

"Are you all right?" Alex asked, grinning back as he pulled her through the cargo hole.

"I'm fine," she answered. "Just a few bruises."

"Damn it," Robert said and held up a mashed box. "I was supposed to deliver these medical supplies to the hospital at Mayo after I dropped you guys off."

"It's leaking," Jan said.

"You're right my lady. It's no good now," Robert said and threw the box to one side.

Alex looked up the slope and then back down. They were about twenty feet from the top and a good hundred from the bottom. The tail of the plane had hit one side of the gully and dug in.

"How about forming a line to the top of this gully and I'll pass the luggage up," Robert said.

"Oh my God!" Jan yelled and scrambled back to the cargo hole. She rampaged through the luggage and came up with her camera bag. Opening the case, she examined the camera. "It seems to be all right," she said with relief in her voice. She swung the camera bag over her shoulder and started up the steep slope.

Alex reached up from behind and pushed Jan up to the top of the slope. He then slid back down to a flat spot between her and Robert. Alex took the luggage from Robert and threw it up to Jan. Fifteen minutes later, they had the luggage piled on top of the slope, and from there they moved it down to the lake.

All of them had cuts and scrapes. Alex hadn't noticed the cut on his forehead until Jan began to wipe at it with her sleeve. "We could use a bandage or two," she said, pulling up her pants to reveal a cut on her leg.

"That looks like a good place to make a fire," Robert said from ahead, pointing to a flat spot of ground and then turned back to take a long look at Jan's exposed leg. "You two get some wood and I'll get my emergency kit from the plane."

Alex and Jan walked away from the lake and found a small, dead tree. Together they dragged it back to the camp site. Alex broke off small pieces and stacked them, ready to make a fire, but they didn't have any matches. They sat down to wait for Robert.

The sun had already disappeared behind the mountain. The only sounds came from the other side of the lake. Alex could hear ducks as they settled in for the night, and an owl hooted its haunting call into the coming darkness. A large fish splashed white foam at the lake's surface as it tried for another bug in the weaning light.

Alex looked over at Jan. She was into her own self, staring off into space with her head tilted to one side. This was her element. She loved the outdoors. She caught his look and smiled.

They heard Robert before they saw him. He walked up to them with the emergency kit over one shoulder and a paper bag in one hand. "Dinner," he said, holding the bag up. "My wife fixed me some sandwiches for the flight to Mayo. I don't think I'll make the flight, do you?" Sitting, he opened the emergency kit and after taking a box of matches out, handed the kit to Jan who proceeded to take care of their cuts.

"By the way I checked the radio, but it's not working, and I found our leak." He struck a match and held the small flame under the leaves and wood.

Alex waited for Robert to say more about the leak, but Jan started talking first.

"They'll miss you tonight and know something's wrong," she said, as she finished with Alex and began to pile small pieces of wood on the blaze Robert had started. Alex added a couple of bigger pieces, and the flames began to grow.

"I'm afraid not," Robert replied. "I was supposed to deliver the medicine to the hospital tomorrow morning, refuel, and fly back home sometime tomorrow afternoon. My wife expects to hear from me then, but won't start looking until tomorrow night. Don't worry, we should make the cabin tomorrow. We can use the radio there to let them know what happened." His face grew solemn. "We may have something else to worry about. The leak I found wasn't an accident. Someone loosened my fuel line."

"How do you know it didn't come loose by itself? I mean through engine vibration?" Alex asked.

Robert looked across the fire at Alex. The fire cast weird shadows across his face. Alex could see the slight tremble in Robert's chin as he held his teeth tight together against his building anger. Robert wouldn't be an easy guy to tangle with when he got mad.

"Because I checked the plane yesterday before I picked you two up. I check it before every flight."

Alex looked at Jan. She had her hand over her mouth. He knew that she was thinking the same thing he was. Robert saw the look and turned from one to the other.

Alex started first. "We saw a man at your plane when we were carrying luggage out. We thought that he had came from a boat next to the plane."

"What man? What was he doing?" Robert asked, leaning forward toward

Alex.

"He was climbing up to the dock from behind the plane," Jan answered. "We couldn't see what he was doing. We said hello to him, but he didn't answer back. We thought it was because we were strangers."

"I'll be damned. Why would anyone want to hurt me? I'm a nobody." Robert asked. He paused and looked at the other two. "Could they be after you?"

"I don't think so," Jan answered. "Who could object to us taking a few pictures and writing a book?"

Robert broke a piece of wood across his knee. "I'd like to get a hold of the bastard who did this," he said.

All of them grew silent. Alex thought about how close to death they had come.

The last rays of sunlight were gone and darkness was settling in. The fire gave a cheerful circle of light against the blackness. Robert divided the sandwiches and produced a canteen of water with plastic cups. They were silent as he gave them a piece of sandwich and a cup of water.

"These are really good," Jan spoke first, between mouthfuls.

"If you think these are good, you should try some of her other cooking," Robert replied proudly.

"It's getting colder," Jan said, drawing her arms tighter around her knees.

Alex walked back to the pile of luggage and returned with two coats and blankets. Jan pulled the coat on gratefully.

Robert stretched his arms high, yawning. "Well folks, I think I'll hit the sack." He picked up one of the blankets and rolled up next to the fire.

"Robert, how far are we from the cabin?" Alex asked as he pulled the blanket tight around his neck.

"Oh, about ten or so miles," Robert answered and turned his back to them.

"That's not too bad," Jan said, yawning. She snuggled up close to Alex

Alex lay in the darkness watching the stars twinkling in the clear sky above. The only sound was Robert's light snoring and the occasional sounds of wild geese on the other side of the lake. He shivered when he thought about the horror they had all been through. In just an instant, they could have been dead. He tried to think of a reason why anyone would try to kill him or Jan. He couldn't think of any. It had to be Robert. Maybe someone had it in for him. Maybe it was the man he'd argued with before he'd picked them up. Alex couldn't keep his eyes open. He moved closer to Jan and drifted off to sleep.

* * *

Alex woke suddenly. It was morning and it was cold – really cold. Jan was tight against him, her head completely under the blanket. It was still dark, but the first hint of light filtered through the trees. He slid from under the blanket and began to lay small pieces of wood on the dying embers. He sat there for a minute staring into the growing fire. Alex heard movement at the edge of the forest as a small animal moved away from the larger circle of light. He turned at another movement closer to the fire as Robert sat up with the blanket tight around him.

"I wish we had one of those geese we heard on the lake last night," he said, "or better yet, the bastard that loosened my fuel line." Alex didn't say anything. "Well, wouldn't you?" Robert asked. He stood and walked around the fire.

"Yes, I guess so." Alex came to his feet, using his part of the blanket to cover the shivering Jan. He knew how Robert felt, but he had always been one to control his emotions instead of letting them control him. But then, Robert had lost his plane and maybe his livelihood. He had a good reason to be mad.

"We'll have plenty to eat when we get to the cabin?" Alex asked, trying to change the subject.

"Oh, there's plenty of food at the cabin. My brother and I keep it stocked all of the time. That is, unless a bear has managed to break in. We have those every now and then."

Jan sat up behind them. "The fire really feels good, and did I hear someone say something about food?" she asked.

Alex turned to her. "Good morning, sleepy head, and we don't have anything to eat. We were talking about eating when we get to the cabin." He moved over to give her a place by the fire. She brought her blanket with her and covered both of them as she snuggled against him.

It was quiet around the small fire. Robert was into his own moody thoughts and Jan was still too sleepy to talk. It was now light enough to see the lake. Alex could hear the wing beats of a water foul, probably trying to get away from the fire. Jan had gone back to sleep. He shook her gently. She sat up and stretched.

Alex rubbed Jan's back briefly and then stood. "I suggest that since we don't have bacon and eggs going, we try to get an early start."

"You're right," Robert said. "It's about that time."

All three walked over to the pile of luggage and stood there for a second, realizing that they couldn't carry even a small part of the pile with them. Without saying a word, Jan starting dumping the contents of a duffle bag on the ground. She opened the suitcases and dumped them, too. She began to pack the duffle bag with things they would need. Jan looked up as Alex joined her. "We can carry the duffle bags easier, and there's no way we can carry all of this stuff. We'll have to come back and get it later."

"Smart girl," Robert said, as he began to help. Soon they had the two duffle bags full. Robert rolled out a blanket and began to make a small pile in the center. When he had the right amount, he rolled the blanket into a tight roll and folded the ends back. Producing a piece of rope from his coat pocket, he tied the blanket, leaving a loop for a sling. He handed the blanket roll to Jan and taking one of the duffle bags, began to make his way up the mountain. Alex took the other duffle bag and fell in behind Jan.

After twenty minutes of climbing, Alex's breath was coming in short gasps. He stopped and looked up the mountain. Jan was leaning forward, climbing with strong, sure steps. Robert wasn't keeping up, but he was a long way ahead of Alex. Alex began to wish that he had gone to the gym more often, something Jan never failed to do. He was pushing himself to the limit and still he was falling behind. He hated to, but he had to call for a rest. He started to yell when he realized that the other two had already stopped.

Alex struggled up to join them. Robert was leaning against a tree, his breathing still hard and heavy. Jan came back to help Alex and smiled at him when he refused her help. She took her camera and climbed further up the hill. Alex slid his duffle bag down next to Robert.

Robert grinned up at him. "I think your wife is trying to walk us into the ground."

Alex grinned back and sat down on the duffle bag, grateful that someone was feeling his pain. The view from their resting place was breathtaking. He could see why Jan wanted to take photos. He looked back down the mountain and figured that they had climbed two miles or so. He could still see the lake but most of it was covered with morning mist. The part that he could see looked like a teardrop of blue against the forest greenery. To the south and down the mountain, the forest teemed with life. A deer paused in a small clearing, a hundred feet below. Alex could hear the whirling of the camera above him as Jan swung it toward the deer. The deer must have heard the sound, because it darted away. Alex looked up at the snow-capped mountains to their north and then to the smaller, evergreen-covered mountains to the south. All signs of civilization had disappeared and time seemed to stand still. It could have been hundreds of years since man had walked here.

Robert tapped his shoulder. He seemed to understand Alex's mood. Any sound now would disrupt the spell of the forest. Without saying a word, Robert swung his duffle bag onto his back and pointed up the hill. Alex followed behind slowly. The duffle bag seemed heavier then before. If it were ten miles to the cabin, they still had around three more miles to reach the top of the mountain, and the climb was getting steeper. The only good thing was the last five miles or so would be downhill.

Jan noticed them moving and began climbing ahead, stopping every now and then to snap another shot and to let them catch up. The climb became even steeper, and Alex began to labor again. The duffle bag seemed to weigh more with each step. Finally, he looked up and saw that Jan had stopped. Robert was fifty yards ahead. Alex wiped the sweat from his eyes and pushed forward the last seventy-five feet to join the other two.

"The climb gets easier just ahead," Jan said, eyeing Alex with concern. "Let's rest here awhile."

Alex didn't need any convincing as he collapsed on his duffle bag. He knew that Jan was stopping mostly for him.

"Boy! I could use about four eggs, bacon, and coffee about now," Robert said. He looked down their back trail. "That climb was a killer."

They both looked up as Jan squealed. With her hand held high, she slowly lowered it to reveal a candy bar. "It was in my coat pocket. I hope it's not too dry." Robert produced a knife, and Jan divided the bar into three equal pieces.

"How far do you think it is to the top?" Jan asked, as she munched on the piece of candy.

"We should have two or three more miles to go," Robert answered.

Alex looked at his watch. It was nine o'clock. "We should reach the cabin by early afternoon," he offered.

Robert stood. "It's not as easy going downhill as you think. Well, are we ready to try for the summit?"

The going was easier as the mountain leveled. They were almost to the top. Alex felt refreshed. He didn't know if it was because of the rest or the piece of candy. Jan was a quarter of a mile ahead now. Alex could see the drop off to the other side of the mountain beyond her. The top of the mountain looked to be about a mile across.

Robert suddenly stopped and motioned Alex to the side. "Stay here," he whispered.

Jan was snapping pictures of something below. Robert left him and began to creep up on her. What in the hell was he doing? Alex started to shout something when a large shape rose from the bushes. It was a giant grizzly. Alex could see a smaller bundle of fur to one side. It was a mother bear and her cub. Alex had heard stories about how dangerous they could be. The mother bear had her nose in the air, pointed toward Jan. Robert was circling the mountain and coming up to Jan from behind. She seemed imperious to the danger. The only sound was the whirling and clicking of the camera.

Alex could see Jan jump as Robert's hand touched her shoulder. She jerked away at the interruption. Robert grabbed her shoulder firmly and began to pull her back from the bear's sight.

The movement caught the bear's attention. The giant grizzly let out a roar. Alex began to search around frantically for a tree they could climb. Jan had finally realized the danger and was on all fours behind Robert, sliding back toward Alex. Alex looked for the bear. It was still in the same spot, but it had dropped to all fours. Alex knew that it was getting ready to charge. It would be on them in seconds. The cub must have seen them, too, because it suddenly ran away toward the other side of the mountain. The mother bear hesitated, turning her head back and forth from the running cub to them. She stood to her full height and let out one last roar before dropping to all fours and following her cub down the mountain.

Alex ran to the other two. "Boy, that was close."

"I know, I'm sorry," Jan said.

"It's a good thing we were upwind," Robert said. "The bear didn't like the sound of your camera but if she had smelled us. . . " He let the sentence dangle. "It's still spring up here and grizzlies can be especially dangerous this time of the year."

Jan grinned at him. "But look at the pictures I'll have."

"Ah," Robert said. "Better your picture as a trophy than your skin."

They all laughed as they gathered their bags and started out again. In minutes, they were back on the top of the mountain and on level ground. Thirty minutes later, they were over the top.

* * *

Going down the mountain was a lot easier, but hard on the ankles. They developed a steady pace and began to make good time. Three hours later, they spotted the blue lake and then the cabin. They were coming in from behind the cabin. It sat against the mountainside a good two hundred yards away from the lake. They stopped for a minute to rest.

"That's the best sight I've seen all day," Robert said. The other two agreed.

They found an animal trail leading down the mountain and, twenty minutes later, they were at the cabin. Jan was the first one to the porch. She paused, taking in the view.

"Oh Alex, it's so beautiful. This is just the way I pictured it."

The front of the cabin was covered with pines and hardwoods. The lake glimmered blue in the morning sun. The air was clean and sweet with the smell of the forest around them. A splash sounded, and the clear waters of the lake rippled as a fish broke the surface and came back down again. A deer, drinking at the lake's edge, raised its head at the sound. Above the lake and to the north, white-topped mountains glittered in the sun.

Jan opened the door and then turned, blocking the doorway. "Who's going to cook?"

"How about all of us pitching in," Robert answered, laughing.

The cabin was one big room. Everything was neatly stacked or put away. A large stone fireplace stood against one wall with cooking pots and pans hanging on both sides. A wood stove sat to one side with its black stove pipe curving back around to disappear into the stone above the fireplace. One full size bed and two sets of bunk beds were to their right against the front wall. Alex could see that they had the cabin laid out for hunting. Six people could sleep here. Three rocking chairs and a curved sofa sat between the full size bed and the fireplace. A huge wood table with eight chairs sat in the center and toward the back of the cabin and beyond that, kitchen cabinets and a sink.

They dumped the duffle bags on the floor and began digging through the cabinets. Robert kicked a bear skin rug aside and opened a trap door leading to a root cellar. He disappeared into the cellar.

"There's a side of bacon down here!" he shouted back. Seconds later, he emerged with a slab of meat and a package.

"Sorry," he said placing the package on the counter. "The eggs are dried."

"Anything to eat is going to taste like heaven," Jan answered. She began to make the biscuit dough while Alex started a fire in the wood stove.

Forty minutes later they sat down to a meal of bacon, gravy, eggs, and biscuits. They washed it down with hot coffee.

"These dried eggs aren't half bad," Robert said, pointing his spoon at the last of the eggs. Alex and Jan shook their heads and he scraped them onto his plate.

"I couldn't eat another bite," Alex said, leaning back in the chair. He looked around the cabin. "Where is the radio? I haven't seen it."

"It's in the closet, I'll get it out in a minute," Robert answered.

"Be quite," Jan said, holding out her hand. "What's that noise?"

"It's a plane," Robert said, jumping up and running to the door. The sound grew louder.

There were two planes and both were circling the cabin. "They see our smoke, but why are they coming here? We haven't called anyone on the radio yet." First one plane and then the other dove for the lake.

"I know the first plane," Robert shouted over the noise. "It flies out of Mayo."

He started running for the lake with Alex close behind. Jan stayed on the porch. Alex stopped and looked back at her. "Go on," she said. "I'm going to make more coffee. Bring them up."

Alex caught up with Robert. He had stopped at the edge of the lake. The first plane was already to the dock. A man jumped from the plane, and another one threw him a rope. The second plane was down and churning through the water toward them.

Robert and Alex started walking out onto the dock toward the first plane. Robert waved at the men, but they paid him no attention. The man on the dock shouted something to another man, but Alex couldn't hear what he'd said over the noise of the second plane. The pilot from the first plane jumped onto the dock to join the others. Robert waved again. The pilot took a long look at Robert and said something to the other men.

Robert slowed and turned to Alex. "I know that bastard and he acts like he's never seen me. Something is wrong here." The other engine died and the second plane drifted toward the dock. Silence hung over the morning mist.

"Hey Herb, are you ignoring me?" Robert shouted, his voice suddenly loud in the still air. The man didn't answer. All of the men on the dock had stopped what they were doing and stood there watching Robert and Alex. Robert stopped in his tracks. A heavy set man had appeared from the second plane and stepped onto the dock. Alex and Robert were twenty yards away.

"That's the bastard I kicked out of my office yesterday," Robert said for all to hear. "Can't you take no for an answer?" he shouted. Robert started walking toward the man.

Alex was two steps behind. He had a funny feeling in his stomach that there was going to be trouble.

"I kind of thought that you might change your mind," the heavy set man said, grinning. Two more men had climbed out of the second plane and stepped up to stand at the man's side. Robert came to a stop. The first two men and the pilot went back to unloading crates onto the dock. They paid no more attention to the newcomers.

That uneasy feeling began to creep through Alex again. Something wasn't right here. These men weren't there to rescue them. He saw one of the men slide his hand inside his jacket.

The truth hit Robert like a brick. He looked at the heavy set man with disbelief. "You!" he shouted. "You're the bastard who loosened my fuel line. You tried to kill us!"

"Not me," the man said, holding his hands up in mock surprise. He was smiling but his gray eyes measured them with a cold hard look

One of the men by his side turned and spoke to the other one in Russian. Alex's mother was Russian, and she had taught the language to all of the kids. Alex was an apt student and could speak it fluently. The words drove fear through him. The man had told the others not to let them get away. Alex saw the glint of steel. The man had a gun.

"Watch out Robert!" he shouted.

Robert was already moving, lunging straight at the three men. He caught them by surprise. The man with the gun was bringing it up when Robert crashed into them like a football player, his leg hooking around the end man and driving all three of them toward the dock's edge. Alex heard a gun fire once, twice, and then Robert and the three men were in the lake.

Alex stood there in shock, watching the water for any sign of Robert. He caught movement at his side and turned just in time to see a wrench coming at his head. Instinct caused him to duck. He lowered his shoulder and gave the man a hard nudge. The man's momentum did the rest, and he joined the others in the lake. Another man ran to the edge of the dock to help his comrades in the water. Without thinking, Alex kicked him in the butt. With a surprised scream, he joined the others. The pilot from the first plane was coming toward him. Alex took two short steps and kicked him in the knee. The pilot fell forward. Alex caught the man by his hair and slammed him face first into one of the posts. He fell back onto the dock without a sound, blood gushing from his face. Another man with a shotgun was on the second plane's pontoon. He leaned against the plane to keep his balance and raised the shotgun. Alex reached out and pushed the nose of the plane hard. The man gave a loud grunt as he lost his footing. The shotgun sailed into the water as the man sat down hard on the pontoon and slid into the lake.

Alex looked for Robert and saw him face down in the water. A crimson stain spread over the surface. Alex jerked one of the ropes from the post and, with shaking hands, began to make a noose. Maybe he could get the rope over him and drag him in. The first throw landed perfectly over Robert's outstretched arms. Alex drew the noose tight and Robert turned over slowly in the water. Sightless eyes stared up at him. Alex drew in a sharp breath. Those bastards had killed him.

A bullet plowed into a nearby post. One of the men had reached shallow water and was shooting at him. Another one was climbing onto the dock. Alex took one last look at Robert. He couldn't help him. He was dead.

Alex ran for the cabin with bullets hitting all around him. Wood splintered at his feet. He looked back as he left the dock and sprinted up the hill. Three men were out of the water. He didn't have much time. He had to get Jan out of the cabin and the hell away from here. Another shot rang out, and then he was out of sight in the thick trees. His legs began to feel weak and he couldn't breathe. He stopped and leaned over, trying to catch his breath. He heard footsteps above him and looked toward the cabin. Jan was running down the hill. She had heard the shots.

"Get back!" he shouted. "Get back!" She stopped and waited on him as he stumbled toward her. His lungs were on fire.

"Where's Robert?" she shouted. "What happened?"

Alex couldn't talk. He grabbed her, pulling her with him toward the cabin. "Dead," he finally gasped. They were at the porch.

"Oh my God," Jan said. "How?"

"They shot him," Alex panted. "The bastards shot him." They were through the cabin door. Alex collapsed into a chair and put his head between his legs. His breakfast was trying to come up. "We have to grab what we can and get out of here," he gasped. He lunged forward to the cabinets and began to throw everything to the floor. "Watch the trail," he shouted. "Call out when you can see them coming."

He found two backpacks in the bottom of the second cabinet. They seemed to be in good shape. Alex started packing, but found that he was making a mess of it. He ran to the window and shoved the packs at Jan. "You're a lot faster at packing than I am. I'll roll up the blankets here by the window."

Jan was on the floor packing before he finished talking. Alex almost had the second blanket rolled when he saw them coming.

There were four of them. The lead man carried a rifle. It looked like an M-16. "They're coming!" he shouted at Jan as he tied the second roll and ran to her side. "Come on, we have to go." She was still cramming food into the packs. Alex pulled at her arm. "We have to go now!"

Alex grabbed a hunting knife and stuck it in his belt. There were no guns in the cabin. He could hear the voices clearly now. They were almost to the cabin. Alex grabbed Jan's arm and together they ran through the back door and into the thick woods.

The tree branches whipped at them as they ran. Alex kept looking back over his shoulder, expecting to see the men coming after them, to hear shooting at any time. They ran until they couldn't run anymore. Alex collapsed on the soft, forest floor, trying to get oxygen back into his lungs. Jan stood over him. He noticed that her breathing was hard, but controlled.

"Which way do we go?" she asked, starting up the mountain again. Her voice trembled with fear.

Alex stood and looked at the sun. If he remembered the map right, it was two hundred miles to anything if they went north. "South," he said. "We flew northwest from Robert's house and Highway 16 runs east and west somewhere south of here. We could go east toward Highway 97, but the cabin's back that way." He got to his feet and followed Jan up the mountain. They slowed almost to a crawl as the climb became steeper.

"My God," Jan said, as she stopped to let him catch up. They were near the top of the mountain and from their lofty perch, could see nothing but rolling mountains and dense forest ahead. "That's a lot of mountains to cross. We'll be lucky to make ten miles a day and it's going to be hard to do even that."

Alex moved forward to a thicket of small pines and laid his pack down. "I know it's going to be hard, but we can't go north and if we go west, we'll have to cross the highest part of the mountains. East is back toward the killers. I know highway sixteen is somewhere south. I think that's our best shot."

Jan was silent for a minute. "What about the cabin?" she asked. "We could circle back and try to get to the radio. They might have left already."

"We can't go back!" Alex yelled at her. "They killed Robert, and I saw them do it. Don't you understand? I can identify them. They won't rest until we're six feet under." Alex could see tears forming in Jan's eyes. He drew her into his arms, cussing at himself for yelling.

She twisted her head back and looked into his eyes. "We might not get out of this," she whispered. "It's all my fault. I should never have taken this assignment."

"We will get out of this, and it's not anyone's fault. I was as willing to come as you. Someday we'll look back on this as the great adventure of our lives." He reached back for his pack. "Come on, we need to put space between us and them."

As Alex turned to go, he noticed the reflection of sunlight on glass below. He walked back toward the lake and suddenly had a clear line of sight to the cabin. Dropping to the ground, he motioned for Jan to keep low and join him. She crawled over to where he lay.

Alex could see movement through the small cabin windows, and then two figures came from the front of the cabin and walked back toward the lake. He could see one of the planes through the tree limbs and part of the second one. The men were unloading boxes from the first plane onto the dock and then onto the second plane. Jan was pulling at his arm. She handed him a case with binoculars inside.

"These were in the stuff you threw out from the closet," she whispered.

"This is great," Alex said as he removed them from the case. He held the binoculars up and searched their back trail. "These are really good ones."

Alex could see no movement or other signs of anyone around the path they had made through the forest.

Jan searched his eyes as he turned toward her. "You're thinking about going back, aren't you?"

Alex nodded his head. "Yes, that idea of yours might really be a good one, but not yet. We'll wait until dark and see what happens, but you're right. They may leave and not find the radio. They know that we can't get very far on foot. If they leave, they won't be able to come back until tomorrow because they can't land on the lake after dark. First, we have to make sure that they don't leave someone to guard the cabin."

* * *

They sat there, through the afternoon, watching the cabin and the lake. The sun was casting long shadows through the trees when they heard one of the planes start and then the other. A few minutes later, the planes left the lake, one after the other, and climbed toward the blue sky. One of the planes turned northwest, and the other headed southwest. In minutes, the air was still and the forest sounds came alive around them.

Alex grabbed his pack. "Come on," he said. "We have to hurry. It'll be dark soon. We have to get close enough to be sure they didn't leave anyone."

They hurried back down the trail, stopping every now and then to listen. It was already dark when they reached the clearing behind the cabin. They sat there for an hour, in the tree line watching every movement and listening to every sound. The cabin and the woods around it were quiet. The only sounds were the soft cries of the wild animals. In minutes, they wouldn't be able to see anything. They had to take a chance.

They slowly made their way to the front of the cabin, stopping to check the lake below. The lake was quiet but it was too dark to see the dock area, so Jan waited, while Alex ran down to the lake. He stopped in the shadows of the tree line and searching the area carefully. The surface of the lake was quiet and still. Nothing moved in the darker shadows of the shoreline. There were still no sounds or other indications of anyone being there. Satisfied, he made his way back to Jan. The cabin was quiet as they eased onto the front porch and opened the door, holding their breath at the squeaking hinges. The inside of the cabin was dark and ominous. The smell of the leftover breakfast drifted through the still air. Alex took out the flashlight and swept the darkness quickly, stopping the beam on any suspicious shadow. The cabin was empty. There was no one there.

They threw their packs on the floor and ran to the closets. There were only two in the small cabin. The dials of the radio glittered in the flashlight's beam, and they both cried out. Alex drug the heavy radio down and set it on the table. He searched for a lantern and found one in the kitchen. He shook the lantern, relieved to hear the slosh of kerosene. The light from the lantern gave a cheerful glow.

Alex set the lantern next to the radio and turned it on. Jan yelled as the dials lit up. The batteries were still good. Alex had never used a radio this old before, but he knew how it worked. The only thing he didn't know was the frequency he needed to be on. He slowly turned the dial until he picked up voices. Someone was broadcasting over the airwaves. He searched for a way to reply. *Wait a minute. There should be a microphone.* Fear struck through his heart when he noticed the empty jack. Where was the mike? They had to have a mike. He ran to the shelf where the radio had sat. There was nothing there. The shelf was empty. Jan jumped as he slammed his fist against the door.

"What's the matter?" she yelled.

Alex sat back down at the table and put his head between his hands. He felt sick to his stomach. The bastards had taken the mike. They were stranded weeks away from civilization. He finally turned at Jan's hand on his shoulder. He took her hand and turned slowly toward her. He could see the fear mirrored in her eyes. She knew something was wrong.

"It's the mike, honey, they took the damn mike. We can't call out."

"It's got to be here somewhere!" Jan cried and ran to the closet. They both searched every inch of the cabin, but there was no microphone. It was gone.

Tears welled in Jan's eyes. "What are we going to do?" she asked. "Are they going to come back in the morning?"

"I don't know, I just don't know. First we need to see how much food we have left in the cabin, and then we'll wait here until morning to see if they come back. If they don't, we can live here until help comes. They'll miss Robert soon and come looking for us. We can last that long."

They began to search the cabin. Jan gave a gasp when she opened the cabinet doors. The once well stocked shelves were empty. Alex threw back the trap door to the root cellar. The meat was gone and so was all of the dried food. There was nothing. The only food they had was in the backpacks.

Alex put an arm around Jan's shoulder. "If we go easy on the food, we'll still have enough to last until the rescue planes come," he assured her. "We'll be fine."

"But what if they come back in the morning?"

"I'm hoping that they think we'll never make it back from this far out, but just in case we'll be ready to run if they do."

They were dead tired. Alex built a fire in the fireplace and they shared a meal of tuna and crackers. Afterwards, they set the radio next to the bed and curled up together under the covers.

The sound from the radio drove a longing through Alex for the comfort and safety of civilization. He had set the dial to a local radio station, but the hours drug on and they heard nothing about themselves. He set his portable clock to go off at six a.m. Jan moved her head against his back. He could tell from her breathing that she was still awake. He glanced at the alarm clock. It was two o'clock. Maybe the radio was keeping them awake. He reached over to cut the power when he heard Robert's name. He felt Jan sit up behind him. They both held their breath as they listened to the news.

"Robert Owens, a well known local bush pilot was reported missing tonight. A full ground and air search will begin tomorrow morning," the radio voice said.

Alex and Jan both yelled at the radio. Alex held up his hand for silence.

"The pilot delivered medical supplies to the Mayo hospital and left word that they were to contact his wife and let her know that he would be arriving home at eight o'clock. He never showed up. As everyone knows, who lives up here, flying over the Rockies at night is no piece of cake. We wish Robert's family all of our hopes and prayers."

Alex and Jan sat there in shock. Jan spoke first. "How could they know? We saw the smashed box. They must have replaced the medical supplies. How could they know about them, and how did they pass themselves off as Robert?"

"These people have to have a lot of connections to arrange something like this. It wouldn't be hard to find out that Robert delivered medical supplies to Mayo. One of the pilots at the dock knew Robert, but to get the medication and deliver it in Robert's name takes a lot of people." Alex paused. "My God! The rescue people will never look for us here. They'll be looking between Mayo and Prince George. The people who killed Robert can do what they want with us. Alex jumped from the bed. We have to get out of here. They'll be here at first light."

"How do you know?" Jan asked. "They took all of the food for a reason. They may be leaving us here to starve. We can live off the land better here at the cabin than we can in the woods."

"They would never take that chance," Alex answered. "They can't know who we've told about this place, and I don't believe these are the kind of people who would leave witnesses around. They know that we can't go far on the food we have. That's why they took the rest of it. It will make it easier for them to catch us. We can't stay here. We can watch the cabin from the mountain to see if they come back."

They grabbed their packs and paused at the door. Alex looked longingly at the radio. He wished that they could carry it with them, but it was too heavy.

"What about Robert?" Jan asked. "We can't just leave him."

"Come on," Alex said and ran toward the lake. They stopped for a second when they reached the lake and then walked slowly out onto the dock, sweeping their flashlights back and forth across the black waters. The lake was quiet. Too quiet, Alex thought, as they neared the dock. It was as if everything alive had left its surface.

They reached the end of the dock. There was no sign of Robert.

"Either they took him with them, or he's under the surface. Either way, we can't do anything about it," Alex said.

"It's so cold out here," Jan said. "Do you get a weird feeling that something's about to happen?"

"I know what you mean," Alex answered. "It's like the quiet before the storm." Jan took his hand as they hurried off the dock.

Jan stopped and turned toward him. "They may just come back and look for us at the cabin. They could give up once they know that we're headed for the deep woods."

Alex didn't answer right away. He kept walking, and Jan fell in beside him. They reached the path up to the cabin. "You may be right, honey, but just in case, we have to be ready to run. If they come after us, we'll have a head start. If they leave again without coming after us, we'll go back to the cabin." They stopped to pick up their packs and headed into the dark woods.

The going was hard in the dark, even with the flashlights. They slowly made their way back over the first trail they had made. Alex swept the light back over the mashed grass and bent limbs. If the killers came after them, they would have an easy time of it. He remembered a vein of rock on the mountain overlooking the lake. He looked at his watch. It would be light in an hour. Maybe he could lead them in the wrong direction just in case they came after them.

The darkness slowly gave way to light. If Alex remembered right, the long climb to the mountain was just ahead. He reached up and pulled on Jan's pack. She turned quickly, startled by his pull.

"We need to cover our path up the mountain and come in from the other side." Alex could see her face in the dim light and knew that she was feeling the same hopelessness that he was. These people were killers. Alex didn't want Jan to worry, but he knew without a doubt that they would come after them. He had seen them murder Robert. They would get away with it if he and Jan disappeared. People were lost all of the time in the Rockies. He looked into Jan's eyes and knew that he didn't have to tell her. She knew already.

They stopped at the trail they had made coming up and back down the mountain and began to straighten bushes. They covered the bent grass with pine straw and dead leaves, trying to remove any sign of the trail they had left. Finally, they circled the mountain until they passed a vein of rock leading up the steep grade toward the top. They walked past the vein and then doubled back, leaving the softer forest floor and stepping onto the rock. They were careful not to leave any marks on the harder surface.

The sun was rising over the mountains to the east when they reached the top. Alex prayed that the false trail would lead the killers in a new direction, but he knew that, at best, it would only slow them down.

Alex searched the mountaintop for the best view of the lake, and they sat down to wait.

They had been waiting for thirty minutes when they heard a plane. It was the wrong color to be one of the planes from yesterday. It came straight over them and began to circle. Jan stood and started to wave, but Alex pulled her back down. She turned on him, her eyes wide with anger.

"We have to see who it is first!" he shouted at her. Jan pulled away from him and tried to stand as the plane disappeared behind the opposite mountain. They could hear the engine change pitch as it circled, and then it came back into view again. It was going to land on the lake. Jan didn't say anything but grabbed Alex's arm and squeezed until it hurt. Alex knew that she was hoping that the plane would bring good instead of evil. Alex prayed that he was wrong.

The plane swung low over the trees and touched down on the clear waters. The pilot gunned the engine and headed for the dock, coming to a rest minutes later. Alex had the binoculars out and could see the plane clearly. A man stepped out of the plane and threw a rope over one of the posts. His head was moving from side to side, searching the shoreline, as he slowly pulled the plane tight against the dock. Alex could see the glitter of a gun as he stepped up onto the dock and walked slowly toward the cabin. Five more men got out of the plane and followed him, one at a time. The first man stopped as he left the dock and waited for the others. Together, they walked toward the cabin. Alex lost sight of the men for a long moment and then they reappeared close to the cabin. He moved around the mountain until he could see the cabin clearly. He felt Jan's cold hand on his arm as she followed him. He turned to her and drew her near.

She pulled back and searched his eyes. "It's them, isn't it? What are we going to do?"

"The only thing we can do, we have to run and somehow stay ahead of them." Alex reached out and touched Jan's face. He felt fear, anger and helplessness. He should be able to protect the one he loved the most, but all he could do, all either of them could do, was run for their lives and hope that they somehow could make it back to civilization.

Alex held her face in both hands. "There are people who live here in the Rockies. Maybe we can find one of them and get a message out." Jan pulled his hands down and turned away. She knew that they didn't stand a chance in hell of finding someone in this wilderness. Alex turned the glasses back to the cabin.

Twenty minutes later, five men came out of the house and walked into the woods. One man was well ahead of the others. He had his head down following their trail. Alex tried but he couldn't see his face. The man was moving fast, and he moved like a ghost, gliding through the underbrush without leaving anything disturbed in his passing. Without knowing anything about woodsmen, Alex knew that this man was an expert in the forest. The other men blundered through the woods like a herd of cattle. *Like me,* Alex thought, as he rolled over and put the binoculars back into the pack.

Alex and Jan pulled their packs on and he led the way down the other side of the mountain. Every hour they would stop, and putting the sun on their left, pick a new landmark. They kept the landmark in sight as they walked. It was morning, and that put them heading south. In the afternoon, they would keep the sun on their right.

Alex stopped and held out his hand. The sound of the plane engine, fainter now, sounded in the still mountain air. Minutes later the plane circled the area twice and then disappeared over the higher mountains to their east. They stood for a long moment watching the sky, hoping beyond hope that a rescue plane would appear and somehow see them. Finally they started out again.

The muscles in Alex's legs began to cramp. Jan stopped and helped him rub the muscles. He cussed himself for holding them up. They didn't talk as they stopped to eat lunch. Alex didn't want to offer any false hopes, and he knew that Jan was trying to forget the whole thing, to pretend that it wasn't happening. They buried their cans and leftovers, covering the fresh dirt with pine straw.

Alex wondered how long it would be before the men would catch up. He drove the thought from his head and pushed his tired legs forward, trying to keep up with Jan. They had to get out of this somehow. They had to.

Chapter 3

Alex and Jan traveled until it was too dark to see. They took the blankets out and huddled together in the cold mountain air. Alex propped the flashlight against his pack, and they ate tuna and crackers by the soft light, washing it down with spring water from the canteen. After eating, Alex leaned over and kissed Jan. Her cheeks were wet with tears. She had been crying silently in the dark. "I know it's bad, honey," Alex began.

Jan put a finger to his lips. "I'm not crying about all of this. It's because of Robert. He was such a nice guy and his family doesn't even know."

Alex felt a growing anger when he thought about how Robert had been murdered. "Don't worry, we'll get out of all of this and make the bastards pay."

"Why did they have to kill him?"

"It's got to be something illegal. Maybe they're running drugs or guns. They're the ones that tampered with the fuel line. What I can't figure is that some of them spoke Russian. What are Russians doing here?" He finished telling her about their encounter at the dock

"Oh my God," she said. "They wanted us out of the way from the very start."

"That's right, they must have been really surprised when we showed up at the dock."

Alex lay awake long after Jan had gone to sleep. He had tried to act brave in front of her, but fear was gripping at his insides. They were in tremendous danger. It was going to take every bit of courage and luck they had just to walk out of this wilderness, but he knew that the killers would never let them leave alive. He went over everything he could think of to give them a better shot at getting away, but nothing he could think of would give them a chance in hell. Jan snuggled closer to him, and he reached out and drew her close. "Please, God, help us," he said softly and closed his eyes.

* * *

Alex woke to the first rays of the sun. The blankets were wet with dew.

He pulled them to one side and stood. A squirrel darted up a tree and sat there chattering at him. In a small clearing below, a male deer raised its head, shook its tall rack defiantly at him, and then disappeared into the underbrush.

Alex looked down to find Jan staring up at him. He gave her a soft smile and reached out his hand to help her up.

"Any sign of them?" she asked.

"I haven't seen or heard anything," he answered as he reached for one of the packs. "What do we have for breakfast?"

Jan brought out a can of spam and the rest of the open crackers. Alex hung the wet blankets over low tree limbs while she opened the spam. They were afraid to build a fire. The smell of the smoke would be a dead giveaway. Alex hadn't eaten spam since he was a kid, out fishing with his father. It didn't taste half bad.

Jan poured the last of the water into the small plastic cups they had brought with them. "We should find water in that valley," Alex said, pointing below.

Jan didn't answer. She was deep in thought. She sensed Alex watching her. "Dammit," she said. "I left the biscuits in the oven. I hope they burned to a crisp before those bastards saw them."

Alex laughed and then Jan laughed with him. They laughed until they couldn't laugh anymore. They were laughing at the desperation and fear clawing at their guts, trying to find someway to drive it away, if only for a few seconds. When it was over, when the laughter stopped, the clawing started again and the desperation grew stronger.

They were silent as they rolled up the wet blankets. "They'll probably mildew before tonight," Jan said in a lifeless voice.

"You're right," Alex agreed. "They'll be heavier to carry, too, but we need them at night."

Alex buried the empty cans and raked leaves over the fresh dirt. He looked at his watch as they started down the mountain. It was seven-thirty and still no sign of the men behind them. Maybe they would make it after all. Give them another day and he couldn't see how anyone could find them, but he knew that it was a false hope. He had a feeling that the tracker could follow their trail anywhere. They stopped briefly to pick out another landmark.

"There," Jan said, "see that funny shaped mountain. It's due south."

Alex shaded his eyes. The mountain, she was pointing to, was a good thirty miles away. The "V" shape between the mountains was easy to see. It would take two or three days to reach it. "You picked a good one," Alex said. "We can use it for the next couple days or longer."

It took a while for Alex's muscles to get limbered up. They were still sore from yesterday. His belt was already loose. Maybe something good was coming from this after all. After they got going, the soreness disappeared, and he seemed to breathe better than yesterday. Jan was walking ahead with that strong, sure stride of hers. Pride welled up in him as he followed his wife down the slope. Nine out of ten women, hell, man or woman, would have given up by now, but here she was, not complaining, pushing on, trying her best to be strong for him.

They picked a spot for lunch, about halfway down the mountain, with a good view of their back trail. Alex searched the woods behind them but couldn't see any sign of movement except for an occasional animal. They took stock of their meager food supply as they ate.

"Looks like we'll have to live off the land sooner than later," Jan said, as she packed the food back into the packs. "We may have enough food for two or three days."

Alex didn't say anything. He didn't know what to say. He could see the tension in Jan from the way her hand shook as she put the food back into the pack. There was nothing he could think of that would give her hope. The territory they would be crossing was some of the wildest he had ever seen. It would take all of their strength just to make it out of here. The men after them would have it easier. They could be supplied from the air. They would have all the food and water they needed. Alex knew that he and Jan would be weak from hunger long before they could get to civilization.

Alex lifted the pack onto Jan's shoulder and gripped her shoulder for a long moment. She turned, gave him a weak smile and, pulling away, started up the trail. Alex felt the same helplessness. Even though they hadn't seen the men that were after them, they both knew that they were there, and if they caught up, the happy life they had known only days ago would cease to exist.

They made their way up the steep side of the mountain following a stream that cut down the mountain to the valley below. The woods were teeming with animals. They could see a river at the base of the mountain. The smaller stream they were following fed into it. As they approached the river, they could see three bears at the water's edge, raking at the foaming water. One of them came out with a large fish and, taking it to the riverbank, began to strip the meat.

Alex let Jan lead the way as they crossed the smaller stream well clear of the bears and made their way down to the river, following it south until it curved and headed east. Jan stopped beside the river and let her backpack fall to the ground. Alex joined her. They needed to be going south and west, not east.

She looked back at Alex. "We'll never cross that!" she shouted over the roar of the running water.

Alex looked across the river. The sound pounded at his eardrums. Upstream from where they were, a waterfall sent foam and mist high into the air. Downstream, the raging waters were turning into an even larger river. They would have to climb the mountains to their north, back toward the bears, until they found a place to cross. The trouble was, they would be heading back toward the men after them.

"We'll have to follow the river north until we find a way across," he said, noticing the quick flicker of fear across Jan's face. "We have plenty of time. We'll be long gone before they can get here." He handed Jan her pack and they started up the mountain.

Alex was breathing easier, even in the high elevation. Slowly he was getting used to this. He turned and took a quick look back down their trail. He still couldn't see anything. Alex wondered if the men had given up and decided to let nature take its course. Even without them on their trail, the odds of getting out of this wilderness were slim.

They left the river bank and made their way back around the bears. Once clear, they turned back toward the river. It was mid-afternoon and he knew that they had to start looking for a place to camp soon, a place that would give them a good view of their back trail and at the same time, keep them hidden.

Alex had his head down, placing his feet carefully on the steep slope, when the ground suddenly leveled out. He lifted his head and looked forward. About a quarter of a mile farther on, Alex could see that the terrain climbed sharply again. He looked around for Jan and saw her disappearing into a stand of trees. He came to a stop and swung his pack to the ground. He had to rest. Alex closed his eyes and let his thoughts drift back to their home in Atlanta. He wished to God they were there now. He turned at a shout and saw Jan running toward him.

"Come on, look!" she said, grabbing his arm. He followed her through the trees to the banks of a small, hidden lake. The lake and a small meadow beside it were beautiful. The small stream, feeding the lake, flowed over a waterfall above and fell into its surface. A natural dam at the lower end of the lake slowed the water to form the crystal clear lake. The stream flowed over the dam and continued its course down the mountain and toward the river. Two otters played on rocks across the lake. Jan ran back to her pack and came back with the camera. She began taking pictures of the otters and the lake. Alex could see that she had forgotten about the men after them. For the first time since they had left the cabin, she was happy again. Alex walked back to his pack and took out the binoculars. He moved behind a large rock so that Jan couldn't see what he was doing and began to search the area below.

He could see for miles. At first, there was nothing, and then he saw movement. He adjusted the glasses and jerked his head back as a man suddenly appeared from the trees. The man had his head down and was moving slowly. He was at the spot where they had headed south. The tiny figure stopped and took his pack off. Alex could see him kneel down to study the ground. Anger swept through him. He cussed at himself for being so stupid. He and Jan had come back over the same trail when they had turned back north. He should have taken a different route. Then the men might have followed the trail south. The figure was too far away to make out clearly, but he was standing and putting his pack back on. He turned and headed straight toward Alex. How had the bastard known which trail to follow? Alex felt the same cold fear creeping through him. Even though he could only see one, he knew that the rest wouldn't be far behind.

Alex glanced around the rock to see what Jan was doing. She was almost hidden in the trees, but he could hear the clicking of her camera. Alex brought his attention back to the man. The figure had stopped and sat on a rock. He was waiting for the others to catch up. Alex looked at the sun. It was about an hour to dark. It would be dangerous for the men below to climb the mountain at night. He and Jan would have a good six or seven-hour head start in the morning. Alex put the glasses in his pack and headed for the lake. He found Jan at the far end. The otters had disappeared and she was sitting by the lake, staring at the blue water. She looked up as he sat down beside her. Alex could see that she had been crying. He put his arm around her and sat there for a long moment without saying anything. "We'll get out of this, honey." He reached out and turned her head toward him. She tried to smile but instead, lowered her head and sobbed quietly against his chest. "We haven't seen them since we started," he lied. "Another two or three days and we'll reach the highway. Then we'll be safe."

Jan dried her eyes against his shirt and looked up at him. "It was just that I was thinking about the pictures and that no one would get to see them." She put her fingers to his lips when he started to say something. "I know you're right. We can't give up." She stood suddenly. "I found a place to cross the stream." She took his hand and led him to the upper end of the lake until they were level with the waterfall. The mist was icy cold as she pulled Alex farther in.

"I'll be damned," he said as she pointed to a level area behind the falls, eaten out by the falling water. The lake was narrow here, and he could see that the natural ledge reached the other side.

"Come on," Alex said, pulling her back. "Let's get our packs and cross over. It will be the perfect place to camp."

It was almost dark when they reached the other side and found a clear area, well hidden from the other side of the lake. Alex found some dry firewood and began to build a fire.

"Won't they see the fire?" Jan asked worriedly.

"We're well back from the edge of the shelf and in these trees, there's no way they can see the light."

Jan ran to her pack. "Coffee," she cried. "We can have coffee."

Alex knew how much Jan liked coffee. She could drink four or five cups a day. Jan dragged out an aluminum cook kit from the pack and soon had a coffee pot going. She fried pancakes, and they had a meal of fried bread, coffee, and syrup.

The hot meal made both of them feel better. Alex felt guilty about not telling Jan about the men below, but tomorrow would be time enough. They would have to get up early. Alex had noticed that the mountain behind them climbed steeply away from the lake and the river. The easy way out would be to head west toward the river, but they could be trapped if there was no way to cross. Alex realized that they would have to climb the mountain and then turn back to the river. It would probably take them all day tomorrow to reach the top. He prayed that the men after them would continue north and not come across the lake after them.

They killed the fire and rolled up together in the mildewed blankets. Jan kissed him good night and pulled him tight against her. Alex went to sleep with the soft sound of her breathing in his ear.

Chapter 4

Alex woke the next morning with a start. It was still dark. He could hear the soft sounds of small animals moving around the lake, but something was wrong. There was something else in the dark, something larger. He rolled away from Jan and gently pulled the blankets up around her neck. The mountain air was bitterly cold. He shivered as he moved slowly away from the wooded area and toward the lake. Alex stopped as he heard a sound from the other side of the lake, a sound out of sync with the natural sounds around him. A cold fear gripped him. Alex turned to wake Jan, but decided against it. First, he had to make sure. How could it be the men after them? They couldn't have climbed the mountain in the dark? He squatted down on the wet grass next to the water and strained his eyes against the darkness. Then he saw a dark shape move and then another one. The shapes seemed to be searching the area on the other side of the lake. They moved through the night with ease, but how could they see in the almost total darkness? The glare of reflected red glowed like a ghost and then Alex knew, they had infrared. They could see in the dark. He turned his face away. It would show up like a Halloween lantern. Alex lay flat down on the ground and crawled slowly back into the shelter of the trees. He moved to Jan's side and put his hand over her mouth. He wished now that he had told her last night. "They're here," he said softly when he felt her move. "We have to pack now and leave."

"Where are they?" she whispered urgently when he released his hand. "Did they find the waterfalls? How did they find us in the dark?"

"I'll tell you later. Right now we have to get out of here."

They rolled up the blankets and quickly stuffed their belongings back into the backpacks. Alex led Jan away from the lake. When they reached the darker shadows of the trees, he pulled at her arm to stop and turned back to see where the men were. As far as he could tell, they were still on the other side of the lake. There was already enough light to see by, but a heavy mist surrounded the lake. Even with infrared vision, the men across the lake would have a hard time seeing. The dim glow of light over the eastern mountains was getting stronger. Daylight was only minutes away. Alex stopped and looked back at their camp site.

"What is it?" Jan whispered, pulling at him.

"I forgot to scatter the rocks and hide the evidence of the fire. They can see it from across the lake when it gets light and be on us before we can get halfway up the mountain."

Jan pulled at him again. "We can't do anything about it now."

Alex took her shoulders. "Honey, I want you to start up the mountain and don't turn back for anything." Jan started shaking her head. Alex could feel her stubbornest. She had to leave now for this to work. "Please, Jan, please do this for me."

Jan hung her head. Alex could see that she was giving in. She grabbed his pack and stood for a second. "I'm waiting two hundred feet up the mountain. If you aren't there in twenty minutes, I'm coming back."

Alex felt the tears on her cheek as he kissed her. He let go and she started climbing. He waited until she disappeared into the darkness and ran back toward their campsite. He lay down and wormed his way the last few yards until he felt the rocks of the fireplace. He could see the shapes of the men clearly now. Soon the night goggles wouldn't do them any good. They would have to take them off. The early morning fog was the only thing protecting him now. He had to work fast. He carefully rolled the rocks away from the fireplace and scattered the unburnt pieces of firewood. Using pine straw, he covered the ashes and burnt wood. Alex felt more than heard something moving toward him from the other side. He lay perfectly still and strained every sense to cut through the darkness. A shadow appeared through the fog coming straight toward him. The shadow stopped on the other side of the small lake, and Alex watched as the red glow moved in a wide arch and then disappeared. The shadow had taken off his night goggles. Alex hadn't realized it, but in another few minutes, it would be light enough for them to see him clearly. The fog was melting away fast. He pulled a handful of pine straw in front of his face and tried to burrow into the ground. The man across the lake didn't move. The minutes passed. If they saw him now, he would run away from the mountain, toward the river, to draw them away from Jan. Alex grimly clenched his teeth. In minutes, the light would cut off his escape to Jan and the mountain. He could still circle to the waterfalls without being seen and hide there. Maybe it would give Jan time enough to get away.

Alex jerked as someone shouted. The shout came from the waterfalls. The man across from Alex turned and ran toward the falls. Alex didn't hesitate. He came to his feet and ran toward the mountain. They had found the ledge behind the falls. The only way out for him and Jan was over the mountain. He left the thicker trees by the lake and started climbing. He cursed when he saw Jan waiting, but deep down he knew that she would be there. Alex was too much out of breath to say anything. Jan saw the look on his face and without a word, handed him his pack and started up the mountain. The mountain was small, but steep. They were halfway up when they heard shouting behind them. The hunters had found their trail.

They climbed without talking, using the small trees and bushes to pull themselves up. Alex's breath came in short gasps. His legs felt like butter. Even Jan was beginning to show the strain. Every now and then they could hear the sounds of their pursuers, and they would climb faster, pushing themselves to their limit. The top was a hundred yards away and then fifty. Jan slipped from ten feet above and slid all the way back to Alex. He caught her and pushed her ahead.

Suddenly, the dirt exploded in front of Alex. The crash of a gunshot sounded. The men behind could see them. Jan was to the top and reaching for him. Alex would have shouted, but there was no air left to shout. He pushed himself over the top and turned to see how close the men were. Alex felt the sudden heavy pull of Jan's hand on his jacket. He turned and took a step toward her, but there was no ground, only empty space. Alex reached for anything to stop his fall. He caught onto a small tree, but his hand was slipping. Jan was dragging both of them down. He could feel her clawing at him. Her hold was slipping. He hooked his arm around the tree and reached down with his other hand to grab her wrist. He caught a glimpse of rocks and trees hundreds of feet below. The small tree was bending. It wouldn't hold them. The cliff side was rushing at him. The tree gave suddenly and swung them hard against the rock face. Jan's weight was tearing his arm off. Alex dug at the rock with his feet, looking for anything to hold on to. He could feel the tree giving away. He saw a ledge below just as the tree dropped them another foot. He had to take a chance. Using his legs, he pushed away from the cliff and then swung back, letting go of the tree just as it crashed into the cliff side. He clawed at the rock face with one hand, trying not to be pushed away from the cliff. Alex had a death grip on Jan. He would never let her go . . .

Alex hit the ledge hard, feeling the air being knocked out of him. He felt the branches of the tree as it swept past. Elation swept through him. They had to be on the ledge. A loud crash sounded as the tree hit the bottom of the gorge. He felt Jan's weight dragging at him. His legs were over the edge. The edge of the shear drop-off just a few feet away. Both of his hands were free. He had lost his grip on Jan. She had slipped down and was holding onto his legs, her feet kicking in the air. Her weight was too much. He was losing his hold. He clawed at the rock as he slid one foot and then another. He could feel Jan trying to climb his legs. Alex felt more than saw a crack in the rock as he slid toward the edge. It might be wide enough to get his fingers in, but he had already slid past it. He struggled toward the crack one inch at a time until he felt his fingers slide in. Slowly, he reached down with his other hand until he could get a good grip on Jan. Alex began to pull her toward him an inch at a time. He could feel her pushing up, trying to help. She must have found a toe hold. Seconds later, she was over the edge, and they both lay safe on the cold rock.

Alex looked up. They were under an overhang. A hole ran a good six feet back into the cliff. He pulled Jan into the hole. She was in shock. Alex rubbed her trembling body with shaking hands. He heard voices and put his hand over her mouth. The men were standing on the top of the cliff, ten feet above his head. Alex dragged Jan further back into the hole. He held his breath as the voices got louder.

"I see the tree limbs moving below," one of the men said. "It must have been them. They're done for."

"Come on, we have to go down," another voice said.

"Why?" someone said. "There's no way they could have survived that, it's at least five hundred feet down."

"The camera," the second voice said. "We have to get the film. She could have taken pictures at the lake. Come on, get a move on. It's going to take us half a day to get down there."

Alex stroked Jan's hair gently until the voices disappeared. He kissed her on the forehead and wiped the dirt from her face. Her eyes had a vacant look. They had to go now. If it took the hunters a half day down and the same back up, Jan and he would have a full day's lead. It could mean the difference between life and death. He wondered how they had known about the camera. These people seemed to know everything.

He left Jan and leaned out over the dizzying height, searching for a way back to the top. A patch of small trees halfway up was just out of his reach. Alex stepped back to the ledge and took off his belt, but it wouldn't reach. He remembered the piece of rope he had put into the pack. He found it and, leaning back, threw it around the first tree. He caught the other end of the rope as it came back and climbed up to the tree. He threw the rope around another tree closer to the top. He climbed up to the second tree and, putting his foot on the tree, pushed himself over the top. He lay there for a second listening to the faint voices of the hunters as they climbed down the mountain. He finally got up and, tying the rope to a large tree, threw it back over the edge. He drew in a sigh of relief as he saw that the rope had reached the ledge below. Using the small trees as toeholds, he climbed back down until he reached the ledge.

Jan lay still in the darkness. There was only one thing he could do. Holding her up, he slapped her hard across the face. She started to scream and Alex slid his hand across her mouth, holding her struggling body tight against the rock face. Suddenly, Jan realized where she was. Alex could see it in her eyes. He lifted his hand slowly from her mouth. She grabbed him and he kissed her face and lips. They stood for a long moment lost in the safety of each other's arms, until Alex gently pushed her away. They had to get going. They tied the packs to the end of the rope, and Jan began to climb as Alex held the rope tight. He climbed after her a minute later and felt her hands on him when he reached the top.

"Where did they go?" Jan asked, as Alex pulled the packs up.

"They think we're dead. They think that your camera is down there with you and went to the bottom to retrieve it. It'll take them a day to reach the bottom and get back up here. We'll be well ahead again by the time they pick up our trail."

Alex could see relief spread across Jan's face. "My God. That means we may beat them to the highway." She grabbed Alex and kissed him over and over again. She finally pushed him back. "Why do they want my camera?"

"Because they think that you may have taken pictures of them back at the lake."

"Oh! I didn't think about that."

"Come on," he said laughing. "We still have a long way to go."

They made their way around the cliffs and started up the next mountain. Alex stopped halfway up and searched their back trail. There was no sign of the men after them. The fear and pressure Alex had felt for the last two days began to melt away. The men would have to travel slow to follow their trail. With a day's head start and only three days or so to the highway, they would never catch up.

They laughed and talked as they climbed, trying to keep their mind off what had happened yesterday. The terrain became steeper and they had to stop every thirty minutes or so to rest. Alex knew that it was more for him than Jan, but he was getting stronger with each mile. The last time they stopped, Alex used the binoculars to scan behind them again. There was still no sign of their pursuers.

Two hours later, they came upon a flat, grassy spot on the mountainside. They could see for miles back down their trail. Alex took the binoculars out and began to search the opposite mountain.

"Do you see anything?" Jan asked.

"No, nothing,"

Jan held her arms out wide. "Oh, Alex, it's so beautiful. For the first time since the cabin, I feel safe. I think we've lost them."

She took out her camera and began to snap pictures. Alex lay down on the grass. Jan finished and lay down beside him. Alex rolled over and kissed her. Jan's eyes grew sober.

"I'm kidding myself, aren't I? I mean, it couldn't be this easy."

"I don't know," Alex answered. "But it really looks like we've lost them."

Jan pulled his hand down to her breast. "Oh, Alex, make love to me. Let's forget about them, and pretend that it's the first time, and we don't have a worry in the world."

Alex knew that Jan needed this to push the fear back, to forget even for a minute that everything was all right and that they were going to make it to safety. He needed it, too, to lose himself in her love, to bring back that hope of tomorrow.

They spread the blankets on the slope and made love in the warm sunlight. Afterwards, they lay on the mountainside, talking about what they would do when they got back. Neither of them mentioned the cabin or the people after them. They pulled the warm blankets over them as the sun sank over the mountaintop and slept like babies, rolled up in the blankets on the soft mat of grass. They didn't notice the flicker of fire in the valley far below.

* * *

The next morning, Alex searched their back trail but still couldn't see anything. They started out in the still morning air before the sun's rays could climb over the tree tops to the east. A mile further on, they crossed another stream and turned back toward the river. They made good time and reached the mountaintop overlooking the river during midmorning. Tall cliffs reached up from both sides of the river.

They were close to the river now and on top of the cliffs. It seemed impossible to cross. Alex took the binoculars out again and searched the mountain slope behind them. He saw movement. It was a huge bear, making its way slowly toward the river. Alex wondered if it knew a way across. Maybe they should follow. He put the idea aside. They would be going back toward the cabin and the men after them. Alex saw movement again behind the bear. This time it wasn't an animal and it wasn't on the ground. The dot in the sky grew larger, and Alex heard a soft hum. The hum grew louder and louder until it was a roar. The dot became a helicopter, and it was heading straight for them.

Alex yelled for Jan and they ran for the cover of the nearby trees, diving to safety just in time. The helicopter circled the top of the mountain slowly, moving closer and closer until it was directly over them. Did they know they were here? Had they seen them from the air? Alex could feel the sound, beating at them through the trees. Jan had her head against his chest. The helicopter seemed to stay there forever. Finally it moved outward in larger and larger circles. Its nose tilted forward, and it disappeared. Alex ran to the edge of the plateau and dropped to the ground. The helicopter was landing at the base of the mountain. Alex had forgotten about a helicopter. They had guessed at the direction they were going and called in a damn helicopter. Five tiny figures got out, and the helicopter lifted. In minutes, it was a dot again in the blue sky.

Alex felt the same cold fear grip his chest. He could feel Jan tremble as she lay down at his side. They were three days away from the road and running out of food. It would be impossible to stay ahead. One of the figures was walking in a larger and larger circle. He was searching for their trail. The tiny figure stopped and waved at the others. From where the figure was standing, Alex knew that they had found their trail. One of them stepped away from the others and looked up the mountain. Alex knew that the man couldn't see them without glasses, but it seemed like he was looking straight at him. Suddenly, Alex heard a soft drone in the clear mountain air. The drone changed to a familiar pitch. It was the helicopter. It came fast from the east and circled over the five men once before it headed straight for them. The men on the ground had given the helicopter the direction. The only good thing was that the helicopter couldn't land on the plateau. There wasn't enough room. Alex and Jan ran for cover again under the evergreens. The helicopter circled slowly with its nose down as it flew up the mountain. Alex could see two men in the cockpit. One of them had glasses. He pushed Jan's head down as they came closer.

The helicopter searched for ten minutes or so and then climbed high into the morning air. It headed east and was soon a small dot in the blue sky.

"They know we're here!" Jan shouted.

"I'm afraid so," Alex answered. He didn't have an answer for the helpless look on her face. He slung the pack onto his back and started down the mountain toward the river. "They have a radio. They can call in the helicopter any time they want." He turned to face her. "I'm sorry, honey, I thought we were rid of them, but it looks like we'll have to push ourselves that much harder. We still have two or three hours lead." Jan didn't say anything but pushed ahead of Alex.

It was rough going. They kept looking for a place to climb down the cliffs. It was afternoon before they saw the most likely place to climb down. Alex searched the mountaintop they had left only hours before. The five men would be there soon and on higher ground. Alex didn't know how far their guns could reach, but he had heard of thousand-yard shots. He followed Jan down the steep slope. There was still no sign of the men when they reached the edge of the cliff overlooking the river. Alex searched the river below with the binoculars.

"We'll never make it across," Jan said. Her voice sounded high pitched and desperate. Alex wanted to grab her and hold her tight, to somehow protect her from the killers after them. There had to be a way out of this.

Alex spotted a section of rock jetting out over the river. The finger of rock almost reached across the river. The gap that was left, seemed narrow from this far away, but Alex knew that it would widen as they got closer. At one time it had blocked part of the raging waters, but years of pounding water, eating at the base, had left only the narrow shelf hanging in the air. The shelf was at the base of the cliff and a long way down. They hurried along the cliff edge toward the rock outcrop. They had to reach the shelf before the hunters caught up to them.

They reached the rock cliff overlooking the shelf two hours later. It was mid-afternoon. They didn't have much time. Every second brought the men closer. The roar of the rushing water drowned out all sound. Jan was shouting at him. Alex leaned over the cliff edge and followed her pointing finger. There was a way down. Giant steps of rock led down to the river and the shelf.

Alex searched both sides of the shelf with the binoculars. A tree had fallen across the gap between the shelf and other side. They had found their way across. He followed the opposite cliff side up with the glasses. It wasn't as steep as this side. They should be able to climb it. Alex looked at his watch. They had to make it down and back up the other side before the hunters could reach the rock outcrop. If they got caught on the cliffs? He tried not to think about it.

Alex started to lower the binoculars when he caught a flicker of light on the opposite side of the river. He adjusted the binoculars. It was a cabin setting back from the top of the cliffs. The light was the reflection of sunlight on one of the few windows. He couldn't see very much of the cabin, but it looked to be in good shape. He grabbed Jan's arm and handed her the binoculars, pointing in the direction of the cabin.

She adjusted the binoculars and then started jumping up and down. "There has to be people!" she shouted close to his ear. "A radio!"

"Don't get your hopes up," he shouted back. "It's getting cold. There should be a fire, but I don't see any signs of smoke. The cabin is probably abandoned, but there could be a radio." Alex cast a worried eye toward the mountain behind them. "We have to get going. We don't have much time."

Holding on to Jan's hand, Alex slowly let her down the first step. She dangled there, a good four feet above the next shelf. He looked down at her, and she nodded her head. He let go and she dropped to the hard rock, rolling once and coming to her feet. Alex let himself over the edge and dropped to land beside her. One by one, they made their way down the steps until they stood on the bank of the raging river.

It was late afternoon. Alex kept looking for the hunters to appear at any time. The last ledge of rock ran three hundred or so yards up the river and about the same down the other way. The rock shelf and the tree were upriver from them and a good hundred feet above that, was a giant waterfall. Spray from the waterfall peppered the tree. Alex climbed up to the tree and touched the slippery bark. This was going to be dangerous. One slip and they would fall into the raging waters. They stood for a long minute looking at the tree and the rushing water below. Alex felt his stomach draw into a knot, but Jan seemed calm as she searched the other side.

"I think we can make it," she said. "The tree limbs will give us a hand hold part-way."

"The other part is what I am worried about," Alex answered. "One slip and it will be all over, and we don't know if the limbs are rotten."

"What choice do we have?" Jan's voice had hardened. She had a determine set to her jaw.

Alex was silent for a long moment. "None."

The trunk of the tree rested on a ledge of rock on the other side. Alex grabbed a tree limb and shook the tree. The trunk rocked back and forth as he pushed on the limb. Six inches either way and the trunk would slide off the ledge and take them and the tree into the raging waters.

"We have to go now!" Jan shouted. "They'll be here at any time."

Alex knew that she was right. It was fear that held him here, but he knew that they couldn't go back. It was all or nothing.

He held the tree while Jan started across. The tree sloped upward making it even more difficult. Jan moved slowly, stopping with every step, making sure she had a good grip before taking the next one. She made it to the last limb and sat down on the slippery bark. There was nothing to hold onto for the next twenty feet. Jan slid forward one agonizing inch at a time. Her hands kept slipping on the wet bark, causing her to fall to one side and then the other, until she caught her grip again and pulled herself back upright. A stab of fear shot through Alex every time her hand slipped. Her hair and clothing were already wet from the spray. He raised his hands and shouted as she finally reached the other side and pulled herself onto the tiny ledge.

It was his turn now. The wet tree limbs were hard to hold onto. He almost fell, trying to make it around the first big limb. His feet kept slipping on the trunk as he tried to push himself forward. The bark was icy cold. Alex stopped at the last limb and slowly sat down, holding onto the limb with all his might. He tried not to look down, but something kept drawing his eyes to the raging waters below. Each time he looked, his insides turned to jelly and he would start to shake. He kept taking deep breaths as he slid out to arm's length.

Alex finally let go of the limb and lay down on the trunk. He began to move forward like an inchworm, reaching out with his arms until he couldn't reach any further and then pushing forward with his legs until his butt was high in the air. Alex would stay there for a second and then start all over again. The spray from the waterfall stung his face and neck. His clothes seem to weigh fifty pounds. Alex kept his eyes on Jan's face as he pulled himself slowly across. He was making headway. She seemed a lot closer. He slid his arms forward for his next hold when, suddenly he felt his legs slipping. Alex yelled, as he slowly slid around the tree until he was hanging upside down. He could hear Jan shouting at him. Alex froze. He couldn't move. He was paralyzed with fear. He drew in long breaths of wet air to calm himself and tried several times to pull himself back on top of the tree, but every time, he slid back to the same position. His arms and legs were getting weak. He saw something move on the tree and looked up to see Jan leaning toward him. She was shouting at him again.

"Alex, cross your legs and climb the underside of the tree."

Alex drew his trembling legs together and, closing his eyes for a second, began to inch up the tree, sliding his arms forward first and then his legs. He didn't look up or down. All of his energy and concentration was on the next inch and then the next. Suddenly, he felt Jan's fingers on his arms, pulling at him. He took another hold and heaved himself forward again, and then he felt Jan's hands on his coat. She had to pry his fingers from the tree and then he was safe, laying on the wet rock, gasping for breath. They sat there holding onto each other for a long time. Jan was crying and kissing his lips, his face. Suddenly, she shouted into his ear and pointed. The men were there at the top of the cliff. Alex saw the reflection of binoculars. They were watching them. They must have passed them by and then doubled back. One of them lowered himself over the first ledge and another man followed him.

"Quick, grab the tree," Alex said. "We need to throw this end into the river."

The tree was wet and heavy. Using all of their strength, they slid the tree to the edge of the ledge and then, with one final heave, shoved it over. The tree hung for a minute and then fell into the rushing water below.

Jan and Alex began to climb up the steep cliff side. Alex turned to take one last look at the men on the other side. They were still there. What were they waiting for? Alex searched the cliffs above for a way up. To his right, a large crevice led almost to the top. Its darkness would give them cover. He caught Jan's coat and pointed toward the crack. She started that way when suddenly the rock exploded above Jan. She screamed and scrambled toward the darkness of the crevice. Rock bits from another bullet cut into Alex's face as he followed her. The crevice was a good thirty feet deep and ran up the cliff side at an angle. There were plenty of hand holds. The sun was low in the western sky, putting them in an even deeper shadow. The men on the other side had stopped shooting. They couldn't see them.

The crevice ran out twenty feet from the top. They would be exposed when they left the shadows. Alex stopped and searched the opposite side with the binoculars. There was no sign of the men. They could wait until dark but then they couldn't see the handholds.

"Climb as fast as you can," he said.

"Don't worry," Jan answered.

The cliff side had rounded over making it easy to climb, but Alex was having a hard time keeping up with Jan. They were halfway there and then three quarters when suddenly the rock shattered next to Alex's hand. A second later, they heard the sound. The one with the rifle had stayed behind. *My God,* thought Alex, *he must be over eight hundred yards away.* They began a mad scramble for the cliff top. Shots peppered the rock around them.

Alex heard Jan grunt. "Are you all right?" he yelled. She didn't answer. He yelled again.

She seemed all right. She had reached the top and then was over. He was right behind her. They dropped to the ground behind a small rise. They were safe.

Alex turned Jan over, moving his hands over her body. "What happened, are you hit?" Then he felt something wet. "My God, you're bleeding."

"I'm afraid so," she answered and smiled weakly at him. "I don't think it's too bad. I seem to be able to move." She stood as if to make her point. "Come on, the cabin's not far away. We can fix it there."

Alex kept his arm around her as they walked toward the cabin. He felt her leaning heavily on him after the first hundred yards. Fear drove through him like a hot dagger. *God, don't let anything happened to her,* he prayed.

The sun was setting when they reached the cabin. Somebody had taken good care of the place. Alex could see evidence of recent calking between the logs. The cabin was small. He guessed it to be about thirty by thirty feet. A set of traps hung neatly against one side of the door, well away from the weather. There was nobody home. It was too quiet. Anyone there would have heard the shots and challenged them before now. Holding on to Jan, he slid the latch down and pushed the door opened.

The one room cabin was empty. "Anyone home!" he shouted just in case. Alex jumped as a squirrel darted across the porch behind him. He lifted Jan through the door and stopped just inside. A large rock fireplace took up one wall of the cabin. Cooking pots and pans hung neatly to both sides. A table and four chairs set toward the back of the cabin. To the other side and well within the warmth of the fireplace was a double brass bed. A chest-of-drawers set next to the bed. In the front corner stood a set of bunk beds. Alex had seen no road up to the cabin.

Whoever owned the cabin had to lug all of this up on a pack horse or by helicopter.

Alex steered Jan toward the bed and took her coat off. The blood stain had spread across her shirt and down into her pants. His hand shook at the sight of the blood. He took a deep breath as he unbuttoned her shirt and pulled it gently away from the wound. He glanced up at her face. She smiled at him, but he could tell that she was in a lot of pain and her face was chalk white.

"I'll make it better, honey," he soothed. Alex gently pulled her sweater over her arms. He could see the wound clearly now. The blood was oozing out slowly, making a small stream down her side. The bullet had exited in the front about three inches from her right side, but he needed to see her back.

"Hold on, honey, I need to turn you over."

Jan groaned as he rolled her gently onto her side. The bullet had entered halfway between her side and spine. Alex tried desperately to remember the pictures he had seen of the human body. The bullet hole was high, but as far as he could tell, it was under the lungs. Jan didn't seem to have any problem breathing. The other good thing was that it was on the side away from the heart. There was no way he could tell if it had hit the intestines or any of the other organs.

The first thing he needed to do was stop the bleeding. He rolled Jan back over and ran to the chest-of-drawers, looking for anything to use as bandages. He found bed sheets and using his knife, cut one of the sheets into strips. He lay the strips on the bed and slid her arms over his shoulders.

"Now I'm not getting sexy here," he said gently as he lifted her to a sitting position on the bed. Jan gave a weak laugh. Alex gently unhooked her bra. She gave a gasp of pain as the pressure was released.

Alex used pads over the front and back wounds and wrapped them with the strips of sheet, starting under Jan's breast and ending at her belly button. He pulled the white cloth tight at each turn and tied the ends. When he finished, he laid her gently back on the bed. Her face was white and drawn. He piled the covers over her half naked body and went quickly to the fireplace.

A pile of smaller wood was stacked neatly by the hearth. It was as if someone had left yesterday and would be back tonight. Alex built a fire and hurried back to Jan.

"I'm going outside for some water," he said. She smiled at him and nodded her head.

Jan grabbed his arm as he turned to go. "How bad is it?" she asked. Her eyes searched his.

In the years they had been married, he had never been able to lie to her. "It looks bad," he said. "I don't think it hit anything major, but you lost a lot of blood. I need to get some food into you fast. You'll be fine, honey, trust me."

"Is there a radio here?"

"I don't know, I haven't had time to search. Let me get some hot food into you, and I'll look." Jan nodded her head and closed her eyes.

Grabbing a pot and a canteen, Alex ran outside to look for water. A well-traveled path led him to a bubbling spring behind the cabin. The owner had built a dam out of rocks and it formed a small pool. Alex filled the pot and canteen and hurried back. He slowed as he came up to the back of the cabin, noticing a set of steps leading down to a wooden door under the cabin. Setting the water down, he stepped down the six or so steps and, sliding the latch to the side, pushed the heavy door open. It was a root cellar. He found a candle and matches on a small shelf by the door. Lighting the candle, he held it high and moved into the cool darkness. The cellar was lined on both sides with shelves. A large wooden box sat against the back wall. He opened the box. It was filled to the top with cured meat, probably deer meat, packed away in salt. He turned to the shelves. There were potatoes and different kinds of roots. Dried onions hung from the ceiling.

Alex carried the pot of water into the cabin. He hung another empty pot on a metal swivel and poured half of the water into it, swinging it back over the fire. Hurrying back to the root cellar, he cut off pieces of the meat and gathered several potatoes, along with onions, peppers, and roots. *The roots must be eatable,* he reasoned, *or why would they keep them?* He took everything back to the cabin and cut them up into the pot. The meat provided the salt. Soon a delightful smell filled the cabin.

Alex checked Jan. Her eyes were closed. He felt her forehead. She didn't have a fever, but he knew that would change. She opened her eyes as he turned away.

"How are you doing?" he asked softly, taking her hand.

"The pain isn't any worse," she said, squeezing his hand. "But my whole side is numb."

"I'm cooking some stew. I found some stuff in a root cellar."

"I can smell it," Jan said. "It smells so good."

"Try to get some rest, I'll bring you some as soon as it cooks." Alex stood, but Jan held onto his hand.

"What about those men?" she asked. "They'll be here tomorrow."

"I don't think so, we pushed the tree into the river. They'll have to go somewhere above the cliffs to cross."

"They can call the helicopter back."

Damn it, Alex had thought of that, but he'd hoped that she hadn't. A feeling of doom settled over him. How would they get away with Jan in this shape? He would have to think of something, and soon.

Something in his eyes gave his thoughts away. Jan squeezed his hand. "Don't worry, we'll find a way," she said.

Alex went back to the fire and put another piece of wood on. The water in the pot was boiling. He saw a bow and quiver of arrows hanging over the fireplace. Funny, he hadn't noticed them before. He took down the quiver and counted the arrows. There were twelve. The bow was unstrung, but the bow string was wound around one end. He remembered the countless hours he had spent on the archery range in college. He had been good enough to win several titles, but that was a long time ago. At least they would have something to fight with. He put the quiver back. Arrows against guns. Who was he kidding? The bow was a modern compound, but it was no match for a gun. He searched the cabin from top to bottom. There was no radio and no guns. Maybe the owner had carried them with him.

Jan had awaken while he searched. She motioned him to the bed. "No radio?"

Alex shook his head no. She held out her hand and pulled him toward her. "I've been thinking. They won't hurt a wounded woman. Leave me food and water by the bed and go for help. You can make it without me to slow you down."

"You know I can't do that. It would take a week, maybe longer, and what makes you think they won't kill you. They have to kill us now."

"Hold me," Jan cried suddenly, holding her arms out to him. "Please hold me."

Alex held her as sobs racked her body. They both cried together until Jan pushed him away. She smiled gently as she lifted her hand and wiped the tears from his cheeks. Her hand felt cold on his face.

"Alex, you know I'm right," Jan said softly. "I can't travel. You have to leave me here, or we'll both die."

Alex kissed her tears away and then kissed her soft lips. Her lips returned the kiss hungrily, her arms drawing him into the bed until he lay beside her. She stroked his hair gently. They lay there without talking while the darkness settled in for good. The strong smell of stew filled the cabin. Their dinner was done.

Alex gently released Jan and went to the pot. He filled a bowl and carried it back to the bed. Jan's face turned white when he pulled her to a sitting position. He waited until the pain eased and began to feed her. She ate half of the stew and then pushed the bowl away. Jan shivered as he pulled the covers tight around her chin. He felt her head. It was hot to the touch.

She drank the glass of water he'd brought and slid down into the bed. She was asleep in minutes.

Alex blew out the candle and slid into the bed beside her. He lay there for an hour in the darkness trying to think of a way out. Maybe he could wait until they got close and draw them away from the cabin. That wouldn't work. They must have binoculars. They would have seen them head for the cabin. Jan needed a doctor badly. She couldn't wait for him to come back. That left him with only one choice. He had to leave the cabin before they got here and somehow set up an ambush outside the cabin. Maybe he could hit one of them and get a gun. His eyes kept closing, until finally he drifted off to sleep. He dreamed of a vacation they'd had together in Mexico last summer.

* * *

Alex jerked awake. It was early morning but still dark. He felt for Jan but she wasn't there. Panic swept through him when he realized that she was gone. The fire had died during the night, leaving the cabin in complete darkness. He jumped from the bed and searched for the candle. Finally he found it and fumbled around for a match. The dim candle light reached out into the darkness as he swung it around. He laughed in relief when he saw her sitting at the table.

"So my beauty is feeling better," he said as he approached her. "Maybe you're feeling well enough to make breakfast."

Alex slowed. Jan didn't move. There was something about the way she sat. He took one step and then another. Fear began to sweep through him like an icy breeze. The small candle made weird dips and jabs into the darkness as his hand began to tremble. He took one short step and then another. Suddenly, Alex gave a startled cry and ran to her.

"Jan, no! Oh God, no!" He dropped to his knees and pulled her to him, sobbing as he rocked her back and forth. He kept brushing her hair and kissing her cold face, hoping beyond hope that she would move, that she would be alive, but her face only got colder and no matter how hard he rubbed, no circulation, no warmth returned to her beautiful limbs. He stayed there with her lifeless body until the early morning sunlight filtered through the tiny windows. Alex finally stood and pushed her body gently back against the chair. He cried out in pain as the growing light showed another horror. A knife was protruding from her chest. Alex pulled her back against him and sat there rocking back and forth. She had killed herself to save him. Jan knew him better than he knew himself. She knew that he would never leave her.

Finally, Alex let her go and, with numb hands, drew the knife from her lifeless body. He pulled her head softly back to his chest. "Oh my darling. Oh my love. You didn't have to do this," he whispered softly into her ear. "Where was that positive attitude you always had? We could have gotten out of this somehow." Alex was sobbing again. His tears wet her cheek. He laid Jan gently back against the chair and stood. Alex turned in a daze, picked up the knife, and walked over to the water pot to wash it. He held the shining steel up to the light and, taking both hands, brought the point against his chest. One quick shove and it would be over. He could be with his Jan again. He hesitated. Jan had given her life for him. He couldn't waste it now. Alex jerked around at the faint sound of a helicopter. He put the knife away and ran outside.

Alex could see the helicopter, a small dot in the clear mountain air. It was headed for the other side of the river. He had thirty minutes. Maybe less. Alex ran back into the cabin and stripped the blankets from the bed. He rolled Jan's body in the blankets and carried her into the root cellar. Laying her on the dirt floor, he pulled baskets from under the bottom shelf. There was a two-foot trench behind the baskets. Alex slid Jan's body under the bottom shelf and into the trench. He sat there for a second and then reached down and pulled back the blanket, revealing her beautiful face. He brushed a strand of hair away from her forehead. Her face was peaceful and young, like a little girl sleeping. Alex leaned down and kissed her for the last time. A stream of tears fell on her face. He gently wiped them away and pulled the blanket back. He piled the baskets over her body and left the root cellar, softly latching the door behind him.

Alex ran back into the cabin and threw the bloody sheets into the fireplace. He wet another sheet and scrubbed the blood from the table and floor and threw it into the flames. Maybe if they didn't see the blood they wouldn't look for her. He couldn't stand the thought of their hands on his beloved Jan. Smoke filled the cabin. It didn't matter. They already knew where he was. He filled a container with the leftover stew and, taking both packs, the bow, and the quiver of arrows, headed for the door. He stopped just outside and dropped the packs. *Jan's camera,* he couldn't leave that for the bastards. He could see the helicopter lifting off from the other side as he gathered his packs again and headed for the root cellar with Jan's camera in hand. They would be here in seconds.

Alex removed the film from the camera. He pulled two of the baskets off Jan's body and pulled the blanket back. Alex lay the camera under her beautiful fingers. He left his hand on the blanket for a long second and whispered a soft goodbye to her before covering her face for the last time. He closed the door softly behind him and ran down the trail leading to the spring. He was a hundred yards into the thick woods when the helicopter dropped from the sky and landed beside the cabin. Even though he would remember little of what he'd done on that clear spring day, he would never forget Jan, cold and beautiful, as he pulled the blanket over her face.

Chapter 5

The next few days were a maze of confusion. All Alex could do was run; run from the hated animals who had killed his wife, run from the grief that threatened to rip his very soul out, run from the guilt that he could have done something, anything to save his beautiful Jan. When the demons had killed her, they had left him with nothing inside. He was no longer human, just a shell of a thing, a wild animal that ran in front of the hunters. At the same time, a tiny light held on, something deep inside, something that kept him from stopping and letting them finish the job. As the days wore on, the tiny light grew until it was a raging flame and that flame became the driving fuel for his very soul. A blind rage and hate took over and fed the flame until it threatened to consume him. The new emotions drove him forward with a purpose, but at the same time, the grief of Jan's death stayed with him like a weight he could never put down.

Alex became cunning and daring, doubling back on his trail to watch the men below and plan his next moves. He had no fear of death now. He would welcome death, but first he had to fulfill this rage that drove him.

On the fourth day he had transferred everything to one pack, leaving Jan's pack by the trail. He hoped that they would think that he was out of food and water. Maybe they would become too sure of themselves and get careless.

* * *

On the sixth day, he broke camp and started out well before light. He knew that they wouldn't be up for another hour. Alex had seen a mountain just before dark yesterday. It would be the perfect spot to wait on them and maybe, if luck was on his side, change the odds.

He made the base of the mountain at first light and began to climb. He was starving. Alex searched his pack for more food but there was none and then he remembered running out of food yesterday. Alex hadn't noticed before, but the forest was alive with animals. Birds fluttered away as he approached, squirrels chattered at him, and a deer stood close as he passed. *That's funny,* he thought, that he hadn't noticed the singing of the birds. Jan and he had spent hours in the woods listening to the different bird calls. He couldn't see any of the beauty that they had once loved. He looked up at a shadow and a crow called out its harsh call. The once colorful forest seemed dull and gray now. He wondered if anything in his life would ever be the same.

Alex stopped and looked up. A squirrel chattered away at him from its perch on a pine limb. He could have killed small animals for food, and soon he might have to do that, but he would have to eat it raw. The killers were always too close to build a fire. Alex stopped halfway up the mountain and studied his back trail. Still, no sign of the men after him. The mountain leveled out, and he stopped to look around. The top of the mountain was almost bare of trees and brush. A huge rock overhang on his left, a good fifty feet off the trail, would be the only place to hide. He began to back up, careful to place each foot back into the faint prints he had made. It took him thirty minutes to backtrack to a vein of rock that led up the mountain and to the rock overhang. When he reached the rock, he slid his pack off and lay down on the hard ground.

Alex rolled over to remove a sharp rock cutting into his side. The sun was behind him. He had made sure of that. There would be no reflection from the binoculars. He raised them again and swept the valley below. A carpet of evergreens covered the mountain and valley. He swung the binoculars back quickly. Was that a movement? There it was again. Suddenly, a single figure came into view. This was the first time Alex had been close enough to the men to make out their features. He adjusted his binoculars to bring the figure in clearly. He was an average built man with high cheek bones and the look of an Indian.

The man stopped; studying the ground before him and then with his head down, glided across the clearing, following the trail left by Alex. They had a tracker. He had known for a while now that one of them was very good at following a trail. He wondered if the tracker was with the people after him or just someone they had hired for this job. It really didn't matter, but he hoped that he was one of the killers. It would make it easier. Alex studied the thick forest behind the tracker but couldn't see anything. Probably the rest were a quarter of a mile or so behind. The tracker would mark the trail for them. Alex caught another glimpse of the tracker between the trees. He was at the base of the mountain now. Soon the trees would thin and he could watch the tracker all of the way up.

Alex reached behind him and brought the bow to the front. He selected an arrow from the quiver and placed it next to the bow. He could see the tracker clearly now in the thinner trees, making his way slowly up the mountain. He heard the others before he saw them, and that was amazing, considering the distance. The tracker had stopped and turned to watch his comrades. Alex brought the binoculars to bare. He could see the contemp on the tracker's face as he watched his party blundering along. Alex held his breath. Would he wait on the others to catch up? No! He was moving again, as if to put more distance between himself and the parade.

Alex studied the armament of the group behind the tracker. The lead man carried a rifle with a scope. Alex's time spent in the army left little doubt about the M-16s carried by the next two men. The last one in line didn't have a gun in sight.

The same five men had been on his trail for six days now. He had been watching, waiting for any kind of an advantage. This spot was the best he had seen. Alex had been without food and water for a day and before that, had only eaten once a day. He knew he couldn't last long now. He was too weak. Tomorrow or the next day they would ... he tried not to think about it. The man with the rifle was always in front of the other four. If he didn't do this right, he could be well within his range, and Alex knew how good he was.

Alex had chosen this spot with care, but a little luck had been with him. The climb was steep enough to keep the tracker looking down, and the sun was behind Alex and in the tracker's face. He looked back down the mountain. The tracker had put more distant between him and the others. Alex brushed his hand over the rocky ground. Picking out a small pebble, he popped it into his mouth. He rolled the pebble around with his tongue, feeling the thick saliva wet his parched mouth. Alex rolled over on his side and looked across the valley to the other mountain. The small stream, trickling down the mountain side was driving him mad. He licked his lips. If he lived through this, he would be able to drink soon.

He turned back. The tracker was gone. Alex grabbed his binoculars and quickly searched the mountainside. What if the tracker had decided to circle the mountain and come up from the other side? Alex cussed under his breath. Wait a minute. There was movement. There he was on his knees by the trail, almost hidden by a small bush. The tracker was having a hard time following the trail across the rock. Alex breathed a sigh of relief. The tracker was still a good six hundred yards away. He would be here soon.

Alex's stomach tightened. He had never killed a man before. He had been trained to kill in the army, but he had never killed. He wiped his sweaty hands on his shirt and took a deep breath, trying to still his mind for what was to come. There was no way out. It was him or them. He knew that they would never give up trying, and he knew that he couldn't.

The tracker was closer. He had stopped three hundred feet down the mountain and was studying the trail again. Alex held his breath. That was the area he had backtracked to. He had tried so hard not to leave any marks on the rock, but then he wasn't the expert that the Indian was. Alex let out a sigh of relief as the tracker stood and began to follow the first trail. Alex eased the bow forward and notched the arrow. He thought about laying another arrow out but dismissed the idea. He would only have time for one shot. His hand shook. The tracker was one hundred feet away and then fifty. Alex was above and to one side of the trail. The tracker raised his head and began to search ahead.

Alex dropped his head down behind the rock. He held his breath. He had to wait until the man was past and to the end of the trail. Hopefully the tracker would turn, knowing that he could be in a trap, putting him face to face with the man he was after. Alex knew he had to shoot at that instant. To hesitate would probably mean his death. He also knew he didn't have much time. The man with the rifle would be in firing range within minutes. Alex put tension on the bowstring and waited. He raised his shoulder to wipe the sudden sweat from his eyes and tried to control his breathing.

The tracker was directly across from Alex now. Alex couldn't see any sign of a gun. He would be killing an unarmed man. He would become just like the killers after him. Alex thought about turning and making a run for it, but then his thoughts went back to Jan and the way she had died. Rage began to build at everything these men had done to him. If he wanted to live, to have his revenge, he had to do this. The tracker had stopped. He was turning. Alex stood and pulled the arrow back against his ear. The tracker saw him and opened his mouth to shout a warning.

Alex's hand trembled. He shouted "now" silently to himself. He didn't feel his fingers let go, but he heard the arrow as it made a soft whirling sound in the still, mountain air. The warning never left the tracker's lips. The arrow hit the man in the center of the throat, cutting through the vocal cords and the spinal cord behind. He fell to the ground without a sound.

Alex could hear the voices from below as he ran to the tracker. He pulled the tracker's backpack from over the jerking arms and quickly searched his pockets. Alex took a knife and compass and, lifting the backpack, stood for a second over the tracker. The man was still alive. Alex could see his chest heaving. He was trying to say something. Alex leaned closer. The tracker's lips clamped together, and he swallowed hard. The man's eyes were searching his. The voices were louder. Alex had stayed too long. "I'm sorry," he said softly and stepping over the tracker, trotted down the opposite side of the mountain.

He circled as he began to climb the opposite mountain face and headed for a thick stand of trees overlooking the tracker's position. Alex stopped when he reached the trees and leaned over for a minute, trying to get his shaking nerves to relax. The face of the tracker swam before him. He gagged, but there was nothing in his stomach to throw up. Sliding the packs to the ground, he began to climb one of the taller trees.

Alex climbed slowly, careful not to move any branches, until he was high enough to see the body of the tracker. The water was closer now and it was maddening not to take a short trip for a cool drink. The tracker probably had a canteen in his pack. Alex cussed himself for not checking before he climbed the tree. The shock of what he had done was still with him, and he began to shake. He hugged the tree tight until the shaking stopped.

The others were coming into view. They saw the tracker and stopped with their guns out. A slender man seemed to be giving the orders. He shouted, and the other three fanned out and began to search the mountaintop. The slender man walked over to the tracker. He stood there for a long moment and then pulled a gun from his waistband. The gun had a round extension protruding out from the barrel. He was using a silencer. Why would he need a silencer out here? The slender man held the gun close to the tracker's head. Alex didn't hear the sound but the tracker's body jerked, and Alex knew that he was dead. The slender man shouted to one of the others, and together they dragged the body to the edge of the steep slope and threw it over. Alex felt a cold shiver go through his body.

The slender man took a small radio from his pocket. Alex knew that they had one, because they had called the helicopter in several times. The man suddenly drew his arm back as if to throw the radio away but instead put it back in his pocket. Good, they were having trouble reaching the helicopter. That would give him more time. The other men were back. They began to make camp. It was too early, and it wasn't a good place for a camp. It would be very cold on the mountaintop tonight. Maybe the slender man figured it would be a good place to try for the helicopter again tomorrow morning.

Alex climbed back down the tree and opened the tracker's pack. He removed the food and a canteen. The canteen was almost empty and the water was hot. He crammed the food into his pack, keeping out a bag of dried fruit. He also found a small tin box with flint, matches and fishing equipment along with a ball of cord for snares. Sudden guilt swept through Alex. The tracker's pack made it too personal. He wondered if he had a family. Alex put the thought from his mind. He took the tracker's sleeping bag and tied it to his own pack. At least he would be warm tonight.

Alex threw the tracker's pack away from him and made his way down to the small stream. He lay on the moss-covered bank and slowly drank the cold water until he couldn't drink anymore. He splashed water over his face and neck. For a second, a sharp image of Jan, as they swam in their swimming pool, flashed through his mind, and he turned to lie on his back, savoring the memory of her slim body knifing through the water. He swallowed hard and sat up.

He filled one of the canteens and looked at the other one. He thought for a few seconds and then filled the tracker's canteen, too. The second canteen would be extra weight, but if it became too much, he could throw it away. He went back to the tree and sat down, leaning back against the rough bark. His eyes began to close. Alex had learned to sleep light in the woods. He would hear the helicopter or the men if they moved.

* * *

It was five o'clock in the afternoon when Alex woke. He stood and stretched before climbing the tree up to the same perch. Alex would watch until dark, and then he would make his move. The helicopter hadn't come. They would be there until morning. It would be a lot easier now that the tracker was gone. In fact, he could never have gotten close to the camp with him there.

Alex took the dried fruit from his pocket and began to munch on it, washing it down with the cool water from the canteen. The water tasted so good. The late afternoon sun filtered through the tree limbs, warming his face. His thoughts drifted back to the airport and Jan. Her beautiful face was there before him again. His hand gripped the branch tightly as he watched the men below.

The sun had gone down behind the mountains, and dark was settling in. Alex shifted his position on the tree limb. His butt was getting sore. He could barely see the men now. They had posted one guard. The guard's position would cover most of the mountainside below, but Alex wouldn't be coming in from that direction. He climbed back down the tree. Early morning would be the best time. He unrolled the sleeping bag and set his watch for six hours. He was asleep in minutes.

Alex woke to the pulsating watch. He rolled the sleeping bag into a tight roll and tied it to his pack. He took another mouthful of the dried fruit and swung the pack onto his shoulders. Alex started along the path he had so carefully picked from the tree, walking slowly, not making any sound. The moon was full and its dim light made long shadows across the mountainside. His pace quickened as he started to climb the harder rock of the mountain. An hour later, he was behind the guard.

After an hour of slowly inching forward, Alex was less than ten feet away. He sat down on the cold rock. Alex had watched their routine countless times from afar. He knew they changed guards every three hours. It was four o'clock in the morning and another hour before the guards would change again. He leaned forward and could hear the man's slow breathing. The guard was asleep, or nearly so. Alex had picked his time well, giving the guard time to relax. If he was lucky he wouldn't make a sound. Alex eased his backpack down and drew the razor sharp hunting knife out. In three quick steps, he moved closer to the guard. Alex tried to remember everything he had been taught in the army. His left hand snaked forward, grasping the startled man's mouth and jerking his head back with the same motion. In the same instant, Alex drew the knife across the man's larynx and continued around the neck to cut through the jugular. The man lunged back against him, and Alex could feel the warm blood spurting over his arm. The body jerked again and then slumped against Alex's hold. There was a soft gurgling sound as he let his hand go.

Alex squatted quickly, trying to quiet his pounding heart and listen for any sounds from the camp. He picked up the guard's M-16 and searched the man's pocket for ammo. He found two clips and shoved them into his coat pocket. He swallowed hard to keep from heaving his stomach out as he wiped his bloody hands on the man's clothing. He felt for the safety on the M-16 and crawled slowly toward the camp. He swallowed hard again, trying to force the hot bile back down. He was weak with fear. Suddenly, a man sat up, and then another. Some sound had awakened them when he'd killed the guard. He would have to make it another night. He could see a pack, five feet in front of him. It must have been the guard's. He reached for the pack and took it with him as he crawled slowly away into the darkness.

He was climbing the opposite mountain when he heard shouting and gunfire from the camp. He had a gun and ammo, and there were only three of them. Now he had a chance. He ejected the clip from the M-16. It was full. He jammed it back. That gave him three full clips. His thoughts swept back to the cabin. If only he could have had the M-16 then. Jan might be alive now. Grief swept through him again. He had been able to push the grief deep within himself for the last few days but now . . . Alex dropped to the forest floor and drew his arms tight as sobs racked his body.

Thirty minutes later, he stood and began to walk again. It was a clear night. The north star was his guide. He was going to put himself between the men and the high ground to the east. They hadn't been able to get a signal out yesterday. With luck on his side, they wouldn't be able to this morning either. The mountains to the east would be the only place high enough to radio the helicopter. Alex needed that helicopter.

He was far enough away to use a flashlight now. He opened the pack and took the tracker's flashlight out. With its light, he put another four miles between himself and the killers. He found a good campsite overlooking the same trail the men had came in on and, unrolling the sleeping bag, settled in for the night. The insulated sleeping bag was a real luxury. He had been sleeping on the ground since the cabin. It was a clear night and the stars lit up the night sky. He remembered the countless nights that Jan and he had laid under the stars, making up stories about the shapes they made, trying to guess how far away they were. He could feel her warmth with him in the sleeping bag.

Alex woke before daylight the next morning. He had plenty of time. They had never broken camp before daylight and that was a good two hours away. He was looking forward to this morning. He was going to have a cup of hot coffee. Their tracker was gone. For the first time, they didn't know where he was. The tracker would have smelled the campfire from miles away, but they couldn't. Alex could still see the tracker's eyes as he stood over him. He shook his head and tried to think about something else.

Alex built a small fire on the north side of a huge boulder that would shelter the flame, just in case. He didn't have the coffee pot. He had discarded all unnecessary weight days ago. Taking a pack of coffee from his pack, he poured a small amount into a large tin cup and filled it with water. Alex set the cup on the fire. Minutes later, the water was boiling. Placing the hunting knife under the handle and using a sock, he lifted the cup from the fire. He drained the coffee through the sock into another cup and squeezed out every last drop. Alex turned the sock inside out and shook the grounds out, scattering them into the leaves. He opened a package of dried fruit and sat there eating and sipping the hot coffee. It was out of this world. It was the first cup of coffee he'd had since . . . .

He drove Jan from his thoughts.

When he was through, Alex stood and kicked dirt over the fire. He packed everything away and headed down the mountain toward a small river. The dim, early light was enough to see by. It felt good to be moving, to be doing something else with his body other than thinking about the past few days. The three men behind him would just now be starting their morning fire. He wondered if they felt fear as they ate, knowing that they were now the hunted. Today, he would take out another man.

Alex stopped at the small river. A rock shelf made a natural dam across its fast-moving waters. Large flat rocks, probably put there by Indians hundreds of years ago, made a walkway across the top of the shelf. Each one was a short jump to the next. It was dangerous, because the riverbed sloped sharply down below the rocks to several steep waterfalls. He remembered when he had led the men over the same rocks three days ago — or was it four. The first rock from the other side had been loose. Not twelve inches from the rock, the river dropped down a smooth rock hollow, curved around a sharp bend, and fell to the bottom of the first waterfall.

He remembered walking up the other side of the river. The series of waterfalls ended two miles below. A slip here would mean a wild ride down the falls. If it didn't kill the lead man, it would surely scare him to death. They had to come this way to reach the higher ground, to call in the helicopter. They had to get another tracker to follow his trail.

Stepping into the icy water beside the rock, Alex used his knife to dig the gravel out from under the lower side. The current was swift against his legs. He had to lean against the pull of the water just to stand. The huge rock was three feet across. The lead man would step on the back side and it would feel solid. Then he would take another step to get closer to the next rock. Hopefully, his weight would cause the rock to give way, taking the man with it. Satisfied, Alex stepped up on the next rock and on across to the other side. He headed down to the lower pool far below. Somebody would be in for a surprise. Alex reached the pool and sat against a small tree to wait. He hoped that he wouldn't hear the helicopter. If they brought in another tracker, it would ruin all his plans. He leaned back and closed his eyes.

* * *

Four hours later, Alex's eyes jerked open. He could hear shouting above the roaring waters of the river. They hadn't been able to reach the helicopter. Seconds later, a man came tumbling down the waterfall. He was moving at an incredible speed, arms and legs wind-milling, the foaming water carrying him like a rag doll. He shot into the pool and surfaced a minute later, gasping for breath. Somehow, through all of that he still had the rifle slung over his shoulder. Alex smiled. He had been hoping that it would be the man with the rifle. The man grabbed a tree limb, leaning out over the raging waters, and held on for dear life. He tried to pull himself out, but the rushing water pulled at him, dragging his body away from the tree. Alex could see that the man's arm was broken. White bone jutted out above his elbow. The man had a determined set to his jaw as he tried desperately to remove himself from the raging river.

Through shear determination, the man managed to throw one leg over the tree limb, but was unable to go any further. The rifle was still over his shoulder, but Alex knew that he would never be able to use it. Alex walked to the river's edge. He was less than five feet away. The man's face lit up when he saw Alex's legs, and then with a tremendous effort he pulled himself higher until he could see his face. Hope faded, as horror took its place. He cried out as he tried to swing his broken arm around to unsling his rifle, but it wouldn't move. He gave up and stared up at Alex with the eyes of a wounded animal.

Alex held onto the tree and waded out into the icy water. He hooked his arm around the tree and braced himself against the pull of the current. Alex took his knife out and cut the shoulder strap on the rifle, catching it with his other hand. He also cut the shoulder straps to the ammo vest the man wore. He threw the vest onto the bank. The man didn't take his eyes from Alex's. Alex felt the rage building.

"You killed my wife with this, you son of a bitch," he screamed into the man's face. The startled man let go of the tree, deciding to take his chance in the river, but his coat caught on a limb. The rushing water kept him at arm's length. He couldn't tear away from the tree.

Alex aimed the rifle at the man's head and then lowered it again. Relief spread over the man's face. The man's gold watch gleamed as he made a surge and threw his broken arm over the tree again, screaming against the pain. Alex leaned forward and pulled the watch from the man's limp wrist.

"Go ahead, take everything!" the man shouted hoarsely. "I'll tell the others to call off the hunt!" His eyes went from Alex's to his broken arm. "I'm not worth a bullet."

Alex threw the hated rifle into the foaming river. He drew his knife and, reaching over, cut the man's clothing from the limb. Holding on to the tree, he raised himself from the water and kicked the man's broken arm from the tree. The man screamed and kept screaming as he tried desperately to swim to the other side, but the raging waters had him in its grip. The stronger current in the center swept him down the river and into the rapids. Alex heard him scream again as his broken arm hit a rock, and then he went under. He surfaced again, clawing at a rock further down, but only for an instant. The river's pull was too much. Alex had taken the long range threat away. They would have to get close to hurt him now, and there were only two left. The animal that had killed Jan was gone. Alex thought that he would feel joy, elation, but he felt nothing, only the cold, hard rage.

Alex traveled until eleven o'clock and began to circle, looking for a spot by the trail. He found a good place and sat down to wait. He saw the two men an hour later. They were walking toward him, searching ahead, looking behind every rock and tree. The lead man had his M-16 pointing outward, sweeping it from side to side. The slender man followed close behind with his pistol out. A squirrel darted out of the trees. The lead man swung his M-16, letting off a short burst.

The slender man yelled at him. "You dumb ass, now he knows where we are."

Alex smiled. Their nerves were on edge. The spot he had picked was at the lowest end of an outcrop of rock overlooking the trail and leading back toward the men for forty yards or so. The men were almost even with the other end of the rock. The lead man ran up the mountain to check behind the rock while the leader waited by the trail.

Alex slid down behind the lower end of the rock and used it as a shield. While the attention of the slender man was on the man above, Alex reached over and hung the gold watch on a bush by the trail. He climbed back to the top of the rock ledge as the man with the M-16 climbed down and joined the slender man. Alex laid down and crawled to the edge of the rock ending up above and to one side of the watch. The man with the M-16 took the lead again. He stopped when he saw the watch. Alex could see his eyes white with fear. "Harris, look at this! My God, it's Thompson's watch. The bastard did kill him."

Alex put Harris's name away into his memory.

"Shut up and let's get out of here!" Harris yelled at him. "We're two days away from getting a helicopter in here. We'll take care of the bastard then."

MALICE

The two men moved down the trail, the slender man in front this time.

Alex waited until the they were well down the trail before he fell in behind. He followed them all day until they made camp and then backtracked until he was a mile behind. He selected a sheltered spot and built a small fire. Alex cooked a packet of dried stew and ate it slowly with crackers, savoring every bite. He scraped the tin cup clean and finished the meal off with another cup of coffee. Alex went back down the trail and strung a cord with two empty cans he had saved, just in case they might try to find him in the dark. He rolled up in the sleeping bag. He would be up before daybreak and have another cup of coffee. It would taste so good. He drifted off to sleep and dreamed of Jan. They were on a beach. She was laughing as he pulled her toward the warm waters.

* * *

Alex woke before daybreak and after a breakfast of dried fruit and coffee, started down the trail. He navigated around a small gully and started up the next mountain. His legs were strong and his breathing shallow. The climb didn't bother him a bit now, but it would have killed him three weeks ago. He was stronger and quicker. He must have lost twenty pounds since the airplane crash. His thoughts went back to Jan. She had always been after him to lose weight.

"Well, I've done it now, honey," he said aloud. He could sense her with him, hear her laughter. She would always be with him.

Alex smelled the campsite before he could see it. As he got nearer, he could hear their voices. They were arguing. *Good, they are still on edge.* Alex crept into a thicket and sat down to wait. The thin trail of smoke from their campfire climbed toward the blue sky, scattered lightly with soft white clouds. He watched the smoke as it fanned out and disappeared. He wondered if Jan's spirit was there in the clouds, watching him. Alex turned back as the smoke changed from a thin stream to a small cloud hugging the ground. They were putting the fire out. Alex stood and moved closer. They finally broke camp and headed toward the snow-capped mountain range.

Alex kept up with them easily. He had to slow down toward noon to keep from getting too close. He darted behind a large tree as he caught the reflection of glass. Harris was checking their back trail again. He waited there until they disappeared behind a stand of spruce trees.

The area they were going through seemed familiar, and then Alex saw the cliffs. They were near the cabin. Alex wondered if the owners had ever come back. Maybe they had found Jan in the root cellar. He stopped to pull out the binoculars and study the cabin. For a second, he thought he saw someone standing in the doorway and his heart leaped, but it was just a shadow. He was tempted to go back and see Jan for one last time. Maybe he would have time to bury her in the mountains she loved so much. He even headed that way and then stopped. His heart ached to see her again, but he couldn't. He would lose the men below. They were still in sight as they crossed the river a good two miles above where he and Jan had crossed, and began to follow the top of the cliff back north.

Alex hurried to catch up and then stayed well behind the men. He took one last look at the cabin as he passed on the other side of the river. Jan seemed so strong with him now. He could feel her hands on him stroking his hair, feel her lips brush his, hear her musical laugher. He passed the grassy area where they had made love only days before and dropped to his knees on the soft grass, stroking the place where they had laid. He couldn't leave her like this, he just couldn't, but in the end his rage won out, and he followed the men's trail toward the spot where the helicopter had landed before. Alex slowed as the men reached the flat-topped mountain and took out his binoculars, searching the high ground ahead until he had the two men in sight. The one called Harris had his radio out. He seemed to be talking to someone. The other man was sitting on the ground against his pack. The helicopter would be there within two hours. He didn't have much time.

Alex studied the area carefully. He could swing around the high ground and come in from the north. There was plenty of cover there. Harris had put the radio down and was studying the cliffs with his binoculars. *He thinks I'm still on the cliffs,* Alex thought. He put his pack on and trotted toward the trees. It would take forty minutes or so to work his way behind them. The helicopter would be there forty minutes or so after he got into place. He should have plenty of time for what he had in mind.

Alex came out of the woods to the east of Harris. He made his way to a small clearing behind the men and then to a small stand of bushes until he could see both of them clearly without the glasses. It was a good hiding place. He slipped his pack off and sat down to wait. The two men were facing their back trail, watching for him. A small black box with a short antenna sat next to Harris. It had to be a homing device of some kind. Alex looked at his watch. It was four o'clock. He was early. It should be thirty minutes or so before the helicopter arrived.

Alex had his eyes half-closed when a thought crossed his mind. He sat up with a start. They would be coming in from the air. He had no cover overhead. The men in the helicopter could see him here. He searched the area behind the men, but there was only one hiding place, an evergreen, stunted in growth by the rock outcrop around it, had low, thick limbs. If he could get under that and behind the rocks, he wouldn't be seen by the two men or the helicopter. It would be dangerous. The tree was less than fifty feet from the two men.

Alex lay down and began to crawl forward, stopping to check on the men every ten feet or so. The time passed slowly, but forty minutes later he was almost there. The tree was only twenty feet away and then ten. He could hear the slow, heavy breathing of the man with Harris. He was almost asleep. No such luck with Harris. He had the gun out and was checking every sound. Alex knew that the man was dangerous and probably a crack shot. Alex stopped and let his breathing slow. All Harris had to do was turn around. Alex was still in the open and ten yards away from the tree. He had to hurry. The helicopter would be here within minutes. He stood and started to move again. A small branch crackled under his weight. Alex cussed silently under his breath as he saw Harris stiffen. He would never make the cover of the rocks. He had to make his move now.

"Put your gun on the ground and turn around slowly!" Alex shouted.

Harris moved slightly to one side, his arm coming up.

"Don't even think about it."

Alex saw the other man move. He was awake. Harris bent forward slowly, holding the gun out in front. Suddenly, with a quick, fluid movement, he fell forward, turning as he fell. Alex caught the movement of the other man swinging the other way. These men were pros. They might have been out of their element in the woods, but here in the open they were experts. Alex fired as Harris brought his gun arm around. The bullet caught Harris in the shoulder, spinning him around. The gun fell from his numb fingers. Alex continued his swing, but the other man had moved. He was quick, but he was off balance as he fired. A bullet tugged at Alex's sleeve as he fired again, catching the man full in the chest. He didn't wait to see the man fall but swung the gun back, searching for Harris. He was crawling toward his gun. Alex fired a burst into the ground inches from Harris's hand. Harris jerked his hand back and rolled over to face Alex. His shoulder was broken but he paid no attention to it. His eyes were cold and calculating and stayed on Alex as he stood. Alex moved forward to put himself between Harris and the gun. He motioned with the M-16. Harris moved back and then again as Alex wiggled the M-16.

His lips curled into a half snarl. His brown eyes darted to the M-16 by the dead man and back to Alex. He could see no edge there. He moved beyond the M-16 and sat down on a rock, keeping his eyes on Alex.

Alex moved forward and picked up the dead man's M-16. He ejected the clip and fired the chambered round into the air. He threw the M-16 down the mountainside and walked over to collect Harris's handgun. It was a thing of beauty. The balance was perfect.

"Must have cost you a fortune," he said as he walked back toward Harris.

"Had it made special," Harris answered, keeping his alert eyes on Alex.

Alex could feel the man ready to pounce at the slightest mistake. He sat down on a rock well away from Harris.

"Who sent you after us?"

Puzzlement flickered across Harris's face. "Ah," he said. "You want to get information out of me." A slight smile broke across his stony exterior. "You want the people behind us. You want to kill everyone." He relaxed and leaned back. For the first time, Alex saw pain flash across his face. "Can I smoke?" he asked, pointing to his pocket.

"Two fingers," Alex warned.

Harris extracted a pack of cigarettes from his pocket with his left hand. Holding the pack in his shaking right hand, he pulled a cigarette out and placed it between his thin lips. He produced a lighter and lit the cigarette. His thick eyelids raised as he drew in a long draw. Harris was a thin man, well under six feet, but the movement Alex had seen only moments ago was that of a man in excellent physical shape. Alex guessed his age to be somewhere in his thirties.

"Don't smoke much," Harris explained. "Bad for your health but what the hell, I don't think I have to worry about that much longer."

"You haven't answered my question," Alex said, raising the M-16 until it was pointed at Harris's face.

Harris smiled again. He reached up with his good hand and brushed his dark hair back. His brown eyes surveyed Alex. "You won't shoot me now. The helicopter won't come down if it doesn't see two people, and I'm the only one left you can use."

"How many men are in the helicopter?"

"I don't know. Maybe two or three."

"What did you tell them on the radio?" Alex asked.

"I told them I had two to pick up, and you were on my trail."

A thin wisp of sound caught Alex's attention. The sound grew louder.

Harris grinned at Alex as he stood. "Party time," he said.

Alex moved next to Harris's bad arm and shoved the pistol into his side. "Easy now. Just stand here beside me and you won't get hurt."

"Smart," Harris said. "It'll be hard to see your face this way."

Alex could feel Harris tense. He shoved the gun harder into his side. "Easy, don't do anything stupid."

The helicopter was coming in fast. Fifty feet above the ground, it leveled out and hovered in the air, rotating to expose its cargo door. Suddenly, the ground erupted around them. Alex couldn't hear the gunfire because of the helicopter noise, but he saw the flashes. A bullet tore through his arm, turning him around. Harris was falling, pulling Alex with him. A red-hot poker sheared across Alex's chest. The wind from the helicopter blades tore at them as it shot overhead and swung wide to make another pass.

Alex pulled himself up and tried to stand.

Harris was tugging at him, pulling him back down. "Play dead!" he shouted. "Wait for them to come close."

"Why are they shooting at us?" Alex shouted back. The helicopter had completed its turn.

"They have binoculars. They know who you are and that I failed, and failure means death." Harris coughed and splattered bright blood into the air.

Alex crawled closer to Harris. "How bad are you hurt?"

Harris pulled at Alex's coat. Alex leaned closer. "I'm sorry about your wife," Harris said.

Alex could see that Harris was getting weaker. The man was probably dying. He tried to pull away, but Harris had a firm grip. Alex wanted to get into the trees before the helicopter made another pass. It was getting closer.

"Wait, let me tell you," Harris shouted over the noise from the helicopter. He coughed and pulled Alex closer. "The man at the lake is Lee Jagger from Detroit. The one above him is Anton Kocyk. He stays in Miami and Atlanta. He's Russian and a real mean shit. Don't fuck around with him. I've heard that a senator is connected, too, but I don't know his name. They won't rest until you're dead. Try to get out of the country."

'Alex burned the men's names into his memory. The helicopter was louder. Alex knew that he didn't have enough time to reach the trees. Harris's hand relaxed on his shirt. Alex looked down. Harris's eyes were blinking rapidly. "I'll see you in another life," he said softly and pushed at Alex.

Alex felt the wind from the helicopter. There was only thing he could do. He lay still, playing dead. His chest was on fire. He slid his hand down. It came back covered with blood. The helicopter blades were making that whomp-whomp sound. Alex closed his eyes.

The helicopter landed and minutes later Alex heard voices approaching. He cracked one eye. Legs came into sight. The legs stopped. He wondered how many they were. He felt a gun poke into his back. The legs moved past him to Harris. Suddenly, Harris rolled to one side. He wasn't dead. The legs jumped back. Gunfire roared in Alex's ears.

Alex rolled the other way bringing up the pistol in one fluid motion. Harris's pistol spit once, twice. The first man fell to his knees with a stunned look on his face. Alex searched frantically for the other man. The noise from the helicopter had masked the soft sound of the silencer. The man hadn't heard the shots. A puzzled look flashed across his face when he saw his partner fall, and then it was too late. Alex fired twice more. There was one more man, but he was by the helicopter. Too far for a shot. The man's head was turned toward the chopper. Alex dragged first one and then the other man behind low bushes to one side. The last man still hadn't noticed him. *He must think they got us on the first pass,* Alex thought.

Alex ran forward to within ten feet of the man and stopped with his legs spread. Some sixth sense must have warned him. He suddenly dropped, turning his gun toward Alex as he fell. Alex's first shot caught the man in the chest, the second one in the throat. The man fell to the ground, reaching out, trying feebly to bring his gun up. Alex shot him again in the head.

Alex turned back to the helicopter. There was no sign of the pilot. He left the last man where he had fallen and ran back to Harris. He was dead. This man had used his last dying breath to save Alex, a man that only hours before had been trying his best to kill him.

Alex quickly went through Harris's pockets, keeping one eye out for any movement from the pilot. He took Harris's billfold and four clips of ammo for the pistol and ran for the back of the helicopter. Alex came in from the pilot's blind side and peeped through the open door. The pilot knew something was wrong. He was leaning against the windshield trying to see where everyone was. Alex rolled through the door, coming to a kneeling position behind the pilot. The pilot felt the weight as the helicopter rocked, but it was too late. Alex already had the gun jammed into his neck.

"Let's get out of here!" Alex shouted, reaching back to slide the door shut. Most of the noise disappeared.

"Where to?" the pilot asked, his voice strained with fear.

"Let's just get out of here," Alex answered.

The pilot didn't hesitate. He increased power and Alex could hear the sound change as the pitch of the blades increased. The helicopter leaped into the air. The pilot rotated the cabin once and the helicopter tilted forward. The next second, they were streaking over the forest below.

Alex didn't say anything for a minute. The cabin and Jan was to their right and becoming smaller by the second. Jan was down there, cold and lonely. He thought for a second about picking her up but changed his mind. Her spirit was already gone. There was nothing left. "South to Vancouver," he said finally, answering the pilot's first question.

"Are you going to kill me?" the pilot asked.

"Not if you do what I say." Alex reached out and patted the pilot down for a gun. He was clean. He pulled his bloody shirt off. A bullet had gone through his left arm, missing the bone, but it was bleeding like crazy. Another one had cut a groove across his chest. It had almost stopped bleeding but was still oozing from the deepest part. Both wounds hurt like hell.

"Do you have a first aid kit on board?" he asked the pilot.

"Clipped to the wall behind you," the pilot answered.

Alex moved to a seat next to the first aid kit. He laid the gun on the seat within easy reach and opened the kit. He took out a bottle of disinfectant and clamped his teeth tightly together as he poured it on the wounds. Black spots danced across his vision, and he began to feel faint. He shook his head to clear away the spots. He couldn't faint now. He just couldn't. Gritting his teeth against the pain, he tied a strip of gauze above the arm wound and pulled it tight to stop the bleeding. He cleaned the wound on both sides of his arm and bandaged it tightly. Alex released the gauze, feeling the sharp pain as the blood rushed back into his arm. He bandaged the deepest part of the chest wound and put his shirt back on. The shirt was so dirty, it would probably infect the wound.

Alex still felt light-headed and dizzy. He leaned back and took a deep breath. He was beginning to pass out. The pilot's voice brought him back, and he slowly leaned toward the voice.

"I don't know if I have enough gas to make Vancouver."

Alex looked through the windshield at the sun. They had been in the air longer than he thought. He wondered if he really had passed out. The sun was settling behind the mountain to their west. It would be dangerous to run out of gas in the dark, but he didn't have a choice. He had to get to a major airport. The people after him would be there with a vengeance when they found out what he had done.

"You had better hope that you do," Alex answered. The pilot didn't reply, but Alex could see his hand shake on the controls. He leaned back and closed his eyes.

Two hours later, Alex saw the lights around the bay at Vancouver. "Do you know a quiet place to land close to the airport?"

"I don't know . . . " the pilot began.

Alex laid the gun against the man's neck. "Do you want to die?" he asked softly. "I can fly this thing if I have to."

"No, please wait, I remember a company I used to deliver to. They wouldn't be open now."

"Good, let's go there." Alex had lied to the pilot. He had been in hundreds of helicopters, but he had never been at the controls.

Alex leaned close to the pilot as he spoke to the Vancouver tower, and seconds later they began to lose altitude. They made a low pass over a line of buildings and swung back to hover over a back parking lot. The helicopter settled softly to the ground.

"Cut the engines, but leave the lights on," Alex ordered.

Alex pushed the pilot through the cargo doors. Keeping his hand on the man's shoulder, he stood there, listening. The building was dark and quiet. Alex pushed the pilot forward toward the front of the helicopter. The helicopter's lights made a dim circle on the pavement.

"Take off your clothes," Alex ordered. The pilot took off his clothing and stood shivering in the cold air. "Now lay face down." The pilot dropped to the concrete.

Alex removed his own clothing and pulled the pilot's jumpsuit on. It was a perfect fit.

"Now put my clothes on," he ordered, throwing his clothing on top of the pilot. He felt sorry for the pilot. He knew that his clothes smelled to high heaven. The pilot finished and stood there with his hands on top of his head. "Now back into the helicopter and lay face down."

Fear spread across the pilot's face. "You're going to kill me, aren't you?"

Alex didn't say anything. He pointed again to the helicopter floor. The pilot hurried to obey.

Alex pushed the pilot's head down and stepping on the pilot's back with one foot, he leaned over and yanked the headset from the radio. Using the wires, he tied the pilot's hands and feet. He didn't gag him. There was no one around to hear. "What day of the week is it?" he asked, as he finished.

"It's Saturday," the pilot answered.

Alex reached back into his backpack and took a water bottle out. "You'll probably be here until Monday," he said. He held the bottle neck against the pilot's mouth. The pilot took a long drink.

"Thanks," he said.

Alex took his pack and the pilot's overnight bag. He stood by the door, taking one last look around. He turned back. He could see the pilot's eyes glued on him. Alex leaned over the pilot's seat and cut the lights. He heard a sigh of relief behind him as he exited the helicopter.

Alex walked to the front of the building. He could make out the outline of a road from the runway lights. In the distance, a long line of aircraft waited their turn to take off. Alex began to walk toward what he hoped was the terminal. The loss of blood was making him weak. Several times he stumbled and almost fell, but he kept putting one foot ahead of the other, determined to make the airport.

Forty minutes later, Alex walked into the airport terminal. He looked down at his watch. It was ten o'clock. The traffic inside the terminal was light. A man and woman hurried to get out of his way. He could see alarm in their eyes. He must look a bloody mess. His chest wound had bled through his flight suit. He hoped that they wouldn't alert security.

Alex headed for the nearest restroom. It was empty. He set the bag on the floor and looked into the mirror. It was strange. He hadn't seen himself in a mirror in three weeks. The tanned, bearded face staring back at him was a stranger. The once plump face was thin and, to Alex's surprise, mean looking. No wonder the pilot had been afraid of him. Dried blood caked his beard and the side of his face. It had to be Harris's blood. The bloody mountaintop seemed a distant thing in his past. The memory of the cabin and Jan was clear and constant.

Alex rummaged through the pilot's bag and found everything he needed. There was even an extra flight suit. After hacking at the beard with a pair of small scissors, he attacked it with the razor. He cleaned most of the hair from the sink and put it into a trash can. Alex splashed cold water over his face again and again. Five minutes later, he was still dabbing at the razor cuts.

Alex went into a stall and pulled off the bloody flight suit. He didn't have anything to bandage the wounds with, but he managed to dab some more disinfectant under the blood-soaked gauze. The bleeding had stopped in both wounds. Alex put on the clean suit. He sat on the stool and took out Harris's billfold. It contained a couple of credit cards, a driver's license, and twenty, one-hundred-dollar bills. Alex whistled at the money. One of the credit cards and the driver's license was in the name of a Walter Stanley, and the other credit card was in the name of Harris Cox. Alex wondered if either was Harris's real name. He must have been ready to change identities at a moment's notice.

Alex put the billfold into his pocket and left the stall. He stopped beside the trash can and stuffed the bloody flight suit into the bottom of the can. Laying his pack on the floor, he took out everything he would need and pushed it into the pilot's bag. He put the backpack into the trash can with the suit and left the restroom. The cold water and change of clothing made him feel like a new man. Alex could still feel the weakness, but he knew it would change as the wounds healed.

Alex started for the airline counter and came to a sudden stop. How could he get the gun through security? All he had was the small carry-on bag. They might think it was funny if he tried to check that. He didn't know much about airport security except that they checked everyone for metal and the baggage were checked for bombs. It had been a while since the Twin Towers in New York. What would they do if he tried to send a gun in the luggage? Alex had a pretty good idea. He needed the gun. It would take too long to buy one and even so, there would be records.

Alex turned away from the airport ticket counter. They would be looking for him to buy a ticket at the nearest airports. They probably knew Harris's fake names. It would be better to take a plane from somewhere in the states. He headed toward the nearest car rental. They might not look for that, and he wouldn't have to worry about the gun right now.

"I need to rent a car," he said to the smiling lady behind the counter.

"Please fill this out," she said, leaning out over the counter as she handed him a form.

He filled the form out, using the name and address on the driver's license. He slid it back with the credit card. That left him with the other card in Harris's name if he needed it. He could have paid cash, but he might need that for later. He suddenly realized that the lady was asking him a question.

"What kind of a car, and how long do you want it for?" she asked. Her eyes took in the flight suit.

"How about a utility vehicle, and I'll need it for a couple of days."

Alex looked at his watch as she checked the credit card. It was eleven o'clock and the pull up lines outside were suddenly crawling with cars, trying to jockey for a position near the curb. Probably a flight was coming in. He turned back to the counter. The credit must have gone through because she was calling the yard. She stood and leaned out over the desk to check a number on the side wall. Her figure was nice but a little plump. She looked back and caught Alex's eyes on her bottom. She flashed another smile at him.

"The bus will be out front in a second to carry you to the yards." She smiled as she handed him the receipt to sign. Alex had put the billfold back into his pocket. He tried to remember the signature as he signed. He messed it up enough so that she couldn't tell the difference anyway. Alex handed back the pen and walked outside to wait on the bus. She mouthed "bye" to him as he left, but Alex only grinned.

Twenty minutes later, he was out of the airport and heading south in a new Chevrolet Blazer. He picked up Highway Five, remembering that it went straight into Portland, Oregon. He could catch a plane from there to Detroit. That way he would be further down before he began to leave a trail again.

The night was cool and the traffic light. Alex began to go over his plans for the next few days. He knew that it would be almost impossible to get to Jagger at his own home. Someone like Jagger would have all kinds of security. Alex went over one plan after another but nothing seemed to work. It had to be at Jagger's house. He could die trying to do this, but he had to try.

Alex was surprised to see the sign for the border crossing. He was making good time. Alex pulled up behind the short line of cars at the check station and rolled down the window. The slight breeze felt good. He moved up a space and then another. The last time he had crossed the border from Canada, they had asked him if he had anything to declare and hadn't searched the vehicle. He wondered if anything had changed. Alex drew in a sharp breath as he got closer. They were searching the cars ahead. It wasn't like the old days. They looked for everything now. He looked around frantically for a way to get out of the line, but there was none. The car behind was too close.

Suddenly his car was next. The guard asked him for his driver's license and to raise the hood. Alex gave the license he had gotten from Harris. The picture could be him now that he had lost weight. Alex saw movement as another guard opened the Blazer's back hatch. He was looking in the back compartment. The gun was there in the bag. He had hid it well but . . . Alex prayed that the guard wouldn't open the shaving kit. He held his breath. The guard with the driver's license had walked back to the other guard and they were talking about something. Alex looked around for a way out just in case, but there was none. He was trapped. Alex jerked back around. The first guard was back at the window.

"What happened?" the guard asked, smiling and pointing to the flight suit. "Did you lose your plane?"

"No," Alex stammered, "it's in Vancouver. I'm down here to see my sister."

"Any thing to declare?"

"No," Alex answered, trying his best to stay calm. He heard the back door shut. Alex took a quick look through the side view mirror and let his breath out. The guard didn't have anything in his hands. The first guard handed him back the license and waved him on. Alex's hands shook, as he pulled into the outgoing traffic and gained speed.

Alex went deep into his thoughts as he fell into the old habit of driving. The pain in his arm and chest was getting worse, and he knew that he had to take care of it soon. Everything seemed so far away, the plane crash, the last few weeks in the deep woods, but Jan was still with him. She was all around. It felt like if he could only turn away for a second and then back, she would be there in the passenger seat laughing, playing, kidding with him. Then he thought about the cabin and a flash of grief swept through him. He had to let someone know. The thought of her being in that cold, dark cellar . . . He shook his head, trying to drive the thought away.

Chapter 6

Keith Barlow turned slowly in his chair at the knock on his door. He looked out at the blue sky over Washington. He loved the feeling of power in this town. He ignored the second knock, but it brought his thoughts back to the person on the other side. Keith was making him wait just for the hell of it. David Carson was an Englishman and Keith was Scottish. Keith just didn't like Englishmen. The other thing was that Carson was thirty years old. Keith didn't like the new breed of agents coming up. They had been brought up with a computer stuck up their butts and didn't know what was happening in the real world. He wished that he had never let him in on this deal, but he couldn't do all of the work by himself. He moved his short frame forward in the chair and brushed his receding hair back over his forehead. His green eyes hardened as he turned toward the door.

"Come," he said and the door opened.

Carson walked in with the sure stride of someone who has mapped out what he needs to do in the next second, minute, hour, or day. He slid confidently into the chair in front of the desk and waited for his superior to speak.

"What happened?" Keith asked simply.

For the first time since Carson had walked into the office, Keith saw a flicker of fear dart across his eyes. Well, maybe not fear, more like unsureness. This made Keith happy. He decided to push the issue.

"Did I read the report right? Our whole team was lost. Who in the hell did you send up there?"

Carson licked his lips. "We sent the best we could find, but these are contract people. You know how that is."

"Who set up that little pilot with wife deal? What did you hope to accomplish with that?"

Carson stretched his muscular neck out of his shirt collar and leaned slightly toward Keith. "That was my idea and a damn good one. We needed time to let the Russians clear the area."

Keith didn't say anything but leaned back in the chair and studied Carson. Carson was a big man, well over six feet with short cut blond hair. His blue eyes had shifted to a picture behind Keith. It was a picture of their boss and Keith knew that Carson had been kissing his ass ever since he had been sent to Washington. Oh, what wouldn't he give to be thirty again. He kept his forty-five-year-old body in shape, but Carson was in his prime and knew it. Keith was looking at his replacement, but that was in the old world.

"Where is our man now?" he asked.

Carson's eyes leveled on Keith. He had regained some of his composure. "We don't know. We have six teams out looking for him. He could have gone anywhere in the helicopter. When we find the helicopter, we'll get a better track on which way he's headed."

"You know that if he's able to tell anyone what he saw, it could blow this whole damn operation. We've been working for eight years to get the Russians in just the right place and heads will roll if we don't pull this off."

"I don't understand. Why wait until the Russians get everything into place? Why don't we take them out now?"

"Because we have to wait until their government representatives are at Camp David for the summit meeting. We have to embarrass them so that we can influence the vote. It's up to you to keep them happy until that happens and that means taking out this bookworm."

Carson stood. He knew that the meeting was over. "I'll keep you informed," he said as he headed for the door.

"Make sure that you do," Keith said to Carson's back. He turned the chair back toward the window and stared out over the city. This whole thing was getting more complicated.

Sometimes he wished he had never become involved, but he knew that he really had no choice. His future here was fast approaching its end. This was his only chance to reach for the gold ring.

Chapter 7

Alex jerked his head back up. He was off the road. He could hear the sound of gravel hitting the side of the car. He brought the car back on the road and shook his head to clear the cobwebs. A sign for the city of Blane flashed by. The next big town would be Seattle. He would be almost halfway to Portland by then.

He saw a sign for a roadside diner. It was open for breakfast. He needed coffee to stay awake and food. His mouth watered when he thought about the food. He was starving. It had been a long time since he had eaten and even longer since he had eaten any good food. He pulled off the road and parked the Blazer behind the diner. The place was half-full of customers; mostly truckers. The wonderful smell of frying bacon and hot biscuits filled the air. Alex slid into one of the booths and, a minute later, a waitress came over carrying a pot of coffee.

"What will it be?" she asked as she poured the coffee.

Alex ordered scrambled eggs, a waffle, and sausage. He sat there listening to the stories of the truckers while he crammed down the hot, greasy food. Alex savored each bite and washed it down with hot black coffee. He finished and flagged the waitress down to order a piece of apple pie and another cup of coffee. He drank the last of the coffee but couldn't eat all of the pie. He took his check with him to pay at the counter.

"Are you going far?" the waitress asked as she took the twenty.

"Not far." Alex could tell that the waitress really didn't care where he was going, but sometimes being nice got bigger tips. She smiled at him when he told her to keep the change.

He felt ten pounds heavier as he walked out of the restaurant. He had never been so full. A sharp pain shot through his arm when he opened the Blazer door. He reached up and wiped sweat from his forehead, wondering if he had an infection.

The car was still warm, but he felt a chill as he pulled out onto the road. An hour later the arm was still throbbing and he knew that he had an infection. He had to find some place to take care of it.

* * *

It was well into the next morning when he reached Seattle. He pulled into the first motel and rented a room for the night, leaving a message to wake him in six hours. He had to drag his bag out with his left hand. He couldn't stand to move his right. Alex reached the room and unlocked the door. Throwing the bag on the bed, he pulled off his shirt and looked at his wounds. The chest wound seemed clean, but the arm was red and swollen. He dabbed more disinfectant on it and fell on the bed. He was dead on his feet. His arm would wait until morning. He had forgotten how good a bed could feel.

Alex woke in a sweat, his arm throbbing. He couldn't wait any longer. He looked at his watch, discovering that he'd only been asleep for two hours. He got up and, pulling his bandages off, headed for the shower. The wound stung with the hot water and pain shot down to his fingers. His arm felt like it was going to fall off. He washed the wounds gently with soap and stepped out into the bathroom to examine them. The chest wound was healing and a light scab was already forming. His arm was a different matter. It was swollen and white around the wound. He could barely touch it. The front exit wound seemed to be the worse. The smaller entrance wound in the back of his arm had almost closed. He needed a doctor, but he couldn't go to one.

Alex went back to his bag and took out the hunting knife. He used a match to heat the point and then waited until it cooled. Alex got down on his knees by the bed and pulled his belt off. He yelled in pain as he lashed his arm securely to the bed post. Reaching over with his other hand he dragged the towel under his arm. He held his head down for a minute to keep from throwing up. Could he do this without passing out? Alex held the knife point over the wound for a second, gathering his nerves. His hand started to shake. He had to do it. He had to do it now! Putting one end of the towel into his mouth and taking a deep breath, he shoved the knife into the bullet wound. The knife was razor sharp and went further in than he intended. Pus and blood shot out as he jerked the knife back. Alex bit down on the towel to cut off his scream. He fell over against the bed as wave after wave of pain shot through his arm and then everything went black.

* * *

Alex opened his eyes slowly and gritted his teeth against the throbbing pain in his arm. He felt something sticky against his face and looked down.

The sides of the bed sheets were covered with blood. He looked at his watch. He had been out for over an hour. He rolled his tongue around in his mouth to get rid of the dryness and released the belt. He reached up and touched his mouth and the dried blood on his chin. He had bitten through his lip. He raised the towel and bit into it again as he poured disinfectant into the wound. He screamed a muffled scream through the towel and waited for the pain to subside.

After a few minutes, he opened the flight bag and took one of the pilot's tee-shirts. He cut it up for bandages. He yelled again as he wrapped the bandages tight around his arm. He listened to see if he had woke anyone, but there was no sound. It was still quiet. He put everything into the bag and left the room. He threw the bag and bloody towels into the dumpster on the way to the car. The manager would raise hell about the blood, but they wouldn't know who he was. Alex was surprised to see that it was daylight outside; a clear and sunny day, the perfect day as Jan used to say.

He drove for three hours and pulled off at a shopping center. Alex went into a department store and bought several changes of clothing and a new bag to carry them in. He then went into a nearby drugstore and bought first aid supplies. He left the drugstore and pulled into a corner gas station to gas up. After he paid the attendant, Alex took the new bag out of the car and walked around to the bathroom. He locked the door and pulling his flight suit off, cleaned and re-bandaged his wounds. The arm looked a lot better already, but it still hurt like the dickens. Alex changed into new clothing and crammed the flight suit into a trash can on his way back to the car.

* * *

Two hours later, he pulled into Portland, Oregon. It took an hour to find a bank with branches in Detroit and Portland and another two to transfer twenty thousand dollars from his bank in Atlanta, five to Detroit and fifteen to himself in Portland. He might not use the five thousand in Detroit, but if anything happened, he would have the money there if he needed it. He waited in the bank until the transfer went through and took the fifteen thousand in cash. He noticed that the bank manager walked out into the lobby as Alex left; watching him. He hoped that he wouldn't report anything to the police. The police couldn't have found out about the men he had killed yet but with the people behind this, it wouldn't be long.

On the way to the airport, he noticed a young man hitchhiking on the opposite side. About a mile past the hitchhiker, an idea came to him. Alex slammed on the breaks and turned around. He slowed as he passed the man again and pulled off the road. He watched in his rear view mirror as the hitchhiker ran up to the car. When he got closer, Alex could see that the man was young; about twenty-five. His clothes were ragged, but he was clean-shaven. The young man opened the car door and stood there, glancing nervously into the car and then over at Alex.

"Where are you going?" Alex asked.

"All the way to Canada," the young man answered.

"Well hop in."

The young man threw his well-worn bag into the car and slid into the front seat.

"Do you have a driver's license?" Alex asked as he pulled out into the traffic.

"Yes," the young man said. "Do you want me to drive?"

"Well, in a way," replied Alex, reaching his hand over. "My name is Bob."

The young man shook his hand. "Mine is Charles. Where are you going, Bob?"

"I'm going to the airport," Alex replied.

Charles looked from Alex to the road and then back to Alex with a puzzled look on his face. "The airport is behind us. I saw the sign a couple of miles back."

"Do you need some money?"

"Sure, don't we all," he answered with a quick hard look on his face. "Look, I'll do a lot of things for money, but I don't think this is one of them. You had better let me out."

Alex laughed as he saw a service station ahead where he could turn around. "I think you have the wrong idea. I need to catch a plane out of Portland in one hour, but I want to turn the car in at Vancouver." Charles's eyes narrowed again. "I didn't steal the car or anything like that," Alex went on. "Everything's on the up and up. The papers are in the glove compartment. You need to get to Canada and I'm offering you a car to drive."

"You said something about money."

Alex pulled off the road into a service station and came to a stop. He turned to Charles. "I'll give you one hundred dollars to drive the car back to Vancouver and turn it in at the airport. All you have to do is drop me off at the airport here and you have a ride all the way to Vancouver. Is it a deal?"

Charles's hard look slowly turned into a grin. "Hell yes, it's a deal." He jumped out of the Blazer and ran over to the driver's side.

Twenty minutes later they were at the airport. Alex took his bag and handed Charles a one-hundred-dollar bill.

"Boy, I can use this," Charles said, as he reached over to shut the passenger door.

Alex stood and watched Charles disappear into the airport traffic. Now it would be hard to track him through the rental car.

He thought again about the gun as he turned to go into the airport. He would have to take a chance. He walked up to one of the porters.

"I'll give you ten bucks for a small box." Alex held up his hands to indicate the size. The porter ran to his counter and produced a box. Alex swapped the ten for the box and headed for the bathroom. He stripped the gun down and emptied the pilot's shaving kit into the box, arranging the gun parts alongside the shaving items. If the box was x-rayed, maybe this would confuse them. He filled the space around the parts with toilet paper. Stopping by the porter's counter, he borrowed tape and was directed to a shipping store down the street. He mailed the box to the Marriott hotel at the airport in Detroit, using the name of Mark Chambers.

Alex ran back into the airport lobby and bought a ticket to Detroit. Alex had enough time to gulp down a sandwich and coke on the way. He had a window seat and he leaned back to watch Portland disappear into the clouds. He felt a cold shiver when he thought about what he was going to do in Detroit. Then his thoughts went to Jan. She seemed so close. He could hear her whispering in his ear. A smile spread across his face as he closed his eyes.

Chapter 8

It was four o'clock and the sky was overcast with that dark look of coming rain, as the plane taxied toward the unloading ramp. Alex followed the line of passengers into the terminal and a few minutes later, caught a bus to the Marriott. It began to rain as he walked through the outside doors at the hotel and stepped into the lobby. He approached the counter and stopped for a second to look around. The lobby was full of people, but no one paid any attention to him.

"May I help you, sir?"

"Yes, I would like a room for three nights," Alex answered, pulling out the credit card with the name of Mark Chambers. Alex signed the card in the same bold writing as the signature on the back. He held his breath as the young woman checked the card. The credit was fine, and Alex picked up his luggage and headed for the elevator.

He watched the people as he waited on the elevator. It was a strange feeling to be around so many people after the past weeks in the deep woods. He almost jumped forward as a blond-headed lady walked by with the same look and walk as Jan. He jumped again as someone touched him on the shoulder. The elevator was there. He was blocking the door.

Alex slid the card into the hotel door and stepped inside. He threw the bag on one of the beds and walked over to the window. He was on the eighth floor. Detroit lay before him. He had been in a lot of Marriotts with Jan. She always tried to beat him to the showers, and he would always be right behind her, crowding in. He could close his eyes and hear her laughter.

Alex stripped off his clothing and headed for the shower. He let warm water run over him for over an hour. Afterwards, he washed his wounds gently. The infection was almost gone in his arm. His chest wound was sore but was already healing. He dried slowly and went back into the bedroom. After bandaging his wounds, he sat on the bed and watched T.V. for a while. A senator was on Fox News talking about the economy. Alex wondered which senator Harris had been talking about. It could even be this one.

Later he turned the T.V. off and crawled under the covers. He lay there staring into the darkness, planning the next day. The sheets had a clean, washed smell. He couldn't keep his thoughts on the plan. Half asleep, he found himself reaching over, feeling for Jan.

* * *

·Alex woke the next morning to the sound of an airplane passing overhead. He turned the lamp on by the bed to check the time. It was four o'clock. Alex reached for the phone book and thumbed through the pages. Jagger was a short list and there were only three Lees. Alex copied the three addresses onto the bedside notepad and tore several sheets underneath until he couldn't see the print. He smiled to himself as he headed for the bathroom. He was getting to be like one of those private detectives he had written about.

Alex showered and bandaged his arm but decided to leave the bandages off his chest. He changed into clean clothes. The clothing was casual, but he'd forgotten to buy shoes. The hiking shoes definitively didn't go with the pants. He would have to take care of that soon.

It was after five when Alex stepped off the elevator. The smell of food drifted across the lobby. He stopped and read the small sign in front of the restaurant. They served breakfast at seven. It was too long to wait.

He stepped out into the morning air and walked toward two taxies waiting on early fares. He slid into the back seat of the first taxi.

The driver turned toward him. "Where to, mister?"

"Do you know of a good place to eat downtown?"

"Sure," the driver said, as he reached over to flip on the meter. "Charley's is opened about this time and he has damn good food."

Alex leaned back against the seat as the driver eased into the morning traffic and left the airport behind. Traffic was already filling the expressways. It was Monday morning and everyone was going to work. Alex remembered when he would help Jan get ready to go to work. They would always have a cup of coffee together before she left, and he headed back to the keyboard. Alex had always loved to write. He wondered if he would ever write again.

* * *

Thirty minutes later, the driver pulled over to the curb in front of a busy café. Alex paid the fare and made his way through the door. The smell of strong coffee and food, filled the air, and the sound of loud conversation blasted at him. The place was crammed. The waitresses ran from table to table hollering out orders to the cook and grabbing empty plates on their way to the next order. Several people were waiting in line. Alex stopped at the end of the line. As the tables and bar stools cleared, the line shortened. His time finally came, and he scooted onto a bar stool.

"Be with you in a minute, honey," a waitress said, as she slid a cup of hot black coffee in front of him. Alex wondered what she would do if he wanted milk. Two young, well-dressed men sat on his right, arguing about the rise and fall of the stock market. Alex reached over and snagged the cream. They paid him no attention. A construction worker sat on his other side with a determined look on his face as he mopped up the last of a fried egg. Alex raised his head to the waitress, and she stopped in front of him with a pad in her hand. The bored look told him that if he didn't order soon, she would disappear.

"What will it be, mister?" she asked, drumming her pencil against the pad.

"How about scrambled eggs and sausage?"

"Coming right up," she said and yelled the order to the cook.

The construction man finished his coffee and held up his hand for the check.

Alex pointed to the paper he had been reading, and the man slid it over. Alex raised the coffee to take another sip and opened the paper to the front page. He almost dropped the cup. One of his old pictures glared back at him. Alex lowered the coffee with a shaking hand and read the headlines.

"Writer goes on a killing spree in Canadian wilds. Wife and a local pilot found dead."

Alex looked around the café. No one else at the bar had a paper. Several people sitting at the tables had one, but he had his back to them. He folded the edges of the paper in to hide the picture even though he doubted that anyone would recognize him since he had lost all of that weight and he was younger in the picture. He felt the beard on his face, lucky for him that his razor was with his gun.

"The body of writer's wife and pilot found in cabin."

The article went on to say that it had been reported that the pilot had delivered medical supplies to Mayo, but that information had proved to be false. The pilot's plane had been found near the cabin. No mention of other bodies.

The bastards had cleaned up. They had found Jan and moved her back to the first cabin with Robert, removed all of their men, and set the scene for the cops.

"Canadian inspector waiting for forensic evidence before final conclusion."

At least the inspector seemed to be open-minded. Alex's heart jumped when he saw a small picture of Jan at the bottom of the column. Her face seemed like a stranger. He reached out with his finger to touch it. The column went on to say that Jan would be buried as soon as the body was released. The newspaper quoted an unknown source, indicating that it could have been a lover's quarrel.

Alex threw the paper down and slammed his fist against the counter top. An angry protest came from his side. Another man lifted his plate and stood. Everyone was looking at him. He had to get out of here. Alex slid a twenty at the cashier, as the waitress yelled at him with his plate of food held high. He didn't stop, but grabbed the paper and pushed his way into the street. He was in a daze. Alex stopped at the corner to read the rest of the column. The paper didn't mention the helicopter pilot he had left at the airport. He was still ahead of them. He had enough time to do what he had come to do. Alex threw the paper into a trash can and hurried down the street.

Jagger had been at the lake. That had been over three weeks ago. He had to be back in Detroit by now. Alex gritted his teeth as he hurried down the sidewalk. It was six in the morning. There was hardly anyone on the street. He had to stop doing things like that. It wasn't good to draw attention to himself. Alex looked up after an hour of walking. The Weston Hotel loomed ahead. It was one of the tallest buildings in North America. Alex drew in a deep breath. Jan and he had stayed there once. They had been able to get a room on the top floor. After dark, that first night, they had sat by the window, sipping wine, trying to pick out different tourist attractions.

Alex crossed the street and made his way into the hotel. The lobby was quiet and empty as he passed by the restaurant and headed for the telephones. It seemed like only yesterday that he and Jan had eaten there. He would never get over his grief for her. Everything he did, today and tomorrow, was meaningless. The only thing left was the rage and his revenge. Alex sat down by the telephones and pulled out the slip of paper from the hotel. He waited for a second and picked up the receiver. The first Lee Jagger line was busy. The second had a recording that said he was out of the country. Alex put a question mark by both and called the third one on his list. A crisp voice answered the phone.

"Can I speak to Lee Jagger?" Alex asked.

"Who's calling?" the voice asked.

Before Alex could answer, he heard another voice. Alex's hand tightened on the phone. It sounded like Jagger. Rage swept through him and he gripped the phone so hard, it began to hurt. Alex took long, deep breaths to calm himself.

"I'm going out," the second voice sounded again.

"Mr. Jagger, I have someone on the line for you."

"Take a message," the second voice said, fading away.

"I'm sorry," the first voice came back.

Alex didn't wait for the rest of the message. He let the phone settle slowly onto the hook and looking around to see if anyone was watching, he tore the page from the book. He spotted a rental car counter across the lobby as he left the telephone booth. Alex walked over to the counter and used the fake driver's license to rent a car. He put the bill on Harris's card. Alex walked outside to wait for the car. It was going to be a beautiful day; another day Jan would have loved. After a brief wait, a blue Ford pulled up to the curb. Alex walked around and handed the attendant a tip as he slid into the front seat. He stopped at a service station on the way back to the Marriott and bought a good map of Detroit.

* * *

It was nine o'clock when he got back to the Marriott. Alex parked the car in front of the hotel and walked through the lobby toward the elevator, changing directions at a wave from the desk clerk. The package had arrived. Clutching the box under his arm, he stepped onto the elevator and pushed the button for his floor.

Alex opened the door to his room slowly, scanning the room for any sign of disturbance. Everything seemed to be in place. He locked the door and, throwing the box on the bed, went into the bathroom for a wash cloth. He came back to the bed and sat down. Alex opened the box, and spread the gun parts in front of him. He wiped each piece carefully before he reassembled the gun. When he was through, he eased the gun barrel back, letting a round slide into the chamber and slammed it home, reaching forward at the same time to flip the safety on. He put the shaving items back into the overnight bag and after taking off his clothes, lay down on the bed. A plan began to form in his head. The plan changed as he went through it bit by bit. It might work. Later, he closed his eyes and went to sleep.

*   *   *

The alarm in his head went off at two o'clock. Alex dressed and then, taking a wash cloth, began to wipe everything he had touched. Afterwards, he packed his bag and used the cloth to wipe both sides of the doorknob as he walked out of the room. He still had two more nights at the hotel, and he might use both of them, but just in case anyone came while he was gone, they wouldn't find anything. Alex threw the cloth into a trash can on the way to the elevator and five minutes later, slid into the front seat of the Ford.

He sat in the rental car and traced a path on the map to Lee Jagger's house. It was two thirty in the afternoon. He would have plenty of time. The traffic was light as he left the hotel behind and skirted the main part of Detroit. Forty minutes later, he pulled into a side street across from a large, three story house on the back side of ten acres or more. The acreage was surrounded by a ten-foot high fence. The side street was uphill from the house, and Alex could see the front entrance clearly. Directly across from him and on the other side of the fence was a thicket of trees. Just down the road from that was the main gate. He turned around and pulled off the street behind a stand of thick trees. He could make out the front of the house and the gate, but it would be difficult for them to see him.

*   *   *

Alex waited there the rest of the day, checking every car that entered or left with the binoculars. He studied each passenger as they got out at the front door. The voice on the phone had sounded like Lee Jagger, but still he had to be sure. He was beginning to wonder, because he hadn't seen anyone who looked like him.

It was after five o'clock when another limousine pulled up to the gate. Alex brought the binoculars to bear. He saw movement above, as an overhead camera swung down to cover the car. First the front window and then the rear rolled down. Alex couldn't make out the driver or the passenger through the open back window. Identification was made and the gate swung open. The limousine moved slowly down the long driveway.

Alex followed the car with his binoculars until it stopped in front of the huge house. He watched carefully as the driver got out and walked to the back door. His hand tightened on the binoculars as the first passenger stepped out. It was Lee Jagger. Alex waited until the car disappeared behind the house and, after checking up and down the street, opened the door to the Ford and sprinted across the road into the shadows of the trees. He could make out the front of the house clearly from here. Alex let his breath slow and rested the binoculars against the fence, studying the front of the house. Everything was quiet, nothing moved, until suddenly a man appeared, leading four guard dogs. The man used the dogs to search the area around the house, and then, one-by-one, he released them. The dogs knew their territory. Two disappeared into the woods surrounding the front of the house and the other two ran to the back.

Alex swung the binoculars back to the front and made a careful search. Set at a radius of about one hundred and forty feet or so from the front of the house were small black posts. During the years of writing spy novels, Alex had researched all kinds of security systems. These had to be sensors of some kind. He studied the front of the house again. Six huge columns rose to a balcony leading out from the third floor. Suddenly, sliding glass doors slid open and Jagger walked out onto the balcony with a cigar in his mouth. He leaned out and yelled at someone below. A man stepped out from behind one of the columns and faced Jagger. After a brief conversation, the man disappeared. Jagger had a guard outside, maybe two or three. Alex swung the binoculars back to Jagger. His breathing quickened as suddenly he was back at the lake. Alex could see Jagger's face clearly as he gave the order to kill Robert. He could hear the gunfire in his head.

The sound of a car came from behind. Alex stepped farther into the shadows by the fence. The car didn't slow. It was almost seven o'clock now and the sun was sinking behind the earth's curvature.

Alex turned to watch Jagger walk back through the sliding door. He tried to see the door jam but he was too far away. He knew there was a sensor. The whole house would be on a security system. Just something he would have to get around. As darkness settled in, the house and yard flooded with lights. The only shadows were under the trees between the fence and the yard. It would be his only way in. Alex lowered the glasses and ran back across to the car.

* * *

He located a motel about five miles from Jagger's house. Alex noticed the golden arches of a McDonald's two blocks away as he stopped in front of the check-in office. He paid cash and drove around to his room. Leaving the overnight bag in the car, he walked to the McDonald's. Alex was starving after missing the meal at the diner. He was surprised to find McDonald's crowded with people of all kinds. . .workers just off work, kids and families. Alex waited in line until it was his turn. A man, just in front, held onto a little girl about three years old. Alex could see the love between the two as the little girl laughed and played with her father. He wondered what Jan's and his children would have looked like. If they looked anything like Jan, they would have been beautiful. A lump suddenly formed in his throat. It was his turn to give his order and the waitress looked at him funny as he tried to regain his voice. Alex finally ordered two cheeseburgers, fries and, a Coke to go.

 Fifteen minutes later, he opened the door to the motel room and threw the bag onto the bed. Propping two pillows against the headboard, he walked over to the T.V. and selected a channel without news. He pulled off his shirt and, laying down on the bed, attacked the cheeseburgers and french fries. He could hear voices in the next room over the sound of the television. They were yelling at each other in Spanish. Alex knew a little Spanish; the guy was calling the woman a whore. Alex turned the television off. The voices had stopped yelling and Alex could hear soft crying. He lay on the bed for a few minutes longer, working on changes in his plan. First, he had to take care of the dogs, but how? He could poison them, but he didn't know where to buy the poison, and he really didn't want to kill them. If only he had one of those tranquilizer guns the zoo used.

 Suddenly, he knew how to get one. In researching one of his books he'd had to hire someone who knew the streets. The guy's name was Jake, and he had told Alex that you could buy anything on the streets if you had enough money. Alex would get someone to steal the tranquilizer gun for him. He lay there for a while longer going over his plan. Everything seemed to fit. He looked at his watch, it was almost time to go.

 Alex stretched his arms high. He could hear the soft drip-drip of the shower. It was a soothing sound and he closed his eyes, only to jerk them open at the sudden slamming of the door from the next room. Alex gave a sigh and swung his legs off the bed, moving to the bathroom to splash cold water over his face. He dried slowly with a hand towel. After changing clothes, he hid most of his money under the mattress, keeping fifteen-hundred out for tonight and stood there for a second with his billfold in his hand. Alex pulled the credit cards out and put them with the money. Anything could happen on the streets. He closed the door behind him, pulling hard against it to check the lock. Satisfied, he headed for the car, stopping as someone came toward him from the direction of the office. It was the manager, hurrying toward the room next door. Maybe he would get some rest tonight.

* * *

Alex took Highway 94 and headed toward downtown Detroit. After stopping several times to ask directions, he finally found the section of town he wanted. It was ten o'clock. The right time of night for the people he was looking for. Both sides of the street were full of liquor stores and run down hotels. Alex plowed to a stop as a drunk stumbled in front of the car. He rolled the driver's side window down and slowly drove down the street, searching. He stopped as four young men came from an alley. He jerked around as a voice sounded behind him. He hadn't seen the hooker come up.

"Don't you want some of what I got, honey?" she asked, placing her ample bosom over his arm. She slid one leg up against the car and pulled her already short dress up to her waist, letting him see between her legs.

Alex shook his head no and moved his arm away from the window.

"Hey, you won't get a better deal than me," she said, shaking an exposed tit at him. The smell of cheap perfume drifted through the car.

The young men had turned and were walking away from the car.

The hooker noticed his attention. "If you're looking for boys, honey, you're looking at the wrong assess. Them boys mean trouble, and I don't mean trouble you can walk away from. What do you want with boys anyway? I can do anything those tight assess can do."

Alex ignored the hooker. He pressed gently on the gas and the car began to move slowly down the street, following the gang. The hooker held onto the car. *She must really need the business,* Alex thought. He eased down on the gas, trying to leave her behind.

"Hey, where're you going? I'm not through with you yet. If you want a blow job, I can do it a lot better than any boy. Thirty dollars and that's as low as I go." She began to laugh. "Get it, as low as I go." Alex increased his speed. "You fuck with those boys and you won't come back!" she yelled, as she let go of the car.

The gang had disappeared around the next corner. Broken street lights left long, dark shadows on both sides of the street. Alex saw shadows moving, drifting in and out of the light. He could hear cries of pain. They were beating someone. Alex stopped the car and waited. The shadows became boys again as they stepped into the middle of the street, leaving a dark bundle against one side of the building.

Alex eased forward again. He could hear their laughter and cussing, daring anyone to come too close. He paused before he got to the dark bundle. It sat up. The bundle was a woman. It was hard to tell her age. His headlights caught her full in the face as he moved closer. The face wasn't a woman. It was a man dressed like a woman. It seemed to be all right.

Alex turned his attention back to the gang. They had reached the next corner and turned right. Alex pressed on the gas. A minute later, he eased around the corner, catching sight of them as he turned. They had stopped at a liquor store. Alex watched as one of them went into the store while the other three waited outside. Coming to a stop twenty feet from the store, he could see them clearly. They were teenagers, the youngest being about fifteen and the oldest around eighteen. Two of them were black and the other one white.

Alex put the car into park. All three turned toward him, and Alex's heart began to race. It was now or never. He slowly opened the car door and stepped out. The teenagers didn't move as he walked toward them.

"Well, what do we have here?" the oldest one asked. "A well-to-do white man coming down here to get liquor from our store."

Alex pressed his hand against his jacket pocket for the reassurance of the gun. The teenager's eyes followed Alex's hand. The other two moved slowly to each side. He could see the other teenager inside as he walked forward slowly. He had a six-pack of beer in one hand and had stopped just inside the door, watching the four of them. He made up his mind and walked over to the counter. Alex wondered if he was going to pay for the beer or rob the store.

Alex's attention turned back to the teens in front.

"You know what," the same teenager said. "I can see that you haven't been to our high class neighborhood. So, I'm going to explain our marketing system to you. If you come down here to buy our superior products, then you'll have to pay for that privilege." The other two laughed.

Alex held his hands up. "Hey fellows, you have it all wrong. I've been watching you. I need someone to do a little job for me, and I think you may be able to handle it."

"What job?" the teenager from the store said, as he came through the doors.

Alex could tell right off that this was the gang leader, and he wasn't a teenager. Alex guessed his age to be about twenty-four or five. He had darker features than most whites. He looked Spanish, but Alex knew that more often than not, the Spanish tended to stay to themselves. His speech didn't suggest any of the three. He had a handsome face with dark, flashing eyes. His muscles rippled under the tight shirt as he shifted the six-pack of beer to the other hand. His empty hand drifted down toward his pocket.

Alex's breathing quickened—then he relaxed. The pants were too tight to conceal a gun. He tried to calm his breathing as the young man's eyes studied his.

"I asked you a question, Mister. Are you going to answer me or stand there with your mouth open?"

"I'm from out of town," Alex began.

"No shit," one of the other teenager's said, spitting a wad of spittle at Alex's feet.

"I need someone to do a job for me. It'll be worth fifteen hundred."

The leader took a step closer. The others moved with him. Alex stood his ground, his hand inches from the gun.

"You have the money on you?" the leader asked. The corner of his mouth curled into a slight smile.

The younger one to his left moved his hand toward his pocket. Alex's fingers moved inside his jacket and touched the cool steel of the gun. The leader noticed the movement. He held out his hand to the rest of the gang.

"I have some of it on me," Alex answered. "You'll get the rest when you do the job."

He couldn't read the leader's poker face. The younger one leaned forward, almost dancing on his toes.

The leader raised his hand again. The younger one jumped at the movement, taking it as a signal. His hand flashed forward, the hard steel of a knife glittering in the street lights. The knife streaked toward Alex with a life of its own.

Not long ago, Alex would have been a dead man, but Alex wasn't the same man. The weeks in the Canadian Rockies, facing death every hour, had changed him. He blocked the knife arm and, with the same motion, stepped in close, rotating the teen to one side and bringing his forearm under his chin. Alex's other hand already had the gun out, pressing it against the boy's ear.

"Drop the knife," he said in a harsh whisper, pulling back hard against the boy's chin. The knife made a metallic sound as it hit the payment

The leader finally found his voice. "Hey, hey, calm down. Joel here is just a little jumpy. Joel, how many times do I have to tell you? Don't try to cut someone unless I give the orders."

"But," Joel said through strained lips, "I thought you wanted the dude taken out."

The leader had both hands up. This man had looked like an easy mark. The money had been theirs, but the man had moved like grease lighting. Suddenly, he was in control and the gang leader could see death staring back at him.

"Enough of this shit," Alex said. "Do you want the deal or not?" Alex glanced through the store window. The clerk had disappeared. He could be in the back calling the police. They needed to finish this quickly. He released the boy and shoved him hard toward the leader, keeping the gun leveled.

The leader eased his hand from under his jacket. "I'm listening."

"You guys know where the local zoo is?"

"Sure, we go there all of the time."

"I need you to break in and steal a tranquilizer gun and spare ammo, like maybe ten shots."

"No problem," the leader said.

Alex reached in with his other hand and guessed at half of the fifteen hundred. He held it out to the leader.

The leader took the money and thumbed through the bills. "Hey man, I thought you had at least half of it? There's only five hundred here."

"I'll give you the rest when you're finished. I figure that might give you a little more incentive. Meet me at the airport by the Delta ticket counter tomorrow morning at ten o'clock. If you aren't there, I'll wait for fifteen minutes—no longer, and you come alone. Leave your little helpers at home." Alex pointed his finger at the leader. "If you don't show up, I'm going to come looking for my money, and this time it won't be to talk."

The leader put his hand out as the others leaned forward. "No problem, man, you bring the cash and I'll have the stuff." He had weighed the cost of getting more money now, or later with the goods. Later had won out. He turned and walked away from Alex with the others close behind.

The instant the gang turned their backs, Alex ran to the car. He slid the gun back out of sight and climbed under the wheel. He looked back as he slammed the door. The street was empty. Alex heard sirens as he turned the corner and headed back to the freeway. The words of the hooker hung in his ears. He would have to be extra careful when he picked up the tranquilizer gun. He knew that they could take the down payment and not show up, but the greed in the leader's eyes made Alex think otherwise. He had seen the clerk come to the door as he drove away. He could have gotten Alex's tag number. Alex wasn't worried. Most of the people here tended to keep their mouths shut. The clerk's only worry was being robbed.

Twenty minutes later Alex turned onto the expressway. The department stores would still be open. He had two more stops to make, and then he would meet the gang tomorrow morning for the tranquilizer gun. That would give him everything he needed.

Chapter 9

Alex woke with a start and sat up in the bed. His whole body was wet with sweat. He remembered the dream now. He had watched Jan die over and over again. A deep feeling of grief and dread swept through him. He had to get up. He swung his feet to the floor and headed for the bathroom. After showering and shaving, he still had that terrible feeling, like something bad was going to happen. Alex sat down on the bed, trying to pull himself together, to feel some kind of purpose in what he was going to do. Finally, he stood and lifted the mattress. He got his money, packed his bag, and hurried from the room.

Alex looked at his watch as he walked across the parking lot to the office. It was seven o'clock. He wouldn't be back to the motel. After tonight, he wouldn't have time to stop anywhere. He had an hour to get to the airport. The motel attendant looked tired, probably from staying up all night with the couple next door. Alex turned the key in and walked back to the car. He threw the bag and the small backpack he had bought last night into the back seat. Alex eased into the traffic and headed for the expressway.

Thirty minutes later, he parked at the airport parking lot. He walked slowly toward the entrance, looking for any of the gang or their leader. Alex couldn't see any of them. Maybe they wouldn't show up, and then what would he do? He was twenty minutes early, they could be late. Alex walked into the airport and checked the flights to Atlanta. Delta had several flights and he headed for the ticket counter. He stopped at the end of the short ticket line and looked around. He thought he saw one of the gang members, but he couldn't be sure.

"Excuse me, sir."

The voice startled Alex. The line had disappeared. He was up next.

"I'm sorry," he said, as he stepped up to the counter. "I need a ticket to Atlanta, Georgia, leaving sometime after seven o'clock tomorrow morning." Alex let his eyes drift slowly across the crowded floor behind him. He couldn't see anyone out of place. He turned back at the brunette's voice.

"That will be four hundred and seventy dollars," she said. "The flight leaves at eight thirty."

Alex raised his eyebrow at the price and slid five one-hundred-dollar bills across the counter. "When does the flight board?" he asked, as he waited for his change.

"The plane boards at gate twenty-eight at 8:00 o'clock tomorrow morning but be here by six." she answered. She handed him the ticket "Have a good flight, sir."

"Thank you," Alex replied and turned away from the counter to scan the floor again. He saw the leader almost immediately. Movement brought his eyes upward. He caught sight of one of the gang trying to hide behind a column and another one at the top of the escalator.

Alex turned slowly, searching as the leader approached, looking for a way out when this was over. There was only one. The same way he'd come in.

The leader stopped in front of Alex. He held out a small case. A smile played across his lips. "I've got what you wanted," he said slowly.

"I told you to come alone."

"Well now, I thought about that on the way over here. We had more trouble getting the stuff than we figured, and that's going to make the cost go up. We figured that you might need a little persuading to come up with the extra."

Alex could see the other gang members moving toward them, cutting off any escape. "How much more?" Alex had the rest of the ten-thousand in the car. It would be worth it to him if he could get the tranquilizer gun and get out of here without a scene.

The leader grinned at Alex. "You know, you don't look like someone who would kill their wife. She must have really been a bitch."

Anger and rage seeped through Alex like a red-hot flame. He took a short step forward and then stopped as the leader nodded toward a nearby police officer. He clutched his fingers into a fist, drawing his fingernails tighter and tighter into the flesh, letting the pain drive through him.

The leader grinned as he saw Alex fighting himself. He leaned forward. "You would like to beat my face in, wouldn't you?"

Alex didn't answer. He noticed that the police officer had moved outside. For a minute, there was an opening through the baggage claim and to the outside street. He could grab the case and run for it. The leader noticed the change in Alex's eyes and jumped back, holding the case behind him. Alex had lost his opportunity.

"I asked how much?" Alex had a feeling of being in a cage with no way out.

The leader smiled. "Let's just say ten thousand dollars. Do you have ten thousand?"

Alex was a few thousand short, but he couldn't let the leader know that. He had to have that gun now. "I've got it in the car."

The leader raised his hand in the air to the rest of the gang.

"Just you and me," Alex said. "Take it or leave it."

"Hey, you don't have a choice. I can have the cops on you in a second."

"Come on," Alex said. "You have stolen property, and you won't get any of the ten thousand if you turn me in."

The leader thought for a second and lifted his hand, waving the rest of the gang back.

Alex led the way with the gang leader close behind. He caught movement on the level above. The rest of the gang would follow, but hopefully they would keep their distance.

They left the airport lounge and crossed to the parking lot. There was no one close except for a man walking parallel to them, pulling a small suitcase on wheels. Alex's eyes drifted over the man and jerked back. The bag still had the baggage claim tickets, and the man was holding something down by his side. The gang leader was covering all of his options. They would never let him get out of this alive. They were there to take everything he had, including his life.

The car was to their left. Alex quickened his steps and turned sharply toward the car. The man with the suitcase was a step behind. Alex hoped it would be enough.

He reached the car and watched the man with the suitcase as he unlocked the door. The man had left the bag and was rounding the car on the next row up. He had a short, stubby gun at his side. It was an Uzzie. The gang leader was toward the front of the car, his hand was sliding to his pocket. He had a gun, too. Alex opened the door suddenly, slamming it into the gang leader, at the same time grabbing the tranquilizer case from the leader's hands and throwing it into the car. The gang leader had his gun out and was bringing it to bear. The other man was a car-length away. Alex caught the gun hand and swung the youth around toward the man with the Uzzie. The gang leader's gun fired and the bullet struck the car beside the other man. He stopped in surprise. Alex brought his knee up hard into the groin of the gang leader and twisted the gun from his hand at the same time. The other man was bringing the Uzzie up.

Alex fired almost without aiming, but luck was with him. The bullet hit the man in the shoulder, turning him around. Alex dove into the car, started it, and was backing out when a stream of bullets hit the side of the car. The gang leader was still on his knees with a shocked looked on his face. Alex let off on the gas and changed into drive, slamming the gas pedal back down. The car shot forward as another stream of bullets busted the back glass out. Alex slowed the car a second later and looked into his rearview mirror. People were running away from the shooting. A lone policeman, with his gun out, came into view and then disappeared as Alex turned onto the exit lane. He couldn't see the other gang members.

Alex slowed for the pay gates. He held his breath as he followed the car in front until it was his time to pay. He kept watching his rearview mirror as the attendant took his ticket. It seemed like it took forever for her to slide the ticket into the machine and tell him how much he owed. Alex's hand was shaking so bad, he had to use two hands to put the money in the tray. The girl's eyes were wide with fright. *I must look like a wild man,* Alex thought, *and the car is a mess.* The gate was going up when Alex saw the flashing blue lights behind him. The police car pulled up three cars behind Alex. Two policemen got out and starting searching the cars as they walked forward. They stopped for a second at the third car back and then approached the car directly behind Alex. The gate was taking forever. Then it was high enough and Alex moved forward. One of the police must have seen his shattered back glass because he sprinted forward, but Alex was already accelerating away. He took a look back as he gunned the car out of the parking lot. The policemen had run back to their car and were trying to get around the traffic. They would never make it.

Alex pulled out onto the main street just as another police car skidded out from the other end of the parking lot. The first police car must have radioed them. He made a sharp turn toward the expressway. Alex increased his speed as he left the ramp and took the very next exit. They would be looking for him toward town. He would circle and come in from the other side. Alex breathed a sigh of relief. The police car took the bait.

Alex still had time to kill before dark. Forty minutes later, he saw the sign for a park and slowed as the exit came up. He pulled into a parking space under several shade trees and cut the engine. A family beside him was getting out of their car. They were all laughing as the kids jumped up and down, pulling at their parents to hurry. The wife leaned over and kissed her husband. Grief swept through Alex as the thought of Jan grew strong in him again. He leaned back against the seat and closed his eyes. It would be the only time he would have to rest. Everyone in the country would be hunting him after tonight.

Chapter 10

Alex arrived across from the house a little after nine. He pulled into a side road overlooking the house and backed under a thicket of trees. He cut his lights and leaned back against the seat. Jagger's house was ablaze with lights. He would have to wait a while.

* * *

Alex sat up in the seat and stretched. It was two o'clock in the morning. The lights went out on the top floor. Everything was quiet around the house. Alex reached into the back seat and pulled the case into the front with him. He smiled as he looked inside. He had a tranquilizer gun and eight darts along with an extra CO_2 cartridge, and all of it had only cost him five-hundred. The gang would be looking for him all over the city. He would have to be careful when he went back to the airport. Alex transferred the gun and darts to his pack. He stepped from the car and swung the backpack over his shoulders, leaving his hands free. Alex trotted softly down the hill and across the road to the fence surrounding the house.

Picking a spot with bushes on both sides and with a clearing on the other side, he dropped to his knees and began to bang the tranquilizer gun lightly against the fence. The noise wouldn't be heard by the guards but would attract the dogs. Ten minutes later, he was still banging the gun against the fence. He wondered if he should hit harder. The darker woods were on his right and an open field of grass to his left. The moonlight gave a yellow glow off the grass. A gentle breeze blew toward the house. The dogs might be able to pick up his scent, but the house was a good thousand feet away. Finally he heard something and stopped banging. A slight sound came from the bushes and then the sound of running paws. The dogs had his scent. They were on the hunt.

Alex stuck the tranquilizer gun through the fence and waited. He could hear their panting now. The dogs didn't bark. They were saving their wind for the kill. The first dog broke through the darkness of the trees and into the opening. The dog was a Doberman and huge. Alex fired as the animal reached the center of the clearing. The dog whimpered but didn't stop. He came straight for Alex. For a moment, Alex forgot about the fence. He stood and backed away. The dog's legs buckled as it plowed into the fence headfirst. Two more Dobermans came straight at him. One of them began to bark as it hurled itself at the fence. Alex shot at the lead dog but missed. His hand shook as he reloaded. He shot at the dog again, just as it hit the fence and hurried to load another dart. The second dog was down, but there was too much noise. The guards would be alerted. He jammed the gun through the fence to get a better aim at the third dog. The dog lunged forward just as Alex shot. The dart buried itself in the dog's neck, but not before its sharp teeth raked across his hand.

Suddenly, everything was quiet except for the panting of the dazed dogs. One of them tried to get up. It strained forward one and then two feet, and collapsed again. Alex searched the darkness for the fourth dog. He looked toward the house. Everything seemed quiet. No lights blazing, and no guards running toward the fence. He banged lightly against the fence again but no dog. Maybe it was behind the house or maybe the guard had taken one of the dogs in. He wiped his hand across his forehead and felt the sting of sweat. The dog had broken skin. Alex loaded the gun again and decided to take a chance. He threw the pack over the fence and began to climb, stopping at the top to search the moonlit grass, straining to hear, but there was nothing—no sound, no movement. Alex dropped softly to the ground beside one of the unconscious dogs. He reached down and patted the dog on the head.

"Sorry, fellow," he whispered softly.

A car suddenly rounded the curve behind him, its headlights outlining him against the trees. Alex dropped to the ground, cursing himself for not dragging the dogs away from the fence. The car roared past without stopping and Alex thanked his lucky stars. He ran back and dragged the dogs into the shadows. He had less than two hours before they came to. Heaven help him if he was still inside the fence then.

Alex kept the tranquilizer gun pointed ahead, searching for the other dog as he ran. He had picked his path while it was still daylight. The oak tree ahead was his landmark. Its huge limbs overhung the sensors. He reached the oak and stopped for a moment to catch his breath, locating first one and then another sensor post in the darkness. Just to the inside of that was a circle of light from the house. Alex stepped away from the tree and studied the large limb above. He had picked the limb because it was almost halfway between two of the posts and out of sight of the guard behind the columns. If he was right, the security fields from the post would overlap each other. The sphere of coverage should be lowest at the center, depending on how much overlap there was, but he couldn't be sure. If he dropped into its field, he was a dead man.

Opening his backpack, he took out a rope. He closed the pack and walked toward the security field. He stopped well short and swinging the pack once, let it go at the top of its swing. The pack arched high in the air and made a loud thump as it hit the ground. Alex dove for the deeper shadow of the oak and held his breath, but there was no alarm—no sound broke the stillness. Throwing the rope over his shoulder, he began to climb. He reached the limb and wrapping his legs around it, began to inch out toward its end. The tree leaned toward the house, and the limb reached a good twenty feet past the sensors. The limb was easy to hold onto at first, but as he scooted along toward its end, it became smaller and smaller. Alex found it extremely difficult to keep upright. He stopped directly over the post, swaying from side to side. If he fell now, it would all be over. Alex lay down on the limb and slid further and further toward the house, until the limb began to bend downward. This would have to do. He would fall if he went any further. Sliding the rope from his shoulders, he tied it firmly to the tree limb and, holding his breath, let it drop to the ground. Alex tensed, waiting for the alarms to go off.

No sound broke the stillness. He was on the other side of the sensors—or maybe they weren't sensors. Maybe he was doing all of this for nothing. Wrapping his legs around the rope, he began to let himself down, hand-over-hand, trying not to swing from side to side. If he set the sensors off, all he could do was to try for the fence. Without the dogs he might have a chance, but there had to be one more dog.

Alex's hand tightened on the rope as a low growl sounded from below. He had found the fourth dog. They had put three dogs outside the sensors and one inside. There must be a sound barrier. The dogs would keep away from the sound, but humans couldn't hear it. Sweat began to drop from his nose as he felt his muscles weaken. He couldn't hold on much longer. Alex prayed that the dog wouldn't bark. He felt his hand began to slip on the rope. He wrapped the rope around his right leg and let himself slide down until it drew tight, clamping the rope against his leg with his other toe. Alex let out a long breath as he stopped. He could see the dark shape of his pack below and then he remembered. *Damn it!* The tranquilizer gun was in his pack. The only thing he had was Harris's gun. Holding on tight, he slid the gun from his belt and flipped the safety off. He would have to kill the dog with one shot. If he didn't, it would make enough noise to attract the guard.

Alex jerked his leg up as the dog jumped at him, touching his foot with its soft nose. Another inch, and the razor sharp teeth would have had his shoe. His hand shook as he leveled the gun at the dog. He tried to hold the gun study, but the rope was swinging. He couldn't get a clean shot. The dog ran forward to lunge again. Two glowing eyes and white teeth rose from the darkness. It was now or never. Alex timed the dog's jump and shot as the dog's razor sharp teeth reached for him. The gun made a soft spiting noise, and the dog fell back without a sound. He had shot it between the eyes. Dropping softly to the ground next to the still quivering dog, Alex lowered the gun and shot again. Alex loved dogs, and he hated killing this one, but there was no way out of it.

Alex turned and dove for the darkness of the bushes next to the house, laying there for a second, watching the giant columns by the front entrance. He knew there was a guard, or maybe he had gone back inside. He crawled over to his bag and dragged it back with him into the bushes. The second trip took care of the dog. Alex took out the tranquilizer gun and loaded a dart. Keeping his back against the wall, he approached the columns. A red glow suddenly lit the darkness. It was the guard. He was on the other side smoking. Alex took a step forward and then another. He could see the guard's dark shape now. He was leaning against the column with his back to Alex. Alex took another step and leveled the gun. It would be a long shot for this type of gun. If he missed, it would be all over. Taking a deep breath and letting part of it go, he squeezed the trigger. He could see the man's hand reach for the dart as it dug into his neck, then the red glow of the cigarette dropped to the ground. A second later, the heavy thump of the guard's body followed. The stuff in the darts worked fast. Alex ran to the guard. He pulled out the dart, removed the man's gun, and rolled him against the wall.

Alex stood there for a minute listening to the house. Everything was quiet. He sprinted across the lighted main entrance and into the shadows on the other side. Jagger's bedroom led out onto the balcony over the entrance. Alex climbed up on the rail. The balcony was still eighteen feet above. He jumped back to the ground and opened his pack. Taking out a coil of rope with a padded weight already tied to one end, he backed up ten feet or so. Swinging the weighted rope once and then twice, he let go. The weight fell over the balcony rail with a clink. Alex froze and waited, but no sound came from the house. He gave the rope a sharp jerk to get the end swinging and let the rope go when the weight cleared the balcony edge. The weight landed with a soft plunk beside him. Putting his feet on the column, Alex climbed slowly up the double rope to the balcony. His arm began to ache but he gritted his teeth and kept climbing. He reached the top and eased over the rail. Alex crouched for a second to get his breath and then crawled to the sliding glass door.

Alex pressed his face against the glass. A dark shape lay on a king size bed. By its size he knew that it couldn't be Lee Jagger. He flipped his pen light on to check his watch. It was 2:45. He had an hour to finish this, giving him fifteen minutes to reach the fence before the dogs and guard woke up. Where was Jagger? He moved the tiny beam of light across the room letting it slide up the bed until it outlined the form upon it. It was a young girl. Alex cut the light and in the pitch darkness, he could see light around a door which seemed to be a walk-in closet. What in the hell was Jagger doing in there? Alex had no choice. He didn't have the time to wait for Jagger to come back to bed and go to sleep.

Alex moved the light around the sliding door until he located the sensor. Keeping his eye on the closet door, he reached for the glass cutter and cut an eight-inch hole in line with the sensor. Latching a suction cup onto the glass and using the plastic flashlight and a piece of cloth to muffle the sound, he tapped the glass until it turned loose. There was hardly any noise. The bedroom remained quiet. Sweat dripped from Alex's nose in a steady stream. Reaching through the hole, he unlatched the door and slid it open an eighth of an inch. Any more and he would set off the alarm. It still wasn't enough to clear the outside metal trim.

Cussing under his breath, Alex pulled out a small D.C. drill from the pack. He put a drill bit in and hoped to God that the soft whirring sound wouldn't attract attention. He used the drill to eat through the outside trim until he could see the sensor button. Using a screwdriver to hold the button in, he slid the door open and reached into his pocket for the ball of quick drying putty cement. Alex pressed the ball around the button and waited. A minute later, he let go of the glue ball. It held. Alex let out a sigh of relief and slid the screwdriver back into his pocket.

Sliding through the open door, Alex closed it softly behind him. His feet made no sound on the thick carpet as he moved quickly to Jagger's side of the bed and slowly slid the night stand drawer open. He knew that Jagger would have a gun there, and he wasn't wrong. He stuck the gun in his belt and circling around the bed, stopped beside the slight form on the other side. The girl was beautiful and young, maybe eighteen or nineteen at the most.

Her blond hair spread across the soft blue pillow. Alex let the flashlight flicker over to the closet door. Now that he was inside, he could hear the soft murmur of voices coming from the room. There might be two or more people. He shifted his attention back to the girl. Alex had to take care of her first.

Taking a roll of two inch tape from his pocket, he tore two pieces from the roll, holding his breath at the soft tearing sound. He turned back to the closet door and waited. Nothing happened—all was quiet. Alex turned back and with one quick movement, pressed the first piece of tape over the girl's mouth, at the same time reaching under her body and pulling her slight weight to the floor. He turned her over and brought her arms behind her back, wrapping the second piece around her wrists in one fluid motion. Alex brought his head up to check again on the door. The voices had stopped. He quickly taped the girl's feet together. By this time she had gotten over her shock and was struggling. He turned her over and, holding her down firmly, leaned over to whisper in her ear. He could see the whites of her eyes in the darkness.

"Stop moving or I'll kill you, do you understand?" Alex could hear her breath coming quick and heavy through her nose. He flicked the flashlight to her face. Her eyes were wide with fright but she had stopped moving. Alex rolled her under the bed and moved to the closet door. Laying his ear against the door, he could still hear the voices but softer now, and further away as if they were in a long hallway.

Alex took his gun out and held his breath as he slowly turned the doorknob. He eased the door open. The walk-in closet was huge, but Jagger wasn't there. Stronger light showed through the rack of clothing at the back. The voices became louder as Alex slid slowly forward toward the light. As he got closer, he could see that the whole back wall of the closet was open and a smaller room was on the other side. Alex saw Jagger through the clothes. He was sitting with his back to the door, talking on a radio of some kind. The person on the other side of the conversation had a thick accent, and Alex drew in a sharp breath. The accent was Russian. Alex moved into the darker shadows of the closet to listen.

"Where is Mr. Hung?" the other voice asked.

"He's in China," Jagger answered. "Your plan is working beautifully. No one knows he's gone. All traces of the business appointments we set up for him will disappear. The housing and electronics for the bomb are inside two sculptures that are arriving tomorrow. The man receiving them has practiced Hung's signature for weeks. When this thing happens, there will be nothing left at the house, but if anything goes wrong, the paper trail will lead to Mr.

Hung and China. The plutonium and trigger will be arriving at your place tomorrow. Just make sure it gets there in time."

"Don't worry about me," the voice said. "My truck will arrive on time."

Alex froze when he heard plutonium and bomb. *My God! What are they going to do? Are they going to build an atomic bomb here in the United States?* The voices were still talking, but lower. Alex missed some of the conversation. He slid closer.

Alex stopped as Jagger's voice suddenly got louder. "Listen, Anton! I told you I had everything under control. You just make sure that you hold up your end."

"You didn't do so well in Canada," Anton came back.

"We'll get him," Jagger said. "Besides, I don't believe he found out anything from Harris."

Alex's mouth drew back into a snarl. They were talking about him, and Anton was the other man Harris had told him about. If he could just find out where he was . . .

"We'll meet at the house at ten o'clock," Jagger was saying.

"What house?" Alex whispered to himself, leaning forward. The hiss from the radio was gone. The conversation was over.

Alex slid forward and pushed the clothing slowly to one side. Jagger hadn't moved. He sat there with his back to Alex as if he were in deep thought.

Alex slid closer. He was two feet behind Jagger. He could hear him breathing.

Alex leaned forward to make his move when suddenly, Jagger turned with lighting speed. There was a gun in his hand. Alex reacted with pure instinct, bringing his gun down hard across Jagger's temple. Jagger grunted with pain, and his eyes rolled back in his head. Alex grabbed the gun from his limp fingers and pushed him toward the end of the small room. Jagger was holding his head to stem the flow of blood as he tried to turn and face his tormenter. Alex shoved him again, and Jagger fell to his knees, turning again to face Alex. His eyes opened wide with shock and surprise.

There was a large open safe behind Jagger. Alex motioned for Jagger to lay down and, putting one knee into his back, began to go through the safe. Stacks of money filled trays on both sides. Other trays pulled out from the back of the safe. Most of them were full of diamonds and other jewelry. Alex whistled softly. *There could be a million dollars here . . .* He hit pay dirt with the bottom tray. A small black book lay with other papers. Alex took the book and held it up to the light. Anton Cacique's name was on the first page.

He thumbed through the book. It was full of names, dates, meetings, and hand-drawn maps. Jagger tried to turn his head, but Alex pushed his face back down with the gun. He looked at his watch. It was time to go. He eased his weight from Jagger and stood. So far, neither of them had said anything. Feeling Alex's weight move off him, Jagger sat up on the floor. His eyes moved back and forth between the safe and Alex. Puzzlement began to register when he saw the money and diamonds still there. Recognition showed in his eyes.

Alex leaned over until his face was inches from Jagger's. "You know who I am, don't you, you bastard. Remember my wife and Robert? Now, you're going to answer a few questions for me." Jagger stared back at him in defiance. Without warning, Alex hit him hard, driving him into the safe door. Jagger began to babble something through a mouth full of blood. Alex jerked him upright and hit him again. Jagger came up slower, snorting blood through a broken nose. Alex kneeled beside him and waited. Jagger spit blood onto the tile floor and stared at Alex with a strange intensity.

"Where is the bomb and who else is involved?" Alex asked. That sick feeling was coming back, but the anger was stronger. Jagger saw the anger.

"You don't understand," Jagger answered, his eyes pleading.

Alex put the gun to Jagger's forehead. "Answer my question or I'll blow your damn brains out."

"You think that will matter a shit? Just the fact that you are here means my death and yours, too, sooner or later. You don't know what you've got yourself into." Jagger pointed to the ceiling. "There's a camera. It's been sending video to my people since I opened the door. The alarm has already gone out. They'll be here in thirty minutes." Jagger spit another mouth full of blood onto the floor and tried to stand. Alex pushed him back. "You damn fool," Jagger said. "Don't you understand? They'll kill everyone in this house to protect this operation, and then they'll run you down and kill you."

Alex looked at his watch. The dogs would be awake in minutes, and if Jagger was right, that wouldn't be the only thing he had to worry about.

Suddenly, a noise came from the bedroom. It sounded like a lamp being knocked over. The girl could be loose. Alex turned back just as Jagger lunged for the safe door. Alex saw the other gun almost too late. Jagger had guns all over the damn place. It was in a holster covered with money, just inside the door. Alex brought his gun up and fired just as Jagger turned. The bullet caught Jagger in the throat. The gun dangled on one finger as he fell to the floor. He tried to reach for it, but it had slid under the safe. Jagger coughed one time and then lay still.

Alex stepped forward and kicked the body over with his foot. Jagger was still alive. His eyes were flickering like a crazy person's back and forth. The bullet had missed the main artery but must have hit the spine. Jagger was gasping for breath. He was paralyzed. His brain wouldn't work his lungs. His eyes were already clouding over. Alex grabbed the book and left, closing the door to the radio room behind him.

The girl was still tied but had made it halfway to the door. Alex left her there and ran for the balcony. Time was running out. The dogs and guard could wake at any time and then, there were the others. He slid down the rope, leaving it where it was. Alex grabbed the backpack and threw it over his shoulders. The moon had disappeared behind the earth's curvature. The shadows between the trees had turned to pitch black. He leaned against the house trying to calm his jerking stomach and tears began to roll down his face. Was the killing ever going to get easier?

Alex ran to the oak tree and looked up at the rope. He didn't have time to go back that way now. He had to take a chance with the alarm. Alex took a deep breath and ran for his life, out of the light and into the total darkness of the woods. The alarm blasted the still air behind him. He could hear people shouting. Light beams cut through the darkness. He heard dogs barking. They had more dogs. Alex lowered his head and ran faster. He crashed into one tree and then another. He had to slow down.

He was seventy-five yards away from the fence when he heard the soft growl. One of the dogs he had left was awake. The street lights cast a glow into the blackness. He could see and ran even harder. He broke through the woods and into the brighter light of the street lamps. The fence was thirty yards away. Alex could hear movement behind him. It was the other guard dogs. He put his head down and tried to get more speed from his tired legs.

A dark shape came at him when he was less than five feet from the fence. Alex stopped and turned. The cries and shouts of the guards were getting closer by the second. His hand shook as he tried to aim the gun. He got off one shot before the shape reached him. He missed. Alex rolled with the weight of the dog, keeping the sharp fangs away from his throat. He tried to turn his gun arm, but the dog latched on, tearing through cloth into flesh. Lights suddenly flooded the area around him. They had yard lights all over the place. With one last effort, Alex dropped the gun into his other hand and shoved it against the dog's head. The gun jerked in his hand, and the dog slumped against him. Alex rolled for the fence and began to climb. He was out of reach when the second dog hit the fence. He dropped to the ground on the other side and ran for the car. Car lights were coming down the road south of the house. He threw the bag into the back and dove behind the steering wheel. The car started on the first try, and he stomped on the gas. Alex left the lights off and turned into the main road seconds before the other car got there. He watched it in his rearview mirror as it turned into the same road. Alex let out a long breath. He felt his arm, there was no blood, he had been lucky. He topped a hill and put the lights on, at the same time slowing down. It wouldn't do for him to attract a cop. Minutes later, Alex turned onto the expressway ramp and headed for the airport. He had one more phone call to make before he left Detroit. He reached into his pocket and slid his fingers over the notebook.

Chapter 11

Paul Dupre poured the coffee slowly. Setting the coffee pot back on the warmer, he flipped the donut box open. *Damn it, they had cleaned the donuts out again.* He walked slowly back to his office, stopping by the office next door. A donut lay next to a steaming cup of coffee. It was his partner's desk. A smile broke across Paul's face. He looked around to see if anyone was watching and snagged the donut. He took a bite as he opened the door to his office.

Dupre was tired this morning. He had come in at two o'clock to get a jump start on the pile of files on his desk. They never seemed to go down. He slid his six-foot-four frame down into the big chair and threw his size twelve shoes on top of the desk. Dupre finished the last of the donut and washed it down with a big swig of hot coffee. Stretching his long arms toward the ceiling, he lowered one huge hand to pick up the top file. He knew what it was before he opened it. He had worked the file every since they had found the bodies. Something was strange about the murders. The pilot and wife were found together at the cabin, making it seem like they had something going on, and the husband, after finding out about the affair that his wife was having with a man she had only met a few days ago, killed them both in a jealous rage. The cabin was a tiny place and unless the husband was out in the woods somewhere, there was no way in hell he wouldn't have known about the affair. The other thing was the plane. It had been reported that the pilot had delivered supplies to a hospital in Mayo, but that information was false. Why would someone give out information like that unless it was to lead the search to another area?

The first indications were that the pilot and the wife had been killed at different times, but they had to wait for the final autopsy. Both had been shot, but the wife had also been stabbed. Usually, when someone shot a person in a rage, they didn't stab them, too. That didn't make sense and neither did the fact that the pilot had water in his lungs. Dupre wondered which wound had killed the women. That was another thing. The bullet hole in the wife suggested some kind of a rifle, but there wasn't a rifle at the site.

Paul brushed the telltale donut crumbs from his beard just as he heard a shout from the other room. His dark eyes already had a look of "who me?" when his partner busted through the door. Joel and he had been working together for more than ten years. Joel was a no-nonsense kind of guy who went after everything with determination. He was all of five eight with a stocky built and huge muscular arms. His nose had been flattened too many times and his brown eyes seemed to be always moving. Right now he looked like a cat that had just found a rat. Joel looked quickly at Paul's desk and hands. His eyes shifted up to Paul's face, looking for any signs of laughter.

"Did you lose something?" Paul asked, trying to keep a smile from breaking across his face.

"I had a donut just a minute ago," Joel answered. He gave Paul another hard look.

"Don't look at me," Paul said, sliding the folder for the lake murders across the desk "What did Doc Raider say about the blood work up and the cause of death?"

"He said that they would have it back sometime this morning. Why? Don't you think the husband did it?"

Paul rubbed his beard with his fingertips. "If he did, he had to be a dumb bastard, and besides that, it just doesn't make sense. The bed covers should have been soaked with blood and the doc said it looked like they were shot at different times. The other thing is, why did the wife have a stab wound? The husband wouldn't do something like that after he'd already shot her."

Joel slid his frame onto the corner of Paul's desk. "There was a blood stain on the dock. We think it was the pilot's blood. Maybe the husband killed the pilot first, and he fell into the lake. The wife runs into the woods. After trying to find her, the husband goes back and carries the pilot up to the cabin. Later, he catches up to her, kills her, and for some reason, takes her back to the cabin, too."

Paul lifted his boot from the table and stood, stretching his powerful arms toward the ceiling. "Maybe you're right, but that's damn weak. For one thing, the country in that area is very mountainous. That means that he would've had to carry her over some rough country to get her back to the cabin. That would have been almost impossible and there's no sign of blood anywhere around the cabin."

The voice from the intercom startled him. "Paul, telephone." Dupre's face froze as he listened to the voice on the other end.

Chapter 12

Alex turned the car in at the rental agency and caught a cab to the airport. He went into the nearest bathroom and took one of the booths, locking the door behind him. Setting the bag on the commode, he took the gun apart and packed it into the shaving kit. He put the shaving kit into the center of the bag and zipped the bag closed. If he was lucky, it would work. He left the restroom and hurried to the ticket counter. Alex set the bag on the scales to be checked in and smiled at the pretty brunet as he handed her the ticket.

"Just the one bag?" she asked.

"That's all," Alex answered, wondering what he would do if she asked him to take the small bag with him. He relaxed when she placed the bag on the conveyer belt.

"That will be gate twelve," she said, smiling at him.

Alex headed for the gate, stopping on the way for a sandwich and a cup of coffee. He ate the sandwich slowly. It tasted so good. He looked at his watch. It was six o'clock. He still had enough time. He could see the telephones as he stepped out of the sandwich shop. Alex stopped beside the phones and looked around. He could see gate twelve ahead as he slid coins into the slot. He couldn't see anyone that looked suspicious. Alex dialed information and got the telephone number he needed. He had to make this short and sweet. He tried to bring everything into his a head as the phone rang.

"Hello," a male voice answered.

"Inspector Dupre please," Alex said.

"Just a minute," the voice said.

A minute later, a deep male voice sounded. "Yes, may I help you?" The voice had that crisp Canadian accent and something else, too, a slight irritation. Alex suddenly realized that the time was a lot earlier there. It was a wonder that the inspector was there at all.

"I'm sorry to bother you so early, Inspector Dupre, but I wonder if I might have a minute of your time."

"Go ahead," Dupre said. His voice sounded softer. Keeping an eye on his watch, Alex began to blurt out his story about what had happened at the cabin. He had gotten to the airplane crash and the meeting with the men on the dock when he noticed two men coming toward him. Alex stopped talking. The men were headed straight at him. One of them looked like a football player and was reaching into his pocket. Alex could see the glint of metal. The inspectors's voice was yelling at him over the phone. Alex slowly let the phone settle back into place. They were too close now. He had only one way to go. Alex could see the gun clearly. How had they found him so quickly?

Alex sprinted toward the end of the corridor. A bullet hit the column ahead of him. He reached instinctively for his gun but it wasn't there, it was in his luggage. Another bullet hit the floor between his feet. Alex couldn't hear the gunfire, they were using silencers. He looked back over his shoulder. They were falling back. The heavy man was having a hard time keeping up. The other man was thirty feet behind.

Someone ran at him from the side. It was a policeman and he was shouting.

"Hey you! Stop! You can't run in here!" The policeman was blocking his way. Alex tried to stop but couldn't. The policeman caught him and spun him around. He was young, in his twenties. Alex tried to shout a warning to him. The next bullet was worth a hundred words. It whined off the corridor floor, not six inches from the officer's foot. Surprise and shock registered briefly on the young officer's face as he went for his gun. He had the gun out and was bringing it up when the next bullet struck him in the chest. His eyes glazed over and his hand grabbed for Alex's jacket. Alex took the gun from the limp officer's hand and dropped to one knee. He eased the sights onto the lead man as another bullet tore at his jacket. Alex squeezed the trigger softy and the lead man dropped in his tracks. The heavyset man slid to a stop. Three more men were coming up behind the heavyset man. *Damn it!* The airport was full of them. Alex turned to the young officer. His eyes were open. He was still alive. Another bullet slammed into the concrete floor, making a white streak. Alex shouted at a man with a cellular phone to get help, but the man ran for the bathroom.

Alex grabbed the young officer and dragged him into a nearby book and gift shop. He saw shoes sticking out from behind the counter and continued on around the end. A young woman was at the end of the shoes and looked at him with fear-glazed eyes. Alex took her shoulder and pulled her toward the officer. He tore the officer's shirt open. The wound was high and toward the shoulder. The officer would live. Alex grabbed a tee-shirt from the shelf behind the counter and placed it firmly against the wound. He took the girl's hands and placed it on the tee-shirt.

"Hold it tight until someone comes," Alex said. He looked over the top of the counter. The shooters had put their guns away and were mingling with the crowd. Two of them were moving forward in the confusion. He had to get out of here. The officer was pulling at him. Alex leaned down. "Thanks," the policeman whispered. Alex patted the officer on the shoulder and came to his feet running.

Gate twelve was behind him, but he couldn't catch a plane now. They were too close. Alex turned into the next gate and, ignoring the shouting attendant, ran down the covered ramp to the plane's opened door. There was room for him to squeeze through and drop onto the concrete below. He heard shouting behind him as he dropped. It was a good twenty feet to the concrete, and the fall jarred his teeth. A bullet whined off the concrete beside him. The people after him wouldn't give up. Alex ran under the plane.

A trailer, filled with luggage, was headed away from the plane toward the main terminal. Alex sprinted for the end car and pulled himself onboard, moving quickly to the center. The driver hadn't noticed him. Two men came running around the plane just as Alex pulled the tarp closed.

He left the trailer inside the baggage area and ran for the stairs just ahead of six security people rushing into the area. He slowed to a walk when he entered the terminal. Everything seemed to be normal as Alex came out through the main entrance and slid into the front taxi. The only thing he could think of was a train station.

"Take me to the nearest Amtrak station," he said.

"That would be on Baltimore Street," the taxi driver said and swung the cab into traffic.

Alex knew that they would probably be there, too, but he had to try something. The cab driver was whistling a tune as he swung in and out of the busy Detroit traffic. Alex's heart was pounding in his chest. Slowly, he calmed down. He wondered how they had found him so quickly. It seemed impossible. Maybe they had just covered every way out of Detroit and got lucky. Somehow, they had known his face. He remembered the camera in Jagger's office. This was going to make everything impossible, but he couldn't stop. Alex knew that his hate was driving him, but now there was this other thing. What in the hell were these people trying to do? A bomb? Russians and people from here in the United States who'd kill anyone that got in their way? Something big was going on and he was right in the middle of it. The cab was slowing. The train station loomed in front of them.

Alex got out and looked around as he paid the taxi driver. The cab had already pulled away when he noticed the three men. They were running straight at him. Two more were coming from across the street. They were trying to box him in. Alex walked quickly up the street and began to run as the men closed in. Fear drove his legs faster. He would never get away. They were everywhere.

The men behind were gaining. They were less than a hundred feet away. He looked back and saw that two of them had disappeared. They were trying to get ahead of him. The man nearest him was reaching inside his coat. Alex put his head down and sprinted away. His breathing came in short, agonizing gasps. People were shouting at him as he pushed them aside to clear a path.

Alex ran one block and then two. The men were falling back. A building loomed ahead. He could see a ramp leading down and then he saw the sign—a parking garage. He ran past the mechanical arms blocking the entrance and began to climb the curving ramp. He had lost sight of the men behind him. Alex slowed and leaned forward as he walked, trying to catch his breath. He saw a door ahead and an elevator sign. He took one last look back as he reached the doors. There was no sign of the men behind him.

Alex stepped back, stunned as the door suddenly swung open, and two men came at him. Panic swept through Alex as they grabbed him and slammed him into the wall. He tried to reach the policeman's gun but both arms were held firm. One of them had a radio and was talking into it. A gun felt hard against his stomach. He had to escape. There was nothing but death here. Alex relaxed in their grip and gathered himself. He could see the other men coming up the ramp. It was now or never.

Alex lunged up and out, jerking loose from the grip of one man and turned, pushing the second man against the wall, grabbing his gun at the same time. He dodged a blow from the first man and slammed the butt of the gun into his face. The man screamed, but Alex had already turned his attention back to the second man. The man tried to hit him, but Alex dodged the blow and hit the man hard in the stomach. The other men were running now. They were almost there. Alex turned and grabbed the door handle, but the second man grabbed his arm and hit him hard in the back of the head. Alex's knees suddenly caved in, and then other hands were on him, holding him, pounding his face and body. Alex struggled to hold on to consciousness and tried feebly to fight back. He struggled back to his feet against the weight of the bodies, but another blow drove him to his knees again.

Suddenly, a shout came from the parking area. "This is the police! Put your hands where I can see them and step away!"

It was a woman's voice. The police. At least he wouldn't die. Alex strained to see through the haze that clouded his vision. He saw one lone figure standing in the center of the ramp, but there was something else. A shadow was behind her. The men beside him were quiet, as if they were waiting. The shadow came closer. Alex tried to shout, to warn her, but his voice wouldn't work. He lunged forward, but one of the men hit him again, driving him onto the concrete. Alex heard a loud sound like a gunshot and felt himself falling. Black spots danced before his eyes. A man's voice sounded from far away. "Wait, not here, take them outside of town." Alex felt hands on him and then the pain faded into blackness.

Chapter 13

Inspector Dupre slid the phone back onto its cradle. Joel stood with his hands out, a questioning look on his face.

"Who was it?" he asked.

"It was the husband," Paul answered. "He was telling me what happened with the pilot and his wife, and then he hung up."

"No shit, it was the husband? How much did he tell you?"

"Not enough, he was just getting to the good part when he stopped talking. I could have sworn I heard a gunshot."

"Someone was shooting at him?"

"I don't know, but something stopped our conversation. He told me about the airplane crash, and then he said there were more people at the dock."

"More people? We didn't see evidence of more people," Joel said.

Paul sat down behind the desk again. "Something isn't right about this case. First the delayed killings and then the possibility of more men at the dock . . ." Paul reached for the telephone.

"I'm calling agent Kurt Heller at the CIA. He called me when the case went public, said that they were working on a case close to the same area. He was very interested in the husband. Maybe he knows something we don't."

It had been over two years since Paul had seen Heller. They had worked together on a kidnaping case. At that time, Heller was F.B.I. He had gone up in the world.

Heller wasn't in, he was in the field. They gave Dupre his car phone, but a message said he would call back at ten o'clock. Paul walked over to his window. The sun was just now coming up over the Rockies. It was a breathtaking view. He loved this country, and he loved his work, especially cases like this one. There was a lot more to it than he had first thought. The voice of the husband sounded tense but honest. Paul wondered where he was. He had heard airplanes in the background. He was probably on his way to another city. He wouldn't take the chance of them tracing the call and being there when they arrived. Paul turned as Joel came around the end of the desk.

"Thinking about the case?" Joel asked.

"You read my mind, buddy," Paul answered, as he turned and headed for the door. "I'm going to be at the lake. It will take a while to get a plane, but I should be back before lunch. Call and let me know about the blood test, and give Heller my phone number when he calls back." Damn if he was going to sit around the office and wait. Maybe there was something he'd missed at the murder site.

* * *

Four hours later, Paul Dupre was in an airplane, circling the lake above the cabin. The pilot made one final turn and straightened out for the short approach to the lake. The plane landed softly on the mirror smooth surface and taxied slowly to the dock. Paul climbed out and helped tie the plane off. He left the pilot at the dock and began walking slowly toward the cabin, searching both sides of the dock and then the path as he climbed.

Paul Dupre got to the cabin and slowly circled it twice. He was looking for any sign of blood but he could find none. There was no need to go back inside the cabin. They had went over the inside at least ten times. He headed back toward the lake, searching both sides of the trail. The sun was on his back and suddenly, something glittered on the right side of the trail next to the water. He leaned over and picked up a bullet casing. It hadn't been there long. It still looked new. Paul recognized the casing. It had come from a seven-millimeter luger. The pilot had been shot with a forty-five and the wife with some kind of a rifle and now a luger. This would seem to back up the husband's story of more people being here. Paul lifted his head at a sound from the dock. The pilot was shouting at him. He looked at his watch, realizing that it was almost ten o'clock. It was probably Heller. He was through here anyway. Dupre hurried to the plane, jumped onto the pontoon, and pulled himself into the cabin. The pilot handed him the mike.

"How in the hell have you been?" the familiar voice said on the other end. "I understand you want to talk to me about your murder case."

"That's right," Paul answered. It was hard to hear because of the static. They were between mountains. It was a wonder that the signal got out.

"I've got some news for you, but it's too much to give on the radio. We need to meet. Also, I got your people to assign you to me on this case, I could use your help. Is that all right?"

Was it all right, Dupre thought, as he tried to keep the excitement out of his voice. It would be good to see new sights. "Hell yes. I'd like that very much. Where do we meet?"

"Our man's just left Detroit, but not before he took out one of the top crime bosses there; someone who we've had under surveillance for over two years. The people over me are really pissed, but our people aren't the only ones who are mad. We think he's headed for Atlanta and someone else is after him. They shot up the whole damn Detroit airport. One more thing, Dupre, put a lid on the case and bring the file with you. I don't want anything else to leak out."

Paul was silent as he digested the information. "So where do we meet?"

"Meet me at the local F.B.I. office in Atlanta, Georgia. Your ticket will be waiting for you when you get to the airport."

Paul motioned for the pilot to start the engine and leaned back against the seat. *Damn! Talk about a turn around.* The pilot reached the end of the lake and Dupre was pressed back against the seat, as the small plane jumped from the restraints of the water and climbed for the blue sky.

Paul fingered the bullet casing in his pocket. *Who did it belong to and what were the other people doing here?* Suddenly, he knew what the husband was doing. He was on a revenge trip. Paul wished that he hadn't hung up. The rest of his story could have tied everything together. The thing was, the husband's life wasn't worth a plug nickel. The bad guys would be after him now with a vengeance. The husband would be lucky to get out of Detroit. His only hope was for him or another law officer to find him first.

Chapter 14

Alex could hear sounds in the distance. It was a voice and it wouldn't leave him alone. He tried to open his eyes against the pain but felt himself falling into the darkness again. Then someone began to pull at his arm.

"Mister, mister, wake up," the voice whispered.

Alex opened one eye, because the other one seemed to be swollen shut. All he could see was a gray mist. He opened and shut his good eye and a face swam before him. Slowly it came into focus, and at the same time he felt the roll and pitch of a vehicle. He could see white walls behind the face and by tilting his head a little, he could see a wire cage between him and the front of some kind of a van. There were two dark shapes in the front. His vision was getting better. Alex turned his head back as far as he could to the face behind him. The blurred features came into focus. It was a young woman in a police uniform. She was laying down facing him. He realized that she must have been the voice from the garage, but he had heard a shot.

"Are you all right?" he croaked, trying to get his voice going again, and then he realized that his hands were tied to the wire cage, and he could see that hers were, too.

"Sh, don't talk so loud," the face whispered. "I'm all right, but I think I killed one of them." Her voice broke. "I really didn't mean to, but he was aiming a gun at me. It's the first time I ever shot anyone."

Alex strained against the ropes to turn further toward her. She was really young, not much over twenty. He could see the fear in her eyes and the tears. Alex pulled on the ropes to test them and his heart leaped when he found that his fingers could reach the knot. He whispered to the girl as he worked on the ropes. "It's fine, honey, you didn't do anything wrong. These men are killers." The knot seemed to loosen. "Did you hear them say anything about where they are taking us?"

"No, they haven't said anything since I woke up. I must have been out for a while. They hit me over the head with something, and my gun is gone."

"We have to get out of here," Alex whispered. "I think they are taking us somewhere to..." Alex stopped at the wide-open look in the girl's hazel eyes. He couldn't think of anyway to break this to her easily. "Don't worry, we're going to get out of this. Are you with me?"

The girl shook her head yes. "They're going to kill us, aren't they?" she whispered.

Alex felt a hand turn loose and sat up on one elbow. He could see through his other eye now. He looked toward the front of the van as he worked on the other knot. The men in front had their faces turned forward. The van noise was covering the sounds of their voices. "Not if we can get out of here," he answered. "Don't think about what they can do to us. Just think about getting out of this van and away from them. Okay?"

The girl's lips firmed. "Okay."

Alex's other hand came free. He rubbed his wrists and began to work on the girl's knots. Hope flashed across her face.

The van slowed down and Alex could hear the voices now. "This looks like a good place," one of the voices said.

Alex could feel the girl tense beside his. "Come on," Alex whispered as the last knot fell away. He pointed toward the back of the van and started crawling backwards, keeping his eyes on the men in front.

The door wasn't locked but before he could turn the handle, Alex was thrown to the side wall. The van must have turned onto another road, and then it speeded up again. Alex took the girl's arm and gave her a hard look. They had to jump now before the van was up to full speed. She understood and leaned forward. Alex opened the door and rolled out in one motion, pulling the girl with him. He felt his feet hit first, and then he was rolling. He lost his grip on the girl. He could feel soft dirt as he left the road and slid down a steep bank.

Alex's breath was knocked out as he hit the bottom—hard. He came to his feet and leaned over, trying to catch his breath. He searched the ditch to both sides, but there was no sign of the girl. Alex ran up the bank and looked for the van. It was about two hundred feet down the road and coming to a stop. They would be back in seconds. The girl had to be on the other side of the road. Alex could hear the tires squealing as the truck swung around.

He ran across the road, searching frantically for any sign of her. He finally saw a bundle of rags, a good twenty feet down the road. It had to be the girl. The fall must have knocked her out. Alex ran toward the bundle and as he got closer, saw that it was the girl. He didn't stop but swooped her light body up in one grab. He would never make it to the other side of the road and the safety of the trees. The van had completed its turn and was already headed back. There wasn't enough time to find a hiding place, and it was all open on this side. The only thing hiding them now was a four-foot high bank. The people in the van would be able to see them in seconds. The girl was moving in his arms, and then he saw the drainage pipe. It ran away from the road and toward a huge factory in the distance. It was their only way out.

Alex dove into the pipe, dragging the girl with him. The pipe was about four feet in diameter and too small to do anything but crawl. The bottom of the pipe had about six inches of thick, brown, foul-smelling liquid. The darkness closed in around them. Alex and the girl were soon covered with the sticky liquid as he dragged her along with him. He stopped when she began to struggle, realizing that she was awake. Alex was trying to set her up when she began to scream. Alex reached for her face, remembering just in time about the sticky stuff on his hands. Using his forearm, he pressed against her mouth.

"Sh, sh, we're safe, we got away." She began to relax, and Alex took his arm away. He couldn't see her face, but he could hear her taking in deep breaths of air, and then her breathing sounded softer, easier.

"Where are we?" she whispered.

"I dragged you into a drainage pipe of some sort." Alex answered. "I don't know where it goes, but I do know we can't go back."

"But . . . " Gunshots stopped her in mid-sentence. Bullets began to whine past them.

"Come on!" Alex shouted. He started forward as fast as he could crawl, pushing the girl in front of him. The gunfire stopped, and he heard voices. They were coming into the pipe.

It became a never-ending journey into the blackness. It was like crawling on a soapy floor. Two slips forward and one backwards. Alex felt the girl beginning to tire and their pace slowed. His nose began to burn. What kind of chemicals were in here? He could hear cussing behind them, and the voices seemed closer. Suddenly, Alex's searching hand fell into emptiness. He moved his hand in a circle, feeling one opening and then another. A pipe crossed the one they were in. They could go either way. Alex pulled at the girl to stop. Which pipe to take? He tried to remember the terrain on the top side, but the pipe could have run in any direction.

Alex could tell that the girl had gone about as far as she could without resting. "Stay here," he ordered and, taking a right turn, began to crawl. Fifty feet in, the pipe became less slippery and the thick sludge became water. The air ahead smelled cleaner. Alex decided to take a chance. He hurried back for the girl. He hoped that she had gotten enough rest.

They crawled for what seemed like hours in the new pipe. Alex's pants had torn through on the rough joints, and he could imagine the bacteria eating their way into the scrapes. The girl was trying valiantly to push ahead, but she was getting weaker by the minute. Alex thanked the gods for the cleaner water. It seemed to be removing some of the slime from his hands and knees. The girl never complained, but she kept stopping to rest. They didn't talk. They were using all of their energy to stay ahead of the voices. It was still pitch black and the strain of reaching out, pushing at the girl, and trying to determine how close the voices were, was beginning to tell. Alex was almost ready to stop and take his chances with the men after them. Maybe he would only have to fight one of them at a time. Anything was better than this dark hell. Suddenly, a dim gray light showed ahead. At first, Alex thought it was his imagination, but the gray changed from a dark to a light gray as they pushed eagerly toward it.

The gray turned to light, and the light got brighter. The water was deeper and cleaner. Alex could hear a sound like a small waterfall. He reached out to pull the girl back, when suddenly she fell away from him. He tried to hold on, but then he was falling too. They were on a water slide plunging straight down. Alex felt himself leaving the slide, and for an instant, he was in space. The next instant, he was under water. He felt thrashing arms next to him as he fought for the surface. His head broke through the water into air and light—blessed light. He could see the girl's head three feet away. She was treading water. The light came from above. Alex could see a grate, thirty feet or so above them and steep walls all around. Steel rings led upward toward the grate. Alex swam to the rings and pushing the girl ahead, started to climb. When they reached the top, Alex pulled himself around the girl. Holding tight to the rings, he pushed upward with all his might. The grate was heavy. No matter how hard he tried, he could only raise it an inch. They were trapped. He could hear the voices again—or was it his imagination? No! It was the voices, and they were getting closer.

Suddenly, Alex felt the girl's body against his. He could hear her grunting as she strained against the grate. Together they heaved with all their might. The grate lifted higher, but the voices were closer. Alex knew that they could be dead in a matter of seconds. Then he felt his shoulder slide into the opening, and he was able to use his back. The grate lifted higher and then still higher, until it fell away with a loud clang.

The voices stopped, and Alex heard a yell and splashing as the men hit the pool. He pushed at the girl and she disappeared. A second later, he joined her. He almost yelled when he felt the warm sunlight and fresh air on his face. Without saying a word, they lifted the grate together and let it fall back over the hole. Gunfire sounded and bullets struck the hard steel. There was a piece of steel beam nearby and they drug it to the grate and let it fall on top. There was no way the men could lift the grate now. They would have to crawl all the way back to the other end.

Alex and the girl fell to the ground, too weak to move. The girl looked awful. Black, sticky material covered her clothing, hands, and face. He knew that he didn't look any better. Her bottom lip began to quiver. All of the tension and fear melted away and her shoulders started to shake. She held her head down and sobbed quietly. Alex wanted to comfort her in some way, but, at the same time, he didn't want to make it worse. He left her alone for a few seconds and then he took her arm and pulled her to her feet.

"We have to get out of here," he said. "They'll be out of the tunnel and after us again before we realize it." Alex could see a paved road leading away from the factory. They started to walk in that direction when suddenly, Alex stopped. The girl turned and stood with her hands on her hips, waiting.

"Come on!" he shouted, starting to run in the other direction. "We can beat them back to the van."

The girl ran easily beside him. "What if they took the keys with them?" she asked.

"We'll try to hot-wire it and if we can't do that, we'll disable it so they'll have to walk out, too."

The van was sitting in the middle of the road. Alex could see the road curving back toward a manufacturing company in the distance. It was probably used as a service road. There was no traffic. He noticed a small, oily looking pond to their right. *My God!* That might have been their grave. He shivered when he thought of how close they had come to death.

Alex opened the van door and shouted. The men had been in such a hurry to catch them, they had left the keys in the ignition.

They climbed into the van, and Alex gave a sigh of relief as the motor purred to life. The windows were up. Alex rolled them down. After being in the closed pipe for half of a day, he didn't want to be closed up in anything. He turned to the girl and held out a greasy hand. "My name is Alex."

She smiled and took his hand, holding it for a moment. "My name is Meg, Meg Harper. You saved my life, how will I ever thank you?"

This was the first time that Alex had gotten a good look at Meg. It was still hard to see the real girl under the slime. Her slightly full face was framed with light brown hair and had a western look to it. Her full lips and big eyes made her seem more like a high school student than a police officer.

Alex pulled his hand back. "You saved mine first, back in the parking garage." He left the manufacturing area and turned onto the main highway headed south.

Meg leaned toward him. "Alex, I need to call in at the first phone."

Alex didn't say anything. He hadn't thought about what he would do when they got away. He had forgotten that she was an officer of the law.

Meg had leaned back and pushed herself against the door. "Are you in trouble with the law?" she asked softly.

Alex gathered himself. How would he explain? After all they had been through together, he felt he owed her the truth, but what would she do? There was an old building on the right side. He could pull off behind the building and not be seen from the road. He slowed the van and made a circle until he finally came to a stop. They were completely hidden from the highway. Alex turned the engine off. They sat there for a full minute without saying anything. Meg was stiff against the door. Alex felt that she was ready to bolt at any time, and he couldn't blame her.

"I'm wanted by the law for killing my wife," he said softly, watching her carefully.

Meg didn't move. Her eyes were on his.

"I didn't do it," Alex said, just as softly. "The men who did, are the ones who tried to kill us." Meg sat quietly but with a question in her eyes.

Suddenly, Alex began to tell everything that had happened to him from the airplane crash to now. He hadn't realized how much of a burden it had been. It was like his soul was being restored as he poured out his story to Meg. She listened intently, asking questions only when he paused. Alex finished and sat there, staring straight ahead.

"You can turn yourself in. I can tell them how you saved my life. You can have help in catching these guys."

"You don't understand," he said grimly. "These people are tied in with the government somehow. They know everything I do. They seem to be one step ahead of me. I know that if I let the police take me in, I will be dead in twenty-four hours."

Meg was silent for a minute. "You didn't have to come back for me and carry me to safety. You could have got away clean. Not many people would have done what you did." She sat there for a second, and then she leaned toward him. She had made up her mind. "Leave me at the next phone," she said. "We're a long way out. It will take them time to get here and when they do, I'll tell them the men abducted me. I won't tell them about you. When I get back, I'll try everything in my power to help you."

Alex looked hard at her, but her eyes met his firmly. He believed her. He started the van and gunned the engine. Two miles down the road they found a gas station with a phone. Alex parked to the side of the gas station. They both ran to the bathrooms to scrape as much of the slime off as they could. Alex brought a handful of paper towels back to wipe the seats. He finished and slid back into the van. He waited for Meg to come out.

Meg gave him a high sign as she came out and headed for the phone. Alex started the van and slowly drove toward the highway. He stopped to wait on the traffic. For some reason he felt a loss. Meg had been the only human being that he had been in close contact with since Jan. It had felt good to be around another person, even though they were running for their lives. He looked back one last time as he pulled onto the highway, then slammed the breaks on and slid to a stop. A truck blew its horn and swung wide to avoid hitting the van. Meg was running after him, waving her arms. Alex leaned over and opened the passenger side door, and Meg was there, sliding into the front seat.

"Drive!" she yelled. Tears were streaming down her face.

Not knowing what had happened, Alex pressed the accelerator to the floor. In seconds, they were flying down the highway at seventy miles an hour. "What happened?" he asked.

Meg turned a tear-streaked face toward him. "They want me for murder. The man I killed in the parking garage was a CIA agent. They say that I killed him in cold blood—that I didn't give him a chance."

Alex was silent for a moment. They had set her up just like they had him, but why would the CIA be in with someone like Jagger and the Russians? If they were, he could see why they wanted to frame Meg. She was a witness. He slowed the car back to the speed limit. The last thing he wanted to do was attract the police. Meg had stopped crying and was staring out the window. She wiped her face with her dirty sleeve, leaving a streak across her cheek. Alex didn't say anything. She didn't seem in the mood to talk. The traffic was light, and Alex was making good time, but he kept looking for the men after them to show up. It seemed that every time he let his guard down they were right there. He saw a sign for Lambertville. It seemed to be about fifteen or twenty miles off the main highway. He wondered what size town it was.

It was getting late. He needed to get rid of the van, and they needed new clothing. All of his clothes and the gun were on their way to the airport in Atlanta. Maybe they would be safe there until tomorrow. Alex pulled off on the ramp for Lambertville and turned west. Thirty minutes later, he passed the city limit sign.

Alex stopped at the first shopping center and parked the van. Meg was still cuddled up against the door. Alex reached out and touched her shoulder. She drew away from him. "I know it's hard, Meg," Alex started. "We have to try to forget what they've done to us and find a way out of this."

Her face softened, and she turned toward him. "I'm sorry, Alex. I know what these animals did to your wife and what that must have been like. It's just that I'm feeling sorry for myself." She tried to smile, but it was a weak attempt. "What are we doing here?"

"We need to get some clothing, and after that we need to get rid of the van."

"Well, what are we waiting for?" Meg opened the door to the van.

People stopped to point at them as they walked through the department store. We must look like something out of the swamp thing movie, Alex thought as he split from Meg and headed toward the men's section. It took an hour to buy the clothes and another thirty minutes to find a motel with adjoining rooms. Alex had just finished scrubbing the slime off and changed into the new clothing when a knock sounded at the adjoining door. It was Meg.

He opened the door to a stranger. Meg was wearing blue jeans and a snug fitting top. The bulky police uniform hadn't done her justice. The picture of a younger looking Jan flashed across his mind, and the pain of her being gone cut through him.

"Well, are you ready to go?" she asked.

He was silent as he grabbed his bag and followed her to the van. He slid in under the wheel and cranked the engine. He started to pull the gear into drive but then hesitated. Meg was studying him from the open passenger side door.

"Is something wrong?" she asked.

"No, no," he said. "It's just that you look a little like my wife, and it brought back memories."

Meg slid in next to him and closed the door. She lay her hand on his shoulder. "We'll get out of this, and when we do, we'll make those bastards pay."

Alex backed the van out and stole a glance at Meg as he did. She had changed. Gone was the self-pity. Instead, she had the determined set to her chin of someone with a purpose. Alex grinned to himself as he pulled onto the highway. He wouldn't want to be in the bad guy's shoes when she ran into them again. He turned onto the main road, and they started looking for a car lot. The registration and tag receipt were in the van's glove box. Meg forged the receipt as Alex searched both sides of the road.

They found one on the other side of the town and after trying four cars, picked out a Honda Accord with low milage. Alex did the trading while Meg waited outside. To his surprise, Meg was sitting in the driver's side when he came out. He got in on the passenger side and adjusted the seat back. Meg gunned the car onto the highway and headed back toward the main expressway. Alex looked at her with a question in his eyes.

She grinned back at the look. "Well, I didn't think you would want to waste any time. By the way, where do we go next?"

Alex took out Jagger's book and patted it. "We're going to Atlanta."

Meg looked at the book. "What's in the book? Is that the one you got from this fellow named Jagger? Was that his name?"

"That was his name." Alex fell silent. He hadn't told Meg about the bomb, but what did he really know? He had no proof. He didn't even know where the bomb was.

"Hey! If you don't want to tell me," Meg started. Her eyes flashed with anger.

Alex looked at her for a long moment. Her eyes met his and then turned back to the road. "I'll tell you what I know," Alex said, finally giving in. He began telling her about some of the facts he had left out the first time; what he had heard at Jagger's house and about the names in the front part of the book. The last part of the book didn't make any sense. Alex hadn't been able to make heads or tails out of the jumble of words.

Meg stared straight ahead, her knuckles white on the steering wheel. "My God! What are they going to do, blow up half of the country? Do you know when they're going to do this?"

"I don't know, but it's got to be soon," Alex answered. "I don't even know where the bomb is, but I do know that I have to try to stop whatever is coming down." Alex reached over and laid his hand on Meg's shoulder. "Meg, you don't have to go any further with me. It's only going to get more dangerous. You can get out at the next town."

Meg took a deep breath. She was silent for a minute. "No! I'm going to stay with you. If what you say is true, I'll never be able to clear my name and besides that, you'll need my help. It's not only that, you and I are the only ones who may be able to save millions of lives. You're right, we can't get help from the authorities. Before we could get them to believe us, it would be too late."

Alex leaned back against the seat. He could force her out, but he didn't know how close the others were. For all he knew, they could be in the car behind them. Deep down inside, he was glad to have Meg with him, but at the same time she was the conscious he didn't have right now. Just her presence might keep him from having his revenge. Alex closed his eyes for a second. He liked Meg, and she was a trained law enforcement officer. She would make a good back up, but she was so young—young enough to be his daughter. Alex prayed that she would come out of this alive. His eyes jerked opened at Meg's voice.

"Get some sleep," Meg said. "I'll wake you when I get tired."

Alex's slowly drifted off to sleep. He thought briefly about what he would do when they got to Atlanta. He needed to call Dupre, but what good would he do in Canada? He thought about Jan, and suddenly her beautiful face was there with him.

* * *

Alex woke up in Cincinnati and took over driving. It was seven o'clock and slowly approaching dark. Meg climbed over into the back seat. Alex looked back at her as he took 75 south toward Tennessee. She was already asleep, curled up in the back seat like a little kid. Alex looked down at the fuel gauge. Meg must have filled up recently, because the tank was full. He didn't remember any of it. He must have really needed the sleep.

The hours passed slowly as Alex kept a steady speed, just over the speed limit. They were in the mountains of south Kentucky now, and the lights below began to wink on as darkness settled in. Alex began to think about the bomb. Could it be in Atlanta? If an atomic bomb went off there, it would kill everyone within a radius of fifty to a hundred miles out, depending on how big it was. He shuddered when he thought about the countless people it would kill. What monster would do something like that? The tires squealed as he rounded a curve. Alex looked down at his speedometer. He was doing eighty. He eased off the gas. He wouldn't be able to do anything if they had a wreck or were stopped by the law, but the feeling of doom kept driving him. They had to get there in time. They had to.

Chapter 15

Keith Barlow slammed the phone down. The damn fools. He could kill every one of them. They'd had Bradley in their hands and let him go. To top it all off, they had somehow involved a police officer. It had been bad enough at the airport and now this. This had to be a tight operation. It was the only way it could work. He jumped as the intercom buzzed.

"It's the director on line one," the secretary said.

Fear drove through Keith as he hesitated. How much did the director know? Keith decided to play stupid. "Hello, sir. How are you doing?"

"What in the hell is this about an agent getting killed at the airport by a security guard? This is sloppy business, Barlow. Does this have anything to do with the sting you're running with the Russians?"

Keith leaned back and let out a long breath. The director didn't know. "No, sir." Keith hesitated, going through what he would say. "It was a rogue agent, sir, but nothing to worry about. We're already taking care of it."

There was silence on the other end of the line. Keith took another deep breath.

"Keith, how long have you been with the department?" the director asked.

Keith felt anger drive through him. He could tell from the director's voice where this was going. He had known for some time that the director had someone slotted for his job—but who?

"I've got twenty-five years in," he answered slowly.

"It's just that the President has been after me for some time to put some young blood down there, and since you're getting close to retirement, I thought maybe I should put someone directly under you. Somebody that you could train to fill your job someday."

Keith's hand trembled on the phone. The son of a bitch was trying to get rid of him. "Do you have someone in mind?" Keith asked.

"Why yes I do. I've been thinking about David Carson. In fact, the President and I were talking about him just the other day. With your training and help, Carson could fill that slot nicely."

Keith felt like he was going to scream. Of all the agents he had, Carson was the one he disliked the most. Hell, he had five more years to retirement, but he knew that the director wasn't talking nearly that long. They would have Carson at his desk in less than a month. The anger drove through him like a white-hot poker. He drew in another deep breath, and then he thought about the other, and the anger began to drain away. A smile came to his thin lips and he leaned slowly back in the chair. What was he getting mad about?

"Are you all right?" the director asked.

"Yes, sir, I'm fine. I think your plan will be great for the department. It's about time I began to think about stepping down from this rat race."

The director's voice sounded relieved. "I'm glad, really glad that you are taking this so well. We don't have to talk about the particulars now. That can wait until next week. Keith, if it's at all possible, get that Russian thing taken care of right away. All of us want the leaders of the terrorists, and I think you are doing an outstanding job, but the President feels uncomfortable with them being in the United States."

"It's almost over now," Keith replied. "Another four or five days and you'll be able to announce the capture of the largest group of terrorists in the world."

A chuckle came from the other end of the phone. "Now that would be a feather in my hat, wouldn't it? I'll be looking forward to that. Well, I see you have everything under control. I'll talk to you later."

Keith lay the phone down. Yes, he had everything under control, but he didn't think that he would be talking to the director next week. In fact, he didn't think he would ever talk with him again.

Chapter 16

Alex leaned back in the car seat and yawned. Daylight was showing across the tops of the mountains to his east. The last sign stated that Chattanooga was sixty miles ahead. That would put Atlanta about three, maybe four hours away. He started looking around, anything to keep awake. A little less than an hour later, Alex spotted the city limit sign. He waited until he passed Chattanooga and reached over to shake Meg.

"Where are we?" she asked, leaning over the seat.

"We're coming into Georgia. I'm wondering if you want something to eat? I see a Waffle House ahead."

"I'm starving," Meg answered, as she crawled back into the front seat. She let down the visor and began to primp in the mirror.

Alex slowed the car and took the exit ramp. There was hardly any traffic as he stopped and then took a right. Meg was putting on lipstick as he came to a stop in front of the Waffle House. He hadn't seen her buy it in the department store, but she had a full makeup kit in her lap. She noticed him looking. "A girl has to have her makeup," she said, smiling.

The smell of coffee and frying food hit Alex as they walked into the Waffle House. A plump waitress came up to them as they sat down. They ordered their food and got a cup of coffee while they waited.

"Where are we going first?" Meg asked between sips of coffee.

"We have to go to the airport and pick up my luggage," Alex answered.

"Why?" Meg asked. "You have new clothes. What do you need at the airport?"

"I need the gun I have in my luggage. It's too hard to get a gun anywhere else, and we don't have the time." They looked up as the waitress set their food down.

* * *

The morning sun was up and the skies were a deep blue as they pulled out of the parking lot and headed for the expressway. Meg offered to drive, but Alex declined. He knew the area a lot better than she did. They could be waiting for them, but maybe they didn't think to check the airport in Detroit to see if he bought a ticket.

An hour later, Alex passed 285 and twenty minutes later, he was in downtown Atlanta. They had missed most of the early morning traffic. The airport was only minutes away. Alex looked at his watch as they pulled up to the curb in front of the airport baggage area. It was a little after twelve. "Get into the driver's seat and watch out for me," Alex said. "Keep the car running just in case."

Meg nodded her answer. "Be careful," she said to his back.

Alex left the car and hurried toward the baggage claim area. He slowed to a walk as he got closer and began to search the area carefully. If they were there, he couldn't see them, but then they could be anyone. Alex came into the baggage claim area from the other side and stood for a long second, carefully checking the terminal floor. Satisfied, he walked over to the counter.

"Can I help you?" the man behind the counter asked.

"Yes," Alex answered. I missed my flight in Detroit but my baggage didn't. He handed over the baggage claim tickets. The man began going through the baggage behind him. Alex nervously drummed his fingers on the counter. He started thinking about what would happen if they found the gun. He let out a long breath when the man sat the bag on the counter.

"Have a good day, sir," he said to Alex's back.

Alex trotted through the airport doors and seconds later, slid into the car. He motioned for Meg to go and directed her toward 85 North. From there they caught 400 North and headed for Alpharetta. There was a Marriott there, and it would probably have rooms this time of day.

* * *

An hour later, Meg pulled into a parking space in front of the Marriott. "Where are we?" she asked as she cut the engine.

"We're in the small town of Alpharetta and less than fifty miles from where the book says Mr. Anton is. Come on, grab your bag. We'll get rooms and start out fresh in the morning."

Alex was mindful of his wrinkled clothing as he and Meg walked across the lobby and up to the desk. The desk clerk gave them a slight scowl, turning to see if there was anyone else he could wait on first, but the lobby was empty. Alex dropped his bag to the floor and fixed the clerk with a hard glare.

"May I help you, sir?" the clerk finally asked, looking everywhere except at Alex.

"I want two adjoining rooms."

"I'm afraid the only thing I have is a suite and that's three-seventy-five a night." The clerk had already started to turn away, believing that would be the end of that. Alex took out Harris's credit card and slid it across to the clerk. The clerk turned quickly to check the credit card. He turned back a moment later and lowering his eyes, slid the registration card across.

Alex filled the card out and took the key from the extended hand. He picked up his bag, and they headed for the elevator.

"If there's anything I can do, sir, please let me know," the clerk said to their backs.

"I don't think there will be," Alex answered over his shoulder.

Alex noticed, when he looked down at his key, that the room was on the ninth floor. The elevator was empty except for one older lady and a small dog. Alex could hear a sigh of relief from behind as they reached their floor and stepped out of the elevator.

The suite had two rooms and a bath at each end. Meg ran for the room on the right and Alex headed for the other one. He threw the bag onto the bed and walked over to the window. He could see Highway 400 far below. The cars looked tiny from this height. Alex turned from the window and walked into the bathroom. It was huge. He walked back to the adjoining door and leaned out.

"I'm taking a shower. I'll be out in a minute."

Meg stuck her head out of the other door. "I'm doing the same thing," she answered. "See you."

Alex took off his clothing and looked at himself in the mirror. The wounds had almost healed except for the dog bite. One of the punctures was slightly swollen. He stepped into the shower and turned the water pressure to full and hot. He let the water sting his skin as he turned around and around.

Later, he walked over to the bag and retrieved the shaving kit. He took the gun parts out and hid them under the pillow. Alex walked back into the bathroom and filled the sink with hot water. He lathered his face with shaving cream and took out the razor. He scraped the thick whiskers off and then dried his face slowly. Alex walked back to the bedroom, pulled the last clean change of clothes out of the bag and began to dress. He had to get more clothes. They had seen him several times in casual pants and shirt. They would be looking for the same. He walked over to the bedside table and picked up the writing pad and pencil. Alex began to make a list of everything he needed. His hand shook slightly as his thoughts went back to his last killing. He felt the same sick feeling in the pit of his stomach. He lay the pencil and pad down and stared into space. His thoughts were on Jan now and their last night together. Everything seemed to come together at the same time—his losing Jan, the killings . . . Alex bent over as sobs racked through his body again. Later, he walked to the bathroom and wiped his face. He stood there for a long moment, staring at himself in the mirror and then turned and walked out into the adjoining area.

"I'll be in the restaurant downstairs," he said loudly to Meg's bathroom door. There was no answer. She was probably still in the shower. He left a note on her door and stepped into the hallway.

It was a little after six when he entered the lobby downstairs. He checked the menu on the board outside before he walked into the restaurant. After being shown to a corner table, he ordered a drink. Alex let his eyes drift over the other patrons with indifference. Not too long ago he would have looked at the other people with interest, looking for signs of characters he could use in his books, but now they were of no more interest to him than trees in a forest. Besides Jan, his only thought was his revenge, the people trying to kill him and the bomb.

Chapter 17

Anton Cacique leaned back against the pillows as he watched his young mistress walk naked toward the bathroom. *God! She is beautiful.* His thoughts drifted briefly back to his wife and a slight twinge of pain flickered across his face. At one time she had been that beautiful, no, even more so. Age had dragged her down as it had him. He stood and stretched his long arms into the air. He was a big man, slightly over six-foot-two. He put his powerful hands on his hips and looked at himself in the mirror. His huge body rippled with muscles. He pulled his once tight belly back into its original shape and then slowly let it out. He still looked good. His sandpaper hair flowed down his back. Not too long ago it had been jet black.

His thoughts went back to the news about Lee Jagger's death. He jutted his square jaw out and his thick lips drew back into a snarl. Lee Jagger had all of the contacts here in the United States. It would take months to establish the same networks. He would have to use people he had never used before, but he didn't have the time to do anything else. This Bradley had killed Jagger and stolen the book. Thank God, part of it was in code. Anton had people all over trying to track him down. He smiled to himself. Even the American government was helping him. He didn't know if it was the FBI or the CIA, but they had government written all over them. It was probably the FBI. The man had crossed state lines. That would put it right in their laps. He wondered if any of the organization's people had been at the Detroit airport, but discarded the thought. All of them were supposed to keep a low profile.

His people thought that the fool was coming after him. The outside of the house was ringed with security. There was no way Bradley could get close. The only other way was by helicopter, but the men on the roof had ground-to-air missiles. A slight fear gripped Anton for a second. He struck out against the fear, slamming his fist into the wall. The woman, coming out of the bathroom, ran for the door. She knew that it wasn't a good thing to be around Anton when he went into one of his rages. One of his men stuck his head inside the room to make sure that everything was all right and quickly jerked it back.

The four men outside of Anton's room tensed as they listened to him vent his rage. They moved away from the door.

* * *

Thirty minutes later, Anton walked through the door, fully clothed, as if nothing had happened. He pointed to one of the men. "Leave two men by the front door, and get everybody else in here."

The man ran to obey. Anton turned to the other three. They were his most trusted men and all of them were from the mother country. Anton knew that any one of them would gladly die for him. He walked over to his desk and took out a Cuban cigar, slowly rolling it in his fingers. He reached for the gold inlaid cutter and cut the tip. Anton flipped the cigar around and around with his fingers as he walked to the window. He stood there while he lit the cigar and blew a ring of smoke out against the glass. He watched it spread across the bulletproof surface. It was early morning. The lake glittered with the sun's dancing rays. Anton wished that he could get into his boat and spend the day in the sun, something he hadn't done much of lately.

"Alex Bradley." Anton mouthed the name softly. His dark eyes narrowed. Bradley had taken out every one of them, and he had started without a gun. After that he had slipped through Lee Jagger's defenses and, with ten men around the house, killed him. His fingers drew into a fist when he thought about Jagger's men missing him at the Detroit airport. Even then Bradley had taken out another man. Then he had disappeared. There was nothing, except for the news about a government man getting shot at the train station. Could that have been Bradley?

Anton had a full report on him. He was a damn bookworm, an author. How in the hell had he killed all of those men? The first five were picked by the Americans. They were trained for this. They were suppose to be the best that money could buy. He turned as the rest of his men filed into the room.

The room was huge. A conference table sat to one side. A long bar curved across the other corner. Anton motioned the men to the conference table. He sat down at the head of the table and waited as the twenty or so men were seated, then he slid his chair back and stood, blowing a ring of smoke out toward the silent group of men.

"Men," he started, "we have trouble." He went on to tell them about Lee Jagger's death and the trouble it would cause the organization. He stopped and sat back down. The men didn't say anything. They knew that more was coming. The rumors had been floating around since yesterday about the man from Canada.

"Now! About this fool running around killing everybody. Some of you know everything that I know but for the rest of you . . . Anton didn't complete the rest of the sentence. We believe that he's coming after me." Anton laughed. A nervous laughter sounded around the table. "The thing is that he will have to come through you." He waved his hand as one of the men started to speak. "I know that all of you want to hunt him down and make him eat his own balls, but that might not be a good thing. We don't have trouble with the law here and we don't want any. The job we have to do can't wait, and it's too important to let this bastard mess it up." Anton paused for a second.

"The truck leaves for Maryland tonight after our little get together. All of you will have short waves tuned to the same channel. The first car takes the lead with the truck next and the second car behind that. I don't want a convoy. Space yourself at least a half-mile apart. If the truck gets stopped by any law enforcement, I want both cars to take them out. You'll have enough firepower to take on a small city. The truck must be protected at any cost. Do you understand?"

The men nodded their answer and rose from their seats. They knew that this meeting was over, and they knew what to do.

Anton put out the cigar in an ashtray provided by one of the servants. He leaned back in his chair and watched his men as they filed out. His superior in the organization would not be please by the latest turn of events. He needed to find out who would take Lee Jagger's place and make sure they were on the same page. He also needed to contact the senator. It was time that he began to earn his keep.

Chapter 18

Alex woke up the next morning. For a minute, he didn't know where he was, and then the last few days came back to him. Anton Cacique and Inspector Dupre were on his list today.

Alex showered, dressed quickly, and walked over to Meg's room. He knocked softly on the door. "Meg, are you up?"

"Yes," she answered back. "I'll be right there."

Alex walked over to the window and watched the early morning traffic. He didn't hear Meg come up behind him.

"Ready?" she asked.

They made their way down to the lobby just as the restaurant opened for breakfast.

"Order eggs and pancakes for me," he said, stopping in front of the restaurant. "I have to make a quick phone call." He watched Meg walk into the restaurant and headed for the gift shop to buy a telephone card. The lobby was empty as he sat down at the telephone. The voice was female and sounded like the same one he had talked to before.

"Is Paul Dupre in?" Alex asked.

"No he isn't," the voice answered in a crisp Canadian accent.

"Do you know when he will be in?"

"I believe Paul will be gone for a few weeks," the voice answered. "He went to Atlanta, Georgia."

"Atlanta? Are you sure? Do you know what time he arrived?"

"Yes, I'm sure," the voice answered. "He's not there yet. I believe he'll arrive about ten o'clock p.m., Atlanta time. Would you like to speak to someone else?"

"No thanks," Alex answered. "But you can do me a favor. Does he have a cellular phone with him?" The voice on the other end hesitated. "I'm a friend, and I really need to get in touch."

"I guess it'll be all right," the voice said. She gave Alex the number.

Alex headed for the restaurant and saw Meg right away. The food was already there and he dove in with earnest. Meg was looking at him with a question in her eyes. When he finally slowed down, he told her about Dupre.

145

"Do you think he will help us?" Meg asked eagerly.

"I don't know," Alex answered, as he finished the last of the coffee and waved to the waiter for more. "He won't get into Atlanta before ten o'clock tonight, and we can't wait until then. I have another problem. There won't be a phone where we're going. My house is just north of here. I think that we need to stop there and get a cellular phone before we head for the lake." Alex downed the last of his coffee. "Are you finished?" Meg nodded her head.

They went back to the room and threw what little clothing they had into their bags. Alex wiped the parts and assembled the gun. He slid it into his pocket. Meg waited by the door while Alex stopped at the counter to check out. As they were walking across the parking lot, Alex noticed Meg watching him. He unlocked the car and turned to her. "What?"

"It's got to be hard on you to go back to your house, I mean with your wife dead. If you want, I'll go in when we get there." Alex started the car and headed for Highway 400.

He didn't say anything until he was on the expressway. Meg sat there waiting. "It's too dangerous," he finally said. "The cops, FBI, or the others could be there." Alex didn't want to go into his house, to all the memories of Jan, but he had no choice. It would take too long to get a cellular phone anywhere else. Meg didn't answer. She stretched her legs out and leaned back against the seat.

Driving up to Roswell brought back all kinds of memories, and they got stronger as Alex got closer to his house. Jan and he had lived here for the past five years and had often talked about getting a house on the lake. Alex swallowed hard, trying to force the lump in his throat back down.

He turned into his subdivision and slowed as he approached the final street. He knew that they would be there, waiting. He was hoping that they would only leave one man, and he would be able to slip around him. Meg leaned forward in her seat, helping him to search for anything out of place. Alex slowed even more when he saw his street and then his house, four houses up from the corner. He drew in a deep breath as he saw something else, a car parked on the curb and two heads through the back window. They were waiting on him, and there was more than one. He wondered if they had anyone in the house. Alex pointed to the car and the two men. Meg nodded her head. Alex let out his breath slowly. He had to try.

Alex circled the block. It was midmorning on a work day, and that meant almost everyone would be away. He turned onto the street behind his house and came to a stop at a clean looking brick house directly behind his yard.

He knew the people who lived there. Ann and Bill Ashley were not what Alex would call friends, but they'd had a few barbecues together.

Alex got out of the car and walked boldly to the back yard. The neighborhood was quiet. He looked back at the car. Meg had moved to the driver's side. She gave him a little wave.

Alex climbed the fence and ran to the back of his house. He paused at the back door and listened for a full minute, but the house seemed quiet. Alex slid his key into the lock and opened the door gently. He ran quietly to the front of the house and peeped out of the window. He could see one of the men on the side toward him. Alex jerked his head back as he caught a glint of reflected light. The man had a set of binoculars. He stepped back from the window and turned slowly, looking for anything out of place. Alex drew in a sharp breath as wave after wave of emotion swept through him. Memories piled one on another, and he slowly dropped to his knees. The fireplace where they had sat for hours, talking about everything or just sitting quietly, close together, watching the flames; the pictures sitting everywhere; his first novel, framed over the mantel. He had wanted to put it some place more private, but Jan had insisted on the mantel. Alex stood and shook his head, but the memories didn't go away.

Keeping away from the windows, Alex ran past the stairway and opened the door leading down to the basement. Everything was quiet. He took the steps down one at a time, straining through the darkness, afraid to turn the lights on. He felt around the wall and found his office. Closing the door softly behind him, he turned on the light. The office was untouched. Everything looked just like the day he and Jan had left. He jerked open the top drawer to his desk and retrieved two cellular phones. He dug through the other drawers until he finally found the car charger cord and then turned the light off. He softly closed the door behind him.

The house was still quiet as he crept back up the stairs. Alex began to breathe easier. He closed the stairway door and stopped dead still. A slight noise had sounded from upstairs. He held his breath, and then he heard it again. Someone or something was upstairs. He had to go by the stairs to get to the kitchen door. Alex eased toward the kitchen. He stopped as he heard the creak of one step and then another. They must have heard. They would see him pass the stairs. He wondered how many there were. Could he overpower them without attracting the ones outside?

Alex slipped to the side of the stairway and squatted. He could hear breathing now. There seemed to be only one. A man's head and then his shoulders came into Alex's field of view. Alex flattened himself against the side of the stairs as the man's head turned toward him, and held his breath as another step creaked. It was now or never. He leaped high, catching the man around his neck and bringing his full weight back down, dragging the man across the banister and down onto the floor. The man struggled violently, throwing his body from side to side, almost succeeding in wrenching himself free. Their struggle seemed loud enough to be heard from the street. Alex knew that he had to end it now. He tightened his hold with his left arm and managed to get his gun out. "Calm down or I'll shoot you," Alex said, bringing the gun tight against the man's head. The man relaxed and lay there breathing heavily.

"Who are you?" Alex asked, keeping an anxious eye toward the front.

"I'm an FBI agent, just look in my inside coat pocket and you'll find my badge. You must be Bradley," the man continued. "You might as well give yourself up. I've already alerted my people, and they have all the exits covered."

Alex searched the man's pocket, laying everything on the floor. The man really did have an FBI badge. Alex wondered if he had called someone, but he hadn't heard any voices earlier. Either way he would have to hurry. He stuck the badge and the man's gun in his pocket. "Get up slowly," Alex said, keeping his gun against the man's head. He pushed the man toward the kitchen and then pulled him to a stop by the telephone. There was still no sound from outside. If the man was telling the truth, they could be waiting for him to come out, and they would have someone covering the back yard. Alex pushed the gun harder into the man's neck as he felt him start to tense and then, without warning, drew the gun back and hit the man hard on the back of his head. The FBI agent collapsed on the floor. For a second, Alex felt pure panic. The whole countryside would be looking for him.

He drew in a deep breath to calm himself and then dragged the man's limp body into the kitchen and out of sight to anyone looking in the front window. He picked up the cellular phones and ran upstairs. There was a large oak tree next to the master bedroom window, with limbs overhanging his next door neighbor's yard. If only he could climb from the window to the tree without being seen, and drop into the next yard, maybe he could still get away.

Alex unlocked the window and raised it slowly. He lifted out the storm window and slid out onto the roof, stopping to listen for any sound. It was still quiet. Alex eased his way slowly to the edge. He looked down, stepping back as he saw the two men below. He would have been dead meat if he had gone out the kitchen door. Alex couldn't afford to wait for them to move. There could be twenty men on their way here by now. Alex looked toward the oak tree. It was a three-foot jump to the first limb, and he knew that the tree would shake when he landed. Alex needed a distraction, but the only thing he had heavy enough to throw was the agent's gun. Alex walked softly across the roof to the other side of the house. He took out the gun and, aiming for the neighbor's window, threw it as hard as he could. His aim was perfect. The gun crashed through the window, making a loud noise. He ran back to the other side and jumped for the tree limb when he saw the agents run toward the sound. He was dropping into the yard next door before the agents reached the other house.

Alex ran onto the street and slid to a stop in confusion. The car was gone. Meg was gone. He heard the squealing tires as the agent's car took off from the other side of the house. They must have found the agent. Alex squatted down behind a bush. His heart was pounding. Meg had deserted him. She was probably with the FBI right now, telling them where he was. Alex got up to run when suddenly his car slid to a stop across the street; Meg was waving. Alex sprinted for the car and slid into the seat just as the agent's car rounded the curve two blocks behind them. Meg slammed the gas pedal to the floor and headed toward the entrance.

"No, the other way!" Alex shouted. "This subdivision has a back entrance." Meg turned the wheel back, bouncing off the curb. The other car was closing on them. They lost sight of the car for a second, and Alex pointed to another side street and then another. The back gate loomed before them, and then they were on the main street, weaving in and out of traffic. Alex looked back. The other car came through the gate and slid sideways to keep from hitting a police car trying to come into the same subdivision. Alex turned back and Meg was already on the ramp for 400 North. He leaned back in relief. The other cars were out of sight. They couldn't see them take the ramp.

Alex kept looking for road blocks all the way to Cumming but nothing happened—no cars chasing them, no flashing blue lights. Alex directed Meg to stop at a restaurant on the other side of Cumming. They hid the car in the back and walked around the building to the front. Alex held the door open for Meg and pointed to a table near the back. She took a seat facing the door. Alex slid into the other side and pulled out the black book he had taken from Jagger. The restaurant was full with people for the lunch hour, and the noise of laughing and talking felt good to Alex. He opened the black book. Meg moved from her side and slid in next to him. There was no address under Anton's name. Alex began to read the page after page of meetings. The writing must have been Jagger's. It was small and neatly done. Several of the meetings were by a lake in Georgia, and Jagger had written down the address. It had to be Anton's place. He was familiar with the roads around the lake and knew that the address was east and going back toward Gainesville. He slid the book back into his pocket as the waitress came to their table.

"Was that the address?" Meg asked as the waitress left with their order. She moved back to the other side.

"I believe so," Alex answered. "It has to be it. We're only about an hour away. Our best chance is after dark, and we can't call Dupre until ten o'clock anyway."

The food was good and they ordered a cup of coffee and piece of pie to kill time. When they left the restaurant, it was two o'clock. It would be another eight hours before Dupre would be in Atlanta.

Alex took the driver's seat and headed north on 400 and then east toward Gainesville. Ten miles later, he turned toward the lake. When they were close, they began to look for the address. It was more difficult than they thought. Half of the driveways didn't have a mailbox or number.

After going through the area several times and checking out every unmarked road, they decided to try the one that looked the most traveled. Alex turned into the gravel driveway and passed the spot where they had turned around the first time. The sounds of traffic fell behind them as he drove deeper and deeper into the heavy forest. As they climbed over a small rise and rounded a sharp bend, Alex saw movement ahead and a metal gate. He came to a stop, and then he saw the two armed men. One of the men had un-slung a rifle and was walking toward the car. Alex could see the reflection of blue water and a house in the distance. The man was lifting the rifle. Alex put the car into reverse and pressed hard on the gas. The back tires threw gravel against the wheel well, making a rattling sound as the car slid backwards around the curve and over the hill. The men disappeared. Alex stopped the car, and they sat there watching the hilltop for any sign of the men. The dust had settled, and the only sound Alex could hear was the soft purring of the car engine. The men must have returned to the gate.

"Boy that was close," Meg said. "Do you think that was them?"

Alex started to turn the car around, when he noticed old tire tracks leading away from the main driveway. It looked like an old logging road. "It must be them," Alex finally answered. "Why else would there be armed guards? Plus, this is the only driveway nearby with a house." He turned the wheel and started up the logging road.

"Where are we going now?"

"We have to find a place to hide until dark and I have a feeling those men will be down this road soon to see if we've left." He stopped the car about three hundred feet from the driveway and got out.

"Stay here," he ordered and started walking back toward the driveway. Weeds and small bushes grew on the road, and the car wheels had mashed them down. He cut a bush and backed down the logging road, brushing the bent weeds back to a standing position. Satisfied that no one from the main driveway could tell that he had been this way, he got back into the car and followed the road through the thick forest. The old road started west and gradually curved more to the north. Alex saw a flash of blue water and stopped the car. He got out and motioned for Meg to come with him.

Alex walked through the woods slowly, searching for any movement. Meg stayed close behind. He could see the lake clearly now and then the house came into view. Alex came to a stop when he noticed movement and motioned for Meg to kneel down. The lake was clear and blue in the afternoon sun. A huge house nestled near the water. Two docks ran from the house and out into the lake. There was a helicopter pad to one side. Men were moving all around the house. There had to be at least ten and no telling how many inside. It had to be Anton's house.

"Is this his house?" Meg whispered.

Alex nodded his head and motioned Meg back. Together they walked back to the car. He got into the car and turned it around. Meg quickly jumped into the other side when he stopped.

"Well, now what?" she asked.

"We wait until dark." Alex leaned back against the seat and closed his eyes. He heard the click of the door handle. "Stay here. We can't take the chance of being seen." Alex could hear Meg settle back into the seat. He smiled and leaned the seat back further. He made a mental note to wake himself before dark.

Alex's eyes popped open a few minutes later at a new sound outside. A blue jay was on a tree limb just in front of the car. Jan loved blue jays. She always fed them when they came around the house. Alex could almost hear her talking to the birds as they fought over the breadcrumbs she threw out. A sadness welled up in him as he thought about Jan, and the anger followed when he thought about what Anton's people had done to her. Alex glanced over at Meg. She had her eyes closed and her breathing was heavy. He closed his eyes again and willed himself to go to sleep. Jan's lovely face floated before him. Alex smiled in his sleep.

Chapter 19

Alex woke suddenly, throwing his arm out and smashing it against the door. In an instant he realized where he was. He sat up and listened. The soft chirping of the crickets and the distance sound of an owl were the only sounds he heard. The dark form of Meg was still in the seat beside him. It was completely dark. Alex looked down at the luminous hands on his watch. It was a little after eight-thirty. He got out of the car and stood for a minute, trying to get his directions. He walked over to the other side of the car and opened the door gently. He shook Meg and she jerked awake.

"What time is it?" she asked sleepily.

"It's almost nine o'clock. I'm going down for a look, and I want you to stay here. If I need you, I'll come back."

"You're going to try and kill him, aren't you?"

"No," Alex lied. "I can't think about that now. I've got to find out about the bomb."

"Then let me go with you. I'll do what you say."

"No," Alex said again. "One of us has to get away and warn the authorities." He handed her one of the phones and checked the charge on the other one. It was fully charged. Alex wrote Dupre's phone number on a piece of paper by the door light and placed it into Meg's hand. "If I don't come back, call Dupre." Alex didn't tell Meg that he was going to call Dupre anyway, but he needed something for her to do, something to keep her away from the danger below. He took her hand. "Promise me that you'll stay here."

"I promise," Meg said softly. "Take care of yourself."

Alex made his way easily through the darkness, picking the same trail he had taken only hours before. He stopped behind the same bush and surveyed the area below. The whole house, and the clearing around it, was ablaze with lights. Alex moved closer, careful not to make any noise. After a few minutes, he spotted figures moving under the lights and became more cautious. He came to the edge of the clearing and squatted down, searching for the guards. Alex spotted one and then two more at the back, but there should be at least five or six. Alex moved slowly around the clearing, stopping every minute or so to search again. There, he spotted another guard and finally another one.

There were guards on both sides of the house patrolling back and forth. It would be almost impossible to get inside without being seen. He had to slip around the outside guard at the back and the two guards nearest the house without alerting the two side guards. Alex took a deep breath and began to move slowly toward the outside guard. He stopped and waited until the guards at each side of the house were near the front.

Alex could hear the sounds of voices and laughter inside the house. There had to be ten or fifteen men and women inside. Even if he was able to slip into the house, he would have to get to Anton with all of those people around him. It was a death mission, but he knew that nothing would stop him from trying. His thoughts went to the bomb. Who were these people with Anton, and where was the nuclear bomb? A bomb like that would kill millions of people and the radiation would kill millions more. Meg was right. He had come here to kill Anton. Alex had pushed the thought of the bomb far back in his mind, away from his drive for revenge. Now he couldn't think about anything else. He closed his fingers into a tight grip. He couldn't do this. He couldn't put all of those people's lives in jeopardy to get Anton. Alex stood and slipped back into the shadows, stopping a good hundred feet away from the house. It was a little after ten now. Dupre would arrive in Atlanta in a few minutes, if he wasn't there already. He would give him a few more minutes and if he was able to reach him, tell him everything he had found out. Then if something happened to him, Dupre would know everything that he knew about the bomb. With his contacts, he could have police all over this place in an hour.

Alex sat down and leaned back against a tree, letting his thoughts go back to the sunny day at the Canadian airport. He could see Jan's face clearly and her green eyes as they smiled at him. Was this quest for revenge, this lust to kill, a way for him to end his own life, a way to be with Jan again? Without his revenge he had nothing. His thoughts drove back to Anton and the bomb. He jerked his head back up and looked around. It was time. Alex dialed Dupre's number. He hoped that he had the phone on him and not in his luggage. The phone rang once, twice, three times, and then Dupre was on the line.

"Yes?" Dupre asked in a slightly breathless voice.

"Mr. Dupre, this is Alex Bradley. We talked before. I called you from the Detroit airport. I'm in Atlanta now."

There was a long moment of silence and then Dupre's voice came back. "My God, what are you doing down here? Don't you know they have half of the country looking for you?"

Alex quickly told Dupre everything that had happened. He shortened some of it but he didn't leave anything out. Again, there was silence at the other end.

"You really need to turn yourself in," Dupre began, but Alex cut him off.

"You can't be serious. These people are going to blow up a good part of the United States, and you're telling me that I have the time to turn myself in."

"Are you sure that these people, wherever they are, have a nuclear device?" Dupre asked. Alex could hear the doubt in his voice.

"I don't know where, but they have one somewhere, and I really need you to get some help up here. Bring enough people to take on thirty or so men. I've got a feeling that they're going to do something soon."

"All right, all right," Dupre said. "I know a CIA agent here in Atlanta. I'll call him right away, and we'll be there as soon as we can. By the way, where is there?"

Alex gave Dupre his location.

"Will you be there?" Dupre asked.

"Not if I can help it," Alex answered.

"Listen, I believe everything you told me, even that Jagger's death was an accident. Turn yourself in, and I'll go to bat for you. You can't run all of your life."

"I may someday," Alex answered, "but not now." He pressed the end button.

Alex stood there for a few minutes thinking about what Dupre had said. What was he going to do when this was all over? He had never thought about the end. He couldn't think about it. The end was an endless void of nothing. Alex turned back toward the house.

Nothing had changed in the thirty minutes he had been gone. It was ten-thirty. Alex crept closer to the house. The guards at the side were close to the front. Just behind the house was a swimming pool and to the side of that, a small building, probably showers and a serving bar. The two guards nearest the back had disappeared and the guard on the outside was making his way to the west side of the building. His path would take him behind the pool house. It was an opening, and if he was quick enough, he could get inside while the guards were on the other side of the building.

Alex darted forward, running with all his might. He came to a stop and flattened himself against the back of the house, next to a set of sliding doors. The light from the doors spilled out into the night. The guard would be around the pool house in seconds and he would be outlined in the light. He peeped through the sliding doors. A sun room was just inside and to one side of that a kitchen and dinning room. Double doors on the other side of the sun room led to the front of the cabin. The whole front part was a giant open room crowded with people. Alex could see out through the open front doors to a deck overlooking the docks and lake below. He entered the sun room and ran to the double doors, squatting down behind one of the two indoor plants to each side. No one inside was looking his way.

In the center of the den was a large stone fireplace and curving upward around the fireplace to a second floor was a stairway. He looked back. He could see the back guard rounding the pool house. He didn't look toward the house. Alex tried to calm his shaky breathing. He was in the open here. Anyone coming in from the back would see him and the guard could turn his head at any moment. The stairway would block him from the room full of people. He tensed, waiting for the right moment to make his move.

Suddenly, he felt a hand on his shoulder. Alex's heart skipped a beat and his knees turned to rubber. He steeled his mind to take on whoever it was. Alex turned in one fluid motion, bringing the gun up, hoping that the silencer wouldn't be heard. His finger tightened on the trigger.

Alex dropped the gun in astonishment. It made a clinging sound as it hit the floor. It was Meg. Her eyes were opened wide with fright. She was already bringing her arm up in defense. How in the hell had she made it here without being seen? She must have been right behind him when he'd made his run. She hadn't made a sound. Admiration grew for her.

Alex pressed his mouth close to her ear. "What in the devil are you doing here? Are you looking to get yourself killed? I almost shot you."

Meg pushed his face away. Her eyes hardened. "I didn't want you to kill Anton. The bomb is more important."

Alex picked the gun up and waited to see if anyone had heard them. Everything seemed to be the same. The noise of the people inside had covered the sound, but they needed to get out of this spot. The guards outside could pass by the door behind them at any moment. The area between them and the stairway was clear. Alex pointed to the stairs. Meg nodded.

Alex ran across the open area and stopped behind the fireplace. The bottom of the stairway was a few feet away, but it was in clear view of the people inside. Meg was right against him. He looked up to the top of the stairs and the balcony above. There was no movement, but someone could come out of one of the rooms at anytime. None of the people below had their heads turned their way, but that could change, too. It seemed hot in here after the coolness of the forest. Alex wiped his sweaty hands on his pants. He made up his mind and, taking Meg's hand, stood to his full height and started up the stairs as if he were a guest, pulling the startled Meg with him. He tensed at every new sound, expecting to hear a shout, a challenge. He had two more and then one step to go, and then they were turning toward the safety of the rooms.

Voices sounded from one of the rooms they had just passed. The door was opening. Alex turned frantically, searching for a place to hide. The balcony ran across the back and down both sides, projecting out over the room below. Alex kept to the wall and made his way across the back and started down one side, trying the doors to the rooms as he went. One of the people had stopped at the opened door with his back to them. Frantically, Alex tried the next handle and the door opened into darkness. Alex pushed Meg ahead and slipped inside. He left the door ajar. Three men came out of the open door and turned the other way, toward the stairs. Alex leaned against the door for a second to gather himself. He could hear Meg's heavy breathing in the darkness. Alex waited for a minute more and checked the hallway. It was clear. He stepped out onto the balcony and motioned for Meg to follow. Keeping to the wall, they headed toward the front of the house and nearer to the crowd of people below. Maybe he could hear the conversations and find out which one was Anton.

A tapestry hung over the railing toward the front of the house, falling down to reveal its design to those in the room below. He noticed another one on the opposite railing. The artwork looked to be Russian. It would be the perfect place to hide from those below, but they would be seen by anyone coming out of the rooms on this side. Alex looked around. It was the only place he could hear the people below. He sat down on the floor behind the tapestry, moving toward the front wall to make a place for Meg. He pulled the tapestry to one side, leaving him a peephole. Meg leaned over his shoulder. He looked at his watch. It was almost twelve o'clock. Dupre would be here soon.

Something was happening below. A tall, powerful looking man was waving his arms to the crowd of people, directing them to a screen being set up by two men. The lights dimmed and a slide projector came on. A map glowed on the screen. The voices died down to a low hum.

"Ladies and Gentlemen," the figure began.

Alex looked around the crowd. He hadn't notice many women, but now he could pick out five or six. He also noticed that several of the men were wearing turbans.

"The time has finally arrived," the figure continued. "We have been working toward this day for ten years, and now all of our fruits will come to bear. On Wednesday, a group of world leaders will be at Camp David, and almost all of the governing body of the United States will be in Washington. I say almost, because many are a part of us and will be taking a small vacation."

The crowd laughed and Anthony leaned forward. The figure was Anton.

Anton waited for the laughter to die down and started again. "For ten years we have been recruiting people here in the United States. They are all over, ready to take over control of the government and the military at a moment's notice. At ten o'clock on Wednesday, a hydrogen bomb will destroy Washington, Camp David, and most of Baltimore. Bombs will also destroy the government in Canada, London, and Israel. In the hours following each explosion, our people will step into leadership positions in each of these countries.

Anton held up his hand as someone asked a question. "Let me finish, please. You may ask why we don't have bombs in Germany, France, Australia, and countless other countries. We could, but we won't have all of the leaders in place because of the time differences.

"When the governments of these other countries hear the news, they will fear for their own lives. At the same time the first bombs are going off, we will have men ready to take over the broadcast networks in most of these countries, and they will urge the leaders to go to the nearest airport where planes and helicopters will take them to safety. Thinking that it's their own government, they will go eagerly. They won't know that the planes and helicopters are ours until it's too late." Laughter drowned out his voice, and he held up his hands again. "We know that our plans won't be successful in all of these countries. It would be too much to hope for. Even so, when all of this is over, most of the world and the world's military will be under our control. The rest will be easy."

Anton paused, holding his arms high, and then he shouted, "In thirty-two hours the revolution will begin and in two weeks we will be kings."

The building shook with the shouts of the people below. A tightness gripped Alex's chest. He could hardly breathe. *My God, what are these people going to do?* All of a sudden, Alex's revenge disappeared and was replaced with a grim determination to stop these people at all cost. He looked over at Meg and could see the anger in her eyes. Alex looked at his watch. *Dupre should be here in less than an hour.* Alex knew what he had to do. He had to find the bomb. He now knew that it had to be near Washington, but where? The crowd had become quiet again and Alex leaned forward against the railing. Meg pushed against him to see.

"The convoy will leave at twelve o'clock," the figure said. "I am giving them fifteen hours to reach the house." The projector changed, and a map showed on the wall. "Those of you who will be in the convoy and working on the bomb will meet at the house tomorrow afternoon at three o'clock. I'll be waiting there for you. The bomb should be assembled by twelve o'clock tomorrow night. Those of you accompanying the truck, remember to keep well apart, and let nothing stop you from the delivery of the parts. The rest of you know your jobs." Anton picked up a drink and raised the glass. "To a new world!"

Everyone drank to the toast and one by one, threw their glasses into the fireplace. A few shouted, "Anton! Anton!" Alex leaned forward. Anger gripped him as he lowered his hand to the gun. It would be an easy shot from here. Maybe without Anton the plot would be stopped. He felt Meg's hand on his. She knew what he was thinking. Alex turned at the sound of a helicopter. Was it Dupre? Had he finally made it? But there was no alarm below. Anton and a few of his people were walking slowly toward the front door. Alex could hear the helicopter settling to the ground. Anton stepped aside at the door and waited until all of the people had left the house. He motioned to his men.

"Burn the paperwork, and clean all fingerprints," he ordered and headed for the door. Alex looked around. Anton's men were all over the house. They were trapped. The sound of the helicopter engine changed, and the noise faded into the night. Alex knew that Anton was gone. He could hear cars and trucks starting. Alex looked at his watch. It was fifteen after twelve. Where was Dupre? They were getting away and there was no Dupre. One of the men was coming upstairs with the projector, and the other six or seven were busy cleaning the area below. Alex motioned to Meg and stood. They had to get that projector and slides. He felt Meg behind him as he ran back toward the top of the stairs. He darted into the same room, with Meg close behind, just seconds before the man's head appeared. Alex watched the man as he reached the top of the stairs and turned toward them. They tried to calm their breathing as Alex closed the door slightly. Alex eased the door shut and stood to the side just in case the man came into their room. He breathed a sigh of relief when he heard the man enter the room before theirs. Alex eased the door open again. The man had left the door open. He could hear the noise of the other men working below.

Alex motioned for Meg to follow and stepped out into the balcony, easing the door shut behind them. He kneeled down by the next door and peeped around the jam. The man inside was busy piling paperwork from drawers in a huge desk onto its top. The slide disks were laying beside the projector. Alex needed both. He held out his hand for Meg to stay back and slipped softly toward the man, his pistol held high. He knew that he would bring it down and shoot if he had to. Alex could hear the rough breathing of the man as he went for another drawer. He stepped forward quickly as the man bent over and brought the gun down hard on his head. The man fell against the desk and rolled to the floor. Alex ran to the hallway and motioned for Meg to come in. He shut the door and locked it. Alex grabbed the projector and slides. He motioned for Meg to help him go through the pile of paperwork.

"We have to tell somebody," Meg said, pulling at his arm. She was crying. "My God, Alex. Don't you know what these monsters are doing? They're going to kill all of those people."

Alex stopped for a second and faced Meg. He knew how she felt. They had known about the bomb and talked about it, but it was something that was going to happen tomorrow, always tomorrow. Now, that they were here, next to the people who were going to do the unthinkable, it was personal. The fear they had been holding back was bursting through, and now they were consumed with the horror of it.

"We can't tell anyone, except maybe Dupre, but even he hasn't been much help. He promised he would come, but he didn't. Maybe he doesn't believe us either. We're two wanted murderers. Who is going to listen to us without proof?"

Meg stood there for a second with her eyes darting back and forth between him and the man on the floor and then without a word, turned to the desk. They quickly went through the rest of the paperwork and laid everything to one side that looked interesting. They were almost finished when one of the men called from below. Alex ran to the door and cracked it opened. The man was yelling for Joe. It had to be the man he had knocked out. He was asking if Joe was finished. Alex muffled his voice and yelled back that it would be a minute. He shut the door and locked it. It was time to go, and they would never get out down the stairs. Alex looked around the room. There were large windows overlooking the swimming pool in the back, but the damn things didn't open. They were built into the frames. A voice called again, but it was a different man and the voice was closer. They were coming up the stairs.

"Come on," Alex whispered urgently as he ran past Meg, grabbing the disks and some of the paperwork. There was a shoulder bag on the other side of the desk. Alex grabbed it and crammed the projector, disk, and papers in. He slung the bag over his shoulder.

Meg didn't need any urging. She was already up.

Alex grabbed the heavy chair by the desk and threw it at the window, but it just bounced off the glass. *Bulletproof glass,* Alex thought frantically. The voices were at the top of the stairs. It was too late to go to the next room. He pulled Meg behind him and drew his gun. Alex held it at a slight angle and fired once, twice and then again, hitting within an inch of the same spot. The gun made a soft spitting sound as it fired. He could hear the ricocheting bullets whining past them. A small crack was forming. Alex fired again and, grabbing the chair, ran at the window just as three men burst through the door. Alex threw the chair at the window and grabbing Meg, followed it through the falling glass. He hit the roof rolling, dragging Meg with him. They couldn't stop if they wanted to. Alex felt the edge of the gutter, and then they were falling into space. He turned in mid-air and looked down in horror. All he could see was concrete and water rushing up at him. The next instant, he felt a jar and then cold water around him. It was the swimming pool. He had missed the concrete, but what about Meg?

He came up blowing water and searched for Meg. God, he hoped that she hadn't hit the concrete. His hands reached for the edge of the pool as bullets pounded the tile around him, driving sharp chips into his face. Meg's head popped to the surface, inches away. Relief swept through Alex. He pulled himself out of the pool in one mighty lunge and reached for Meg. He couldn't believe it. He was still holding onto the bag. He pulled her over the pool's edge, and then they were both on their feet, running for their lives, trying to keep the pool building between them and the flaming guns. Alex turned to look over his shoulder as bullets from a different angle hit close. Two men were coming out of the back of the house, firing as they ran. Alex and Meg were at the edge of the woods. He pushed Meg behind a tree and turned. He tried to calm his breathing as he aimed his gun at the closest man and fired. The man fell with a bullet in his knee. More men were coming from the house. They were spreading out, moving to each side. Alex knew that they would be trapped if they stayed here any longer.

He yelled at Meg to head for the car while he covered her. He fired the last of his clip, causing the men after them to run for cover. Alex bent over and followed Meg, moving as fast as the trees would allow. He could hear the men cussing the thick underbrush as they crashed through the darkness, but he had an advantage. He had been through here before, and he knew where he was going. Alex made the car just behind Meg. He reached for the key and slid behind the wheel. The passenger door slammed shut as the engine came to life. A bullet crashed through the window as he pressed the gas pedal to the floor and turned the lights on. In seconds, they were at the driveway and two minutes later, onto the main road.

He had until Wednesday to warn the government about the bomb, but they didn't have the time. It would take forever for anyone in the government to believe them in the first place. By that time it would be too late. Alex needed to find the bomb first, and then he would have the evidence. He saw a service station ahead. They needed gas and a map. He would figure out what to do on the way.

Chapter 20

Dupre stared at the phone for a minute. Alex had hung up on him. For some reason, Dupre believed everything he had been told. He had to call Heller. It took three tries to get him.

"Where are you?" Heller asked. His voice sounded tired.

"At the airport, and we've heard from our boy just a few minutes ago."

Heller's voice became reserved. "What did he have to say, and where is he?"

"He's here in Atlanta, and he told me everything that's happened to him since his wife's death. Let me tell you, Heller, I've heard a lot of tall tales but I believe him. The damnedest thing is, that he's at this Anton Kocyk's house, one of the people he believes is behind the thing back in Canada. He's telling me this Anton has a bomb, set to go off somewhere here in the United States."

"A bomb, what kind of bomb?" Heller asked. He didn't wait for Dupre to answer. "His story is a little far out isn't it? I think he's trying to take our attention away from him. By the way, I know he's here in Atlanta. He overpowered an FBI agent at his house this afternoon. He's got a girl with him and get this, she's wanted for killing an agent in Detroit."

"Then why would he leave there and go to Anton's house at Lake Lanier? The normal thing would be to get as far away from Atlanta and his home as he could. I'm telling you, he's following a lead. He told me he found a book with the names of a terrorist organization at Jagger's place. He also told me that the bomb is a nuclear device."

"He's at this Anton's place now?" Heller's tone had changed.

"Yes, and he's waiting on us to bring people up there. Why would he do that if he's not telling the truth?"

Heller was silent for a full ten seconds. "I'll tell you what, give me the directions, and I'll send men up there. In the meantime, I'll pick you up. The fact that they have a nuclear device changes everything. I haven't told you, but we've been on to this terrorist group for a while now. We knew that they were up to something, and now I know the perfect place for them to place a nuclear device. A group of NATO leaders are having a meeting at Camp David Wednesday. If the bomb is big enough, they could wipe out Washington, too. Enough talk, I'll pick you up in twenty minutes."

Dupre walked through the terminal to the baggage claim and waited for his baggage. Twenty minutes later, he walked through to the outside with his bag in hand. He dropped the bag and sat down on it. *Damn! This thing is big.* Heller had just confirmed everything Alex had said. If this thing went off, the federal government would be no more. The whole system of government in the United States could collapse. He tried to think about something else. He hadn't talked to his wife and kids in a while and wondered if he should call them, but then decided against it. They would want to know how long he would be, and he didn't have any idea.

Fifteen minutes later, Heller pulled up next to him in a Jeep Cherokee. Dupre threw his bag into the back seat and slid in next to Heller. Heller gunned the Cherokee into the airport traffic and seconds later, took the ramp to 85-75 North. Dupre looked over at Heller. He hadn't changed much since the last time. His red hair was shorter and he still had the same stony, hard look to his face, like he hadn't cracked a smile in years. Heller had cold, blue eyes that seemed to stare right through a person. He was a smaller man than Dupre, but he didn't have an ounce of fat on him. He moved quick and easy with a sureness that left little doubt of his power.

"Where are we headed?" Dupre asked.

"My men just reported in," Heller said. "Anton's place is empty. They must have the bomb in Maryland somewhere, and they are probably on their way there. It's the only target we can come up with. I've sent every agent I have up there already. I've also got cars ahead of us on all the main roads. Maybe we'll get lucky and catch them before they get to the bomb." He handed Dupre a pad. "These are all the tag numbers we have registered to Anton. If we can find them, maybe they will lead us to the bomb, and even if they don't, we have airborne devices to detect the radiation."

"Any sign of Alex or the girl?" Dupre asked.

"No," Heller answered. "Either they're after Anton or he caught them and took them with him. Either way, I believe we'll find them when we get to Maryland."

Dupre leaned back in the seat. The only trouble was, the longer they took finding the bomb, the less chance they would have of getting away from its blast before it was too late. Dupre wondered how large the blast area would be. There was no way of knowing. It would depend on how large the bomb was. He looked down at the list of tag numbers. Each one gave the name and make of the vehicle. That really helped. He wondered what had happened to

Alex. He had to be telling the truth. His voice sounded like someone that Dupre would have liked. He hoped to God that Anton hadn't killed him and the girl.

* * *

Thirty minutes later, they passed under the 285 loop around Atlanta and in another thirty minutes, they were approaching the Buford exit. Heller had told him that this would be where Anton would come onto Hwy. 85. Dupre leaned forward in the seat and started checking the vehicles, even though he knew that Anton would be well ahead of them by now. Dupre looked over at the speedometer; it was rocking between 90 and 95. That would draw a lot of attention Dupre thought, and sure enough as they passed a shopping mall on their left, a state trouper fell in behind with blue lights flashing. Heller got the trouper on the radio and after two minutes of talking, Dupre could see the patrol car back off.

"What do you have on this Anton?" Dupre asked, turning back from checking another vehicle as they flashed by.

"He used to be in the Russian army in his younger days, fairly high up in rank from what we could gather. Anton ran a very profitable black market business while he was in the army and continued after he got out. He showed up here in the United States about ten years ago and since then has gotten his citizenship. We didn't want to interfere with what he was doing here, because he was a lead to the organization he worked for in Russia, and that allowed us to track a lot of drug activity."

"So you stood by while a Russian criminal became a citizen of the United States?"

"Well, we win some and lose some," Heller answered. "The thing is, we may have never known about this bomb if not for the surveillance on Anton."

Dupre didn't answer. The sign for South Carolina flashed by. He could feel a tightening in his chest as they grew nearer. The whole thing seemed like a dream. He had come down here to catch a fugitive, and now he could be headed into the very pits of hell itself.

Chapter 21

Alex pulled into the service station and filled the car with gas. It was after twelve o'clock and there was only one car in front of the station. It probably belonged to the attendant inside. Meg headed for the restroom as soon as the car stopped. Alex walked into the station and found a map of the eastern United States. The attendant was young, maybe in his teens, with stringy hair hanging down to his shoulders. He grinned at Alex, showing teeth that needed dental work, as he handed the change back. He had a set of earphones on, and Alex could hear the faint sound of hard rock. Alex started to ask how far it was to the next town but decided that he wouldn't be heard anyway. He pointed at the key to the men's restroom, and the attendant tossed it to him. He turned and headed out of the station, passing Meg on the way. He came out a minute later to see her inside at the counter with drinks and sandwiches. She held up two sandwiches and the drinks with a questioning look. He walked back inside to pay, and they headed for the car.

"How far do we have to go?" she asked, as they climbed back into the car.

"I really don't know," Alex answered. "We need to hold up somewhere and try to read the stuff on the projector or maybe get an address from some of the paperwork."

"Do you want me to drive?" Meg asked, taking a big bite from one of the sandwiches and handing the other one to Alex.

"I'll take it for a while longer."

The traffic was still fairly heavy on 85 north, but Alex was able to make good time. Anton's people were about an hour ahead, but the trucks would slow them down and since they didn't want to attract attention, they wouldn't go much over the speed limit. Alex was sure he could identify the truck he had seen at the house, but even if they caught up to it, he wouldn't be able to do anything. They had too much firepower. The best he could hope to do was to follow it.

* * *

It was almost one o'clock, and Alex could hardly hold his eyes open. He should have let Meg drive. They had to stop some place soon to go through the stuff from Anton's house. He saw the sign for Charlotte ahead and past that, a service station with a motel to one side. He pulled into the station by the motel and filled the car up again. It was getting late. They might have a hard time finding another station open. After paying, he headed for the motel. A heavyset man stood up as they entered and slid over a registration card. There was only one room available. The man was eating pizza and drinking beer. The mixture ran down the corner of his thick lips and a drop dripped onto his already dirty shirt. His eyes drifted slowly over Meg, and he gave Alex a knowing smile. Alex resisted the urge to drag his fat ass over the counter and instead slid the card back. It was two thirty when they checked in.

Alex held the door open for Meg and followed her in. He could smell a slight perfume smell as they walked in, covering up the body odor of the thousands before them. He threw the bag down on one of the two twin beds and dumped the contents. Meg took the slide projector and began to check to see if it was dry. Satisfied, she sat the machine up on the dresser and turned back to Alex.

"What do you have?" Meg asked, as Alex handed her a receipt for a shipment of furniture to a Mr. Hung in Maryland. The address was on the receipt. Why would Anton keep something like that unless it was important?

"Do you think the bomb is there?" Meg asked.

"I don't know, but it's a good start," Alex answered. He pointed to the projector. "Let's see if we can find the slide showing the route the trucks took."

Meg aimed the projector at the blank wall behind the bed. Alex cut the lights and she began going through the slides, stopping when she got to the same map they had seen at Anton's house in Georgia. The map had a red "X" marking an area just to the north east of Washington, close to a town named Greenbelt. Alex went to the car and brought the map in. They traced the route onto the road map. It was the same area as the address on the receipt. They knew where the bomb was.

Alex called the desk to wake them in two hours, and cutting the lights, they each took a bed. He said goodnight to Meg and closed his eyes. He remembered a motel that Jan and he had stopped at while driving back from a book review in Philadelphia. The motel was just outside of Baltimore on the upper end of Delaware Bay. She'd kept him up most of the night taking pictures of the moon and the water. Slowly, he drifted off to sleep.

* * *

Alex woke with a start. The telephone was ringing. "Wake up call," a voice said. Alex could hear Meg in the darkness. She was already up and heading for the bathroom. Alex rolled out of bed and gathered up the papers and slide projector. He loaded them into the car and stopped for a minute to look up at the star sprinkled sky. It was another thing that Jan had loved. She had installed a skylight in their bedroom so that they could watch the stars at night.

Meg was already out of the bathroom and drying her hair when he got back. Alex took a quick shower and was ready to go in twenty minutes. He stopped and waited while Meg ran into the motel office and left the key. The traffic was light, as Alex left the ramp and slowly increased his speed.

Alex pulled into a Waffle House five miles up the road, and they ordered breakfast. It was Tuesday morning and twenty-seven hours away from the biggest catastrophe the United States had ever known.

Alex looked up to find Meg watching him. The waitress gave him a slight grin as she set two cups of coffee down. Alex reached for the cream. Meg hadn't said anything since they'd sat down. He looked at her. She still didn't say anything. "Well?" he asked simply.

"You think about your wife all of the time, don't you?"

Alex poured the cream into his coffee slowly. He lifted the cup to take a sip, letting his eyes rest on Meg's. Down inside he felt that his thoughts of Jan were personal and just for him but, at the same time, Meg had been through hell with him. "Yes, I do," he answered. "It's hard to let go of her."

Meg reached over and lay her hand on his. "I'm really sorry about what happened. She must have been quite a lady."

"She was more than that. She was a part of me." Alex shifted his attention to the parking lot outside as he felt a choking feeling coming into his throat, ending the conversation. They finished their breakfast in silence and headed for the car. Meg slid into the driver's seat. Both of them were quiet until they reached the main road.

"That was nice of you back at the restaurant," Alex said. "I mean to ask about my wife." He held up his hand as she started to answer. "This is going to get nasty. I just want you to know that I can't think of anyone I would rather have with me, but you and I both know that neither one of us may make it out of this alive. I'm asking you again. Are you sure you want to go through with this?"

Meg pulled out to pass the car in front. She took a quick glance over at Alex. "I'm not afraid to die, Alex. I'm young, but I know danger when I see it, and I know what you say maybe true. You and I are the only two right now who can stop this thing, and neither of us can turn our backs on it. So I guess you're stuck with me."

Alex didn't say anything. The closer they got to Maryland, the more he felt the horror of what might happen there. His mouth went dry when he thought about all of the people who would be killed if the bomb went off.

Chapter 22

Anton walked back and forth across the huge foyer. He stopped in front of the portrait of the previous owner of the house. The owner had gotten home early and found them in his house. Now he was laying in a ditch at the back of the estate. They had picked this place for the isolation and the fact of it being in the center of Washington, Baltimore, Fort Mead, Annapolis, and Camp David. Anton smiled. This would destroy the leadership of America. Soon this great country would be his. Well, maybe not all his. His thoughts went to the organization in the United States. They were his partners. He wished that he could cut them out, but he knew that would be impossible. Their men were in every aspect of the government from the state level on up. They had been working for the same ten years, moving their men up into key positions. Even he didn't know who most of them were. No, he would have to put up with them, but maybe later when they began to take control . . .

Anton walked back to the front window. He knew that the truck wouldn't have had time to get here yet, but he couldn't wait. They would have to work into the night to assemble the bomb and hoist it up to the top of the tower. That would give them just enough time to get outside its ring of destruction. Tomorrow morning would be the greatest day of his life. Everything had to go right. His thoughts went back to the call last night. The fools in Georgia had let Bradley get away. Somehow, he had gotten into the house before they could destroy everything. Bradley could even know the location to this place. Anton slammed his fist into his palm. That meant that he was headed here. Anton could feel a slight fear creeping through him, and then he forced the anger to drive it away. He had doubled the guard around the house, and what could one man do? What sane man would try to come against all of the men here? He would need help, and it would be impossible for him to get it. Every law official in the southeast was looking for him, and who would believe him? Anton laughed out loud and headed outside. He was worrying too much. Nothing could stop him now.

Chapter 23

Dupre jerked awake as the car made a sudden turn to the right. "Where are we?" he asked sleepily.

"We'll be there in an hour," Heller answered. "I'm stopping for a gas refill. Use the bathroom while I'm gassing up. We'll grab something to eat inside the station and be out of here in five minutes."

Dupre looked at his watch as he walked slowly back to the restroom. It was nine o'clock. Nine o'clock on a Tuesday. He wondered if they had enough time. His mouth watered at the smell of frying food at a Waffle House next door.

As Heller had promised, they were on the road five minutes later. Dupre munched on a stale donut and tried to force the black coffee down. He had seen no sign of the vehicles they had been looking for. "How do you know where we're going?" Dupre asked as he opened the window and threw the rest of the coffee out.

"I talked to my people while you were asleep. The helicopter reported a hot spot just outside Greenbelt. We're going to check it out now. My people will be right behind us."

Dupre sat up in his seat and pointed out the exit sign to Greenbelt.

Heller slowed and put his turn signal on. He came to a stop at the bottom of the ramp and then turned east. They drove through the outskirts of Greenbelt and turned onto another road by a subdivision of older homes. The subdivision disappeared behind them as the car speeded toward the rising sun. Dupre held on as Heller turned sharply into a long driveway. He could see a large mansion in the distance, and then Heller turned the wheel hard, jumping over the curb and into the woods. He cut the engine and turned toward Dupre.

"We need to get closer. I don't know how long my men will take. We may be able to do something before they get here." Heller drew his gun and stepped from the car.

"What about me?" Dupre pointed to the gun.

Heller pointed to the glove compartment and Dupre flipped it open. A pistol was inside. He stepped out of the car and stuck the pistol in his pocket.

They made their way through the woods to the back of the mansion. Most of the twenty or so acres around the mansion were covered with trees. A pool lay close to the back of the house and a two-acre flower garden was between them and the mansion. The building was four stories high and on top of that was a tower, reaching toward the sky. Several men were working at the tower. Dupre could make out a huge black, bullet-like object. *My God! It must be the bomb,* he thought. The top of the tower had to be at least a hundred feet above the mansion. He had read somewhere that the higher a nuclear device was, the more destructive force it had.

Dupre could see several guards to the sides and back of the mansion. Heller eased forward, and Dupre followed close behind. They moved from the woods and into the garden, using the thick hedges as cover. Dupre stayed close to Heller as they crept closer and closer to the back of the house. They made it to the edge of the garden and crouched down behind the last hedge. There were men all over the area behind the house. More men were unloading a truck and carrying canisters into one of the four garage doors. Dupre drew in a deep breath to calm his shaking nerves. Thoughts of his wife and children flashed through his mind. Heller raised his hand, and Dupre looked over his shoulder. The guards at the back were walking toward the men at the truck. They were laughing and talking to each other. Their backs were to Heller and Dupre. Dupre rose with Heller and ran forward, skirting the pool and stopping at the back of the house. No alarm sounded. One of the doors to the back of the house was open and seconds later, they were inside. Dupre drew in deep breaths of air. He wasn't used to running like that. He checked the safety on his gun. Heller was already moving forward. Dupre said a little prayer and followed him into the kitchen. The kitchen and dining room were quiet, but voices were coming from ahead. A short hallway opened to the front of the house. They flattened themselves against the wall and crept forward.

Dupre could see the huge room in front of them clearly now. It could have held a small house. Large double windows reached from the floor to the thirty-foot high ceiling. To his left, a beautiful curved stairway with marble steps wound its way to the second floor. Crystal chandeliers hung from the ceiling, glittering with thousands of tiny lights. The room had two fireplaces, one at each end. The twin doors from the hallway were open.

There were three men inside. The rest had to be either upstairs or outside. Heller moved back to Dupre and whispered, "The middle one is Anton. If we can get him, maybe we can hold the rest at bay until my men get here. You go to the left, and I'll go to the right. We'll come at them from both sides."

Without waiting for Dupre's answer, Heller slid through the doorway and around the wall.

Dupre took a deep breath and went the other way. He had closed the distance to ten feet when one of the men turned toward him. Dupre didn't have a choice. He pointed his gun at the man's head. "Don't move a muscle," he said softly. He moved forward quickly, covering the three men and trying to look over his shoulder to see where Heller was.

The man that Heller had pointed out as Anton, turned slowly with his hands in the air. He had a slight grin on his face.

Dupre pointed his gun at the floor. "Get down on your knees." Anton lowered his hands slowly, but didn't move. "I said get down on your . . . " Dupre stopped in mid-sentence as he felt the cold steel of a gun against his neck. Where in the hell was Heller?

"Drop the gun," Heller's voice said from behind. Dupre slowly let the gun fall to his side. Disbelief and then anger boiled over inside like an exploding bomb. Heller was one of them. The bastard had been with them the whole time. Dupre felt sick. Heller stepped over to join Anton.

Anton's grin had broadened at the look on Dupre's face. "You got to be careful who you run around with," he said and starting laughing. The other two joined in, but Heller stood there with a grim look on his face.

"Your guards suck," Heller said. "You're lucky it's me. What if it had been someone else?"

Anton turned to Heller. "Come on, Heller, we saw you coming in. The old man had a video system that covers the whole perimeter. A rabbit couldn't get through." Anton motioned for Heller to followed him.

One of the men produced a set of handcuffs and jerked first one and then the other hand behind Dupre's back. Dupre's mind had calmed. He was planning, thinking. He knew that he was dead. There was no way they could let him live. His only chance was now. Without thinking, he drove an elbow into the stomach of the man behind him, turned, and threw a kick at the back of Anton's head. Anton fell like a rock. Heller was turning toward him. Dupre's anger turned him into a madman. He moved forward and aimed a kick at Heller's head, but something stopped him in midair. Blackness engulfed Dupre and Heller's startled face disappeared. The man who had hit Dupre stepped forward and placed the gun against his head.

Anton was coming to his feet, holding the back of his head. "No, Wait! Don't kill the bastard yet. I've got a better way."

Chapter 24

Alex stretched back against the seat. It seemed like hours since he had taken the wheel and they had left Hwy. 85 but he knew that it was less than three. He saw the bypass around Washington and minutes later the sign for Greenbelt. He made his way over to the right-hand lane. Alex looked over at Meg. She was leaning against the passenger door with her eyes closed.

He began to think about what he was going to do when he got there. He couldn't go to the law without some kind of proof, and Dupre had been useless. He probably had all kinds of law enforcement looking for him back at Anton's place right now. Something in Dupre's voice had led Alex to trust him, but then actions speak louder than words.

It was a little after ten o'clock and Alex reached for the last pack of crackers from the convenience store. There was just enough coke to wash them down. The traffic around Washington had slowed him down more then he had figured. He pressed down on the gas pedal to make up the time.

* * *

Alex saw another sign for Greenbelt. The exit was two miles ahead. He started to let off on the gas when suddenly, a blue light flashed behind him. Alex's hand slammed down on the steering wheel. *A cop! A damn cop!* Meg sat up in the seat next to him. Alex looked down at his speedometer. It was falling slowly from ninety as he let off on the gas. He could have been doing a hundred. He cussed himself for not being more careful. The gun, he had the gun. Where could he hide it? They might get out of this, but if the officer found the gun . . .

"Do something with the gun!" he yelled at Meg. She was already rolling down her window and looking back at the patrol car. Just as Alex left the pavement, she threw the gun over the fence.

Alex hit the button for the side window and came to a stop. His hand shook as he pulled the emergency brake back. He drew in long breaths of air to calm himself.

Alex sat there watching the police officer as he slowly got out of his car and approached them. The officer bent over to study the car tag as he walked forward. He stopped and wrote something on the clipboard.

"Do you think I should show him my badge and tell him that we're on a case?" Meg whispered.

"No," Alex whispered back. The officer was almost there. "Your badge is from Detroit. They probably have a wanted out on you by now; hide it." Meg slid the badge between the two seats. The officer was at the window. Alex turned and tried to put on his best smile.

He wondered, as he looked up at the officer, if he could make a run for it, maybe take off on the ramp to Bowie and lose him in the traffic. The car was still running. He gave up the idea. Maybe the officer would just give him a speeding ticket and let him go. He had Harris's I.D. and driver's license.

The officer was thirty, maybe thirty-five. He was clean shaven, with clear blue eyes and a firm chin. His lips were drawn back into a hard line. He looked more like a line backer for the Jets than a police officer. Muscles rippled under the long sleeve shirt as he lifted one huge hand to his hat.

"Please cut off your engine, sir," the officer said, pushing his hat back on his head.

Alex reached for the key. It was too late to do anything but hope that the officer had drank his coffee this morning.

"Going a little fast there, weren't you?" he asked.

"Yes, officer, I was," Alex answered. "I just wasn't watching what I was doing."

"Could I see your driver's license and registration please?" The officer's eyes were searching the car as he talked. They stopped on Meg and after staying a little too long for official purposes, switched back to Alex.

Alex saw the name tag with Joe Raintree in gold letters on the officer's shirt. He wondered if it would be too personal if he called the officer by his first name. His hand shook as he handed the officer his license and the title for the car.

The officer studied the license and then Alex's face. The car was suddenly stuffy in the cool morning air.

"Step out of the car, sir."

Alex's legs were stiff as he stepped out of the car and faced the officer. He felt sick inside. He could tell by the officer's face that he was suspicious.

The officer leaned toward Meg. "You stay right there," and then he turned back to Alex.

"Step to the back of the car and stay put."

Alex walked to the back of the car and turned to watch the officer as he got back into the police car. The morning sun was in his face, and he could feel the sweat wetting his shirt. He prayed that Harris's license was clean. The officer talked on the police radio for what seemed like an hour, but Alex knew it couldn't have been over five minutes. The officer would look down at his clipboard and then back up at Alex. The seconds ticked by. Alex thought about telling him about the bomb, but he would never believe him without proof. He looked through the back window and could see Meg looking back at him with a worried look on her face.

The officer was talking on the radio again and finally he finished and stepped from the cruiser. He walked toward Alex with his hand on his pistol. "Turn around and put your hands behind your back," he ordered.

"But Officer," Alex said, "we really need to get to this job interview. Couldn't we work this out some other way?"

"There's just too many things that don't add up," the officer answered. "You have a car registered in Michigan, the picture on the license doesn't look like you, and you were going twenty miles over the speed limit. We'll just check both of your fingerprints at the station and you'll be on your way in no time."

Something in the officer's voice told Alex that it would be useless to argue. He was silent as handcuffs were put on, and he was led to the back of the police car. He felt the officer's hand on the back of his neck as he was pushed gently into the back seat. Alex watched as the officer walked back to the car and handcuffed Meg. She gave Alex a stiff smile as the officer pushed her into the back with him. Alex turned and took a last look at the location of the car. They would probably pull it in sometime today. If by some miracle he could get out of this, maybe he could find the gun. He turned his head and could see the bushes where Meg had thrown it. He tried to memorize the area around him, but his mind was in a turmoil. His fingerprints would put him under the jail, and they wouldn't believe anything he said. Meg would be no better off. The only chance he had was to use his telephone call to contact Dupre, but then Dupre hadn't believed him the last time. Alex leaned back against the seat in defeat. It didn't matter anyway. Before he could get anyone to believe him and stop Anton, the whole countryside would be gone. The police officer didn't know it, but he was a dead man.

The police station turned out to be only a few miles from where the officer stopped them. Officer Raintree parked the car and a second later, opened the back door, motioning Alex and Meg to get out of the car.

The station was small. Alex made out two, maybe three officers. A drunk, with a pair of handcuffs holding him to the seat, slumbered against a side wall. The smell of strong coffee drifted through the air. Officer Raintree led Alex and Meg toward the back of the room. Another officer came out through a door to the back as they stopped in front of the fingerprint area. Alex could see a caged area leading to the jail cells. God! He was going to end his life stuck in an iron cage. He watched as Raintree took Meg's fingerprints and led her to a spot on the floor. She stood there holding a small sign on her chest while her picture was taken and then was led away toward a desk in the corner. Raintree returned for him. Alex blinked as his picture was taken.

"Hey Joe, got yourself some hardened criminals there," another officer yelled from across the room as Raintree led Alex to a chair next to Meg. Meg's eyes frantically searched his as he leaned over to sit down. She looked straight ahead as Raintree sat down and turned toward them.

Raintree didn't answer the other officer. He turned and rolled his chair over to the desk behind his. A slightly plump, fairly attractive lady police officer looked up and smiled.

"What can I do for you, Joe?" she asked, sliding the paperwork she had been working on to one side.

Raintree handed her the cards with Alex's and Meg's fingerprints. Alex's eyes followed the card with a sick feeling in the pit of his stomach. He wondered how long it would take them to find out who they really were. He had the same feeling when he'd held Jan in his arms—lost, confused, like it was the end to everything.

"Run these through the FBI files," Raintree said.

"Will do," she said and put the cards on top of her paperwork.

"Thanks, Paula," Raintree said over his shoulder as he turned back to Meg and Alex. He pulled a keyboard toward him and turned the computer on. He looked at Alex. "Richard Harris. Is that your full name?"

"Officer, you've got to hear us out," Alex said. "We can explain everything."

Raintree leaned back in his chair with a smile on his face that said he had heard this a hundred times a week.

"Come on Harris, or whatever your name is. Just answer the questions."

"But there's a bomb in a house close to here that's going off sometime tomorrow. We were headed there to stop it."

Meg leaned forward. "He's telling the truth, Officer. You could check it out in a few minutes. You have us here in jail. What harm would it do?"

Laughter cut through the air behind them. "You have a couple of terrorists there, Joe," one of the officers said. "Don't let them get too close." More laughter sounded.

Raintree leaned toward Alex. "I'm only going to ask you one more time. Is that your name?"

Alex leaned back in defeat. He looked over at Meg and saw the same feeling in her eyes. They would never believe them without proof.

"Yes," Alex answered the question. He could see that this would be a slow process as he watched Raintree hunt and peck at the letters on the keyboard. He looked around the small station, looking for any way out. It would be impossible. There were three officers besides Raintree. He wouldn't make it out of the chair before they would be on him. He looked over at Meg and tried to give her a reassuring smile while Raintree's attention was on the keyboard, but he knew that the smile came out badly.

"Where are you from?" Alex's mind wandered to Anton and the bomb as Raintree asked him question after question. It must be getting close to lunch. The afternoon would pass by, and then it would be dark, and then after that, the last day of his life—the last day of everyone's life for miles around. It would probably be the last arrest Raintree would ever make. Finally, Raintree finished and turned his attention to Meg.

Thirty minutes later, the lady officer took Meg away. Meg touched Alex on the arm as she was led past. Raintree motioned for Alex to stand.

"Don't I get a phone call?" Alex asked, as he stood and looked toward the telephone on the desk.

Officer Raintree pushed the phone toward him. "Make it quick."

Alex's mind raced. He had a lot of friends, but no one who could get him out of this mess quick enough. Dupre was the only one, but he hadn't shown up the last time. Alex didn't have a choice. He dialed Dupre's number and held his breath while it rang. Once, twice, three, and then four, until a female voice came on the line informing him that the cellular customer couldn't be reached. Raintree could tell by Alex's face that he wasn't having any luck. He motioned for Alex to hang the phone up. As Alex lay the phone on its cradle, his heart skipped a beat. On the empty desk across the aisle was a handcuff key, laying right out in the open. He weighed his chances. Even if he got the key it wouldn't do him any good in the jail cell. They took your handcuffs off anyway, but it was something, a small hope for later—if there was a later.

Alex held back as Raintree motioned him toward the back door. He stubbed his toe on the chair leg and fell forward across the desk, grabbing the handcuff key before Raintree could turn around. Alex pushed himself back from the desk and popped the key into his mouth, rolling it to the side with his tongue. Raintree jerked him forward and then pushed him against the desk. He began to pat him down. Satisfied, he turned Alex around.

"Open your mouth," he ordered. Alex opened his mouth wide, hoping that the key wouldn't show between his teeth and cheek.

"Okay, let's go," Raintree said and shoved him toward the door.

With his back to Raintree, Alex spit the key into his hand and slid it into his front pant's pocket. He put his hands against the door jam and pushed back toward Raintree. He could see that the officer was getting angry, but Alex had to try one more time.

"I have an address. At least look at it."

Raintree stopped and studied Alex. Anger flickered in his eyes. For a minute, Alex thought that he was going to hit him, but then he gave a sigh and held out his hand for the address.

Alex pulled the handcuffed hands up to his shirt. "Here in my left pocket," he said. He put his hands back down as Raintree reached for his pocket and pulled out the piece of paper.

The other three officers had gathered around. One of them laughed. "They'll say anything to stay out of that jail cell for one more minute," he said.

Another officer leaning over Raintree's shoulder shouted, "Hey, I know that address. It's old man Hung's house. Last time I heard, he was over in some other country."

"Where did you get this address?" Raintree asked. "Were you going there when I picked you up?"

"Yes, Officer," Alex answered eagerly. Hope shot through him. "We were getting off at the next exit."

"If something was wrong, why didn't you tell me when I stopped you?"

"I know it sounds like I'm crazy," Alex pleaded, "but I'm telling you the truth. This guy Anton and the people with him are going to blow up half of the countryside if you don't stop him, and that includes this station. They are putting together a nuclear bomb right now at that address. Why would I make something like this up? My God! What can it hurt to send one car out there?"

"You had better call out the psycho unit," an officer said and walked away.

"Come on," Raintree said and pulled roughly on Alex's arm.

Alex gave up and followed Raintree through the back door and into one of the cells. He sat down heavily on the lower bunk as Raintree shut the cell door.

Raintree paused and turned back. "It's lunch time," he said. "We usually feed the prisoners about this time. What can I get you?"

Alex was hungry. He wondered what time they would feed him tomorrow morning. It would be his last meal. Hell, it would be everyone's last meal. "Anything would be all right," he answered. "Would you mind getting something for Meg and drinks?"

"A sure thing," Raintree said and turned away with a puzzled look on his face.

He's probably wondering why I sound so sane one minute and crazy the next, Alex thought.

He looked down the row of jail cells. A small hand suddenly stuck through the bars in the back cell. "Meg, is that you?"

"Yes," Meg's voice came back. "I heard you yelling at Raintree. Did he believe you?"

"No," Alex answered back. "If I don't get to talk to you again, I want you to know I couldn't have had a better partner or a better friend."

"The same for me. You know, it's funny. I never knew my father. He died before I was born, but I always pictured him as being someone like you. I hope you don't think that I'm trying to make you too old or something."

Alex swallowed the lump in his throat. Jan and he had talked a lot about having a child, and both of them wanted a girl. "I don't think that at all," Alex yelled back. The door suddenly opened and an officer stuck his head through. "Cut out the yelling. If I hear you again, I'll stick a sack over your head."

Alex lay down wearily on one of the bunks and stared at the ceiling. The cell was small with a bed against each wall, a commode, and next to that, a sink with one small shelf. Alex swung his legs off the bed and went to the sink. He turned on the cold water and splashed it over his face and cupping his hands together, drank gulps of water. He went back to the bunk and lay down, closing his eyes. Jan's smiling face filled the void and the tensions of the last few days began to drain away. Death held no fear for him. He welcomed it with open arms. He would be with his beloved Jan again. Even his drive for revenge was something far off—like a dream. The only thing he worried about was Meg. The minutes turned into an hour. He jerked his eyes opened at a pecking sound on the bars. It was Raintree with his food. Alex slid off the bed and walked to the front of the cell.

"I got you meatloaf, a couple of vegetables, and ice tea to drink," Raintree said, sliding a plastic tray through the slot in the bar. I got your girlfriend the same. Raintree stood there as Alex took the tray and walked back to the bed. Alex looked up at Raintree as he sat down.

"Look, I'm getting off at four o'clock," Raintree said slowly. "I can drive past the old man's place and check it out for you. I have to go close to there anyway on the way home."

Alex could see that Raintree was a decent guy after all. He set the tray on the bed and walked back to the bars. "Thanks, Raintree, thanks a lot, but you be careful out there. These men are killers. Just promise me one thing. If you see that I'm telling the truth, please get all of the backup you can to stop this thing."

"Don't you worry, I can call for help in a second." Raintree turned back as he walked away. "I'll see you tomorrow. Maybe we'll get the prints back, and you can get out of here."

Maybe Raintree could stop this thing. Maybe there was hope after all. He ran to the bars and taking a chance, yelled the news down to Meg. There was laughter in her voice as she yelled back. Alex ate the food and finished off the large cup of ice tea with gusto. It had been a long time since breakfast. Alex lay back down on the bed and slowly drifted off to sleep. There was nothing he could do but wait.

* * *

He woke at the rattle of his cell door. It was dark. The only light was in front of the cell. Alex rubbed his eyes and looked at his watch. It was five o'clock in the morning. The cell door opened and two officers came in. They must have been the graveyard shift because he had never seen them before.

"Hold your hands out," one of them ordered. Alex could feel the cold steel of the handcuffs as they handcuffed his hands in front, and then he was pushed toward the door.

"Where are you taking me?" he asked.

"You're going to the big city of Washington," the lead officer said. "The Feds want to see you."

Alex was fully awake now. The Feds. They knew who he was. He had crossed several state lines. They could be sending him back to Canada to face the murder charges. They could be out of the area when the bomb went off. He tried to turn to see if they were taking Meg, but one of the officers pushed him forward. The next thing he knew he was outside and being shoved into the back seat of a parol car. Someone was already sitting on the front passenger side. It was Meg. She gave him a smile, and then the door shut and her face became a dark shadow. The other officer got into the back with him.

Alex could see that the police officer sitting next to him, was really nothing more than a kid. He looked to be in his early twenties. The driver peeled rubber out of the police lot, and after a right, swung hard left onto the ramp leading onto the expressway. Alex was thrown sideways toward the kid as the car turned the sharp corner. The kid pushed him back and flipped the strap up on his gun, facing Alex with his hand on the butt. Alex smiled at him, and the embarrassed young officer slid to the other side and looked straight ahead.

Alex could see his car on the other side of the expressway as they flashed by. They hadn't gotten around to pulling it in. If he could just get away in the next few miles, he could walk back to the car, and then he remembered. They had emptied his pockets last night. He didn't have the damn car key. He had the handcuff key, but it wouldn't do him any good now. The kid was watching him like a hawk. Alex noticed that the driver had thrown a bag onto the dash as he got in. He wondered if the bag held their belongings and the car keys.

The miles clicked off. They were already too far from the car even if the bag had contained the keys. The driver slowed as the traffic blocked his way. The kid leaned forward, pointing.

"Hey Josh, see that girl in the blue Chevrolet. I knew her in school. I used to date her sister. Now you talk about a looker."

Alex couldn't believe his eyes. He drew in a deep breath. The kid's gun strap was still unsnapped. The gun was inches away from Alex's hand. The driver was looking at the girl in the blue Chevrolet. It would be the best opportunity he would get. Alex lunged forward, slamming the kid against the wire cage and pulling the gun out at the same time. The kid was a fighter and drove back against Alex, trying to get the gun. Alex flipped the gun around and hit the kid just behind the ear. The kid folded onto the seat without a sound. The driver was turning his head to see what had happened.

Alex stuck the gun through the mesh and against the driver's head. "Take the next exit or I'll blow your brains out right here." The driver slowed to take the exit and came to a stop at the bottom of the ramp. "Take a left and head back toward the station."

"You won't get away with this," the driver said. "The Feds will be expecting us. When we don't show, they'll have half the countryside looking for us." His eyes were wide with fear.

Alex didn't answer. He was trying to remember the address. A moment of panic swept through him. Raintree had taken the piece of paper with the address. He had the name. If he could just remember the number. Suddenly it came to him, and he gave it to the driver. They passed the turn off to the police station, and Alex could see the driver tense. "Josh, isn't your name Josh?" Meg had pushed herself against the passengers' door.

"Yes," the officer answered stiffly.

Alex could see that Josh was quiet a bit older than the kid. "If you want to live, you'll keep those thoughts out of your head. Just keep your eye on the road and take me to the address, understand?"

"Yes," Josh answered curtly, but Alex could see his hands tighten on the wheel.

Josh took the next exit and turned left. After a few miles, he took another road to the right. Alex recognized the road. It was the one they had picked out from the map. Alex read the number on a mailbox as the car's lights flashed by and then the next one. The numbers were going up. The house couldn't be far away. They passed the entrance to a park on their left. A thought came to Alex. "Turn around and go back to the park," Alex ordered.

"This isn't it," Josh said. "It's a good four miles ahead." Alex pressed the gun tighter against his neck. "Okay, okay, I'm turning." Josh slowed the car and turned around. Seconds later, he turned into the park entrance. Alex directed Josh to a side road, and they began to climb a steep hill. He ordered the officer to stop when they reached the top. Alex could see several buildings below next to a small lake. "What are those buildings?" he asked.

"It's the restrooms and a place to change to swimsuits," Josh answered.

The kid was moving at Alex's side. He had to hurry. "Down there," he ordered. "Next to the buildings." Josh drove slowly down the hill, looking from side to side.

Alex knew that Josh was looking for a way out. If he were in his shoes, he would do the same thing. Alex was sweating. He was still handcuffed, and he had the wire mesh between him and the driver. This wasn't going to be easy.

Alex pressed the gun forward. "Stop here, cut the engine, and unlock the back doors." Alex waited, but no sound came from the door. He leaned forward. "I'll shoot you if I have to and take my chances on getting out." He heard the sound of the door unlatching. "Now sit there with both of your hands on the wheel." When he saw both hands on the wheel, Alex took the handcuff key out of his pocket and reached toward Meg. "Unlock your cuffs, take his gun, and get out of the car on your side."

In seconds, Meg was outside the car, pointing the gun at the officer.

Alex opened the back door and walked around to the driver's side, motioning for Josh to get out. He held out his hands and Meg unlocked his handcuffs.

"Turn around," Alex ordered as the officer stepped out of the car. He moved to Josh's back and stooped down to check his legs for anything hidden. There was nothing.

"Take your partner and carry him into there." Alex pointed to the building.

Josh picked up the kid's limp form and walked into the first restroom. The concrete floor was wet and had the smell of a place that hadn't been cleaned in a long while. Alex ordered Josh to sit down on the wet floor and motioned to Meg. She handcuffed him to the toilet drain. They dragged the kid over to a commode and handcuffed him. Josh hadn't said a word. His eyes were glaring into Alex's.

"I'm leaving you here so that you can be found tomorrow, if there is a tomorrow," Alex said. A flicker of puzzlement shot through Josh's eyes. Alex didn't bother to explain but turned on his heels and followed Meg out. If the bomb did go off, maybe the hillside would protect them, maybe they would live.

Meg looked around before she got in the car. "It's got hills all around. You put them here to protect them, didn't you?"

Alex didn't say anything but jumped into the driver's side. They were running out of time.

He swung the police car out onto the road and pressed the gas pedal to the floor. It was seven o'clock. They had three hours. They checked the bag on the dash. It was all of their belongings including the cellular phones.

He shot past the address and swung the car around, cutting his lights as he turned into the driveway. It was already light enough to see, but that meant they could be seen, too. The long winding driveway led toward a huge mansion in the distance. A tower rose from the four-story house like a dark finger. The dim outlines of a bullet-shaped object hung on the inside of the tower. Alex knew that it was the bomb. The house was dark and silent as he left the driveway and pulled into the bushes.

"What in the world is that?" Meg asked. Then recognition dawned in her eyes. "Oh my God! It's the bomb!"

Alex released the clip from the police gun and checked the bullets. It was full. Meg was doing the same with Josh's gun. He motioned for her to stay behind him and, keeping to the bushes, approached the house. There were no vehicles in sight and from what Alex could see, no guards.

Alex rounded a patch of thick bushes and stopped suddenly, catching his breath. A police car sat thirty feet off the driveway. The lights were off, and the car was quiet. It had to be Raintree, who else could it be, but he had come here last night. He should have been long gone by now. Had they captured him? Was he in the house?

Alex made his way quietly around to the other side of the car. He could feel Meg right on his back. The passenger door was open. Holding his breath, he slowly approached the door. A dark shape began to emerge as he grew closer. A person or body was laying still in the front seat. Alex squatted down beside the car and watched the house for a full minute before he moved to the open door. The body was about the same size as Raintree. It lay face up with one arm thrown forward, covering the face. A sick feeling crept through Alex's stomach. He reached out and pulled the already stiff arm away from the top part of the body. Raintree's head reached almost to the floorboard. His hair fell down into a pool of blood. Someone had almost cut his head off. Alex drew back from the car, pushing Meg back and falling to his knees on the damp grass. He stayed there on the grass for a full minute. He heard Meg give a sharp gasp as she looked into the car. Alex took in deep breaths, trying to keep from throwing up. The sickness slowly turned to anger. They didn't have to kill him. They could have tied him up. Hell, he would have been dead in a couple of hours anyway. Alex slowly climbed to his feet and looked at his watch. It was seven-fifteen. He should do something with the body, but there wasn't time.

They approached the house with caution, but nothing moved. There was no sound and no light. The huge mansion had four floors above ground. The grounds were well kept. Two stone lions guarded the steps leading up to the entrance. The driveway was lined on both sides with head-high shrubbery which circled to within thirty feet of the house and then turned toward the back. Large iron gates led to driveways on both sides of the house.

Alex ran behind the shrubbery until he came to the gate and then motioned for Meg to join him. There was still no sign of life. Anton had said that the bomb was set for ten o'clock. They didn't have much time. They needed to be at least forty miles or more away before the bomb went off. Alex prayed that they would have enough time.

Alex decided to try the front first. He eased around the house until he was up against the steps. The early morning light reflected off the windows, making it impossible to see inside. He motioned for Meg to stay where she was and crept up the steps one at a time until he was pressed against the huge doors. Two narrow windowpanes were to each side of the door. Alex peeped around the frame. He could see Meg coming up the steps out of the corner of his eye. He'd known that she wouldn't stay back.

The morning light extended into the large foyer but fell short of a darker area in the back. Alex's eyes adjusted and then he saw a shape. He drew in a sharp breath. The shape was a man, and he seemed to be tied to a chair. Alex could see no movement anywhere in the foyer. The man didn't move. Could he be dead? Alex was at too much of an angle here. He needed to be on the other side. Alex ran to the other side and pressed his face against the glass. Meg ran across to join him.

Alex could see the man clearly now. He was big and had a beard. Who was he and why was he there? He jumped back as the man suddenly opened his eyes and stared straight at him. Alex pecked on the glass and pointed to the door. Maybe the man would know if there was an alarm. The man moved for the first time, shaking his head from side to side. He stopped and stared at Alex again. It was clear that he was warning Alex away from the front door. Alex made a circular motion indicating that he would go around to the back. The man started shaking his head "no" again. The whole house must be boogie trapped, but how? He looked at his watch.

"What do you think?" Alex asked Meg.

"Whatever we do, we have to do it now. It may take all of the time we have left to get the hell away from here. There's no time for us to get someone here to disarm the bomb."

Ten minutes had passed since they'd left Raintree's car. Meg was right. They had to do something now. The glass looked to be double pane. Alex would have a hard time shouting at the man. He was almost certain that there was no one else here.

Alex made up his mind. There was no time to do anything else. The frame of glass beside the door was a good two feet wide. He took out the gun and swung it hard against the glass. The pane shattered, showering glass everywhere. He used the gun to break out the smaller pieces and stepped through. The man was shouting. The words became clearer as they ran toward him.

"Get out! Get out! There's not enough time. Gas is going to be released in less than a minute." The man was staring at a point behind Alex. Alex looked back as they slid to a stop beside the man. A large clock was on the front wall. The minute hand was almost at seven-thirty.

Something was going to happen when the minute hand reached the number six on the clock. Meg started to untie the man's feet, and Alex went to the back of the chair. The man's arm was bent back at an awkward angle. They had stuck one arm through the oak cross section of the chair and handcuffed his hands together. His legs were tied with a rope. Meg was already working on the rope. They had thirty seconds. The man was screaming for them to get out and something about a senator. Meg had the handcuff keys, but they didn't have time for that. Alex jerked his gun out and sticking it close to the handcuffs, pulled the trigger. The handcuffs parted and he grabbed the man's arm. Meg had the rope untied and she grabbed the other arm.

The circulation must have been cut off in the man's legs because he could barely walk. They began to pull him toward the door. Alex glanced up at the clock. The hand was three seconds away. He threw one of the man's arms over his shoulder and heaved the man onto his back. He was thirty feet away from the door and then twenty. Meg was behind, pushing. Small banging sounds came from above and then a mist settled toward them. Alex put every bit of energy he had left into a lunge for the open window and the outside. He tripped as he dove through the window and fell down the stone steps. He could feel Meg stumbling beside them. He came to a stop with the man on top. The man was pulling at him and pointing to the house. A gray mist was rolling out of the door and down the steps toward them. All three ran away from the house and the mist.

The man stopped at the trees and turned toward him with his hand out. He was trying to get his breath and had to whisper. "Thanks for saving my life. My name is Paul Dupre." Meg stepped in and unlocked the handcuffs.

Alex stared at the man. Now he knew why Dupre hadn't shown up in Atlanta. "My name is Alex, Alex Bradley," he said with a smile. "This is Meg Harper."

An astonished look came across Dupre's face and then he began to laugh. Alex and Meg joined him. All of the tension of the last few days began to drain away. It was remarkable when he thought about it later. Here were two men and a woman standing in front of a house with a nuclear device about to go off, and they were laughing like they had just heard the greatest joke in the world. The laughter stopped, and they looked at each other. They had to get out of there."

"Do you have a car?" Dupre asked.

"Yes, come on." Alex ran toward the car with Dupre and Meg Close behind. Dupre hesitated when he saw Raintree's body, but kept running.

They reached the car and Alex took the driver's seat, Meg jumped in next to him, and Dupre took the back. Alex saw the question in Dupre's eyes when he saw the police car but he didn't have time to answer.

Alex started the car and headed toward the highway. "Do you know where we're going?" Meg asked, turning back to face Dupre.

"I heard everything when I was tied up in that room. But then they thought I would never leave the house. They're going to use an electronic device to activate the bomb. It's going to be done from a senator's house. I have his name but not his address. Do you have a cellular phone?"

Meg handed over the phone. "I hope the batteries are still good."

Dupre cut the phone on. "Oh, still plenty of juice." He looked over at Alex. "By the way, I never believed you were guilty about that thing with your wife, ever since I first talked to you." He began to dial a number.

"Who are you calling?" Alex asked. "And which way do I turn?" He had reached a dead end.

"Back to the expressway and then go north toward Baltimore," Dupre answered. "I believe they went northeast, and I'm calling my office. They can get the address to the senator's house a lot quicker than I can."

Alex could hear the phone ringing at the other end, and then a female voice came on the line. He turned on the expressway and headed north.

"Anne, this is Paul," Dupre said. "No I didn't check in, I was detained. Yes, I'm all right, but right now I have something very important for you to do. Yes, you can call my wife, but before you do that, I want you to get an address in Maryland. Don't do anything else until you get the address. I want it ten minutes ago." He gave her the senator's name. "I'll call you back." Dupre cut the phone.

"What kind of gas was that back at the house?"

"Some kind of a blood gas, very deadly and fairly fast acting. You have to have full body protection because it goes right through your skin. It breaks down your body cells and you bleed to death. Anton told me what it was going to do to me before he left. The canisters will keep going until the bomb goes off. No one can get into that house now without a full chemical suit. They even have canisters on the tower in case anyone tries to climb up to the bomb or come in from the air."

"Sounds to me like Anton didn't like you very much."

"I don't suppose he did after I kicked him in the face. I just wished that I had kicked the bastard harder, but that's another story." Dupre looked around at the car. "Where did you get the police car?" He was looking hard at Alex.

Alex grinned. "We didn't kill anyone." He could see Dupre relax. He was a policeman and they tended to stick together. He couldn't blame him for wanting to know after seeing Raintree. He explained about Raintree and how they had came to be driving the car they were in.

Dupre leaned back in the seat and looked down at his watch. "It's time to call back." He took the phone out and dialed the number. The phone rang three times before it was answered. "Did you get it?" Dupre asked. He reached over the seat and grabbed the policeman's clipboard and began writing. "Thanks, Anne, I owe you one. Now I have one more thing for you to do." He called off the names of other countries. "Get everyone in the office to help you. Tell them that a nuclear device is going off at ten o'clock eastern standard time and it's located at their national government center. The time won't be the same over there, but it will be after midday. Tell them to get as many people into the bomb shelters as they can. He laid down the phone and held out the clipboard for Alex to see. The address and directions were written on the board.

"How did you get the address so quickly?" Alex asked.

"We have a national data base. It's got all the bad guys and most of the top leaders around the world. She got the address and then the direction from the computer's map program." Dupre looked at his watch. "It's ten after eight, and we have a long way to go. It's going to be tight. That's a 25-megaton bomb back there. The senator's house is in the very outer ring of its destruction. If we're lucky, we may be able to get to Anton before he can push the button, but there's no way they can find the other bombs in time. I just hope that Anne can contact all of the other countries before they detonate." He held out the telephone. "I've got to call all of the people I know in Washington and Canada just in case Anne and the others don't get through."

Alex looked at the gas gauge and reached up to cut the blue lights on as Dupre's voice droned on. The speedometer hand was pushing ninety. If they didn't kill themselves first, they would make it. He slowed and took 95. The sign said Baltimore.

Dupre knew a lot of people in and out of Washington. He finally finished and handed the phone to Meg. She had relatives in the bomb's range. "Damn fools," he grumbled. "They didn't want to believe me, but I think I got them worried."

Alex slowed as a truck got in his way and then pressed the gas pedal back to the floor. They were doing over a hundred. Alex had already made up his mind not to stop for anything. He could hear Meg talking. He was glad that she was able to reach someone.

"Slow down a bit," Dupre said as Alex almost ran into a car ahead. "We can't do anything if we don't get there."

Meg's voice droned on as she reached one after another of her relatives.

Alex looked over at her as she lay the phone down. "I've reached everyone I can, but I couldn't get all of them," she whispered and lowered her head. Alex stroked her hair as she leaned over the dash and cried.

He looked down at his watch. It was eight thirty. They had one and a half hours to get away from the bomb.

Dupre began to tell them what had happened to him since he had received the call from Alex.

"It sounds impossible," Meg said. "Crime bosses, CIA, Russians. How many people are in on this?"

"I don't know," Dupre answered. "I do know that we have to somehow use the information we have to stop this thing."

Alex began to tell Dupre about Jagger and what he had learned there. It was twenty minutes after eight when he finished, and they had gone another thirty miles. The turn-off had to be close. His hands gripped the steering wheel as his thoughts turned to what lay ahead.

Dupre didn't say anything for a second and then he reached over and laid his hand on Alex's shoulder. "I would have done the same thing to that bastard," he said softly.

Another ten miles flew by. Alex could see another intersection coming up and let off on the gas. Dupre threw up his hand and pointed. It was their turn.

Alex made the turn and pressed on the gas pedal. Somehow, the statement from Dupre made him feel better.

"How large of an area will the bomb cover when it goes off?" Meg asked.

"From what Anton said, it's a hydrogen bomb. You saw the tower they had it in. From that height it will do a lot of damage. I think I heard Anton say that the destruction would reach Baltimore."

"Oh my God," Meg said softly.

Chapter 25

Keith Barlow slowly closed the bag and took one last look around his office. He almost hated to go. He had spent the last ten years of his life working his way up to this office. There had been a lot of good days and then, he mused, a lot of bad ones—specially during the last few years. The one thing he had always enjoyed was the power that went with his position but glory was a fleeting thing, because there was always someone above him ready to take it away. Over the years the political climate changed, new people moved up and old ones moved down. He was one of the ones on the downward move now, but this time there was something he could do about it.

He turned at the rattle of the doorknob. He had locked the door to keep prying eyes away. Even then, most of his fellow employers would knock before they came in, except for Carson. Anger swept through Keith. The bastard had been impossible since he'd found out that he was taking over Keith's position. The rattle stopped and a loud knock sounded. Keith looked around the office to see if he had missed anything. Oh yes, there was one more thing. He reached into the bag and pulled out the pistol and then the black silencer. He slid the bag under his desk and walked toward the door, screwing the silencer onto the barrel.

"Yes, who is it?" He asked, finishing with the gun and sliding it under his belt.

"You know who in the hell it is. Let me in," Carson said.

Keith waited a minute more just to piss Carson off and then unlocked the door.

Carson stormed into the room swinging his head from side to side. Satisfied that everything was in place, he slid into a chair. "What are you doing locking the door? Trying to bug the room?" He looked around the room, trying to find something he had missed. "It won't do you any good. I'm stripping everything and going over it with a fine tooth comb."

Keith walked back around the desk and slid into his big leather chair, at the same time easing the gun out and holding it between his legs. "Now, would I do anything like that?" he asked, smiling. "I'm just gathering my things together. I'll have everything out of here by tomorrow."

"Tomorrow hell," Carson said. "I'm moving in this afternoon. It's about time we got some new blood in here. By the way, about your Russian project, it's over as of now. I just got off the phone with the director and told him I wanted you out of the building and out of my hair."

A big smile settled over Keith's face. He could see that it startled Carson.

Puzzlement showed in Carson's eyes as he leaned forward. "What in the hell are you smiling at? I'm serious about this. I want you out of here now." He leaned back and grabbed both sides of his jacket, pulling them together with a snap, as his eyes flashed with anger.

Suddenly, a siren began to sound. Keith knew that it was a warning to get to the bomb shelter. There was one in this building, deep under the earth. What in the hell had gone wrong? There wasn't suppose to be a warning. Had someone found the bomb? Carson jumped up and hurried for the door.

Keith raised the gun and pointed it at Carson's back. "Sit back down," he ordered.

Carson froze at the tone in Keith's voice. Astonishment showed on his face as he turned and saw the gun. "What in the hell are you doing? That's a bomb warning. We have to get to an elevator." Ignoring the gun, he started toward the door.

Keith aimed the gun and squeezed the trigger. Carson screamed as the bullet tore into his knee. He tried to keep his balance but the leg gave way, throwing him to the floor. Keith stepped over him and locked the door.

The room was almost soundproof. Keith couldn't hear anything outside, but he knew that the hallways were a mass of confusion as people hurried to the elevators. A shadow blocked the sunlight and he ran over to open a window. The sound of the helicopter blasted into the room. His ride was here. Keith turned as Carson got to his feet and lunged forward. Keith sidestepped the wounded man and calmly shot him in the other knee. Carson cried out as he fell and drew both legs tight against his body.

"You bastard," Carson screamed. "You won't get away with this."

Keith reached under the desk and pulled his bag out. He slowly set it on the table and walking across the room to a chair, began pushing it over to Carson. Reaching under Carson's arms, he pulled him into the leather chair. After a few seconds, Carson's screams turned into moans. His knuckles were white from gripping the chair arm. Keith rolled the chair slowly over to the window and turned it until Carson was facing northeast. "I have already gotten away with it," he finally said. "Don't you want to know why I'm not killing you?"

Carson remained silent, but he never took his eyes off Keith. Blood ran down his chin as he bit his lip against the pain. Keith sighed and turned toward the desk.

"Tell me!" Carson screamed, his eyes wide with fear.

"The Russian sting, the one you just took away from me?"

"Yes! Yes!" Carson screamed again.

"Well it wasn't a sting. It was real."

Carson's eyes widened even further. "Are you telling me that there is a bomb and that the fucking thing is going to go off?"

Keith leaned over toward Carson. "That's what I'm telling you," he whispered into Carson's ear. "You can see now why I fixed it so that you couldn't walk. I didn't want to deprive you of that great moment when you look into the face of God." Keith looked at his watch. "It should happen in about forty-five minutes. I'm going to leave you now. My transportation awaits."

Carson screamed against the pain as he pushed himself out of the chair and tried to drag himself across the floor after Keith. "Please don't leave me. I'll do anything you want, please."

Keith stood with his hand on the doorknob. "Hey, you should be happy. You have your office early." He waited until Carson dragged himself the last few feet, until his hands almost touched Keith's feet, and then opened the door and stepped into the hallway. The hallway outside was empty. Everyone was on their way to the bomb shelter. Keith closed the door softly and locked it. The hallway was empty. There would be a lot of people in the bomb shelter. He could still hear Carson's muffed screams as he turned and headed for the stairs. Maybe the walls were not as soundproof as he'd thought.

Chapter 26

Alex slowed as Dupre pointed to the right at the bottom of the ramp. Later he slowed again to turn onto a small paved road on the right. Alex took the right and crossed a bridge over the rapid flowing waters of a small river. On the other side, the road began to climb a small mountain, and after ten minutes or so, Alex saw a large mansion cut into the mountainside near the top. Below that the grounds around the house were surrounded by a tall rock wall. Alex stopped the car well short of the wall and backed into the bushes. Keeping to the cover along the road, they ran toward the wall. He could see the glitter of naked wires on top. *Electric wire,* Alex thought to himself as he stopped to let Dupre and Meg catch up. Both of them were breathing heavily.

"Man, you can run," Dupre said as he came to a stop beside Alex.

Alex looked at his watch. "We have twenty-five minutes."

They were well hidden in the thick bushes by the road. An iron gate stood just ahead and to the inside of the gate, two armed guards waited. They didn't have time to go around the guards. They had to go through. Alex turned to Dupre.

Dupre had read his mind. "I know, we have to take them out." He pointed to a tree, leaning close to the stone wall but on the other side of the road. "You're lighter than me. Can you climb up there and make it across the wall? I'll distract them by walking up the road and Meg can come in from the other side just in case." Dupre turned to Meg and she nodded her head in agreement. Without saying a word, she disappeared into the trees. Dupre grabbed Alex's arm as he started out. "Good luck," he whispered.

Alex kept to the trees as he ran toward the guard house and then stopped, waiting until the guards were looking the other way. The guard by the gate turned and walked behind the stone wall. It was his chance. He sprinted across the road and up the hill to the wall. He stopped there until he could see Meg. Alex was impressed. She was waving at him from the other side of the road. Meg had made it to the wall before him. Alex picked a tree next to the wall and began to climb. He reached a limb overhanging the wall and stepped lightly onto the top, careful to avoid the electric wires. He eased himself over the wall and hung there for a second, listening to the sounds around him. Alex could hear the guards talking and laughing. He wondered if they knew about the bomb, that millions of people were going to die. He could see the house clearly now. It was built from stone with large areas of glass to the front and sides. Alex let go of the wall and hit the ground hard, rolling to take up the shock. He lay there for a minute listening. Everything sounded normal. He got up and crept slowly toward the guard building, keeping to the shadows, careful not to make a sound. Alex rounded the guard house and stopped less than ten feet behind the men. He eased the pistol out as he inched forward. They had no idea he was there, their attention was on the road.

Alex could see Dupre now, walking boldly up the center of the road as if he owned the place. He couldn't see Meg, but he knew that she was there. He moved forward, cutting the distance to five and then three feet. If only he could do this without shooting and alerting the house. The guard on the left was aiming his gun at Dupre when Alex stepped softly up to him.

"Easy boys, don't make a sound and nothing will happen to you." The second guard lowered his shoulder. He was getting ready to turn. Alex reversed the gun and hit him hard across the temple, bringing the gun back quickly to the first man. By that time, Dupre was at the gate and Meg was coming in from the other side with her gun covering the first guard. Alex ran to the guard house and hit the gate control. The gate slid easily to one side. They didn't have time to tie the other guard. Alex slammed the gun into the guard's head, dropping him like a rock. Meg took one gun, and handed it to Dupre, and threw the other one into the woods.

All three stayed in the shadows of the wall as they ran for the house. It was ten minutes to ten when they reached it. They tried to catch their breath as they eased around the wall to look through the window.

The room was enormous and full of people. A giant stone fireplace took up one end. Everyone inside was turned toward a man by the fireplace. They all held champagne glasses high and seemed to be watching a clock over the fireplace.

"It's Anton," Dupre whispered. "Look, he's got a control box in his hand."

Anton was making a speech and everyone's attention was on him. *Of course,* Alex thought, *they are going to celebrate the end of the United States.* Alex looked back to Meg and Dupre. They both nodded their heads. They would never have a better time.

Alex looked at his watch. Another minute had passed. Dupre and Meg were checking their guns. Both of them had a spare clip. Alex had the feeling that none of them would come out of this alive, but they had to try. All three ran toward the back of the house.

Alex stopped at the door. "Take out as many as you can," he whispered. "I'm going for the control box." Dupre nodded. Meg's face had turned to stone.

They had one guard at the back, but they were on him before he knew it. Alex brought him down with one swing and then they were in the kitchen, running straight at a startled cook. Dupre hit the cook without stopping and he crumbled to the floor behind them. They stopped by the inside kitchen doors. Alex pushed the door opened slightly. The big wall clock was straight across from him. The hands were almost to ten o'clock. Anton had moved closer to the clock. The people behind him were chanting. Another man had moved up to stand beside Anton.

"Heller," Dupre hissed from behind Alex.

They could hear the sound of arriving helicopters outside. The chanting in the main room was drowning out most of the sound. *They must be here to take Anton's people away after the bomb goes off,* Alex thought.

Alex raised his gun high as a signal to the others and started to push the door open when suddenly, all hell broke loose. Dupre grabbed his arm and pulled him back. Men were crashing through every window in the great room with guns blazing. The helicopters were louder. Anton's men were dropping like flies.

Anton's face was frozen in shock. Alex kept turning to watch the windows and doors in the kitchen, but so far, no one was coming in that way. They were safe for now. He turned his attention back to the confusion inside the great room.

It was over in seconds. Alex knew that some of the men had to come from the woods. They had seen Alex and the others come in. They knew where they were. Alex turned to Meg and Dupre. The same shock was in their eyes. Were these the good guys? Was it all over?

Anton's people were being herded into a corner. He stood by himself facing Heller. Heller had a gun pointed at Anton. *Whose side is he on?* Alex thought.

Alex turned to Dupre with a question in his eyes. Could Heller be undercover after all? Was Dupre a pawn that Heller had been willing to give up to get all of the terrorists? Alex could see only puzzlement in Dupre's eyes. He turned back to the scene inside the great room.

"Why? Why?" Anton was shouting at Heller. He suddenly reached into his jacket, but a shot rang out and a bullet shattered his elbow. Anton bent and caught the control box in midair with his other hand. He held it high, his other arm hanging limp at his side. "I'll set the bomb off."

Heller smiled at him and low laughter swept through the room.

An astonished look crept across Anton's face. "You want it all for yourself. You! You. . ." The rest of the words died on his lips. The room turned quiet.

Heller brought his gun forward. "You must have known that we would never have trusted you to keep your end of the bargain." He aimed the gun.

Anton rushed Heller, at the same time pushing the button on the control box. Heller shot him between the eyes. Anton fell face down at Heller's feet.

Alex felt Dupre pulling at him. "We have to go. They can't leave us alive."

Alex couldn't believe it as they ran through the kitchen doors and into the yard. There should be sounds, or terrible winds. He had seen Anton push the button. Relief swept through him. Maybe the bomb hadn't gone off. Then they were away from the house, and he saw the mushroom cloud reaching for the sky. There was a deadly quiet, and the air seemed to shimmer. A bright light suddenly lit the sky like a giant lightbulb. Alex turned his face away from the intense heat. When he was able to open his eyes again, a wind began to sweep the mountaintop, soft at first and then increasing until it was a terrible howling force. The sun disappeared and a darkness settled over the once blue skies. A helicopter, hovering above, suddenly slammed to the ground. The three couldn't move. It was the end of the world.

Suddenly, bullets cut into the ground at their feet. Alex hardly noticed that someone was shooting at them. *My God, they did it,* Alex screamed to himself. *They killed millions of people.* A rage swept through him. He wanted to go back and kill all of the monsters, but he couldn't. He would just become another pile of dust among the dead and dying. He had to live to bring them to justice. He turned with the others and ran toward the wall.

Dupre pulled himself over the wall, and Alex pushed Meg to the top. He looked back at a sound behind him. A Humvee was rushing toward them. He would never get over the wall. Alex sat down against the wall as bullets chipped at the stones around him. He leveled his gun at the vehicle, firing round after round into its windshield. He could hear guns on the wall over his head. Meg and Dupre were there, covering him. Suddenly, the Humvee curved to one side and came to a stop. Alex could see the driver slumped over the wheel. The other men inside were now on the ground and running toward him. Alex pulled himself over the wall and dropped to the other side. He ran to catch up with the others.

They reached the car and Alex climbed behind the wheel. He started it and pushed the gas pedal to the floor, spinning backwards onto the road. Another Humvee rounded the curve behind them. Dupre fired through the back glass. The car began to fishtail as Alex fed gas to the huge engine, and they began to leave the Humvee behind. Suddenly, an explosion threw dirt into the side of the car. Alex looked back in the rear view mirror. One of the soldiers was hanging over the windshield of the Humvee with a rocket launcher pointed at them. Fire erupted again from the tube. The road exploded fifty feet to the front, and a tree fell across the road. Alex turned to the right until his tires were on the edge of a shear drop-off and hurled toward the top of the tree. He felt the car go up on two wheels as they hit the tree, and then they were sliding down the road on the other side. He hit the break pedal, and his foot went back to the gas as the back of the police car began to come around. After sliding for one breathtaking moment toward the drop-off, the car straightened and hurled down the mountain. Alex let off on the gas and began to ease down on the brake. He managed to slow the car a little, but the bridge was coming up fast. The car slammed onto the bridge and almost bounced over the edge before Alex felt the tires begin to hold. He turned the wheel hard toward the skid and pressed the gas pedal to the floor. The car slid sideways as he turned onto the main road and headed east. The Humvee had disappeared.

Dupre had the map out. "Head north on highway 95 and then west on 70. I know a retired general who lives north of Peterborough, Canada, near Warsaw. Even though he's British, he knows a lot of military leaders worldwide. The only advantage we have is that Anton bragged too much about what he was going to do when the bomb went off. Heller's organization has people ready to step into government and military leadership positions around the world. I know we don't have much time, but if the general could short circuit that change of leadership in just a few key positions, we may be able to stop those bastards."

Alex slowed as the traffic began to fill the expressways. People were fleeing the bomb. Suddenly, they were crawling along at ten miles per hour. Every second counted, but Canada was on the moon as far as they were concerned.

Alex's hand gripped the wheel. He could hear Meg crying softly in the back seat. She had lost loved ones. Alex felt sick. All of those millions of people. A bird flopped onto the hood of the car and then fell to the road. There was death everywhere—behind them, in front of them, even in the very air they breathed. They were trapped. They couldn't get away from it.

Chapter 27

Keith Barlow's hands were still shaking. The fierce wind from the bomb had almost driven them into the ground. Several times he'd thought that they were going to die. The fact that they were coming around the east side of the mountain when the bomb went off saved them. He leaned forward and pointed a trembling finger to the large house on the hilltop below. The helicopter cabin tilted forward as the pilot changed direction. He could see a burning helicopter in the yard and dead men on the ground. Heller must have had more trouble with Anton than he figured. Men below were motioning for them to land in front of the house. Keith could see Heller running toward them as the helicopter touched down.

Keith was facing west as he climbed down to the ground and he could see the large mushroom cloud climbing toward space. Fears drove through him and something else, dread. They had released the power of the universe, and what they had started could destroy the world.

Heller was there and motioned for the helicopter pilot to keep the motor going. He waved Keith away from the noise.

"How did it go?" he shouted.

"Not so good," Keith said in a normal voice as he got farther away from the helicopter. His calmness surprised him. "Someone tipped off Washington about the bomb. They knew forty-five minutes before it went off."

Heller stopped with a shocked looked on his face. "The hell you say. How in the hell did they . . ." He stopped in mid-sentence. "It was Dupre and that damn Bradley. They were here. Part of this was caused by them. Bradley somehow found Dupre and they must have warned Washington and anybody else they could."

"We need to stop those bastards. They could ruin everything," Keith said.

"No! Forget about them. They can't do anything now. We have to make sure we finish taking over the military. With forty-five minutes warning, the President, his cabinet, and a lot of Congress must have gotten away. They'll be headed straight to Colorado. I just got a message from Dover. Our people have taken control. I'll talk to them on our way there and we'll get planes in the air to intercept Air Force One. We'll use Dover as our base until we get the word from the others to the west and south." Heller motioned toward the helicopter. More of his men were already climbing in along with Senator Tim Rivers, the next President of the New Republic.

Other helicopters were landing behind them. They lifted into the air and headed east. Twenty minutes later, Keith saw another mushroom cloud to the northeast. It was the bomb in Canada. He began to feel better. Everything was going according to plan. He wondered if the director had gotten out of Washington and if so, what he was thinking now.

Chapter 28

Alex was stuck. A sea of traffic went on as far as he could see. The mushroom cloud had flattened out, and the sky overhead was already getting darker. The radioactive dust would be falling on them soon. Next would come the sickness. The people on the road were shouting and blowing their horns, trying to get those ahead to move, but no one could go anywhere. Some of them had made the traffic worse by leaving their cars and walking.

"You can leave the road there!" Dupre was shouting as he leaned his head out of the window and pointed. "There's a sign for an airport ahead. Maybe we can get a plane."

"What good would that do?" Alex asked. "All of the pilots must have left hours ago."

"I'm a pilot," Dupre said as he drew his head back in. "If they left a plane, we may be able to fly out."

Alex left the highway and climbed the slope toward a fence at the top. He pressed the gas pedal to the floor as they began to slide, and the car jumped forward, crashing through the fence and over the top of the bank. Then they were sliding down into a gully on the other side. The car finally came to a sudden stop, throwing everyone forward. Alex tried to give the car gas and turned the wheel from side to side but they were stuck. They would have to leave the car.

"Is everyone all right?" Alex asked as he climbed out.

"I'm fine," Meg answered.

"Me, too!" Dupre shouted. He was already climbing the bank on the other side. "I can see the airport!" he shouted as he reached the top. He disappeared and Alex and Meg ran to catch up.

Alex could see a road on the other side of the gully and beyond that an airport. Relief swept through him when he saw ten or so airplanes sitting beside the one hangar. He caught up to Dupre. Meg was close behind.

"There's a Cessna," Dupre panted. "It's good on gas if there's any gas left."

"We can refuel it," Alex said.

"That may not be as easy as you think," Dupre answered. "The electric power that drives the pumps may be off and unless there's a refueling truck . . . " He let the sentence dangle.

Minutes later, they were at the plane. Alex looked around, but he couldn't see anyone. The whole place seemed deserted. Dupre had already climbed into the plane. Alex stuck his head inside the door. The plane could hold four or five people.

Dupre leaned out and shouted down to them. "It's full, the damn thing is full of gas!" He reached out his hand for Meg and Alex climbed in behind her. Dupre began to flip switches.

Suddenly Alex was startled by the roar of the engine, and he felt the plane begin to move. Dupre let the plane sit there for a minute to warm up and then headed for the other end of a long runway. Meg sat in the front with Dupre, and Alex in the back. He reached over and opened the window on his side. The air felt good. Meg was shouting and Alex leaned forward. There were two, no three, figures running toward the plane. As they got closer Alex could see that it was a woman and two small kids. Meg shouted at Dupre to stop. Finally Dupre gave in and the plane began to slow. The woman had fallen on the concrete and was trying to crawl toward them. Alex and Dupre jumped out of the plane and ran to her.

"Look!" Dupre shouted, pointing toward the hangar.

A dozen or so people were running toward them. Alex realized that they must have been in the hangar. He reached the woman. She was trying to stand. Alex picked her up in his arms and started back to the plane. Dupre took the little boy and girl, one under each arm, and followed. Alex could hear the people behind them shouting. They wanted to go with them, but they couldn't. There wasn't enough room. The woman was getting heavier and Alex had to slow down. All he could manage was a fast walk. Suddenly, Meg was at his side helping. The people behind were gaining. They were within a hundred feet when Alex and the others reached the plane. Meg took the little girl, and Alex pulled the woman and boy into the back seat with him.

Dupre pushed the throttle forward, but hands were already on the door, trying to get in. Dupre increased Speed. One man dropped off, but another refused to let go. Dupre turned back toward Alex. "You have to get him off. It's too much weight."

Alex felt the plane began to lighten, and he knew that they were taking off, but the plane wasn't gaining altitudes. They all would be killed if the man held on. He pushed the boy toward the woman and opened the door. The man reached for Alex trying to drag himself inside. Alex hit the man full in the face and followed it with a kick. The man fell, but caught the wing strut. He held on for an agonizing moment. Alex could see the fear and desperation in the man's face, then he let go and disappeared from sight. Alex said a little prayer that the man would live but for how long? The radioactive dust would be here soon. Alex closed the door as the plane jumped into the air. Dupre circled toward the north and began to climb, motioning for Alex to shut the window. As Alex turned back, Meg shouted and pointed north. Alex felt a terrible dread as he followed her pointing finger. Another mushroom cloud was reaching for the sky.

Chapter 29

Heller pulled the headset down and turned to Keith as the helicopter began to lose altitude. A smile played across his face. "We just got word that we now have control of the communication satellite over Colorado and half of the defense radar. Four of our pilots have taken off to intercept the President's plane. In two hours, there will be no federal government. Give us a week, and we will be in control of the whole damn country, and then the world."

"Do the pilots know that it's the President's plane?"

"Yes," Heller replied. "These are our men, put into place years ago. We couldn't send any of the regular air force pilots yet. They think that we are fighting the terrorists and we want them to keep them thinking that."

"What about the rest of the military? Without them we'll be spitting in the wind."

"Don't worry. We have people from the very top right down to the sergeant level. We've been putting our people in for ten years now. Remember, all we need to do is takeover the top ten percent of the leadership, and we can control the rest. When we have that control, we'll go on national television and declare a state of emergency. By then we'll have a military presence in all of the main cities. The people will think that the government will be restored in a few short months. We'll use that time to strengthen our positions, and then it will be too late. We will *be* the government."

"Have you heard anything from the other countries?" Keith asked.

"It's too early. We'll just have to wait. Don't worry. Everything is going our way."

Keith could see the blue line of the ocean ahead and minutes later, they were over Dover Air Force Base. Air police surrounded the helicopter when it landed. *It's amazing,* Keith thought. *Ninety percent of the people here didn't know that the enemy was already in control, that the whole military was being taken over from the inside.*

Keith looked around as they hurried across the concrete toward headquarters. The base was on full alert. The roar of the aircraft landing and taking off made it hard to talk. Fire trucks, with sirens blaring, raced toward an airplane that had overshot the runway. He looked back as he felt a pull on his sleeve. They were being led into the building. A one-star general met them in the hallway and motioned for them to follow. Keith wondered if he was one of theirs. They followed the general into a large conference room.

"Sit down, gentlemen," the general commanded and left the room.

"Is he one of ours?" Keith whispered.

"I don't know," Heller answered. "I do know that our general is already here."

They looked up as a dozen people filed into the room led by a three-star general. He was a tall, thin man who looked to be in his fifties. His thin lips were drawn into a firm line and his blue eyes looked straight ahead. When everyone was seated, the general held his hand up and pointed to Heller. "If you're who I think you are, you'll know my name."

"Taylor," Heller said softly.

"And who is this?" the general asked, pointing to Keith

"Keith Barlow, formally CIA, head of the Washington branch."

General Taylor grinned. "It looks like you're out of a job," he said, nodding his head at Keith.

Soft laughter drifted around the table.

"I don't need to tell you to be extremely careful who you talk to," General Taylor began. "Most of the enlisted men here are loyal to the United States of America and will stay that way until we brainwash them into believing otherwise. Most of the top command structure is under our control, and those that didn't see it our way are no longer with us. I took over command here two weeks before the bomb went off. I made sure that the men got to see me a lot, and I believe most of them will follow every order I give."

He turned to Heller. "We got your message about the President. It is now 1200 hours. We picked up their planes on satellite radar a few minutes ago. We have scrambled the four planes I told you about and more are taking off from other bases. They should be enough to take care of the President's plane and their escort before they get close to Colorado. In two hours, there will be no more Federal Government." General Taylor turned to include everyone at the table. "Gentleman, I have some more great news. Two more bases are under our control. By the end of the week, we should have all of the military with us and then phase two will start." Shouts rang out around the table.

Keith tried to show enthusiasm, but his shout was weak. His hate for the system had led him to strike out against it. Everything was going as planned. The country would be theirs. The future looked bright, but all he could see ahead was a black void.

Chapter 30

Alex jerked his eyes opened and looked at his watch. They had been in the air for over an hour. It was twelve o'clock. He leaned across the front seat. "Where are we?" he asked

"We are coming into a small airport to the west of where the general lives. I've already called for transportation."

"What's the general's name?"

"General Miles Weaver," Dupre answered as he dropped the left wing and started his descent. "He's one of the best military minds I know. My father served with him."

Alex could feel the plane lose speed, and for the first time he saw the long strip of runway ahead. Dupre brought the airplane in line with the runway and minutes later, the wheels touched down softly on the concrete. He opened the door and turned to them.

"Stay here," Dupre ordered. "I've got my papers, and I can explained better than you." A car with a flashing light was approaching fast. Dupre jumped to the ground and waved to the car. It slid to a stop and he ran to meet the man stepping out of the passenger side. After ten minutes of intense conversation, Dupre waved at the others to join him. Alex grabbed the boy and helped the woman out of the plane. Another vehicle had joined the first one. Airport security motioned for the woman and two children to get into the second car. The woman ran back to Alex and, after hugging him, went to Meg and then to Dupre. The driver of the first car had the back door open and was motioning to Alex and Meg. They walked over and slid into the back seat. The driver then went to the plane and climbed in, leaving the man from the passenger side to drive the first car. The man slid into the driver's side and Dupre took the other side.

"This is Captain Ambros with customs," Dupre said from the front seat. "The good captain knows the general and has offered to drive us to his place, which I'm sure he wouldn't do under normal circumstances."

Alex could see the plane start up as the car headed toward other side of the runway. The driver could handle a plane too.

The car left the airport and gained speed. The few buildings disappeared behind them and soon, tall trees blocked what little sunlight there was left. Dupre was chatting away with the captain.

"But that's impossible," Dupre was saying. "You can't get the military to do anything?"

"Nothing," replied Ambros. "The radioactive cloud is headed this way, and they should be here overseeing the evacuation, but we can't get them to move their butts. It's as if no one is in command."

Dupre held up his finger as Alex started to say something. Alex leaned back in the seat. Maybe Dupre was right. If they told the captain about the takeover, it would just cause panic or maybe he was in with the others. Alex sat up and began to watch the captain carefully.

An hour later they turned off the main road and onto a narrow driveway. The captain shifted gears as they began to climb. Streaks of light were glittering over the layer of fog below. They turned through a huge iron gate and followed a paved driveway, breaking clear of the trees just before the top of the mountain. The top was about twenty acres or so of level field. White wood fencing divided the field into sections ending at a large, well-kept barn. Alex could see horses in one of the sections. As they rounded the barn, a giant three-story log house loomed before them. A porch circled the lower floor and a large parking lot was to one side. The car circled a well-kept flower garden to stop in front of a pair of huge double doors. A tall, gray-haired man stood in front watching the car approach. There were several other cars already in front of the house.

"Paul, it's so good to see you!" the man shouted, hurrying to the car and grabbing Dupre's hand before he could get out of the car. The general stood to one side as Dupre introduced Meg and Alex. Dupre thanked the captain and he waved goodby from the open window as the car disappeared into the trees.

"Come on in the house." General Weaver stepped aside and glanced at their tired faces as they passed by. The foyer led into a giant open den with a stone fireplace at one end. Alex caught a glimpse of a library to one side. Shelves full of books reached from the floor to the ceiling. They were led to a couch and chairs in front of the fireplace. General Weaver looked much younger than his years. His brown eyes were quick and intelligent.

As they sat, the general barked orders to a maid. "After you eat, I'll take you to your rooms. All of you look like you haven't had any sleep in a week."

"We don't have time, General," Dupre said. "We have important information about the bombs and the people behind them."

General Weaver's face changed, and he took a chair close to Dupre. "All of us have been talking," he said. "By all of us, I mean my comrades in the military, both here and in the United States. Our theories range from any one of a dozen countries to a terrorist group." He turned toward Alex. "I feel so sorry for you and your countrymen. Like us, you have lost most of your leadership."

"Maybe not, General," Alex said. He began to tell the general about their warning to both governments forty-five minutes before the bomb went off.

General Weaver jumped to his feet and threw his arms out. "My God, man, that means that some or all of them got out." The food arrived, but no one paid any attention.

The general grew quiet and sat down again as Dupre related everything he had heard while he was a captive.

"It's hard to believe that they've taken over our countries from the inside. For this to work, they have to destroy both of our governments," General Weaver mused. Suddenly, he jumped to his feet. "Your President and Congress will try to get to the command center at Colorado. That means these bastards will have planes in the air looking for them. We have to try to get word to Air Force One somehow." He ran from the room shouting for them to follow.

They followed the general toward the back of the house and down a flight of stairs into a huge basement. He stopped at a metal-covered door set into the concrete back wall of the basement and, taking out a set of keys, unlocked the door. He led them down a short hallway and through another door.

Alex stopped in amazement. The giant room was filled with radio equipment, computers, and wall screens.

General Weaver threw a breaker and the whole room lit up. "I've already been down here this morning. I wondered why over half of the United States and Canada's radar and communication systems were out. I figured that it was because of the bombs, but two bombs aren't suppose to reach out that far." He keyed the mike on a shortwave radio and started broadcasting. Five minutes later, a voice blasted back at them. "Miles, you old son of a gun," the voice said. "It's been a long time since you called me. What can I do for you?"

"Doug, do you think you can use your shortwave to get a message to an airplane crossing near your station?"

"Hell yes. Since that bomb went off, it's about the only way you can communicate. Most of the airports closed down when the bomb cut out fifty percent of air traffic communication from the east. Just give me the call sign." The general reached for a thick book next to the radio. He keyed the mike and gave Doug the call sign.

The radio was silent for a full minute, and then the voice blasted in again. "This is Air Force One we're talking about?"

"Yes," General Weaver came back.

"What in the hell is going on?"

"I don't have time to explain all of it," the general said. "Let's just say that at least part of the bastards setting off the bombs are from the United States, and they're taking over the government and the military."

"Holly shit!" Doug came back. "What's the message?"

"Tell them to change their flight path." General Weaver stopped for a minute. "Damn it, if we put their destination out over the airwaves they'll pick it up." The general keyed the mike again. "Doug, how far out do you think the plane will be when they pick up your message?"

"I'm west of Kansas City," Doug came back. "I would say that it would be over Kansas City."

"Good, tell them when they see Kansas City, turn due north and drop down under the radar. You and I know that the other bastards will pick up the communication. Here's what we will do. Call me and let me know when they make the turn. We'll meet them with another plane before they get to Minneapolis and lead them in. Got it?"

"Got it," Doug came back.

General Weaver turned to his guests. "The satellite covering that area will be out of range in a few minutes. That should give Air Force One enough time to get away from those bastards before it can come back around again."

"But how will the other plane know where to meet the President's plane?" Dupre asked.

"Spotters," the general answered. "I'll call a few of my radio buddies on the plane's path and have them watch out for Air Force One. They'll use the radios as little as possible until the two planes connect. Then there will be total radio silence until they get here. Hopefully, we'll keep the plane away from the enemy until then."

"Where is here?" Alex asked.

"I believe that the airport at Peterborough has a runway long enough," General Weaver answered. "Go get some rest. I can take it from here. My housemaid will show you to your rooms. Don't worry, I'll wake you before anything happens. I have a few of my friends already here and I'm calling every military person I can get a hold of. I'll have this house full of people before you wake up."

Alex followed the maid to a large bedroom with a breathtaking view of the surrounding countryside and a king size bed. He took off his shoes and laid down for a second on the bed before undressing. That was the last thing he remembered.

Chapter 31

Heller and Keith were in the chow hall eating when a sergeant came up to them. "Sir, the general wants to see both of you." Keith wolfed down the last bit of food and fell in behind Heller. The sergeant led them back to the same conference room. General Taylor and most of the command were sitting at the table.

The general stood as they came through the door. "We have a problem," he said. "The President's plane didn't show up. We kept ten planes in the air until they had to return for refueling. We are just now getting refueling planes into the air so that they can stay up longer. Just before they were supposed to arrive at the intersect point, our radio people intercepted a shortwave message, instructing them to drop under the radar and turn north. We've sent more planes after them but so far, haven't had any luck. The satellite is out of range. It won't be back over the area for at least another hour."

"We have to destroy the government!" Heller shouted. He pounded a fist down on the table. "If they escape and are able to get some of the military behind them, it will be all over. We can't get the rest of the military to fight their own government. For this thing to work we have to establish complete control and to do that, the old government has to be destroyed. You have hundreds of planes damn it! Why can't you use one of your surveillance planes to find them?"

General Taylor faced Heller with a hard look. "By the time we could get one into that area, they'll be gone. It's not the only thing we have to worry about. There's been a lot of chatter on the shortwave bands. It seems that they have a command center somewhere in Canada. They're getting a network of retired military and reserves together and from the talk, they're trying to contact the people on the bases we control. I've restricted all calls coming into the bases and locked everything down, nobody in or out, hoping that will stop any contact with the personnel. Another thing, we can't get into the command center in Colorado. For some reason, our people weren't able to take over. They've already redirected another satellite to replace the one we blacked out. They must know something is going on, I mean more than the bombs going off."

"Can't we get enough military out there to take care of it?" Keith asked.

General Taylor pointed to a map. "It depends on what you mean by, 'take care of it'. The whole center is under a mountain. It's built to withstand a direct hit from a nuclear bomb. We can't move on it until we know that the military bases around that area are under our control, and so far we haven't heard from any of them."

"Then we're up shit creek!" Keith shouted. "Since we can't move on Colorado yet, I suggest we get our asses up to that command center in Canada and take it out. At least we can hold on to what we have." He nodded to Heller, and they both stormed out of the room.

Chapter 32

Alex woke with a start. Someone was knocking at the door. He slowly got up and looked around the strange room. It was dark outside. The only light came from a small lamp in the corner. He walked over to the lamp and looked at his watch. It was two o'clock, but then he didn't know what time zone they were in. Suddenly, everything came back to him—the bomb, the airplane, the general. He stumbled over his shoes as he walked toward the door. He still had his clothes on. "Yes?" he said, as he reached the door.

"General Weaver wants to see you in thirty minutes," the voice said.

"Okay, I'll be there," Alex answered through the door.

Alex could hear a knock on Meg's door as he headed for the shower. The bathroom was huge. He took a quick shower, letting the water run cold for a minute to wake up. He dried and looked in the mirror at the thick beard on his face. The bathroom had everything; razors, shaving cream, and even aftershave. After scraping off his beard, Alex dressed and hurried downstairs. He stopped at the top of the stairs in astonishment. The whole bottom floor of the house was full of people. Some were in military uniforms and others looked military, even though they were wearing civilian clothes. No one paid attention to him as he slowly walked down the stairs. He jumped at a hand on his shoulder.

"Just me," Dupre said from behind. "It looks like the general has a lot of friends."

"You can say that again." They both turned as Meg joined them.

"Who are they?" she asked.

"We don't know," Dupre answered. "But I believe we're going to find out soon."

General Weaver was heading toward them. "Did you get any rest?" he asked, smiling. "Let's get you something to eat. I've had my cooks working around the clock to feed this crowd." He led them to a table full of food in the dining area.

Alex was starving. He followed Meg around the table, piling his plate full of food. The general pointed to empty chairs against the log wall, and the three sat down. He pulled up a chair facing them.

"Go on," General Weaver said, as they began to put their plates down. "I'll talk while you eat. The first thing I have to tell you is that the President and half of the United States Congress are safe. They landed at Peterborough hours ago. From there, they were picked up and taken to a safe place. They have gotten together with what is left of our government and agreed that both will work together as one until this thing is over."

"Why didn't you bring them here?" Dupre asked.

"I've had several shortwave radios going around the clock, and we've been able to get out over some cellular phones. We've been talking for hours now to military bases, friends, state governments, and anyone else who would listen. You were right. They are taking over military bases, but we stopped them cold at several important bases, and the word is out. A few more bases, and we'll have control back. Then we'll take back the broadcasting stations one at a time until we have full control of the airwaves again. The sooner the people from our two countries know that most of our government survived, the sooner we can start taking back our countries.

"Now back to why we didn't bring them here. The other side must be picking up our radio activity and will know what we're trying to do. It would be in their best interest to take us out." The general saw the look on Meg's face. "Don't worry. We haven't been sitting on our hands here. The woods around this place are full of commandos, and we have countless ground-to-air missiles. If we are attacked, I want you to go to the war room in the basement. Someone will be there to show you a tunnel, which comes out on the other side of the mountain. When you arrive at the other end, my people will take you to safety."

Alex stopped eating and slowly set his plate down. "I don't want to run," he said softly. "I take it you are going to defend the place?"

"That is correct," General Weaver answered. "I just didn't want to place you in harm's way. After all, you did your part when you uncovered these bastards and saved your President's life."

"I don't mean to cut in," Dupre said, "but you keep saying 'our' two governments. How many of the Canadian Parliament got out?"

"Oh! I'm so sorry," the general said. "I completely forgot to tell you. Your warning was in time and over half of the Parliament escaped before the bomb went off. I'm sorry to say, quite a few were killed."

The three had finished eating and Alex stood. "General, if you will give me a gun and tell me where you want me?"

"I'm staying with Alex," Dupre stated.

"Me, too," Meg joined in.

General Weaver looked at them for a long moment and suddenly laughed. "I was hoping that you would say that. We need every man and woman we can get." He threw up his hand at a tall man in a military uniform. "Captain, would you arm these people and show them where you want them." The general turned back to them. "Good luck," he said gravely.

Chapter 33

Keith checked his side arm as he watched the helicopters drift out of the darkness like giant dragonflies to settle softly onto the concrete runway. He watched Heller with the general and a group of military leaders. He and Heller were suppose to be equal in all of this, but they hadn't even invited him over. Keith knew why they were going on this mission. It was to fix the damn mess they were in.

He and Heller, along with countless others, had spent the past ten to fifteen years, digging up all of the dirt on government and military leaders, driving them out of office, making sure that they would be replaced by the right people. What did the rest of these assholes do except step over to the other side?

Keith turned and walked slowly to the first helicopter. He wondered how many people they would have to kill. Their best guess was that the President and Congress were at the Canadian command center. Some of their own people were probably there, too. Only he and Heller knew who they were, and that information could be very useful when they got there. He felt resentment rip through him as he watched the ease with which Heller handled the people around him. He should be the one out there taking charge, giving orders.

Heller left the group and ran toward Keith. "Ready?" he asked.

"It's been a long time since I've gone on something like this," Keith replied, trying to hide his emotions.

"Don't worry," Heller said. "It's like riding a bicycle. We'll be on the fourth helicopter going in. These are top trained soldiers from Fort Benning. It shouldn't take them over an hour to take these amateurs. We'll be back in time for lunch."

"Where do these men think they're going? Are you sure they'll fight against some of their own countrymen?"

"According to the general, they believe that they're going there to wipe out the terrorists that set off the bomb. They are trained not to listen to any propaganda when in combat. They will close their mind to anything the people at the control center have to say."

The captain in charge of their helicopter shouted and waved at them. It was time. Keith followed Heller to the helicopter and slid into a bench-like seat. The other soldiers looked straight ahead. The whomp-whomp of the blades changed to a roar, and the helicopter slowly lifted into the night air. Keith felt his stomach draw into a knot as he leaned back against the webbing. He wasn't supposed to do this. He should be somewhere else, living like a king, basking in the glory of command.

The hours droned by. Keith looked up as the shadowy figure of the captain suddenly stood in front of them. "Men, we are five miles northeast of our target. Put your infrared goggles on and get ready to repel down."

My God! Keith thought. *I don't know how. I can't swing out the door and slide down some fucking rope.* He turned to Heller, but Heller had stood and moved toward the door.

"Three minutes!" the captain shouted.

Suddenly, the sky lit up as a helicopter next to them exploded. The helicopter they were in shook and fell away to one side as the hot air blast hit them.

"They have ground-to-air missiles!" the captain shouted as another helicopter disappeared in a ball of flame. "Land! Land!"

"There's no clear spot, Captain!" one of the pilots shouted back, sticking his head out of the cockpit. "The only open place is next to the house and that is where most of the firepower is coming from."

The helicopter shook again as another missile exploded. "I don't care if it's on top of the house!" the captain shouted. "We're getting killed up here!"

The helicopter made a sudden turn and dropped like a bullet for the earth. Keith leaned forward and threw up on the floor. No one noticed.

Chapter 34

Alex, Meg, and Dupre were led to a stone wall on the east side of the house. Alex leaned the M-16 against the wall and sat down. He leaned back against the stone wall and looked up at the moonlit sky. The moon was almost touching the curvature of the earth. It was getting close to the start of another day. He could feel Meg lean toward him.

"Alex," she said softly. "Do you mind if I ask you something personal?"

"No, go ahead."

"Do you remember when we were in jail and I said that I wished I could have had a father like you?"

Alex was silent for a moment. A warm feeling began to wash through him. It was the first emotion he had felt in a long while. "Yes, I remember," he answered.

"Well, do you think if we ever get out of this, you might . . . I mean."

Alex could feel the tremble in her voice. He reached out and put his arm across her shoulders. "Yes I could," he said gently. " I would be very proud to call you my daughter." He felt tears brimming and turned his head.

Meg cried softly and kissed him on the cheek.

"Well now," Dupre said from the darkness. "I could be a godfather."

They all laughed and then one by one, they fell silent as they thought about the coming day.

* * *

Alex could hear the helicopters long before they arrived. He picked up the M-16 and turned toward the sound. Suddenly, the roar of missiles filled the air and exploding balls of flame fell from the sky. It seemed that nothing could get through the barrage of missiles, but dark shapes were dropping out of the darkness to land in the shadows. The sound of small arms fire sounded below and then blinding light turned the fields into daylight. Dozens of men in military camouflage were caught in the open. They were pouring out of the few remaining helicopters and running toward the house. Alex realized with horror that they were American soldiers. Bullets ripped into the stone wall. How could he kill his own countrymen—but they were trying to kill him. He had no choice. The dark shapes were getting closer. Alex aimed low, cutting the legs out from under the first soldier he saw. The dark figures began to fall by the dozens as gun fire cut into them from both sides. The gunfire slowed and then stopped. Only a few soldiers were left standing. The rest were unmoving dark mounds. As suddenly as it had started, it was over. Pockets of soldiers still fired their weapons, but most of them were giving up.

Alex turned in surprise as Dupre ran forward shouting. "Heller! It's Heller!"

Two lone figures were running toward one of the helicopters. The helicopter blades were turning. The two shapes dove into the helicopter and it took off, tilting its fuselage toward the darker side of the mountain. Dupre stopped and shook his fist at the disappearing helicopter.

Alex felt drained as he walked slowly back to the general's house. He didn't want to look at the field. The sight of the dead American soldiers sickened him. Everyone there must have felt the same way because silence hung like a heavy weight. The general was motioning to him, so Alex changed directions. General Weaver had a group of men with him.

"Alex, do you know what this Heller looks like? The one that was with the attackers."

"No, sir," Alex answered. He turned to look for Dupre. "I saw him briefly at the battle, but Dupre was held captive by Heller and knows him a lot better than I." Dupre walked up as he finished. The general turned to Dupre.

"Yes," Dupre answered. "I probably know him better than anyone here."

General Weaver hesitated. "I hate to ask you, but we really need your help. There are two helicopters down there that can fly. We want to use them to follow their helicopters back. We have to catch up to them and become a part of the returning force. They won't be expecting us to do that." The general paused and looked out over the battlefield. There was a sick look in his eyes when he turned back.

"We know that most of the military at Dover aren't terrorists. They believe that they're fighting on the right side. If we can isolate Heller and the others, we can present our side to the other military men and try to get them to join our side. Heller will be sticking close to the other terrorist leaders. They have to be located and taken out. That's why we need you, because Heller seems to be one of the terrorist leaders and you know what he looks like. I want the two of you to go with the first strike force and pick him out for us.

"We have the helicopter pilots here, and we have a supply of uniforms on the field. If we can get the helicopters in the air quickly, we can fall in right behind them. We got their call signs from one of their wounded. We can radio a message to them that we made it off, but that we have a lot of wounded."

"What happens when we land?" Dupre asked.

"The uniforms will be bloody. When you land, they'll think that you are wounded soldiers coming in and rush you to the base hospital. We're hoping that no one will think to look too close. Once you're in the hospital, you'll put the staff to sleep with a special gas that we'll supply. You will then move from the hospital to the headquarters building. The terrorists should be there. You'll take over the building and hold it until we arrive."

"General, how do you know the base is Dover?"

"One of the wounded soldiers told us," General Weaver replied. "The soldier is begging to go back with us because he knows now that we're not the bad guys, but I'm afraid that his wounds won't allow him to do so. From what we can gather, the commands are coming from six men: four generals, Heller and Barlow, who seems to be Heller's second in command. If you can capture or take out these six men, we can turn Dover AFB back over to our side and you'll save thousands, maybe millions of lives."

"Dover is a big base, General," Alex said. "Where are you going to get enough men for the job? You were able to surprise them here. That won't work at Dover. As soon as we move in they'll know that you'll be right behind."

General Weaver grinned. "We won't need many men. In fact, we'll only need one."

"The President of the United States," Dupre finished softly for him.

"That's right," the general said. "Once the soldiers and airmen on Dover see and hear the President, the whole thing will be over. Without the head, the snake will die."

"Won't that be putting the President in danger?" Dupre asked.

"We've already thought about that. The first helicopter in will have loudspeakers. The President will broadcast from another helicopter, well out of harms way, until the base is secure."

"Please, General, can I go?" Meg asked. " I saw a medic uniform. It would be more realistic to have at least one woman."

General Weaver looked at Alex and Dupre. Both of them nodded their head. Meg had been in this from the start.

Uniforms were shoved into their hands, and they ran toward the house. In five minutes, they were ready to go. Alex grabbed a pistol as he ran out of the door. The two helicopters were waiting with engines already running. Alex slid in next to Dupre and Meg. A soldier was going down the line, marking everyone's face with black grease. Alex looked up and down the interior of the helicopter. With the grease on their faces, they looked just like the soldiers they were replacing. With a soft roar, the helicopter lifted into the dark skies.

* * *

Someone was shouting at them, explaining the mission. They would be at Dover AFB in less than forty minutes. Alex looked forward to meeting the bastards that had ordered Jan's death. He eased the pistol out and checked the clip. It was full. He slid the gun back into his front pocket and looked around. Half of the soldiers carried rifles. Others didn't have a weapon. They were like Alex, playing the wounded, but everyone had two canisters of gas and a sidearm hidden away.

Alex leaned back against the webbing and closed his eyes. Jan's face swam into view. Her smile was sad. He remembered how she hated violence. Guilt suddenly swept through him at the thoughts in his head. "Forgive me, my darling," he whispered.

Chapter 35

Keith held his hands together to stop the shaking. One of the wounded soldiers screamed. Only four had made it into the helicopter with Heller and himself. He wondered how many more made it out. Cold wind was blowing in through the open helicopter door. He thought about getting up and closing it but then thought, to hell with it.

Heller was screaming at the top of his lungs. "How in the hell did this happen? The best men we could get, and they beat us like we were school kids."

"We underestimated them," Keith answered. "We should have come in through the trees."

"And how in the hell could we do that!" Heller screamed at him. "The field was the only place to land."

The pilot stuck his head back from the cockpit. "Sir," he said. "Two more of our helicopters made it out, but there are a lot of wounded."

Heller slumped down into the seat. "Damn it, damn it all to hell! We'll have to go back to the base and regroup. We'll send in twice as many men this time."

"Do you mean we're going in again?" Keith asked, horrified.

"We have to," Heller replied. "If we don't, everything will be lost."

"But what about the other countries? We could leave here and join one of them."

"We cut ourselves off from most of the others when we killed Anton," Heller replied. "Besides, we won't know for another day or two how successful they were. Don't you understand? Even if they are successful, without the military power of the United States, it will never hold up. We have no other choice except to take out the government here. They're already broadcasting all over the damn place. We have to destroy them or they will turn the military against us, and we will be lined up and shot like the traitors we are."

"Not so loud," Keith warned, pointing to the wounded soldiers.

Keith could see the landing lights of Dover ahead. They would be on the ground in minutes. Heller was silent. Keith dreaded going back into the horror of battle again, but deep down inside he knew that it was the only way.

Heller went to the cockpit to talk with the tower. He wanted another attack force ready to go within the hour. Keith could hear him shouting at one of the generals. He jumped from the helicopter as soon as it landed and followed the running Heller toward headquarters.

They burst into a war room bristling with activity. General Taylor turned toward them. His lips were grim with anger. He didn't say a word but motioned them into the conference room. The other three generals stayed in the war room.

"What in the hell happened up there?" he shouted.

"They were waiting for us!" Heller shouted back. "They had ground-to-air missiles. They tore us to pieces before we could land, and after we landed, they had the field of fire. That's what happened."

The general slammed his fist down on the table. "The few bases we had west of Chicago have been taken back from the inside. It seems that the command post you were suppose to take out have been filling the airways with the news about the President and about us."

Heller ran his hand through his hair. "Are we still in control of the bases here on the east coast?"

"Yes," General Taylor replied. "But we won't have them for long if this keeps up."

"Put a bombing mission together. Go in with the bombers first and follow it up with the fighters. After that, we'll go in again to clean up. Have everything ready to go in two hours."

"How many men did you bring back with you?" the general asked.

"Just the ones in the helicopter we were in and in two more behind us. They should be coming in about now, but I believe most of them are wounded."

"I'll call Fort Brag to fly up more men. Our bombers will be ready to go within the hour. The men from Fort Brag should be here by that time."

Keith leaned back in the chair. He was dead tired. He should eat, but the bitter taste of bile was making him sick. He wished to God that he could undo this and go back to the way it was. He had a cold empty feeling that he could be living the last week of his life.

Chapter 36

Dupre punched Alex in the arm and pointed forward through the opening between the pilot and copilot seats. The lights of Dover showed ahead. He could hear the pilot shouting into the mike that he was bringing wounded in and to have ambulances ready.

Alex watched the field as the pilot circled to find the He-lo pads. He drew back at every flash of light expecting to see missiles climbing toward them. Then they were under the radar and Alex sat up in the seat as the helicopter dropped toward the concrete below. He looked over at Meg. She had a firm set to her lips and was staring straight ahead. Alex prayed that nothing would happen to her. He felt the helicopter bounce once and settle to the ground. The flashing lights and blaring sirens blasted at him as he leaned over to begin the acting job of a wounded soldier.

Suddenly, he felt Meg with her arm around him shouting at the ambulance attendants. "He's shot in the chest!" she screamed, as she dragged him to the waiting ambulance. She helped the attendant lay Alex on one of the stretchers and hurried back to help Dupre onto the one beside him. When the ambulance was full and the doors shut, it sped away. The attendant reached down to strip Alex's shirt off but looked up in surprise as Meg moved against him. He didn't know what hit him as he breathed in the gas and sank softly to the floor. Alex and Dupre jumped to their feet.

Alex looked through the back window. "We're almost there," he said. "Get ready. Remember to hold your breath. The gas is heavier than air but hold your breath each time until it has a chance to settle."

The truck stopped and started backing up. It came to a stop and the back doors sprang open. The driver stood aside as two attendants came through the double doors of the hospital, pushing a gurney toward the van. Alex reached out and sprayed the driver, remembering to hold his breath, and jumped over the falling body to the two hospital attendants. Meg and Dupre were right behind him. The attendants never knew what hit them.

"Quick, get their jackets," Alex ordered. They stripped the jackets from the men and put them on as they ran to the back of the hospital. Alex looked inside through the double doors and could see three more attendants running toward the back. He motioned Dupre and Meg to the side and stood there in front of the doors as two men and one woman rushed out. They didn't have much time. Another ambulance was already rounding the corner of the hospital. The three attendants stopped, confused by the lone man in front of them. Alex shoved the spray can into the face of the biggest one and turned, but Meg and Dupre already had the other two. The three attendants fell to the floor without a sound. They turned as one and ran toward the second ambulance. It was already backing toward the next parking place. He took a deep breath and flattened himself against the first ambulance.

The second ambulance came to a stop. Alex ran forward as the driver opened his door, forgetting about the rear view mirror. The driver saw Alex and slammed the door outward just as he reached it. Alex was falling backward as the driver dove out of the door. He grunted as he hit the hard concrete with the driver on top of him. His wind was knocked out, he couldn't breathe. The man held the wrist with the can and was bringing it down toward his face. Alex was too weak from lack of air. He couldn't stop him. Suddenly, the man collapsed, and Alex could see Meg's grinning face. She reached down and helped him to his feet. He leaned over for a minute to collect his breath and then ran to help with the rest of the ambulances.

Twenty minutes later, the fourteen man team stood outside the hospital. The sleeping attendants and drivers were in two of the ambulances. They had to move now. The hospital staff would be wondering why none of the wounded soldiers were coming in.

"Stay together until we get there," the major in charge whispered. "First, we'll take out the guards. I've been to this base before. The war room at headquarters has two entrances. Seven of us will come in at each entrance. Take the guard's weapons. We may need them."

They ran together toward the headquarters building. They were shadows in the early morning light. No one saw them.

Alex could hear the heavy breathing of Dupre as they came to rest against the building. There was heavy fog over the base. He could make out the dim figures of two guards at the front entrance. Two of the major's men moved forward and, seconds later, two darker shadows merged with the guards and the first shadows disappeared. A shadow stepped out from the building and motioned them forward, continuing on around to the back. They had two more guards to take care of. Alex hoped that they hadn't killed the soldiers—they were only following orders.

The twelve waited until they saw one of the men wave to them from the other end of the building, and then five split off and ran to join them. The rest paused at the outside doors while the major slowly pushed them open. After looking inside, he motioned for the others to move forward. Alex couldn't see the other end of the hallway, but this end seemed clean. He pushed Meg behind and followed Dupre. The men ahead advanced slowly, covering every doorway with their rifles. Alex couldn't see the others yet, but he knew that they were coming in from the other end of the building.

Alex jumped as gunfire broke the silence, but he couldn't see the flashes. Their other half had already engaged. The major ran forward with the others on his heels. A man ran through the doors at the end of the hallway and shouted when he saw them. He was too far for the canisters and Alex was the only one with a silencer. The major turned to shout at him, but Alex had already brought the gun out and with one fluid motion, shot the man in the chest. The major grinned at him.

There was more gunfire on the other side of the double doors. They ran over the dead man's body and threw themselves at the doors. The space on the other side was a war room. There were at least twenty men in the room and most of them had a weapon. Their comrades had thrown a table over and were in a gunfight with the group just in front of Alex.

Alex and the others dove for cover. He grabbed Meg's jacket and pushed her down behind a filing cabinet. Dupre went the other way. Everything was like a slow-moving motion picture. A general had his hand out, pointing at them and shouting at his men, but before they could do anything, Alex rushed him. He felt others with him, but his full attention was on the general. Bullets plowed into the floor at his feet. Alex ducked under a rifle and tried to spray a man with the canister—it was out of gas. He threw it to the floor and drew the pistol. He heard gunfire behind him and saw the general grab his shoulder. A pistol hit the floor and bounced. Meg had saved his life. The rest of the team was moving in from the other side. Another terrorist fell. Two generals stood with their hands high. Alex looked around for Heller, but he couldn't see him anywhere.

The major was shouting at his men to drag a desk over to the doors. The gunfire would wake everyone on base. They would be there in minutes.

Alex and Dupre searched the room.

"They aren't here," Dupre said. "The bastards got away."

Alex grabbed one of the generals by a wounded arm. The general screamed. "Where are Heller and Barlow?" he shouted.

"Go to hell," the general said.

Alex saw a door leading to another room. He and Dupre ran to each side of the door. Alex nodded his head and opened the door. They both rolled through and came to their feet. The room was empty. Alex started to leave when Dupre motioned overhead. A two-foot ceiling tile was missing.

Before he could stop her, Meg ran down the hall, shouting back at them, "I'm going to check outside!"

Alex tripped and fell as he tried to run after her. The military on the base would be all over the building in minutes. Together, he and Dupre followed Meg down the hallway and saw her disappear through the doors at the other end. In seconds, they were through the doors and outside but Meg was nowhere in sight.

They heard tires squealing and ran toward the sound, rounding the corner just in time to see a van speeding toward the runway.

Alex ran toward a line of vehicles when suddenly, bullets hit the pavement around them. Two half-trucks full of soldiers were heading straight for them. Alex looked around frantically for Meg. She was nowhere in sight. Fear struck through his heart. She had to be in the van, but Alex and Dupre had no choice. The soldiers were too close. They ran for the safety of the headquarters building.

They were halfway down the hallway when Alex heard the sound of something hitting the floor behind them. They dove over the desk blocking the door just as the dull thump of gas grenades went off behind them. It was tear gas. They would rush in behind the gas. The major was already yelling as another canister, spewing gas, rolled down the hallway. A gas mask and a M-16 were pushed into Alex's hands. He pulled the mask on just as more tear gas grenades went off. He felt the M-16 bucking in his hands as he sprayed the hallway, aiming low. Cries of pain and frustration came back through the cloud of gas. A quietness settled over the hallway. The major pulled Alex and Dupre back. They had found fans. The gas was blowing back the other way. The major was shouting.

"We've contacted the President's party. They're coming in. They're already broadcasting the President's voice and talking to the control tower. So far the tower doesn't know what to believe. Without orders coming from any of their leaders, the whole base is in confusion."

"Good," Alex said. "How soon can we get out of here? Our friend has been taken by some of the bastards that started this."

"It shouldn't be long," the major answered.

Alex could hear the faint sound of loudspeakers. The sound got louder and closer. The minutes passed as they waited. The hallway was still quiet. The gas slowly cleared, and then they could see that the whole hallway was empty. They slid the desk back and advanced slowly toward the open doors. There was no sign of the attacking men. The major held up his hands at the doorway. A dozen military men stood outside with their heads turned toward a helicopter hovering slowly in the morning sky. The men paid no attention to the men behind them. They were in shock.

The loudspeakers blasted down at the men below. "This is the President of the United States speaking. I have with me the Speaker of the House and the Secretary of Defense. You have been following the orders of terrorists who have taken over command of your base. The men who have taken over your headquarters building are soldiers for the United States of America. Please cease all hostilities."

Another voice came over the speakers. "Men, I am the Secretary of Defense and I am here with your supreme commander. I want all officers to meet in front of the control tower now." The helicopter turned and the President's helicopter fell from the skies to take its place. Seconds later, the second helicopter landed in front of the control tower. Three more helicopters appeared from nowhere to hover over the grounded helicopter. Some of the military personnel were running toward the grounded helicopter while others wandered around in confusion and then slowly at first and then faster and faster, more men started to stream toward the President's helicopter. Alex and Dupre could hear the President speaking to the hundreds of soldiers as they ran for the nearest vehicle.

The President's voice was blasting away at the soldiers. "We have ten bases across the United States that have been taken over by the terrorist. We need a new command structure now. I am putting the Secretary of Defense in charge until we have a chance to pick someone else to replace those who would take over our government. I want all officers to step to the front." A line started to form in front of the helicopter and the Secretary stepped out.

Alex found an air force truck with a full tank of gas. He jumped into the driver's side and turned the key. Alex gave a sigh of relief as the engine purred to life. Dupre was already in the passenger seat. The Secretary's voice faded as they headed for the west gate. There was no guard at the gate. "Which way?" Alex asked.

"They will head north. There's no way they would go back toward the bomb." Dupre had opened the glove box and pulled out a map. "Here we go. Turn right at the next road. We need to get to highway 13. That's the way I would go."

Fifteen minutes later, they were on the ramp above highway 13. Alex looked out on a sea of abandoned vehicles. They were still fleeing from the effects of the bomb this far north. Tracks of vehicles, taking to the grass, wove in and out between cars in the medium and to both sides of the expressway. Alex could see one vehicle moving in the distance but no sign of the van. His heart sank. Maybe they had come the wrong way.

Alex turned to Dupre. "Which way do we go? We can see for miles and they couldn't have gotten far in this mess."

Dupre hesitated for a second. "We have to go back to the base and try to talk the command out of a helicopter. It's the only way we can find them."

Alex swung the truck wide and pushed the gas pedal to the floor. Dupre shouted at him as the truck slid sideways at the gate leading into the base. "Slow down!" he yelled. "We won't do Meg any good if we're dead."

Alex headed straight for the President's helicopter. Groups of men were spreading out, running toward different parts of the base. Alex saw the major to one side. He knew that the major wasn't in the United States military. He was a Canadian officer, but Alex hoped that he had some pull. The major turned toward them as they stopped and jumped out of the truck.

"We did it!" he yelled. "We did it!" The laughter died on his lips when he saw the look on Alex's face. "What's the matter?" He asked.

"They have Meg," Alex, said out of breath. "We need your help to get a helicopter."

"Come on!" the major shouted and started running toward the President's helicopter.

Alex and Dupre stood back as the major talked to a few of the officers and then to the Secretary. Minutes later, he came back with a young lieutenant and a smile on his face. "You have a helicopter, and this is your pilot, Lieutenant Tom Jackson."

After thanking the major, Alex turned to the young pilot. "Where is your helicopter?

"It's imperative that we get into the air right away."

"Follow me," the lieutenant said and ran toward the other side of the tower where a line of helicopters set in line. He motioned the others into a helicopter and jumped into the pilot's seat. He began to flip switches and the helicopter blades started to turn slowly. Alex checked his M-16. It had a full clip. Harris's pistol was in his pocket along with four extra clips. Finally, the helicopter blades began to turn faster, and a few minutes later the Apache helicopter lifted into the air. The nose tilted west and in seconds they were back over highway 13.

"Which way?" the lieutenant shouted back.

"Let's try north first and then we'll search south. We'll leave east and west for later," Alex answered.

The helicopter skimmed over the sea of vehicles. There were few people. Most had left their vehicles and walked out. The only thing moving were a few four-wheel drive vehicles and trucks. Ten miles up the road, Alex began to notice a few people walking on both sides of the road. The people waved at them, trying to get them to land. Alex knew that they probably needed food and water, but they couldn't stop now. They had to find Meg.

Another ten miles and still no sign of the van. People crowded both sides of the road. They waved and shouted at the helicopter. There was no way that the van could have made it this far. Alex tapped the lieutenant on the shoulder. "Let's try the other way."

The lieutenant made a climbing turn and headed south. He stayed high over the country side below until they reached Dover and then came down low over Hwy. 13 again. Washington was to their west. Alex began to see some of the effects of the bomb. Dead bodies lay on both sides of the road. They covered ten miles and then twenty. More bodies lined the road. Alex drew his arms tight to stop the shiver running through him. He could almost see the bomb's blast as it swept out from the center. Everything inside a radius of seven miles would have been totally destroyed. At a radius of eleven miles, only forty percent of the people would have survived. Most of those would die in twenty-four hours from the massive radiation. Alex realized that he was looking at some of them. All of the survivors outside of the eleven-mile radius would be fleeing for their lives. Hundreds of them would be sick from the radiation and would probably die in days or weeks. Some of the stronger ones would last for months.

The helicopter swung to the east and began to climb. "Need to get above the radiation!" the lieutenant shouted. "The weather has the jet stream coming directly from the west. It's carrying the radiation east."

Alex looked to the west but couldn't see anything. A huge cloud of dust and black smoke hung over what must have been the Washington area. Nothing would be left of Washington and the area for miles around. It would be a dead zone for years to come. The helicopter began to drop toward the ground again.

"They couldn't have made it this far," Dupre said. "I suggest that we head north again. They may have heard or saw us coming and hid."

The lieutenant nodded his head and brought the helicopter around. He dropped closer to the road and slowed his speed.

The expressway below was jammed with vehicles. People were moving in a study stream toward the east. Alex saw a sea of white to one side. He pointed it out to the lieutenant, and the helicopter changed directions. Alex drew in a sharp breath as they got closer. The solid white turned into individual spots. It was tents, thousands of tents. People were moving like ants through the spaces between the tents. Alex motioned for the helicopter to land. There was a clear space just to the north of the encampment. The helicopter was still in the air, a few feet above the ground when Alex saw hundreds of people running toward them. He almost ordered the helicopter to take off again, but the lieutenant saw the people and dropped to the ground before they could get there. The landing jarred Alex's teeth. The mass of people surrounded the helicopter and began to cheer as they stepped out. A man in a white, blood-sprinkled shirt, stepped forward with his hand outstretched.

"Thank God," he said. "Someone has finally sent help." His eyes searched the helicopter with puzzlement. "Where are the supplies? Are they coming later?"

"We didn't bring any supplies, but when we're airborne again, we'll call someone to help," Dupre said.

"My name is Doctor Thomas. We need everything—medical supplies, food, water. We are boiling the water, but we don't know if it's contaminated with radiation. The boiling may not be doing any good but we don't have a choice. We have tried to call on our cellular phones, but no one answers. We've seen other military helicopters and tried to signal them, but they pay no attention. Dozens of people are dying here every hour."

Alex felt compassion for the man in front of him. Dr. Thomas's head was held high but his eyes were begging. Alex took his hand. "We'll get high enough to radio the base at Dover. We'll get help to you right away. I promise."

A young woman pushed to the front. She held a small girl in her arms. The little girl's eyes were closed, and her tiny face was a deathly white. "Please, mister, would you please fly my daughter to a hospital? Dr. Thomas can't do anything for her. She has less than an hour to live if she doesn't get to a hospital."

Alex glanced at Dr. Thomas. The doctor's eyes were diverted. What could he do? His drive and his need was to find Meg, but he knew that he couldn't turn this woman down. Dupre was nodding his head yes.

Alex grabbed the young woman's arm and led her under the whirling blades to the helicopter. Dupre was shouting something at him. Alex turned toward him. "I'm staying here," Dupre said as he got closer. "Maybe they passed this way. Somebody could have seen them. Pick me up on the way back." Alex was already pulling the seat belt around the woman's waist. She was crying and thanking him over and over again.

The lieutenant brought the helicopter up fast and tilted the nose toward Dover. He was on the radio as they climbed. An ambulance would be waiting and helicopters would be leaving within an hour to help the people they had just left. Minutes later, they were dropping toward the landing pads at Dover.

The base was a beehive of activity. An ambulance met them at the pad. The attendants took the little girl from the woman's arms. She turned briefly to hug Alex, and then they were gone.

Alex turned to tell the lieutenant to take off when a familiar voice shouted at him. It was the major. He stuck his head into the helicopter.

"Did you find them?"

"No," Alex answered. "We had to bring a little girl in. Have you heard anything?"

"Nothing," the major answered. "We're getting more and more bases over to our side. The terrorists are running like rats. Heller and Barlow will have to leave the USA. They won't have anywhere to go. They probably know that already. We were able to find Heller's records. He can fly a plane. There's an airfield on the southwest side of Washington, outside the bomb's destructive path in a little town called Manassas. We found a map at headquarters marked with that location. We believe Heller's headed there. He would have to swing around the radiation in Washington. The town is on highway 66." The major shoved the map into Alex's hand. "Good luck."

Alex grabbed the major's hand. "We'll see you later," he shouted and slid the helicopter door shut. The lieutenant took off and climbed toward the gray skies. Seconds later, the helicopter dipped its nose toward Washington. They had to pick up Dupre and swing south. Heller had to be there. Time was running out.

Chapter 37

Meg pushed herself back against the side door of the van. She tried to pull her shirt back together, but there was no button. The man sitting beside her had torn it when he'd dragged her into the van. She bit her bottom lip hard to keep from screaming, not at them, but at her own stupidity. Her own aggressive nature had gotten her into this, and now she was probably going to die.

She leaned over and tried to look out of the van window, but the one called Keith reached over and dragged her back into the seat.

"Sit still, or I'll tie you up and throw you into the back," he growled.

The one in the front had to be Heller. He was cussing and banging the wheel. Meg leaned back and closed her eyes. She took deep breaths and tried to calm her fear. At least they had stopped the bastards. She would die happy in that knowledge.

Keith leaned over the seat. "What are we going to do with her?"

"We might need her if they catch up to us," Heller said. "Oh shit," he shouted as the van slid to a stop.

They had stopped at the top of the ramp leading onto an expressway. Meg could see thousands of stalled cars as far as she could see. She turned to looked the other way. No one was going to travel either way in that mess. She breathed a sigh of relief. They couldn't go anywhere. Maybe Alex and Dupre would catch up to them. Meg had no doubt that her two friends were already after her. A calm feeling began to replace the paralyzing fear.

"What in the hell do we do now?" Keith asked.

Heller was already backing the van up. When he got to the top of the ramp, he headed west on the two lane road. There were cars all over the two lanes, but Heller managed to get around them until after five or six miles, they came to a cross road. Stalled cars and trucks were everywhere. Heller stopped the van and walked to the center of the road. Keith pushed Meg out of the van and followed. Both roads were completely blocked. There was no way to get the van through. The banks on either side were too steep for the van to go around. Heller climbed up on the top of a truck and looked west. He climbed back down. "We walk," he said simply and started out between the cars.

Keith pushed Meg to the front and pushed her again when she tried to look back. "Keep your damn eyes to the front!" he shouted.

Meg looked around as they threaded their way through the cars and trucks. An eerie quiet surrounded them. There was no life anywhere—no people, no dogs or cats, no birds. It was as if all life on earth was gone and they were the only ones left. She followed Heller as he walked on, mile after mile. The sun was covered by a gray overcast but it was still hot and like an oven in the thick military clothing. Soon, the clothing began to feel like a wet blanket. She kept her eyes down and her legs going. She got satisfaction in keeping well ahead of Keith. She grinned to herself every time they had to climb a hill, and she could hear his labored breathing. Heller kept up a steady pace. He seemed to be in good physical condition.

Heller had just topped a hill a hundred feet or so to the front, when he shouted and disappeared over the hill.

Meg increased her pace, leaving the slower Keith behind. He yelled at her to stop, but she kept going. Heller had stopped halfway down the other side of the hill beside a vehicle. It was a fairly new, green Chevrolet Blazer. Heller had the door open and was sitting inside when Meg got to the vehicle. She could smell an odor, like something decaying. Meg gave a sharp gasp when she saw the two dead people laying in the ditch beside the vehicle. Dried blood covered their faces, and a cloud of flies moved over them. Heller acted as if he didn't notice the bodies. He looked up at her, his eyes blazing. "The damn thing is out of gas."

Meg couldn't help herself. She grinned at him. The next thing she knew, she was sitting on the ground, and Heller was standing over her with a murderous look on his face. Keith arrived and grabbed Heller's arm as Heller swung another blow at her face. She had no doubt that the blow would have killed her.

"You said we might need her."

Heller jerked his arm away and went to the back of the Blazer. He opened the back and pulled a gas can out.

"Where are you going to get gas?" Keith asked.

"From the other damn vehicles," Heller said, pointing up the road to the line of stalled cars and trucks. Heller walked to the next vehicle and opened the hood. A knife flashed, and he pulled a long hose from the engine. Going to the gas tank, he loosened the gas cap and stuck the hose into the tank. Holding the hose almost to the ground, he leaned over and sucked on the hose. He spit as a stream of gas shot out onto the ground. He transferred the hose into the gas can and waited until it was full. Two hours later, and after many trips from the stalled cars to the Blazer, the gas tank was full.

The four-wheel drive made it easy to get around the road blocks, but they still couldn't make good time.

"We have to leave the country, but where can we go?" Keith asked. "When you killed Anton, you limited the countries that will take us."

"We're going to South America," Heller said softly, turning in the seat, his eyes shifting from Meg to Keith. Keith grew silent and leaned back in his seat.

Meg knew that Heller didn't care if she knew where they were going, and she also knew that the information would mean her death sooner than later. The second they didn't need her anymore, they would kill her. She stilled her mind for what was to come.

Chapter 38

Alex looked at the map the major had given him. The small town of Manassas was circled with a red marker. The helicopter swung to the east, and he could see the white of the tent city below. A tight knot of grief welled up in his stomach at the families torn apart by the destruction of the bomb. There were millions dead and hundreds of thousands would die in the coming weeks. Anger replaced the grief when he thought about the men they were after. No death they could suffer would begin to be enough.

The lieutenant was shouting something at him. "There's your friend!" he said, pointing.

A rush of affection went through Alex as he looked down at the small figure waving up at them. Dupre was trying to keep the people back as the helicopter settled to the ground. He turned and ran forward as the helicopter came to a rest. Alex opened the helicopter door and Dupre slid in. The doctor was right behind him with a question in his eyes.

"Help will be here within the hour!" Alex shouted at him.

"Thank God!" the doctor cried back, and a smile broke across his tired face.

Alex waved the doctor back and pulled the door closed.

"Have you found out anything?" Dupre asked.

"We think we know where they're going," Alex answered back and showed Dupre the map. The tent city became a white speck below as the lieutenant brought the helicopter up and tilted the nose south.

* * *

Thirty minutes later, the helicopter turned to the west. They began to see some of the bomb destruction on the south side of Washington. Nothing moved. It was a quiet place of death. The dust had settled, but a gray mist hung over the ground like a blanket, as if to cover the millions of dead. No one said anything as they passed by the mass destruction. Alex took a deep breath and tried not to scream at the devils that would do something like this. He knew that this was only one of the many bombs that had gone off. It would take years for the earth to recover. The bright sun glared at them, and he turned his head to the west, to the fulfillment of his revenge.

* * *

The gray mist was behind them when the helicopter began to lose attitude. Alex leaned forward and looked through the window as the tiny specks turned into buildings, and then he could see cars moving on the highway. There was no sign of the bomb here. If it hadn't been for what he had seen only an hour ago, Alex could almost believe that everything was normal, that all of the horror was only a bad dream.

The helicopter dropped even lower as the lieutenant began to search for the airport. He had been talking into his microphone, and after several changes of directions, they hovered over a small airport. The helicopter settled slowly to the concrete. Alex could see a truck with flashing lights headed toward them. He slid back the door and stepped out.

The truck came to a stop and a thin man in coveralls got out of the passenger side and walked slowly toward them. "Where are you folks from?" he asked as he got closer.

"From Dover AFB, on the other side of Washington."

Disbelief spread over the man's face. He turned back to the driver who was coming up from the other side. "Did you hear that?" the thin man said. "They're from the other side. There are people alive over there." He turned back to Alex. "We heard that the bomb killed almost everyone on the east side of Washington, and the ones it didn't kill, died from radiation." He looked close at Alex. "You look all right."

"We're fine," Alex replied. "Please, have you seen two men and a woman arriving here sometime in the last few hours and has a plane taken off during that time?"

"No strangers have been here all day and no one has taken off that we know of," the thin man answered.

Alex turned to Dupre and the lieutenant. "Is it possible that they're still on their way here?"

"It's more than possible," Dupre answered. "We had the helicopter. They had to come over land. Probably they would go around Washington to the north and then head south on the west side back down to here. With all of the traffic jams, they probably won't get here for hours."

The lieutenant ran back to the helicopter and brought the map back. "They would go west from Dover until they could cross the bay," Dupre said.

"There's no way they could go south from there," Alex added, tracing his finger along the map. "It would be too close to the bomb path. They would have to take highway 301 north to 70 and from there go west to highway 15 and then south to here."

"I know this area," the lieutenant said. "That's a good 200 miles. At the speed they will be going there's no way they could be to highway 15 yet."

"I agree," Alex said. "I think we should take off and intercept them where highway 15 intersects with highway 70." They grabbed the map and ran for the helicopter. The two men were yelling something at them, but they paid no attention. The men they were after wouldn't hang onto Meg long. Alex prayed that they would be in time.

Chapter 39

Meg drew a deep breath in horror as they left the long bridge over the bay and turned north on highway 301. Dead people were everywhere—hanging out of their cars, laying on the side of the road, mothers with little children in their arms. Suddenly, a breeze of foul air blew over her face. Keith had rolled down the window on his side.

"You crazy fool," Heller yelled from the front. "Do you want to contaminate all of us?"

In his hurry to hit the window button, Keith rolled the window further down. Heller turned in the driver's seat. "If you roll down one more window, I swear that I will shoot you." A gun had suddenly appeared in his hand.

Keith quickly rolled the windows back up. "I didn't think about the contamination," he mumbled to himself.

Even though the windows were closed, the foul smell of the air still lingered in the car. Meg could picture the radiation spreading through her with every breath. She tried to breathe small breaths, holding them as long as she could. She looked through the front window, trying to see any clear area ahead, any place that they could get out of this destruction, where they could roll the windows back down to flush out the smell of death.

An hour later, they began to see live people on the sides of the road. The traffic had stopped. Most of the people were out of their cars, walking down both sides of the road. Heller left the road behind and headed west through the fields and pastures. Finally, they ran across a dirt road going in the right direction. They followed it for miles until they saw the expressway in the distance. As they got closer, they could see moving cars and a fence. They followed the fence until they came to an intersection. Turning right and then left, Heller made his way to the ramp on the other side. The traffic below was moving, but Meg could see hundreds of vehicles blocking most of the four lanes. The traffic was weaving in and out between the stalled cars. With the advantage of the four wheel drive, they began to make fairly good time.

Meg rolled down both back windows, and the foul air seemed to be leaving the car. The traffic was getting better since they had left the northern part of Washington behind. She was thrown to the side against Keith as Heller took a ramp and headed into the sun. Meg could see a sign to highway 70. She wondered where they were going. She leaned back in despair. Alex and Dupre would never find her now. Either these men would kill her or take her with them. She had no doubt that they were planning to leave the country. She had to get away. So far they had been watching her like a hawk, but as time went by, they would let their guard down and she had to be ready to act, even if it meant her death. She had no choice.

Chapter 40

Alex looked out of the helicopter window as they skimmed over the countryside below. Everything here looked normal. He turned to the front as the helicopter began to lose altitude. The thread that was the highway became wider.

"We're almost there," the lieutenant said. "How do we find out which car they're in?"

Alex looked down at the highway below. The traffic was light. He could see the intersection of highway 70 just ahead. To the west was a small stand of trees.

"Do you have field glasses and a radio?"

"Sure, they're in the back." The lieutenant pointed to the area.

Alex retrieved the glasses and the radio. "You two land on the other side of those trees and wait for my call. I'll scan all of the vehicles coming off the ramp and heading south. When I see them, I'll call and you can pick me up."

"I'll go with you," Dupre said.

"It would really be better if I'm alone," Alex answered. "They would be less likely to see only one of us."

Dupre nodded his head. "You have to promise that you'll call as soon as you see them."

"I will," Alex promised. The ground was only twenty feet under them now, and then it was only four. Alex hopped to the ground.

"Wait!" the lieutenant shouted over the helicopter noise. "Take this." He shoved a M-16 into Alex's hands. Alex stood watching as the helicopter lifted and disappeared behind the trees. He ran to a small ditch with tall grass on both sides and laid down, facing the ramp from highway 70.

Alex laid there for what seemed like hours, checking all the vehicles coming off the ramp. He had never gotten a really good look at the two men. Maybe he should have let Dupre come with him. It was too late now. Several times, he almost shouted into the radio as he would spot two men in the front of a car or truck, only to discover that it wasn't them. He looked up at the sun. It was only a few hours until dark. What would he do then? He would never be able to make them out.

* * *

Alex looked up as a green Blazer came down the ramp. There was only one man in front. Alex lowered the glasses. As the Blazer got closer, he could see two more heads in the back. He brought the glasses back up and shouted. He could see Meg sitting in the back seat. He grabbed the radio and yelled into it. The Blazer had picked up speed. Alex shouted his frustration into the air. The helicopter would never get here in time.

Chapter 41

Meg moved closer to the door handle. She took a quick look at it, memorizing its position. She would have to make her move soon, and she would have only one chance to grab the handle and jump. She wondered what it would feel like to jump out of a car moving this fast. She probably wouldn't feel anything. She would be dead. She had to wait until the car slowed down. She couldn't jump when the car stopped. They would shoot her before she'd gotten ten feet. No, it would have to be while the car was moving, to give her enough head start before they could turn around. It would have to be close enough to cover—trees, bushes, a building—just something to put between herself and them. She glanced over at the one named Keith. His head was leaning back against the seat, and he had his eyes closed. Meg leaned forward in the seat. If only Heller would slow down, but she realized that she would need more than that. She would need more luck than she had ever had in her life. She moved her hand closer to the door handle just in case. Meg read a sign for an intersection ahead. She tensed when she saw the highway number. It was the same road Heller had mentioned only thirty minutes earlier. Another sign, for highway 15 flashed by. It was only one mile ahead. He would have to slow to make the off ramp. Heller was moving over to the left-hand lane, and then they were on the ramp. The car didn't slow. In fact, it seemed to move faster as if Heller had known what was on her mind. Meg was so deep into her plan, that she jumped when Heller shouted. They were already off the ramp and onto highway 15. Meg felt their speed increase.

"Keith, get your ass up! I saw something to the west!"

Keith sat up and leaned over. Meg tried to see, too.

"What is it?" Heller shouted, looking back over his shoulder.

Keith narrowed his eyes as the black spot got bigger. "It's a damn helicopter, and it's landing on the side of the road. Wait a minute. There's a man running toward the helicopter."

"Damn it to hell, they were waiting on us," Heller shouted. He swung the wheel hard to the right.

Meg held on for her life as the Blazer bounced high into the air and then settled back down as it left the road. There was a gap in the fence. Trees and a ditch loomed ahead, and Heller had to slow down. Keith had been thrown to the other side of the car. It would be her only chance. Meg threw the door open and hit the ground rolling. She could hear Heller shouting at Keith as she left the van. She came to her feet running, thanking God that she was in top shape. Thick trees were just ahead. She was going to make it. Suddenly, something slammed into her back and she stumbled and fell. She couldn't get up, but she could still crawl. The bushes were only a few feet away. It was so hard to move her arms and legs. Something else pushed into her again. Meg felt no pain, but she couldn't move anything now. She tried, but nothing seemed to work. She could hear the Blazer drive by, but she couldn't turn her head. Everything was frozen. Blackness began to settle in. Something brought her toward the light for a second. It was the sound of a helicopter. *Good,* she thought as she settled back into the blackness again. Alex and Dupre were coming for her. Everything would be all right.

Chapter 42

Alex watched the back of the vehicle and then turned as he heard the helicopter coming in. He ran toward the open door and swung into the dark interior. Dupre grabbed him as the helicopter shot toward the sky and headed south down highway 15. The Blazer was nowhere in sight. Alex grabbed the field glasses and moving to the open door, began to sweep them back and forth. He spotted something on the ground and swung the glasses back. It was a form, a human form. Alex reached for the lieutenant's shoulder. "There, check that out!" he shouted, pointing to the disappearing form.

The helicopter made a wide turn and began to lose altitude. The body was a good two hundred yards off the road. Alex drew in a sharp breath as they got closer. He could see the long hair fanning out onto the green grass. He raised his hands in anguish. It was Meg. She wasn't moving. Alex prayed that she was all right. Some sixth sense warned him as they dropped closer to the ground. Dupre was shouting something at him and then the words began to register.

"There's a reflection in the trees!" he was shouting.

Alex felt the helicopter start back up, and then the windshield shattered. The helicopter tilted to the side and dropped swiftly toward the ground. Dupre was shouting at him and climbing into the front of the helicopter. The lieutenant was hit. Dupre was trying to move him aside, to get to the controls. The ground was close, too close. Alex could see Dupre's hand on the control stick, and then the helicopter shifted the other way and then sharply back. Alex felt his hand slipping and suddenly there was nothing but air. The green trees below were rushing up at him, and then he hit a tree top. The M-16 was torn from his hand. The tree branches grabbed at him like something alive, and then open air again and the ground rushing at him. One foot hit first, and then he was rolling. His arm was on fire, and he felt himself come to a stop. He lay there, trying to keep from passing out, but everything seemed to fade away. His last thoughts were that this must be what it felt like to die. Poor Meg, no one could help her now.

* * *

Alex opened his eyes and wondered for a second where he was. The sound of the helicopter brought him back to reality. He rolled over and yelled at the pain shooting through him. He felt like he had broken every bone in his body. The helicopter was two hundred feet above him, going round and round in circles. He caught movement to his right and rolled that way. Two men were standing in front of the trees. The Chevrolet Blazer was to their right with the doors open wide. One of the men had a hand gun and the other one, a rifle. Horror swept through him when he realized that they were shooting at the helicopter. Dupre was trying to fly the damn thing. He couldn't get away. They would kill him.

Alex tried to stand, but his ankle gave way. His left arm wouldn't move. He put more weight on his ankle and found that he could stand, but something was bad wrong with his left arm. He couldn't move it. He could feel warm blood. He stood there for a minute, letting the wave after wave of pain sweep through him. Black spots began to dance in front of his eyes. He shook his head and made himself look at his arm. Something was sticking out of it. It was a piece of a tree branch going all the way through just above his elbow. Blood was pouring out. He took a quick look at the two men. All of their attention was on the helicopter. Dupre was still going round and round in circles. Alex fell to both knees and noticed something in the grass to his right. It was the M-16. He crawled over to the rifle and pulled it toward him. Putting the M-16's strap in his mouth, he grabbed the stick with his right hand and pulled with all his might. He almost passed out as the stick came free. Blood spurted out as the dead arm fell to his side. Alex pulled his belt off with his right hand and placed it around his arm above the wound, at the same time biting his lip to keep from passing out. He pulled the belt tight, and the bleeding stopped.

He must have screamed, because the men had turned toward him. The one nearest him was pointing a gun. Alex rolled to one side as bullets cut into the ground at his side. He brought himself to his feet and, screaming like a mad man, rushed the two men. A bullet grazed his leg as he raised the M-16 with his right arm. Another bullet bit into his side, but he kept running, refusing to stop and take cover. At twenty yards, he began firing, sweeping the M-16 in short arches. One of the men fell, and the other one dropped to one knee. Alex was close enough now to see the man's face. It was Heller. Alex suddenly realized that he was laughing and yelling. Heller had a shocked look on his face, and then he was up and running into the trees. Alex stopped for a second to catch his breath and to shake the black spots away, and then he was running again, following the moving bushes.

    Alex didn't know how far he'd run, but the sound of the helicopter was a dim roar behind him. He wondered if Dupre had been able to bring it under control. He prayed that his friends were all right. Suddenly, the helicopter noise stopped, and quietness settled in around him. Alex stopped to adjust the belt and then tighten it again. He knew that he stood a chance of losing his arm, but that wasn't important now. All that mattered was Heller, the monster Heller. He stopped and dropped to the ground. The movement had stopped in front of him. His heart was pounding like a sledge hammer in his chest. He took deep breaths as he crept forward, pulling himself along with his good arm. He willed the pain to go away.

    Every sense in his body was on the forest ahead. The trees around him were mostly oak, hickory, and pine. The thicker pines ahead had covered the forest floor with a blanket of pine needles.

    Alex used the rifle to pull himself to his knees and searched the trees and bushes carefully. There was no movement—no sound. Heller could be anywhere. Alex wondered how bad Heller was hurt. He dropped back to the forest floor and checked the wounds he had received. The leg wound was nothing, but the wound in his side had cut through his muscle and was beginning to hurt like hell. He pulled his shirt off and rolled it into a wad. He yelled in pain as he pushed it into his pants over the wound. He wished that he had another belt to put pressure on it. Blood was soaking his pants. He knew that he didn't have long to find Heller. He would pass out in a few minutes.

    Alex stumbled forward slowly, searching every hiding place. A slight noise came from his right. He rolled softly behind a tree and carefully pulled himself to his feet. Alex tried to calm his shaky breathing. The sound had come from a thick stand of trees thirty feet ahead. The ground sloped upward. Heller would be on higher ground. That would give him an advantage.

    Alex slowly made his way forward, always keeping cover between himself and the sound. He made it to the trees and began to climb the slope. His side was burning now, and he had a hard time lifting his right leg. Pain shot through him with every step. Something on the forest floor caught his attention. It was blood—bright red blood. The drops on the brown pine needles were big and fairly close together. Heller was hurt bad, too. A tight grin played across Alex's face. He dragged himself along, following the blood trail, searching ahead for any sign of the monster. He was almost to the top of the grade.

He stopped to gather enough energy for the final push. He saw a flash of color. Something was moving. It was coming toward him. The bloody, screaming madman rushing down the hill toward him wasn't a man, it was a demon—a horrifying demon of death. It was firing at him as the distance closed. Bullets clipped the trees and bushes like angry bees. Alex tried to throw himself to one side, bringing the M-16 up, holding the trigger down, firing on full auto, but he was too late. Bullets tore into him. He didn't feel himself falling, but the ground was suddenly there, inches from his face. He felt his flesh give as his face hit the leaves and pine straw. Pine needles were suddenly in his mouth, and he was rolling down the hill. He didn't feel the tree as he slammed into it. He couldn't see the demon either. He wondered what had happened to it. He tried to spit the pine needles out, but his mouth wouldn't move. It was funny. He couldn't see the trees anymore, but he could still see the sun. The brightness rushed to meet him.

Chapter 43

Dupre slowly opened his eyes. Something was attached to his arm. He looked up slowly at the tubes leading down to his right arm. The sounds of a hospital filled the air around him. He tried to sit up, but blackness settled around him.

* * *

Dupre woke up again. He wondered how long he had been out. It could have been minutes or hours. Everything seemed the same. He moved his finger to the controls for the bed and pressed the button, feeling the bed start to rise. Someone was coming toward him. He could smell the soft scent of perfume.

"How do you feel?" a female voice asked.

Dupre tried to say something, but his mouth was full of cotton. He motioned to his mouth for water, and a hand came toward him. He felt the coolness of the water as he sucked on the straw. He tried to raise his head, but a wave of pain shot through him. Dupre could feel the warmth of the sun through the windows, but everything in the room seemed dim. The nurse was a darker shadow moving around him. She was doing something to the tubes. The maddening tubes. He felt a warmness spreading down his arm, and suddenly he was back in the green mountains of his beloved Canada. He was sitting beside the clear, blue waters of a lake and he could hear his wife in the background laughing.

* * *

The next time he woke, he felt much better, and he was hungry. He pressed the button for the nurse. She had a big smile on her face as she came into the room.

"Mr. Dupre, I see you are doing better this morning. What can I get you?"

"How long have I been under?"

"I believe this is your sixth day."

"What happened to my friends?"

Memories filled his head as he asked the question. Meg laying on the ground, the lieutenant getting shot, and Alex falling out of the helicopter. He remembered the bullets crashing through the helicopter as he pushed the lieutenant out of the seat and tried to take control. One bullet hit and then two. He'd finally gotten the damn thing to go down—landing hard.

The lieutenant was still alive, and he knew that Alex was, too, because he saw him following one of the two men into the woods. Together, he and the lieutenant were able to find Meg and Alex and drag them into the helicopter. Both of them were barely alive. Dupre knew that they would probably never make it. He didn't know if any of them would make it. Between the lieutenant and himself, they had been able to fly the helicopter, but they never made it back to Dover. The last thing he remembered was going down onto a grassy field. There were military trucks there. His thoughts jerked back to the hospital room as the nurse leaned closer.

"I'm sorry, Mr. Dupre. They were taken somewhere else. The last thing I heard, they were not doing very well. Your wife is here. She has been outside for days now."

Dupre tried to get up, but the nurse gently pushed him down. Then she was at the damn IV again, and the painkiller eased through his veins. "Please?" he asked. He grabbed her arm. "Find out about my friends, and I want to see my wife."

Chapter 44

Meg lifted the handkerchief to wipe the streaming tears away. She felt a hand on her arm and turned to find Dupre at her side. He stood tall and stiff, his face upturned to the sky. His wife and children were at his side. Her eyes lifted over the funeral site to the north Georgia mountains. It was Alex's home. She was sure he would love it here.

Meg flinched as the honor guards fired guns into the air. She looked down at the casket for the last time and then joined her friends as they walked toward the waiting cars. Dupre said something to his wife and turned toward Meg. She was surprised as Dupre's wife got into a car, and it drove away. Dupre waved and walked toward her. Meg had come to the funeral in the same car as the lieutenant. They had been in the same hospital and had become fast friends. He moved from the car to stand beside her.

Meg noticed two men walking up behind Dupre. She knew that Dupre had been working closely with the CIA since he had gotten out of the hospital. He had been released three weeks earlier than she and the lieutenant, but he had visited them almost every day. Meg had not been able to see Alex. Dupre had told them that he had died in a hospital in New York City.

Meg smiled at Dupre. "It seems that you've let your ride take off."

"Oh well, I'll get another one." His eyes grew sober. "I've got a favor to ask you and the lieutenant. We want you to take a short plane ride with us and meet with someone from the CIA. Let's call it a debriefing on everything that's happened to us."

Meg thought for a moment and looked at the lieutenant. He nodded his head yes. They both trusted Dupre. "We're yours," she answered simply. Dupre had saved their lives. There was nothing they wouldn't do for him. "Give us time to pack," she continued.

"Our friends have already thrown a few things into bags for both of you." Dupre nodded to a car across the road. A window was down and a man was holding a bag up.

Meg hesitated and then without a word, started to walk toward the car.

She sat in the back with the lieutenant and one of the CIA men and Dupre sat in front with the other one. She saw the sign for highway 400 south flash by and leaned back in the seat to take in the sights. She had never been to Atlanta until she'd met Alex and she hadn't seen much of it either time. It seemed like a nice place, but she missed her home state. She had been calling from the hospital almost every day, trying to find any of her family, but hadn't been successful. She knew that Alex hadn't been her real father, but she had never been closer to anyone in her life. It was like she had always known him—that he had been in her life since she was born. Meg turned her head to the side as tears filled her eyes again. It was so unfair to lose him.

She leaned toward the window as they passed through the main part of Atlanta. The crowded city with its thousands of cars took her away for a moment from the horror she had seen in Washington. She wondered if the United States and Canada would ever recover.

The main city of Atlanta disappeared behind and minutes later she could see the Atlanta Airport. They pulled through a gate before they got to the terminal and approached a small jet sitting to one side. Meg and the lieutenant followed Dupre to the jet. She turned at the top step and looked north toward the mountains. In her mind, she was saying goodby to the best friend she'd ever had.

Meg felt her stomach leap as the jet took off and slid through the white clouds until all she could see was a sea of white below. It was two o'clock and the sun was on her right. They were headed south. She smiled. Alex had always been so good with directions. She seemed to have picked that up from him. She turned as Dupre slid into the seat next to her.

"Is this really about meeting with the CIA?" she asked. "Another thing, no one has really told me anything about what has been happening around the world since the bombs. The TV stations haven't given out much. It's as if someone is keeping them quiet."

Dupre was silent for a minute. Meg noticed that the lieutenant was leaning across the isle to hear Dupre's reply.

"Okay, I'll tell you everything. If anyone deserves to know, it's you two." Dupre leaned back in the seat and closed his eyes. "As you know, the two bombs that went off here and in Canada destroyed a large part of our two governments. Thank God, half of our elected officers lived through it. Other countries weren't as lucky. The terrorists took over the government in Russia, France, Germany, China, and parts of South America. There is still fighting in the streets across Israel, but they seemed to be holding their own. Several of the Islam nations have been taken over. A bomb went off in London, but the English took back their country fairly quickly. The world is a mess. The

United States has joined Canada and now for most purposes are one nation. Terrorists took over part of Mexico and came across our southern borders into Texas and California. We're pushing them south but are losing a lot of men doing it. The military is in shambles down there." Dupre opened his eyes and turned toward Meg.

"What do you have to do with all of this?" Meg asked.

"Both governments have asked me to help bring the remains of Canadian intelligence, along with the FBI and CIA together. Our job in the short term is to rid this country of the hundreds of terrorist involved in this mess. Most of them have run like rats. We caught some, but a few made it to other countries. A lot of them are still here, and we don't know where they are or what they're capable of. For all we know, they could have twenty more bombs here in the United States and Canada."

"My God," Meg said. "This may be just starting."

"That's right," Dupre said.

They had been in the air for over an hour now, and Meg's ears began to pop. They were losing altitude. An island appeared through the clouds below. It was the main Bahama Island. Meg had been there before. She looked over at Dupre, but he had his eyes closed. Why in the hell were they going to the Bahamas?

Chapter 45

The taxi pulled into the front of the condo and came to a stop. Meg got out and stood there for a second, looking around. The condo was one of many strung out along the ocean front. The blue waters on the other side looked inviting. She could see herself, laying on the sand, letting the warm sun bake all of the memories from the last two months away. The smell of the fresh ocean air was wonderful. Dupre had stopped and was waiting on her.

"Who are we meeting inside?" Meg asked.

"Just one person," Dupre answered.

"What is the name of this CIA person?" Meg asked.

"His name is Larry Carson."

Meg followed Dupre through the door. The condo inside was big and beautiful. The huge opened foyer led to a den with a view of the beach. The whole back of the building was glass which would let in the morning sunlight. A curved archway led to a large kitchen to the right and onto a sunroom. Meg could see a deck across the back of the condo with steps leading down to the beach. To one side of the foyer, a curved wrought iron stairway led to the second floor. Meg looked around for the CIA man they were supposed to meet, but the condo seemed empty. She turned to Dupre, but he was already past her and walking through the sliding doors leading to the deck. As Meg followed, she could see a man sitting there facing away from them. The shape, the back of the head seemed familiar. Suddenly, she cried out and ran toward the figure.

Alex turned in the chair and threw up his arms to protect himself against the onrushing Meg. She hugged him and patted him all over to see if he was real. Finally, she pushed him back and stood with her hands on her hips, her eyes blazing.

"Why? Why did you do this to us?" Meg turned to include Dupre.

Alex motioned to the bench at his side. "Sit down. Dupre and I will tell you everything."

Meg slid in next to Alex. She reached over and hugged him again to make sure it was real. Lieutenant Tom Jackson joined Dupre on the other side and finally got to shake Alex's hand. The lieutenant was thinner than Alex had remembered, but then the hospital could have done that. His handshake was firm and strong.

Alex turned to his friends with a broad smile on his face. He had been with Jan for the last three hours, remembering the fun they'd had on this very beach. Her laughter still rang in his ears. He laid his hand over Meg's. "I'm so glad to see you," he said. "And you, too, Tom. How's the arm?"

The lieutenant raised his arm and moved it back and forth. "It's fine, thanks to Dupre. I would have lost it if it hadn't been for him."

"I'm glad," Alex said, never taking his hand from Meg's. He glanced over at Dupre. "I'm afraid that Dupre will have to tell you most of what's happened. I was out of it, probably much like you two." He held out his hand to Dupre.

Dupre leaned forward. "First, I don't believe the lieutenant needs to hear this for his own good." He turned to Tom. "Would you mind taking a walk and I'll tell you what I can later?"

Tom looked a little hurt, but he went along with it. When he was out of ear shot, Dupre turned back to Meg. "Meg, I know that you know everything about how Alex killed those men in Canada." Meg shook her head yes. "The trouble is," Dupre went on. "Half the country has a warrant out on Alex. It's going to take some time to clear him. There is another reason, and I will tell both of you later." Alex cut his eyes sharply at Dupre, but Dupre kept talking as if he didn't notice. "The killings are not the only reason we want him dead for now. In the end, his record is going to be cleared. It's going to read that he was in the CIA before any of this started." Dupre stopped and looked at Alex. "Alex, there's something I haven't told you either." Dupre hesitated again. "Heller isn't dead. That's the other reason we want you to lay low for a while."

Both Meg and Alex jumped forward in their seats. "Not dead! I thought you told me in the hospital that he was," Alex cried.

"I didn't want to excite you," Dupre said. "You may not have known it, Alex, but you were on your death bed. All of the doctors thought that you were going to die."

"But how could he get out of there?" Meg said. "He was shot, wasn't he?"

"Damn right he was," Alex said, standing up. "I was following a blood trail."

"I followed the same trail back over the hill where I found you," Dupre said. "There was no sign of him anywhere. The one named Keith was dead, but Heller was gone."

"That means he knows where all of the terrorists are. If they have any more bombs, he will know where they are, too!" Alex shouted.

"I know," Dupre said. "That's why I wanted you two here today and the lieutenant. This is a big job I've been given. Only the three of us know what Heller looks like. We have to find him or this country will really be in bad shape. I guess that I'm asking both of you to join me until this is over."

Alex got up from the table and slowly walked over to the rail around the deck. He stood there silent, watching the waves as they rolled in. Meg walked over to join him. Dupre headed down the steps toward the beach.

"You know we have to do this," Meg said as Dupre hurried to catch the lieutenant.

"I know," he answered. "I don't have anything else to do." He turned to her. "What about you? You're young. You have your whole life ahead of you."

Meg looked up at him. "It's no more dangerous than being a police officer, or have you forgotten?"

Alex looked hard at her and then a big grin broke across his face. He put his arm around her, and they stood there watching Dupre catch up to the lieutenant. The two turned and started back toward Alex and Meg. The lieutenant was nodding his head, and Alex knew that he would join them. He wondered how Dupre would get him released from the Air Force, but he had a feeling that Dupre could do almost anything when he set his mind to it. He felt Jan inside him again, and he saw Meg give him a puzzled look as he grinned down at her. He had a strong feeling for this young woman. She was like the daughter he and Jan had never had. He could almost feel Jan agreeing with him.

Alex stepped away from Meg and placed both hands on her shoulders. Her trusting eyes looked up at him. "You know in Canada, when you said that I was the father you never had."

"Yes," Meg said, smiling.

"I just want you to know that I'll be there for you always."

Tears filled Meg's eyes, and she hugged him. Dupre and the lieutenant had reached the bottom of the steps. Dupre smiled up at them. The lieutenant had a different look in his eyes. For the first time, Alex realized that Tom's eyes were the same color as Meg's. He also realized that the look had a touch of jealously in it. Alex smiled. He might have to adopt a son-in-law before long, but for now? Alex walked away from the others, down the steps and toward the breaking waves. He needed to talk to Jan.

* * * *

Printed in the United States
5977